Praise for *The Bone Witch*

★ "Mesmerizing. Chupeco does a magnificent job of balancing an intimate narrative perspective with sweeping worldbuilding, crafting her tale within a multicultural melting pot of influences as she presses toward a powerful cliffhanger."
—*Publishers Weekly*, Starred Review

★ "Fantasy worldbuilding at its best, and Rin Chupeco has created a strong and colorful cast of characters to inhabit that realm."
—*Shelf Awareness*, Starred Review

"Readers who enjoy immersing themselves in detail will revel in Chupeco's finely wrought tale. *Game of Thrones* fans may see shades of Daenerys Targaryen in Tea, as she gathers a daeva army to unleash upon the world. Whether she is in the right remains a question unanswered, but the ending makes it clear her story is only beginning."
—*Booklist*

"Chupeco delights. Exceptionally written from beginning to end."
—*BuzzFeed*

"Chupeco craftily weaves magic, intrigue, and mystery into a captivating tale that will leave readers begging for the promised sequel."
—*School Library Journal*

The

BONE
WITCH

ALSO BY RIN CHUPECO

The Girl from the Well
The Suffering

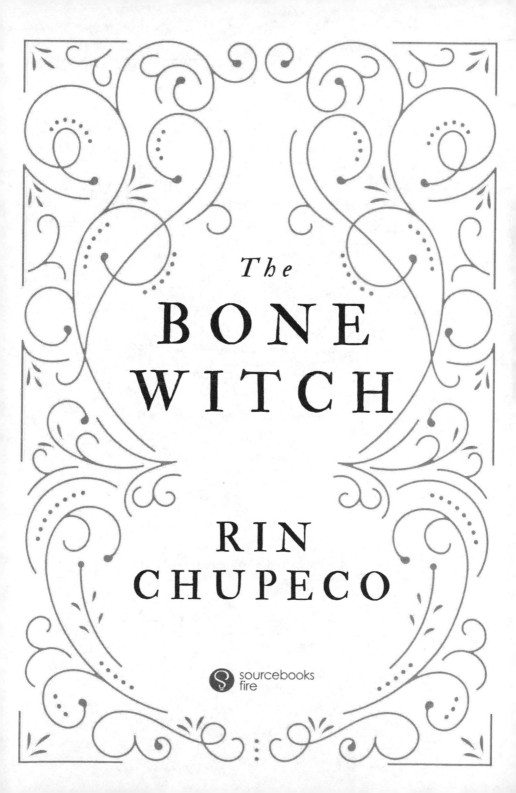

The

BONE
WITCH

RIN
CHUPECO

sourcebooks
fire

Published by Sourcebooks Fire, an imprint of Sourcebooks, Inc.
P.O. Box 4410, Naperville, Illinois 60567-4410
(630) 961-3900
Fax: (630) 961-2168
sourcebooks.com

The Library of Congress has cataloged the hardcover edition as follows:

Names: Chupeco, Rin, author.
Title: The bone witch / Rin Chupeco.
Description: Naperville, Illinois : Sourcebooks Fire, [2017] | Summary: Tea's
gift for death magic means that she is a bone witch, a title that makes
her feared and ostracized by her community, but when an older bone witch
trains her to become an asha--one who can wield elemental magic--Tea will
have to overcome her obstacles and make a powerful choice in the face of
danger as dark forces approach.
Identifiers: LCCN 2016016719 | (13 : alk. paper)
Subjects: | CYAC: Magic--Fiction. | Witches--Fiction. | Fantasy.
Classification: LCC PZ7.C4594 Bo 2017 | DDC [Fic]--dc23 LC record available at https://
lccn.loc.gov/2016016719

Source of Production: Marquis Book Printing, Montreal, QC, Canada
Date of Production: November 2022
Run Number: 5028728

Printed and bound in Canada.
MBP 16

Dedicated to the countless bowls of ramen,
who have supported me throughout the writing of this book
and have still continued to do so long after I was done.

And also to Ramen Santouka, for supplying said ramen.

THE WORLD
OF THE BONE WITCH:
THE EIGHT KINGDOMS

*T*HE BEAST RAGED; IT PUNCTURED *the air with its spite. But the girl was fiercer. She held no weapons except for the diamonds glinting like stars above her brow, against hair like a dark mass of sky. She wore no armor save a beautiful* hua *of mahogany and amber spun from damask silk, a golden dragon embroidered down its length, its body half-hidden by her waist wrap. She raised her arm, and I saw nothing. But the creature saw, and its wrath gentled, until it did little but whimper.*

"Kneel," the girl ordered, and—against all expectations—the daeva obeyed. It sank to its knees and bowed its head.

Seventeen, I thought. She could not be older than seventeen years. Seventeen could explain the poetry of her face, with her skin brown and unblemished. Seventeen explained the pertness of her nose, the determined tilt to her chin. But seventeen did not explain the oldness in her eyes, large twin pools of black from where no light could escape.

The girl stood beside the fiend. It was four times as tall and weighed a hundred tons, but it shrunk from the touch of her hand. It was an elephant-like beast, with a hide the color of dead trees and a mouth full of teeth as large as tusks, but it did not attack. It bore fangs like knives, each canine more jagged than the next, but it was afraid. They made for a bizarre sight: the girl and the monster on a beach of ash and silt, while waves crashed against the shore and sent up sprays of seawater and salt.

The beast watched her with its dull, white eyes. It whimpered again.

The girl smiled. She stroked its misshapen jaw and leaned toward the hideous, yellowing teeth as if she had a secret to share.

"Die," she whispered.

The daeva sighed, a relieved sound. It toppled onto its side, raised its head beseechingly at her one last time, and died.

The girl rose to her feet, slipping a knife out of her sleeve. Her hand traveled past the beast's jaw and neck, searching. She paused at a spot halfway down its throat and sank her blade into the roughened flesh. Black liquid, slick as oil and thick as congealed syrup, bubbled from the gaping wound.

I turned my face away. My last meal rose in my throat unbidden, and I forced it back down with effort.

Blood and grime dripped down her fingers. From within the depths of the creature, the girl withdrew a perfectly round stone. It was as large as her hand, smooth and polished, and it glittered red, the color of giant rubies. As she did, the monster crumbled, reduced to a mountain of dust in an instant.

"A bezoar," she said for my benefit. "The mark of every daeva. This creature is called an akvan, *and its bezoar can sense all known magic. But it does not explain you here in my domain."*

Despite the masterful craftsmanship of her hua, *there was something unusual about the dragon woven on it—its snout was too long, and it too had tusks instead of sharp teeth and whiskers. It was an imperfection I was not accustomed to in such fineries.*

The gown was slit on one side, and I saw the long, white scar that climbed her right thigh. She made no move to hide this flaw and stood boldly, with her legs apart, so that the beaded dragon looked to have burst out onto her dress from the puckered skin. She wore her waist wrap loosely, in defiance of tradition; like her hua, *it was black, but with chrysanthemums stitched in gilded thread. One of the great atelier Arrakan's creations, I surmised; intricate gold embroidery was his specialty.*

She wore a beautiful chain around her neck, and on it a heart-shaped pendant. I had my own heartsglass of the common glossy, apple red. I expected hers to be of a bright silver, a soft, swirling mist contained within the tempered glass, as expected of an asha. Instead, it was as black as the night.

The akvan *had not been the first death on that lonely shore. Bits of other bones lay scattered around the desolate beach, their skeletal remains victims of the relentless tides that sent them crashing at intervals against sharpened rocks. Large rib cages glistened despite the soot-ridden light. Empty skulls gaped back at me, silent and accusing.*

The girl turned to face me, and I saw the grave behind her for the first time. It was a slab of headstone lying on the only patch of grass that flourished in the otherwise barren landscape of sand. It bore no inscription, and I wondered who lay buried within, whom she mourned.

"They call you Tea of the Embers," I said.

She said nothing and waited.

"I collect stories," I continued. "I was born in Drycht but was banished when I came of age for my freethinking ways and for singing against the tyrant kings. Since then, I have made my living on tales and ballads. I have seen with my own eyes the endless wars of the

Yadosha city-states. I have broken bread with the reindeer people and have danced with the Gorvekan tribes on the Isteran steppes. I have seen princes poisoned, have watched a Faceless follower hanged, and have survived in a city that's been swept out to sea. My name is known in many places; my reputation is more than modest.

"But I know very little of the workings of the asha. I know of their dances and of their weapons and of their legends but not of their quarrels and their gossip and their loves. And until today, I have never seen one slay a daeva."

She laughed; it sounded bitter. "I am no longer an asha, Bard; they are beloved by the people, and I am not. My exile here, at the end of the world, is proof of that. They have another name for those like me. Call me a bone witch; it suits me better. But I have no need of you, and you are in my way. Give me one reason why I should not cut you down where you stand."

I am used to pleading for my life, and so I said, "You are an asha, and you must know how to discern truth from lies. Put me to the test."

The girl moved closer. From within the folds of her hua, *she took out another stone and placed it in my hand. I was no magic adept, but even I could feel the strength of the spells woven into her dress, though I did not know what they enhanced—her beauty, which such magic was commonly used for, or her power, which was formidable enough without them.*

"If you speak the truth, it will flare a brighter blue," she said. "Tell me lies and it will shine the deepest black. Choose your words carefully, Bard."

"I had a dream. I saw a bright-blue moon in the sky. I followed it across the clouds until it shone over a gray, empty beach littered with the bones of sea monsters of old. On it stood a young girl with her hands stained with blood but who promised me a tale beyond anything I could ever imagine. 'If there is one thing people desire more than a good story,' she said, 'it is when they speak their own.' When I woke, I saw that same moon, as blue and as real as you and I, looking down. I trusted my instincts and followed the road the way it had been mapped out for me in my dream. It is here I find that same beach and that same girl. I have heard all the tales they speak of you. It would be my honor to hear yours. Give me leave to sing your story, and I will do it justice."

The waves lapped at the shore. Vultures circled overhead. The sapphire in my hand shone the purest blue.

She broke the silence with more laughter, the stillness shattering at the sound. "You are confident and curious. Some would say that is not always a healthy combination." She took back the bezoar and turned away. "I leave in seven days. I will give you until then."

I followed her, my heartsglass heavy with questions. Of everything I had heard, I had not expected her to be so young. Seventeen did not explain why she stood on that strange, graying beach, alone, with monsters' corpses for company.

I

LET ME BE CLEAR: I never intended to raise my brother from his grave, though he may claim otherwise. If there's anything I've learned from him in the years since, it's that the dead hide truths as well as the living. I have not been a bone witch for very long, whatever the stories you've heard, but this was the first lesson I learned.

I understand now why people fear bone witches. Theirs is not the magic found in storybooks, slaying onyx-eyed dragons and rescuing grateful maidens from ivory towers. Theirs is not the magic made from smoke and mirrors, where the trap lies in the twitch of the hand and a trick of the eyes. Nor is theirs the magic that seeds runeberry fields, whose crops people harvest for potions and spells. This is *death* magic, complicated and exclusive and implacable, and from the start, I wielded it with ease.

There was never anything unnatural or mysterious about me.

I was born in Knightscross, one of the smallest villages that dotted the kingdom of Odalia, surrounded by a lovely forest on three sides and rolling plains on the other. My only claim to strangeness was that I read fiercely, learned thirstily. I read of the history of the Eight Kingdoms, about the Five Great Heroes and the False Prince. It was here that I learned of the magic-wielding asha and their never-ending war against the Faceless, the people of the lie, practitioners of the Dark, sworn to the False Prince. Sometimes I would pretend to be the asha, Taki of the Silk, whom the fabled King Marrus took to wife. Or Nadine of the Whispers, who ended the war between the kingdoms of Istera and Daanoris with her dancing.

"You think in the same way men drink, Tea," my father once said, "far too much—under the delusion it is too little." But he brought me books from distant fairs and encouraged my clutter of parchment and paper. Some days, I would read to him when his work at the forge was done for the day. It was a sight to see: him, a tall, muscular man with a heavy beard, reclining in his favorite chair and listening as I read children's fables and folktales in my high, piping voice.

It was true that I was born at the height of an eclipse, when the sky closed its only moon eye to wink back at the world, like my arrival was a private joke between old friends. Or perhaps the moon read my fate in the stars and hid, unwilling to bear witness to my birth. It is the kind of cataclysm people associate with bone witches. But surely normal children have been born under this cover of night, when the light refused to shine, and went on to live perfectly normal lives?

Necromancy did not run in my family's blood, though witchery did. But my older sisters were witches of good standing within the community and did not go about summoning dead siblings from graveyards as a rule. Rose was a Forest witch; she was plump, pickled brown from the hot sun, darker than even the farmers who worked the fields from dawn to dusk. She owned an herb garden and sold poultices and home remedies for gout, lovesickness, and all other common ailments. Lilac was a Water witch; she was tall and stagnant, like a deep pool. She was fond of donning veils, telling merry fortunes, and occasionally finding lost trinkets, often by accident.

She had cast auguries for me and found nothing amiss. "Tea shows an inclination to be a witch like us, if she wishes to," Lilac told my mother. "I see her wearing a beautiful amber gown, with bright gems in her hair and a handsome prince on her arm. Our little Tea is destined for something greater than Knightscross, I think."

Even those who knew nothing of the witching trade considered Forest and Water magic to be reasonable, respectable professions. And Rose and Lilac made for reasonable, respectable witches.

Had I known the color of my heartsglass sooner, I might have been better prepared.

On the third day of the third month of their thirteenth summer, children gathered at the village square for the spring equinox and because it was tradition. Boys and girls wore delicate heartsglass on chains around their necks. Some were simple cases their parents bought cheap at the Odalian market; those who could afford it purchased them from famed glassblowers in Kneave.

A witch—some years it was Rose, and others it was Lilac—
traced Heartsrune spells in the air until each empty glass sputtered
and flared and filled with red and pink hues. As was the tradition
in Odalia, my father and mother wore each other's heartsglass—
his was burned and ruddy, like the endless fires of his forge, and
hers was coral tinged and warm, like the hearth. Most of my
brothers and sisters wavered between their colors, though purple-
tinted hearts singled Rose and Lilac out for witching. I was only
twelve years old then, thought too young to appreciate my heart's
value. Having a heart was a responsibility; young children were
heartless creatures anyway—or so said Mrs. Drury, who lived
three cottages away and was the acknowledged village busybody.
But I never believed that grown-ups took great care of their hearts
either, because my older sister Daisy, seventeen and the loveliest of
us Pahlavis, was constantly losing hers. She gave it to Demian Terr
and then later to Sam Fallow and then again to Heath Clodbarron,
and Rose or Lilac had to draw new Heartsrune spells each time
her romances ended. It was all right, Daisy insisted, because the
hearts she'd given away faded over time, and she could always ask
for one anew.

"Never give your heart freely or as often," Rose or Lilac would
reprimand her. "The wrong kinds of people can place spells on it to
gain and keep power over you."

I wasn't sure why anyone would want power over Daisy,
because I couldn't imagine her doing anything involving work. And
Demian and Sam and Heath, obviously the wrong kind of people
for my sister, wouldn't know magic if it kneed them in the loins.

I once asked Rose why Daisy's heart never lasted longer than her courtships, while Mother's and Father's heartsglass never needed replacing. "Hearts only last when you put in work to *make* them last," she responded. She was, however, more forgiving of Daisy than Lilac was. "She can't help herself," Rose said. "Sometimes you can't help who you love or for how long."

•• ⫶⫶⫶ ••

With my sisters named the way they are, you might wonder about my unusual name. My mother had high expectations of her children—and of her daughters in particular. Fine, upstanding young ladies, she believed, needed fine, upstanding names. My sisters were named Rose and Lilac, Marigold and Daisy; by the time I came along, she had abandoned flowers. I grew up to the sounds of squabbles and running feet and love, and, despite my preference for ungainly books, I was unremarkable in every way.

But Fox? Fox was the family tragedy. His heart was a solid and dependable umber, bronze when held in the right kind of light. He was like a second father to me and is one of my earliest childhood memories. As the oldest, he looked after me when the rest of my siblings occupied my mother's time. He joined the army when I was ten, and for two years, I read his letters home to my parents. There were no shortages of ill-mannered nobles who raised banners of gold and silver and called the throne their own, he wrote, and so King Telemaine sent soldiers like him, armed and primed for war, to force them down from such high, insolent ledges.

And then Fox wrote of strange and terrible tidings. These rumors sprouted up like bindweed along the edges of the kingdom and gorged themselves on whispers and fears. They told of daeva—strange and terrible monsters, maimed creatures assembled from scale-slicked bodies and yellowed fangs and spined limbs and horns. I was familiar with the legend: the daeva are the False Prince's final curse on the world, and the Faceless are said to command them. Occasionally, the curse would take hold once more, and a daeva would rise from the dead to wreak havoc. Fox was periodically assigned to patrols that guarded Odalia's borders and had seen one of the creatures for himself. But their commander had ordered a retreat; it was the Deathseekers' job to kill the beasts in their stead. Fox had been impressed by these elite, magic-wielding fighters.

Shortly after that, Fox was killed "by creatures unknown," as General Lode's letter read. Military speak for daeva, Father said. There was nothing else—just a simple pine coffin, three months' worth of his wages, and a single note that felt indifferent and regretful all at once.

My mother and sisters wept; they could have flooded Knightscross with the strength of their grief. My father and brothers held vigil for three days and three nights and said nothing with their impassive faces and wet eyes. I was only twelve, and I couldn't see the kind, playful Fox I had known in that rigid body. I couldn't recognize him in that pale, grim face. This was *my* brother, who had raised me and fed me and carried me on his shoulders, and it hurt to see him so still.

I was quiet when the mourners pulled the coffin lid shut. I was silent when they set the wooden box in the hole they had dug. Only when they poured the last shovelfuls of dirt onto the new grave did I speak. Even now I can recall how heavy those words felt when they fell from my lips.

"You can't put him there. He can't get out."

"Sweetheart," my mother wept, "Fox isn't coming back."

"You're wrong," I said. "*You're wrong*. I saw him move. As sure as I know my own breath, I *saw him move*, but he can't get out." The syllables tripped on my tongue, tasting old and formal. It felt as if they came from someone using my mouth as a passageway through which words not my own raced. I had heard Fox. I had seen him move. In my mind's eye, I had seen past the heavy stone, past the soil and the dirt and the rot, and I had watched my dead brother open his eyes.

I dashed toward the grave. Wolf and Hawk barred my path, but I ducked underneath their strong arms and slipped past. For a moment I imagined myself as my brother's namesake, strong and sly, shaking hounds off the length of my tail. But the illusion soon passed, and I was a child again, tripping and falling. The ground slashed at me, marking both my knees and the palms of my hands with the sharpness of knives. Blood dripped down onto the cold gravestone and spilled across the ground.

A chorus of noises thrummed inside my head, a peculiar buzzing that also carried with it my brother's voice, asking and pleading and yearning, answering a question I had not yet asked aloud: *Yes, Tea*, Fox whispered to me in my head. *Yes, I am willing*.

It was *wrong* of them to put him in the ground when he did not want to die.

A strange symbol burned before me. Without thinking, my bloodied fingers traced the pattern in the air, again and again and again, until my brothers took me by the waist and dragged me away.

"What has gotten into you, girl?" My father was shaken and angry. "There is no excuse for behaving in this manner—and at your brother's wake, no less!"

What other reprimands he intended died on his tongue when the ground began to move. A terrible rumbling and heaving began underneath us, beneath the fresh dirt that made up Fox's grave. There was a muffled splintering inside that small mound, like something within the coffin had escaped its confinement. As we watched, a cold, gray hand rose up, scratching and stretching, and gripped the tufts of weeds growing close to the grave. The strange being lifted itself out of its earthly prison with little difficulty and brushed the dirt off its tall, thin form. My mother fainted.

When it raised its head, I saw that it had my brother's face, drawn and bloodless and dead.

"Tea," the figure said.

But then it smiled, and it was Fox's smile, quiet and kind.

*T*HE CAVE ITSELF WAS SPARSELY *furnished—two chairs, a stool, a long, wooden table, and a small, polished mirror hanging from a wall from where another smaller table stood, littered with glass bottles of various sizes. There was an impressive arrangement of flowers: a burst of color in otherwise somber surroundings. A wooden divider foraged from driftwood marked off a separate area, presumably for changing and sleeping. It made for impressive accommodations, despite its suggestion of impermanence.*

A small cot lay near the entrance—mine for the duration of my stay, I was told. The girl placed the two stones she carried at the end of the wooden table, adding them to a row of six other gems similar in shape though boasting different hues. A small, jeweled case lay at their center, polished so it gleamed.

"Most asha fall sick that first time," she said. "Some may encounter no more than a small wave of dizziness or a fever lasting a few hours. But for bone witches, it can be fatal. It took me three days to recover.

"I had the most curious dream then. In it, I found a black cat, which I hid in my room. It was a beautiful kitten with the shiniest fur and the softest paws. People came and went asking for it, seeking with their blurred faces and watchful eyes. I was never sure why I lied, only that it was important that they not know I

was keeping him, that something terrible would happen should they discover him.

"My kitten would change form at odd times. Sometimes it was a black dress and then a dark mask and then a beautiful obsidian gemstone. It didn't worry me in this dream that I owned a cat that didn't always stay one.

"Finally, it turned into a majestic-looking sword, as black as shadows—its hilt to its blade steeped in creeping, moving darkness. I knew then that I need not hide it any longer and raised up my sword.

"But the dream ended, and I woke."

She took a sip from her wooden bowl and laughed softly. "Would events have been different, I wonder, if I had died then? Perhaps the dream was some kind of prophecy, a portent of what was to come. But I cannot predict the future like the oracle or even my sister Lilac. That is not the kind of magic I wield."

Her fingers moved lower, tracing the long, raised scar on her thigh.

"The only sight I seem to possess nowadays is hindsight."

2

SHE WAS A BEAUTIFUL WOMAN. Her long hair billowed out behind her like a cloak of sun-kissed yellow, and her eyes were dark caves from where blue gems glinted. She was young, in the way a woman of sixty might carefully tuck away the years around her to appear twenty. She looked nothing like a bone witch ought to look. She was soft and willowy and comely, and everyone in Knightscross was afraid of her.

My mother told me later of the fear the lady inspired when she first rode into Knightscross. Her horse was a beautiful palomino with a glossy chestnut mane, and the woman herself wore a robe of varying blues and dark greens, as if to mimic the colors of the ocean. Silvery fish adorned the edges of her dress, swimming into view and back out again whenever her skirts rustled. She wore a waist wrap of pale lavender with an embossed pattern of pearls. Gemstones attached to long pins were woven into her golden hair, and they glinted each time she moved her head.

On a chain around her neck, a heartsglass swung. It had metalworks of hammered gold and tiny jewels, the surface glossy mirrored and silver sharp.

But it was also empty.

"Crone," muttered the bravest in the crowd. "Crow." But even the most courageous of the lot melted away at her approach or were led away by those with better sense. The villagers knew she was the worst of witches, a demon in womanskin. But the king had decreed otherwise, and whatever their breed of cowardice, they were neither traitors nor fools.

She arrived within two days of the attempted funeral, though the news had not yet traveled to Murkwick, the nearest township fifteen leagues to the east. She strode down the path leading into the square without a word, villagers trailing behind her despite themselves. She marched straight into my home, where my family had shut Fox up in the forge, away from the terrified mob.

"Milady," she said to Lilac, "I would be grateful if you could calm the people gathered outside. It wouldn't do to have your family's livelihood burned for so poor an excuse." Next, she turned to Rose. "And might I ask you, milady, for a treatment of wortroot and farrow, lavender oil and bathwater."

Rose and Lilac—reasonable, respectable witches by comparison to the frightful woman, an accursed *bone witch*—hurried to do as she commanded.

"Where is she?" was her next question, and my father showed her the room I shared with my sisters. She found me curled up on my small bed, forehead burning from the strain of the magic.

I was in no condition to remember what happened, but my mother told me everything. The witch bathed my face and chest with bitter herbs and sweet water. She measured sage and fallowtree in a bowl and spooned small doses of the concoction into my mouth. When evening came to dust the sky with tiny, twinkling stars, my fever had broken. The furnace in my mind reduced to kindling, I slept undisturbed until dawn the next day while the witch stood guard.

The sickness was gone when I awoke, and in its place was the woman, sleeping in a chair at the foot of the bed. I rose to a sitting position and stared at my visitor. A soft haze surrounded her, a subdued light both familiar and frightening.

"My dead father was my first summon," the lovely woman said without opening her eyes. "Don't know what came over me, I'm sure. I was his daughter, but he thought I fared better as his property. Denied me even the smallest freedoms and imprisoned me in petticoats and sewing lessons. Had he lived longer, he would have confined me to a convent or deeded me over to a wealthy merchant to wed. Perhaps I did it to show him there was more to me than as someone else's dowry. He was not as imposing dead as he was alive though, and he was most unwilling, so I sent him back quickly. Sick as a dog for four days for my trouble. You seem to have fared better, with only two nights' worth of illness. My name is Mykaela. You might have heard of me."

Six months ago, a visiting merchant told my father of a daeva that terrorized the town of Lardbrook ninety leagues away. A strange woman they called Mykaela of the Hollows had killed it, he said. Surely no one else in Odalia had hair so pale or skin so light.

I trembled. "Yes. They call you the bone witch."

"Your parents tell me you're quite the precocious child." The woman smiled, two rows of pearly whites against scarlet lips. "That's not the worst they call me, and that will not be the worst they will call *you*."

Bone witches were not a respectable trade. They said bone witches gave sleeping sicknesses to innocent princesses with the prick of a finger, and they said bone witches ate the hearts of children who strayed too far into forests. Bone witches did not truly serve the Eight Kingdoms as they claim, because they dabbled in the Dark runes just like the False Prince and his Faceless followers. Bone witches raised armies from the dead. Bone witches could raise daeva—like the one that had killed Fox.

My heart beat faster, my chest painfully tight. "Will you send my brother back?"

"No." The witch traced an obscure pattern in the air. "That is not how this works. He is your creation, not mine. Your brother did not know when he asked, and you did not know when you answered, but unlike my father, I suspect Fox Pahlavi is where you both want him to be. You can summon the dead, and they will come at first, because they are creatures curious of the life they once tasted and long to savor again. But you cannot bind dead folk without their consent, and you cannot make them stay. That is the first rule of the Dark. There are only two types of people you cannot raise from the dead: those with silver hearts-glass like ours and those who are not willing. And your brother is very willing."

I felt sick all over again. I did not want to be a bone witch. I could *not* be a bone witch. Lilac had promised me gems and dresses and a handsome prince. "And if I don't want to?"

The lady's bright eyes looked back at me, knowing. "Do you know that it is considered in poor taste to lie to the one who saved your life?"

I averted my gaze because she was right. I did not want the woman's presence in my room, tainting the air with a truth I had no desire to hear. I did not want to think about my brother, torn between the living and the dead by my own hand. But I had wielded the magic, and I had liked its flavor. Even then, my fingers itched to trace that exquisite rune in the air again, to sample it with my mind. The spell's aftertaste still lingered in my mouth— like sweet peaches, like silken honey that had burst underneath my tongue and ran smoothly down my throat.

"The Dark are greedy runes. Draw them once, and they ruin you for any other magic. The Dark are also jealous runes. We cannot channel Fire and Water and Earth and Wood runes any more than we can attack with the shadows on the walls. But most importantly, the Dark are seductive runes that steal into your head and make free with your thoughts when you least anticipate them. And for that, you will require watching."

"I don't need watching," I said out of a desire to be stubborn.

The witch guffawed, a strange sound from one who looked so elegant. "Yes, child. You need no watching, and I should have stayed in my asha-ka in Ankyo and let the Dark sup on the waste of your bones. And then your family would have two funerals instead of one." She sighed. "We have little choice, you and I. It is the law: if you do not serve the kingdoms, then the Faceless shall seek you out. Which path would you prefer: bone witch or traitor?"

I took a long, shuddering breath. This was true; I owed her my life if not yet my trust. "What's going to happen next?"

"We leave for Ankyo as soon as you are able."

I froze. I had never left my village, much less traveled to Kneave, Odalia's capital. I knew that Ankyo was even farther than that, across Odalia's borders and into the kingdom of Kion.

Mykaela of the Hollows smiled at my stricken face. "There are many things that I need to teach you, Tea, and it would inconvenience me to have the villagers' fear running underfoot when it is most inappropriate. Your family may visit if you wish them to. It is a long journey, but if your studies go well, we can arrange to have their expenses paid for by our House. And we shall take your brother with us."

"Will you make him better?"

Lady Mykaela turned to me, and only then did I see how terribly old the woman was. Not old from the passage of years but from seeing too much of what most would rather see little of.

"You can't make the better of the dead, sweet child," she said, "though I reckon death could make the better of us."

Fox showed no inclination to eat anyone once the doors were unbarred, though food could have improved his features. He was too ashen, his eyes red rimmed, but he stood obedient while Lady Mykaela made her inspections. A crowd still gathered as news of my condition had spread. Mrs. Drury stood to one side and gave me the evil eye, and when the people muttered and whispered, they looked at me the same way they looked at the bone witch.

"You're in better shape than most I've seen." She reached up and smoothed Fox's hair, and my mother's hand twitched in response. "All your fingers and toes and the wits still in your head. Do you feel at ease in this skin?"

"I am not uncomfortable," Fox replied.

"I am sorry," the lady said, this time to my parents. "Tea will not be safe here. Not from the villagers' prejudice, which can be rectified. Your daughter must have training or the Dark will chew holes into her heart, eat her from the inside out, until she shall be more husk than the dead we trade in."

"Do you want to do this, Tea?" Father asked, like he believed I still had a choice.

I did not want to, but Fox was now my responsibility, the way I had been Fox's in those days before he went to war. "I am going to protect my brother," I said slowly, trying out the words to see how they sounded.

My brother smiled at my gumption, though it did not quite reach his eyes.

"We must go soon," the bone witch said, "but before we do, I owe you one more thing at least. You will not have a chance to enjoy your Heartsrune day, so I hope this is of some consolation." She held out to me the most beautiful heartsglass I had ever seen—gold spun into intricate leaves winding through the glass on all sides. Small stones of ruby and beryl balanced out its paleness. Shivering, I allowed my sister Lilac to clasp it around my neck.

Lady Mykaela of the Hollows drew a shape in the air, and I felt nothing more than a small tug at my chest as the bone witch coaxed my heart out and into the glass. In that early sunless dawn, it shone—not pink and red, as my parents' and siblings', or even purple like my witch-sisters', but a dazzling silver white.

S HE PREPARED OUR MEAL WITH *simple tools, in rudimentary fashion—a metal pan over a small fire, oyster shells for spoons, coconut husks for bowls. Mine was a feast worth more than I was: a leg of turkey stuffed with sage and thyme and dripping in gravy, freshly baked bread as if just from the ovens, and fish swimming in a tangy sauce made from chopped apples and glazed lemons. There was wine of the finest vintage from Tresea's famed vineyards.*

"I came prepared," she said, smiling at my astonishment. "A merchant from a nearby town supplies my needs and asks no questions. In many places, money speaks louder than one's beliefs. Did you think I would come here to forage for scraps when I have other skills at my disposal?"

In contrast, her meal was simpler: a glass of water, choice fruits and raw vegetables, and servings of sliced runeberries. "I never did acquire a taste for runeberry wine. I prefer to eat them raw."

"These are not from Stranger's Peak." The runeberries that grew in that desolate region were smaller and rounder, like brown peaches. These were larger and paler in color.

"They're from Murkwick. Have you heard of the place?"

"But, Mistress Tea, these runeberries are of a lesser quality than even asha apprentices are given to eat."

"That's true. But they remind me of my years spent as a novice

in my asha-ka. I hated the acrid taste and yearned for the day I was old enough to take them in wine, as every proper asha did. But when I turned sixteen, I found the wine bland and disappointing. As terrible as the fruit was, I had grown used to the taste."

She selected a large slice, lifted it to her lips, and bit down. She chewed briefly and closed her eyes.

"Sometimes it is good to remind ourselves how bitterness tastes."

3

W E ARRIVED AT THE VILLAGE of Murkwick four hours
later, to purchase supplies for our journey to Kion and
also to find horses for Fox and me to ride. Murkwick differed
from Knightscross in two ways. While my village dabbled mainly
in farming produce, the people here involved themselves in the
runeberry trade. And unlike Knightscross, they welcomed bone
witches with open arms.

Runeberries are a willful, intractable breed, Lady Mykaela
told me. They grow only where their forebears had and wither
away when uprooted into unfamiliar pastures, even with soil
richer for farming. And so they grow in places like Stranger's Peak,
where the cold bites at the marrow and only strong, foul-tasting
kolscheya can chip away at the blood that freezes in your veins
each night but where the fruit is the best and most expensive of
its kind. Or as far away as the desert bluffs of Drycht, where they

prize the stems better than the crop and sell them to the most fashionable ateliers in all eight kingdoms to be woven into cloth. Or in the village of Murkwick, where its species of runeberries, owing to the moderation of the seasons and its contradictory nature, produces a far inferior quality. For all that, it remains highly sought after among those who cannot tell the difference.

The village chief refused to accept payment for the runeberries Mykaela purchased, and the people treated her with gratitude verging on worship. I learned the reason for it much later, when a young girl approached me and shyly asked if I was the asha's daughter.

"She's a bone witch," I said without thinking, "not an asha. And I'm not her daughter."

The girl's smile vanished. Before I could react, she delivered a stinging slap against my cheek, and I stumbled back. "You dare insult Lady Mykaela!" she snapped and raised her hand again.

Fox's fingers closed around her wrist. The girl yanked her hand away and the anger left her face, leaving only fear. She hurried away without another look back.

"Bone witches *are* asha, Tea," Fox said to me, "although most would use the former as an insult."

My cheek burned where the girl had struck it. I had no idea of the offense I'd given. Lady Mykaela was exquisite, and she certainly wore the type of clothes I imagined an asha would, but I couldn't envision her beloved by the people or entertaining the rich and ennobled the way the asha in my books did.

"She's loved by the villagers of Murkwick," Fox pointed out.

"The magic she uses might be taboo to some, and Odalia as a whole is suspicious of spellbinders—but there are still parts of the kingdom where that makes little difference."

I wanted to ask him more questions, but I hesitated. I couldn't look at my brother and not see a walking, talking corpse, and for all Lady Mykaela's patient explanations, I was afraid death might have changed him somehow—that something else had returned in his stead and wore his face. He could no longer maintain a heartsglass, the pallor never left him, and sometimes his legs creaked and spasmed when he moved, but Fox made no complaints and bore his death with a restraint I did not have. Unlike us, he did not need sleep or food and spent his time standing guard while Mykaela completed the rest of her purchases.

I noticed something else. Where Fox walked, he cast no shadow. With a quick look behind me, I was relieved to see that I, at least, still had a shade to my name.

If the villagers knew of my brother's condition, they gave no sign of it. He was quiet and said very little, the way he'd always done in life. But something was missing. He was calm and confident, and his eyes were still kind, but that tiny, indefinable spark that made Fox Pahlavi *Fox Pahlavi* was gone. This secret guilt I would carry around with me for many long months afterward.

Fox smiled at me. He didn't talk much for the rest of the day but remained close at hand. I think he knew my fears but could not assure me otherwise.

Lady Mykaela took me to the village runeberry fields to watch the fruit ripen. Planted only the day before, Murkwick's runeberries sprouted overnight from tiny budding shoots to slender stalks of unopened blossoms heavy with potential. As I watched, delighted, their petals unfolded to reveal bright orbs with shifting diamonds at their centers, dimming slightly when I approached but bursting into color when they thought no one saw. The villagers gathered up the black seeds that fell as the fruit was plucked to sow again once the harvest was done.

"This will tide us over until we get to Kion," Mykaela said. Rather than press the fruit and serve it as wine, she asked the villagers to carve them into slices, to eat with gooseflower tea. Its bitterness stained my mouth, but Mykaela insisted. "Once every morning for a year, starting today. Twice a month after that, more if you are able."

"I don't recall my sisters ever eating these for breakfast." I hated the way the berries took command of my tongue and forbade all other taste for hours afterward.

"You are not a Forest witch and neither are you a Water witch. Your sisters are medicine women, not spellbinders. They do not weave the kinds of magic we can. Bone witches like us need their strength—and for good reason. Runeberries will put the iron in your blood and the steel in your spine."

"Why do you call yourself a bone witch and not an asha?"

Lady Mykaela busied herself, storing bundles of runeberries into her horse's large saddlebags before replying. "I *am* an asha, Tea. I am also a bone witch. I cannot be one without being the other. And it would do both of us good to remember that there will always be people who ignore the first in order to condemn me for the second. The secret is to find pride in both,

Tea—the good as well as the bad. It will help you do what needs to be done, regardless of what they see you as."

"Mistress Mykaela?" One of the villagers approached us—a young boy with pleading eyes and smatterings of blue across his heartsglass.

I did not understand, but Lady Mykaela did. She reached into the bags and pulled out a small pouch and signaled for Fox and me to follow.

The boy led us to one of the smaller houses. Inside, an old woman lay groaning on the bed, her eyes clouded with fever. Lady Mykaela gently lifted the blankets off her and glanced at her heartsglass, green tinged and clouded against her chest. "Bonesmelt," she said. "Common for her age but already at an advanced stage. What is your name, boy?"

"Tanner, milady."

"Boil me some hot water, Tanner, and fetch me a clean bowl."

Lady Mykaela took packs and jars from her pouch, all containing assortments of dried herbs. She mixed some of each into a bowl—a pinch from one, a larger dose from another—before dividing them into smaller portions, pouring all but one into folded paper packets with the efficiency of one who did this often. The last she added to the hot water. "This is a mixture of enderroot, sage, and adalt. Your grandmother must drink a bowl of this three times a day, after every meal," she instructed. "When the potion runs out, boil her a fresh batch. One packet for every pot. Remember that. They should last you four months, but I should be back before then."

"Mistress Mykaela?" There was someone else at the door.

This time it was a young woman whose husband had broken his leg in a fall.

We followed Lady Mykaela as she moved from house to house, treating the sick and the injured. I could not figure out how the asha knew their ailments with only a glance at their heartsglass, but I noticed a pattern: the sickly were green hued, family members' blue with worry. There was orange for disinterest, yellow for fear, and red if their owners were healthy and happy. My mentor asked for nothing in return, and my confusion grew with each visit. My books told me that asha could heal the sick, but I had always assumed it was through magic. The reality was very different.

The villagers gave us a simple meal of bread and vegetables, but the asha ate no more than a few bites. It was evening by the time she was done making her rounds, and the village chief asked us to stay for the night, citing the lateness of the hour.

"There's something troubling you, Garen," Lady Mykaela said, smiling. "I can see it in your heartsglass."

I looked and saw faint blue ripples across the surface of his pendant.

"You're right, Mistress," the old man apologized. "I am worried. It will be the seventh day of the seventh month tomorrow, and I wonder… The time is growing close to when that… that *thing* rises again. Murkwick is the nearest village where it could vent its fury, and I am very much afraid—"

"I have not forgotten, old friend," Lady Mykaela interrupted him. "Rest easy. I will deal with the matter tomorrow, as I always have."

"We are, as always, in your debt, Lady Asha. Is there anything else you require?"

"There are two things. I would like a shovel and perhaps a small sword for Sir Fox over here."

"I will have them ready before you leave." The old man bowed. The blue of his heartsglass faded until only its red hue remained.

They gave us the largest room at the Dancing Rune, Murkwick's only inn, at the village chief's request. The innkeeper offered Fox another, but my brother turned it down, calmly pointing out that the dead had no need for sleep. I'm sure it unnerved the man, but Fox had never been one to mince words.

I could sense Fox while he occupied himself in the village and was surprised to learn that a connection existed between us, however faint.

"What did you expect?" Lady Mykaela asked, sitting on her bed. She had traded in her beautiful blue-and-green dress for a silk robe more suitable for sleep. Even the woman's underclothes were stunning. The rough chemise I had brought along looked ungainly and coarse in comparison. "The bond between an asha and her familiar is strong and difficult to break. You'll learn more once we return to Kion."

"What's going to happen tomorrow?"

The woman took something round and carefully wrapped in paper from her pouch. When she pulled back the sheets, I saw a black stone, crumbled and decayed and covered in mold. "This is a bezoar," she told me. "When fresh, it is a powerful antidote to many illnesses. But in a few days' time, not even ashes shall remain. Tomorrow, we shall bring back a fresh specimen." She slid into her bed, took a quick glance back at me. "You may ask me any other questions you have in mind. You must have many."

"I could see the colors of the villagers' heartsglass changing. I've never noticed that before."

"Using the Dark runes for the first time made you more attuned to magic. That is all. Most people know three kinds of asha, Tea. The first are performing asha, known for their dancing and their singing, though their magic may be weaker than others. The second are fighting asha, known for their magic and their prowess, though they may not be the most gracious of hosts. The third are Dark asha like us, the strongest of them all."

"Does this make my sisters asha as well?"

"Your siblings can sense magic, but purple hearts prove they are not powerful enough to be even the weakest of asha. They make for good apothecaries and ateliers, that is true, but they cannot harness magic strong enough to shape it according to their will. *Asha* means two things in old Runic. The first is 'truth'; the second, 'spellbinder.' That is what we must do—we bind the magic and force it to do as we command. Rose may be a good healer, but she cannot see illnesses in heartsglass. And Lilac might be a good diviner, but she is not strong enough to summon so much as fire. They can draw Heartsrune, but that remains the extent of their abilities. Do you not find it odd that it is the custom of even the most remote villages to wear heartsglass?"

"When my parents wedded, they exchanged them as proof

of their love. They have never lost their hearts in the twenty years since their marriage." My eyes betrayed me; they wandered to Lady Mykaela's neck, to her empty heartsglass. I jerked my gaze away, but already Lady Mykaela's smile grew pinched, like she had tasted something tarter than runeberries. For a moment, she looked so sad that I worried I had given offense yet again.

But she only said, "Then that is evidence of your parents' fidelity. But one of the original purposes of heartsglass was to find people who can wield the magic to take them to be trained. And then there are the rare few like you, who do not wait until they are thirteen years old to make their presence known. It was only by a stroke of luck that I was at the right place and time to sense the Dark you drew to summon Fox; you would have fared worse otherwise."

I worked up my courage. "Lady Mykaela, what happened to your heartsglass?"

Her silence was the only reply I received. She turned and blew out the candles, and the room was plunged into darkness. I lay in bed and listened to the rustle of her clothes, the squeak of the mattress as it settled beneath her. When she spoke again, her words rang out like steel hammers. "That is enough questions for tonight. We rise early tomorrow."

It was not easy to fall asleep in strange surroundings. I missed my small bed in my little house in Knightscross, and already I missed my family. I thought about the heartsglass my parents wore, about the hearts Daisy was constantly losing. Now that I knew the truth, I couldn't help but feel cheated. Her explanation of them sounded so commonplace, less exciting than my books led me to believe.

And I was to be an asha. After everything that had happened, I had little time to appreciate my situation. All my childish play at pretending to be the famous asha of my stories now felt ridiculous. Did Taki of the Silk and Nadine of the Whispers feel this way? I wondered. Were they uprooted from the families they loved and sent to unfamiliar places because the magic that brought them their fame first gave them no choice?

I fell asleep with those melancholy thoughts. In the midst of my strange circumstances, Fox's quiet presence in my mind was reassuring. Dead as he was, he was the only familiar thing I had left.

*T*HE WIND BLEW HEAVY POCKETS *of sand across the beach, blanket-
ing everything with grit and ground, but the grave remained
pristine, free of mud and soil. The girl knelt, polished the heavy stone
at the head of the tomb. She watered the small, budding flowers that
sprouted up along the green edges.*

"What do people say of me?"

*"They believe that you have turned fully to the Dark, my lady,
that you have joined the ranks of the Faceless, and that you are preparing to lead the people of the lie to war."*

"And do you believe them?"

I chose honesty. "I do not know, milady."

*"I cannot blame you. The three who claim to lead the Faceless
also draw in the Dark; most cannot tell us apart. Usij leads the southern
faction—he makes a fortress out of the mountains in Daanoris and calls
himself king, but he is all bark and bluster. Druj is wilier—he sows
his discord in the west, and all city-states in Yadosha would pay a dear
amount of money for his head. And as for Aenah, the last leader…"*

*She pauses. A curious, bitter smile is on her lips. "Not much is
known about her save that she originally hailed from Tresea."*

"Mistress Tea," I asked, "who is buried here?"

*The grass stained her dress as she lay beside the grave, laid her
cheek against the ground.*

Sadly, she said, "A boy who died for me."

4

THE SMALL MOUND LAY TWENTY miles away from Murkwick, hidden in the woods. There were no paths, and it seemed like you could find that exact spot only if you knew it was there to begin with.

"This creature used to haunt these woods undeterred for many years, killing stray villagers," Lady Mykaela said, "until an asha who lived over a hundred years ago realized it was a daeva and put an end to its rampage. I harvest its stomach frequently, as I travel to this part of Odalia often. Even dead, however, it can be dangerous. I learned this the hard way, when I was much younger. My shoulder still aches when the weather grows cold."

"Its *stomach*?" I stared at the mound with growing nervousness and fear.

Fox crouched beside the knoll, his eyes strangely eager. His hand played with the hilt of the sword strapped to his waist.

"Keep your distance, Fox," Lady Mykaela told him. She drew out the decaying bezoar and set it down on a large rock. "There is no telling what it may do."

"All the more reason to keep near," he replied. "I have seen daeva before, and I have read as much of them as Tea has. I know what to expect."

"There are many things they leave out of books. And learning about them in stories and learning through experience are two different things—and as I recall, you did not fare so well in the latter." The asha drew out a thin knife and, to my shock, made a small nick on her forefinger. "Take Tea behind those trees. You will not wish to view this daeva up close. And whatever you do, do not look into its eyes."

I tugged at Fox's sleeve without waiting for him to obey. As Fox led me away, she sketched out a strange rune in the air with her cut finger. The blood trailed after her movements; rather than drip onto the ground, it remained suspended, painting the symbol she drew red and pulsing, as if it had a life of its own.

The wind crackled around me, and I felt the small clearing charge with unseen energy, enough to make my hair stand on end. I understood how the asha could have sensed me when I had raised Fox; this must be what it felt like to be struck by lightning but without the pain. I felt the magic gather around the rune before dipping into the mound, and I felt it burrow deep into the hill's center.

But this was different. When I raised Fox, it had felt right. Here, hovering on the edges of Lady Mykaela's magic, my mind brushed against something foul and putrid to my senses—a stench of thought rather than of smell.

The bezoar blazed up and crumbled abruptly into dust, until no trace of it remained.

The creature burst through the mound, roaring in rage. It was a hideous beast, a hodgepodge of animal parts sewn together to form one body. It was the size of a large bull, fat and corpulent, and its head a cross between a badger and a lion, with the latter's mane. Its legs were as long and as limber as a stag's, and its hooves were cloven. It turned toward us, froth dripping from jaws that widened to fold its face nearly against its ears. It bore no gums, only teeth that took up the width of its mouth, sharp and ridged. Any allure it might have possessed was in its eyes, which resembled silver gemstones striped with red.

It howled, and the sound was terrifyingly human.

I remembered the asha's warning too late. Perhaps it had sensed that I was the weakest of its prey, for it came stumbling out of its grave with its eyes already trained on me, and I froze.

It crooned. There was something hideously seductive about its ruby-like gaze on mine, and as much as I wanted to run away, I remained rooted to the spot, unable to move.

The beast bounded toward me, but Fox stepped forward, placing himself between us. His sword was leveled at its body. Unfazed, the beast snarled and leaped forward until it was almost on top of him.

"*That is enough!*" I felt Lady Mykaela release the energy she had been holding at bay around the rune, directing it toward the creature. The spell wove itself around the daeva, stretching tight like a rope to bind the daeva where it stood. The thing stumbled, its ugly snout inches away from Fox's face. Its roar was cut short, and for several moments, it wavered. Fox did not back away and stared stonily back.

Its jaws closed. The creature took a hesitant step backward.

"*Kneel*," Lady Mykaela commanded, her voice soft.

The monster dropped to its haunches. It bowed its head.

"*Let her go.*"

I sank down to the ground, shuddering, able to move again.

"Amazing," Fox said, lowering his blade.

"It is a *taurvi*," Mykaela said. "Swift as the wind, and it sings a splendid lullaby. The bezoar in its stomach is worth more than what a popular atelier can make in many years. That is also how it entices its victims—it paralyzes them, keeping them immobile and docile before it swallows them whole. *Return to your grave.*"

The fight had gone out of the *taurvi*. It was almost meek as it slunk back into the mound it had sprung from. It yawled only once—a thin, almost beseeching cry, like a young girl's.

"*Die.*" The asha's voice was cold and grim.

The creature died. It collapsed into the hole it had climbed out of as soon as the word left Lady Mykaela's lips.

The woman approached the beast, her knife at the ready. Four quick slashes at its midsection, and a bright-yellow bezoar lay in the palm of her hand. The creature turned to ash almost as soon as she retrieved the stone.

Lady Mykaela pulled her cloak closer around herself and sighed. "Take the shovel from the saddlebags, Fox. Return the mound to the same state it was in when we first arrived."

"I'm sorry." I was still shivering. The sudden disappearance of the spell around us had a strange effect on me; I wanted more of it to linger, more of it to sample. Fox placed an arm around me, and I leaned into him, grateful.

"You were not in too much danger." Lady Mykaela lifted the *taurvi*'s bezoar up, admiring the way it sparkled against the light. "But it is a good lesson for you to learn. I trust that you will be more cautious next time."

"*Next time?*" I echoed weakly.

"Why did you take that stone from its stomach?" Fox asked as he shifted earth into the empty hole in the ground.

"Daeva were created by the False Prince with death magic so complicated that not even asha today know how to recreate them. They were born dead, and even dormant, the Dark constantly replenish their bones. The Five Great Heroes discovered the means to kill the daeva—and slew six of the seven. Yet, every few years, they must be forcibly raised, divested of their bezoars, and sent back to their graves. For *taurvi*, harvesttime means visiting this mound once every ten years. There is an *akvan* a hundred leagues away in Daanoris's Sea of Skulls that must be put down in four years' time, and along the Kion borders, one must retrieve a green stone from the tail of a *nanghait* every seven years. Their bezoars slowly decay as the day of their resurrection draws near, and when they disappear, the creatures rise, and we repeat this cycle all over again. It is important that we raise them within a specific time frame—seven days before they revive, at the least. They are dormant before that and do not respond even to the Dark. Dig this grave a year from now, and it will carry no trace of bone. Dig it a week before today, and you will find a complete body."

"And if you do not raise them," Fox said slowly, "they will climb out of their tombs at the peak of their strength and kill again, as one killed me."

Mykaela nodded. "A *savul*, I believe. Sakmeet was in charge of it; she is a Dark asha who lives in Istera. We have had no word of her, and I fear the worst. The only way to kill them again is to rip the bezoar from their bodies—a messy endeavor, even for an average asha. The False Prince's final curse is a heavy burden."

"You say the Great Heroes killed six of the daeva. What of the seventh?"

"The *azi*, the fiercest and most powerful of the daeva, eluded even them. No one knows where its mound lies. It is the most reclusive of the beasts and has not been seen for many millennia."

"And you do all this?" Was this to be my responsibility as well? The thought terrified me.

"I have been doing this for close to fifteen years. Other asha, Deathseekers, and those skilled enough in the magical arts can slay these creatures, though with more difficulty. Only bone witches can control them long enough to deprive them of their bezoars. The people of Odalia may not like us, child, but a reason for their dislike is having to be beholden to us." Mykaela tucked the topaz-hued stone into her waist pouch. "And in exchange, we acquire priceless ingredients. Mix the bezoar with elderbark juice and mushroom tart, and you also have an antidote for consumption."

The effects of the spell Lady Mykaela had woven, combined with the strange paralysis I suffered, still lingered in me. While I had not liked my first brush with the creature, the magic the asha used to contain it had not been unpleasant. My fingers twitched, and I reached out without thinking, seeking for remnants of the magic that remained—

—and felt the full force of Mykaela's will bearing down on my mind. The asha was forcing me to draw in more magic than I could handle, the pleasure so great it was almost painful—

"*Let go.*"

—only to find myself abruptly cut off and on the ground before I could move.

"It will always feel good," Lady Mykaela said softly, "at least at first. But the more you draw in such a short time, the harder it will be to put up barriers in your mind, until all you will concern yourself with is drawing more power until you die from the darkrot. It is an addiction that many bone witches could not overcome, and that is why we are so few in number. I compelled you the way I compelled the creature to show you the consequences of taking in too much, of letting your guard down and allowing someone else an opening to take over. In time, I will teach you control. I will teach you restraint. I will decide the next time you can draw the rune again, and it will be different."

"You put her in danger!" Fox accused, dropping to his knees beside me. I could sense the anger in his thoughts.

"I slew a fellow sister-witch once when I was younger. The daeva took her over, and there was no other choice. I am ruthless now because I have no intention of doing so ever again." Harshness took the place of the asha's melodious voice. "Do you understand me, Tea?"

"Yes," I breathed, squeezing Fox's hand in reassurance, my mind clearer. Lady Mykaela was telling me the reason bone witches were feared: not because we could control daeva but because daeva were not the only ones we could choose to compel.

*D*ID YOU LIKE KNEAVE?" *I asked.*

The girl sat and stared at the ocean from underneath the bones of a monster long dead, for there is a reason they call this place the Sea of Skulls. Water swirled around her ankles and stained the bottom of her dress the color of rusted blood. The skeletal monster loomed above her, its remains an arc against the hot sun that scorched the black earth around them. I remembered the elephant-like daeva she had slain mere feet from where I stood, staring out at the world through unseeing eyes with loops of viscera halfway out its stomach. I held my breath, but no foul odors wafted from the spot. No flies buzzed from where its carcass used to lie. Despite the blazing heat, I could see no maggots combing the earth for flesh. Only the bones from other monsters remained—dead monuments, offerings to the sea.

"No. I found the people strange. I found them suspicious of all those who don't look and act like them. Doubtless they held the same opinions of me but for the opposite reason. You came from Drycht; you understand full well the tyranny of the old guard, the inflexibility of the ruling class. The bourgeois of Kneave entertain more liberties; a Drychta might kill an asha and believe it only follows the will of gods. A Kneavan will claim the higher ground and preach clemency but kill when no one else sees. The runeberry trade influenced Murkwick's beliefs, but the rest of Odalia takes its cues from its capital city. Even Knightscross.

"But the world will always look different when you open your eyes to what you previously refused to see. It was the same for you, wasn't it? When King Aadil outlawed the songs that made you famous everywhere else and they took you from your mother's house to languish in his dungeons for three months."

"How did you know that?" From above us, the skeletal beast watched, knowing.

She gestured at my heartsglass, at the colors that ebbed in and out of view. She smiled. "You are easy enough to read. I did not like Kneave, but entering that city for the first time remains one of the strangest and most exhilarating experiences of my life. Perhaps because everything felt so new. Perhaps because I was realizing how much wider the world was than the Knightscross-shaped one I had occupied.

"I never got over my dislike of crowds, though I have performed before them hundreds of times. I never liked being the center of attention, which is unusual for an asha. But despite the people's aversion to us, I had fond memories of my first night in Kneave."

"Why is that?"

"In my life, I have only ever been attracted to two men. And what is even more unusual was that I met both that very same night in Kneave, though not in the best circumstances."

5

KNEAVE WAS THE CAPITAL OF Odalia, and a celebration was in progress when Lady Mykaela guided us through the winding streets, she riding on her palomino and Fox riding behind me on the gray dapple she'd purchased in Murkwick. I had never seen so many people packed together in so small a space before.

Knightscross constructed its houses according to the natural paths of the land, and so I was used to broad roads. I've lived in Kion for many years, but I've never grown used to the narrow, constrained lanes of busy cities like Odalia. Adding to the feeling of close confinement are the groups of people who have gathered to watch noisy bands of musicians cavorting through the streets, dressed in confusing swirls of clothing and color. Some carried tambourines, while others chose drums or trumpets. All were not shy about making as much noise as was possible.

People built small fires around the city square and took

turns leaping over them while others watched and applauded, laughing. The sight of those flames, coupled with the smallness of the spaces and the largeness of the crowds, alarmed me. I clung to my brother, fearful that the fires might spread, that parts of the city might burn before long. Despite the heat and the smoke surrounding us, his skin was cold to the touch.

"They celebrate the spring equinox," Fox said as boys and girls alike leapfrogged over the pyres, daring each other to jump higher at every turn. "Fire is a cleansing tool, and to leap over it is to clean themselves of all sickness and evil in anticipation of the coming year."

"But we don't do this in Knightscross." The closest thing we have to a large fire was my father's forge, and I could only imagine his reaction should the villagers elect to jump over it.

"Farmland is not an appropriate venue for fire building, Tea."

"I'm not sure cities are made the same way."

The festivities quieted somewhat when we passed. People stopped to stare—at Lady Mykaela's empty heartsglass and then at the silver tints of mine. They tried to melt back into the crowd, to give us room, though the paths were small and gave them difficulty. Fox received a few of those stares for his lack of heartsglass and for the plain silver sword at his hip, as none of the revelers wore weapons that I could see. Not for his absence of shadow, I tried to convince myself, and certainly not because they knew he was dead.

Kneave was nothing like Knightscross. It may seem ridiculous to imagine I could compare the two. But Knightscross was all I'd ever known, and not even my books prepared me for the shock of the city. My village was simple and muted against a backdrop of forests and stone, where the forge and the gossip were the noisiest sounds.

But the city of Kneave wore its people for emphasis, like giant exclamation marks that walked in every street and loitered at every corner. Its citizens attired themselves in bright and stunning dresses that called to the eyes. None of the women back home wore veils; it would be an awkward garment to wear when working in the fields. Some of the Kneavan women wore these loosely about their persons, and others wore them coiled so tightly about their heads that I could not tell the color of their hair or even if they had any. A few took this a step further; they had on masks and long, flowing robes that hid everything but their eyes.

Many of the people's faces were smooth and polished, at times prettier and handsomer than they first appeared. It felt to me that there was something strange about their features—they were a little too refined and a little too contrived, like a whetstone had given them precision but also left them too sharp for nature to allow for. To my eyes, it was like each person wore two faces that shared the exact same space, one pressing down on top of the other—one too pretty and affected to be natural, and the other too flawed and regular to be artificial.

"Glamour," Lady Mykaela said over her shoulder without looking up from her book. I would later learn that it was her habit to read as she walked and read as she rode. She had given me a book from her collection so I could do the same, but I was unused to riding horses, and sore buttocks soon distracted me from turning the pages. "The smallest of magics. Harmless for the most part. It allows the people their vanities, but we asha can see them all the same."

We rode past colorful banners and vibrant pinions. The marketplace was awash with sights and smells—from the fresh, minty scent of potted plants to the tantalizing aroma of fried foods and baking bread that reminded my stomach I'd had nothing but a strip of beef jerky in the last few hours. Signs calling for prosperity and luck graced every door. Carts wheeled by, and children raced past older folk, who bore armfuls of clothes and baskets. Occasionally a carriage would pass, too rich and ornate for its inhabitants to give us more than a second glance.

I expected Lady Mykaela to make for the harbor. She had told me that the fastest way to Kion was to take a ship from the port of Odalia in Kneave, as opposed to the monthlong journey it would take on land. When she rode past the street leading down to the rows of ships anchored at the dock and onto the road leading to the Odalian castle, I was surprised.

"We shall stay at the palace for the night, at King Telemaine's request," the asha said. "It is the spring equinox, and I draw Heartsrunes for the children in Kneave every year. We'll leave at first light tomorrow and catch the earliest ship to Kion. Speak up, Fox. I can see the question on your face."

"I do not mean to cause offense, Mistress. But many Odalians consider it bad luck to offer bone witches a place to stay, even for a night. For the ruler of Odalia to do so would be disastrous in their eyes. How did you manage to convince the king?"

"It was his idea. The royal chancellor and the palace steward have been taken into his confidence, albeit reluctantly, and no one else is aware of our housing arrangements." She smiled faintly. "And in case you wondered—no, I did not compel him to do it. Drawing Heartsrune for so many at once is a tedious task, but I do it in gratitude to His Majesty."

I wasn't sure what to think of the king I deemed responsible for Fox's death, but my brother only shrugged and said that it was a soldier's life, and if they blamed the king for every cut and kill and death that they take, there would be no army left in all the kingdoms.

"But wouldn't that be better?" I asked as we dismounted. Stablehands from the royal stable hurried forward to take the horses' reins. "No armies would mean no war."

Fox laughed suddenly, though his chest did not rise and fall. "Silly girl. You are not yet an asha, and you already understand the games kings and queens play? I certainly don't."

The castle was open to all who came at this time of the year because, like the spring equinox, this was the custom. The people wore magic on their brows. They painted their lips scarlet with the spells' fullness and dusted their cheeks with its rouge. I could feel the enchantments woven into their clothes. Lady Mykaela took her time pointing out some of the spells to me so I could commit to memory how they looked and what they felt like. Many arranged elegance in their feather bonnets and solemnity in their tailcoats. Composure adorned a lady's majestic hat. It didn't work on me; the overabundance of feathers made her look like she had assaulted an ungainly duck in a past life and wore its skin, and the thought made me giggle.

"Why do they do that?" I asked Mykaela. "Why do they waste magic this way?"

"It is the way of the rich," she replied, shrugging one silk-clad shoulder. "They commission the ateliers to spin it into their clothes and call it fashion or have apothecaries paint their faces and call it beauty. You are village born and do not understand the way the city's mind works. The city rich are not like bees in a hive that work together to share honey for all. The city rich are like the jungle apes; they show off their red bottoms and beat their chests because they fear to be culled from the herd if they show weakness. Even the most inferior of runeberries can suffice for this magic, so we let them be."

"Is that why you don't wear magic like they do?"

Lady Mykaela grinned at me. "But I *am* wearing magic, little one. The difference is that it is woven so finely into my *hua* that you cannot detect it."

The people in this part of the city recognized her too and gave us a wider berth. I walked through the crowd with my head down, the ground suddenly more interesting to study than people. Lady Mykaela was used to the silence and walked with her head thrown back and a secret smile on her lips. Fox brought up the rear and paid no attention when those standing closest shrunk back.

The king and his son stood at the castle gates, welcoming visitors. King Telemaine was a large man of unexpected height. It was easier to imagine him in the smoke of battle or in the aftermath of a bloody duel, not dressed in rich satin robes of dyed purple, with a crown two sizes too small for his head. He had a great black beard clumped against his chin to hide a thin, nearly lipless mouth and bright-green eyes that were more shrewd than clever. His heartsglass was built to size, twice as large as my own but adequate when framed against his massive chest. Beside him was a young boy a year or two older than me, wearing a smaller crown and his father's eyes. But where King Telemaine's eyes were a hard and opaque jade, his son's were deep and gentle emeralds that smiled back despite his serious face. He was easily the most handsome boy I'd ever met. When he caught me staring, I looked away, frantically willing my blush to fade.

"Lady Mykaela." The king stepped forward, large hands folding over one of the asha's and hiding it from everyone's view. "Thank you for coming, as always."

"It is my pleasure, as always. There is a good crowd here. How many heartsglass are present?"

"Four hundred and eighty in all."

I started. In Knightscross, it would be a good year if there were more than twenty thirteen-year-olds for the equinox.

"We have even less reason to delay, then. The night grows old. This is my apprentice, Tea Pahlavi, and her brother, Fox."

"I am enchanted." King Telemaine was an experienced statesman. The faintest spasm of orange flickered across his heartsglass, but only for the briefest second. I felt an irrational surge of resentment and forgot my embarrassment.

"No, you aren't."

Both King Telemaine and Mykaela turned to me; the man was curious and the asha cautioning.

I could understand his disinterest of yet another bone witch in his kingdom, but Fox was a different matter. "My brother died. You told him where, and he went like a good soldier to fight and got nothing but a coffin for his troubles. Surely he deserves more than your indifference"—I gave his heartsglass a pointed glance—"even if it is well concealed."

Some of those in his retinue gasped, alarmed by my frankness. Lady Mykaela said nothing.

The king threw his head back, revealed two rows of square, white teeth to everyone present, and laughed aloud. "Such spirit in this one! You've chosen well, Mykaela! She'll grow your fangs soon enough."

"She shows much promise," Lady Mykaela murmured. "She seems to have learned to read heartsglass with little training."

King Telemaine turned to Fox. "I am grateful for the services you rendered your kingdom, young man, and I am sorry for the situation that finds you here. I shall talk to my stewards and ensure that your family will want for nothing. It is small compensation, but it is the least I can do."

"You are too kind, Your Majesty." Fox bowed.

"It was a bad business. I remember that order, but I had little choice. I could not afford to have my northern borders terrorized by some nameless creature. We never did find the daeva, but my men must have injured it, for the attacks ceased soon after. What are the chances of it slinking off to whatever lair it calls its own to die?"

"With much respect to Your Majesty," Fox said, with his usual gravity, "I hope it did not."

The king laughed even harder. "I see that you have your hands full with these siblings, Mykaela. Fire and calm, these two, water and flash. Much like my sons. This is Prince Kance."

The boy smiled at me, and I felt my cheeks prickle with heat again. "It is my honor to meet you, asha." He bowed low, and his heartsglass swung with the movement. Like his father's, it was set in silver and adorned with an intricate working of the royal family crest along its edges: a lion's silhouette emblazoned against the sun.

"I'm not an asha," I stammered. How could a simple smile work such wonders to my heart? "I'm…I'm—"

"An apprentice," Lady Mykaela interrupted, taking pity on me, "due to take up her novitiate in Ankyo."

"But a bone witch all the same, eh?" The king winked at me. "It has been a rare year. The first new bone witch in decades! Two of you from Odalia, when many other kingdoms are forced to do without. Doesn't Istera only have that one old crone left, Mykaela? Of course, we don't have Kion's heartforger, but he's old and getting on in years."

"Heartforger?" I asked before I could stop myself.

King Telemaine gestured at my heartsglass with a thick hand.

"Their heartsglass are silver white, like yours. But they don't wave magic about like you do, only fire up memories and forge them into new ones."

Two others approached the king—one a royal councilor, judging from the robes he wore, and the other a young boy in a brown cloak and hood. I read the blue and yellow palpitations on the older man's heartsglass, an irregular heartbeat of fright. The other's was easier to discern—his was beet red with anger, directed at us. I didn't bother to look at their faces, keeping my eyes on the councilor's heartsglass instead.

"Your Majesty," he stuttered. "We shouldn't—shouldn't keep the children waiting."

You cannot spend so much time on those witchfolk, the man's heartsglass seemed to whisper. *What would the people think, seeing their king consorting with these pariahs?*

"He is right." Lady Mykaela laid a firm hand on my arm. "We had best get started. Four hundred and eighty children are waiting."

"Kings and queens may be let off with ungracious behavior," she murmured once we were alone again. "Bone witches may not. Speak in that manner to the king or to anyone else in the palace, and I will box your ears and have you clean the city outhouses for a month. We are welcomed in most of Odalia because of his generosity and are outcasts without."

"I promise," I said meekly, because Lady Mykaela was the kind who carried out anything she threatened, if our time at the daeva mound was any indication. "What did he mean by heartforgers?"

She tapped at my heartsglass. "A different magic but with the same color. They're of more use to the people than bone witches, so they aren't as reviled. They can take memories and break them into bits and pieces, distill them down into potions and spells, and build them back up into new hearts, bright and counterfeit, so that even we can't tell one heartbeat from the other. Fortunately, some artificial hearts cost more than a kingdom, and so few people bother."

"But why?"

"For noble reasons and for horrible reasons. Give your heart to the wrong person and they can abuse that trust, and there are spells to prevent you from drawing one anew. When you have enough enemies, it is sometimes necessary to speed up what nature did not intend. The strongest spells require memories. There are many people who wish to forget, and there are many rich enough to pay for the privilege."

"But that's terrible!"

"People can be terrible, Tea." Lady Mykaela's empty heartsglass winked against the light as she turned away, and I wondered what in the asha's past was responsible for making her so sad.

•• ＞||＜ ••

Only one asha was necessary for the equinox ritual, so I stood aside, watching from the sidelines while Lady Mykaela attended to her task. As her apprentice, I was given a spot among the most junior of the king's staff: on the edges of the crowd but able to watch the proceedings without looking over everyone else's heads. Fox, not quite as fortunate, stood somewhere in the middle of the group. It did not matter; I could feel him there, and that was enough.

We were part of a large audience looking on, where at the center of the town square, a group of children around my age stood expectantly. They were dressed in their prettiest and most expensive clothes and held their empty heartsglass in their hands.

After presenting themselves to the king, the boys and girls waited as Lady Mykaela moved down the line, tracing runes as she went.

Each heartsglass case seemed to me even more elaborate than the next. I could feel poise and composure incantations woven into the dress of one girl so that the crowd marveled even as she fidgeted and squirmed in her lace and satin best. One boy dug a finger into his nose with undue diligence, the spells on him muting the action. *It was simpler back in Knightscross*, I thought. *We were too poor to afford but to behave.*

Behind me, a chorus sang, and instruments were played by unseen hands. Lady Mykaela continued, fingers working at the air, and the people watched, their faces enchanted to hide their disdain of the bone witch—to all but those who can see through the magic and through them.

"They say you can bring back the dead."

I looked behind me. A boy stood there, his hostility obvious.

"They say you can bring back the dead," he repeated. "Well? Can you?"

Most of the people in Kneave had gone out of their way to ignore me, and so his pointed derision took me by surprise. "It depends. Do you require raising?"

It did not appear to be the answer the boy wanted.

"Can you, or can't you?" A black cloak many sizes too big swallowed him up, hid his heartsglass from my view. I could not see the color of his hair, could only see the lower half of his face and one of his eyes, which was hooded and gray. If only I could see his heart, I thought, and tell whether he had reasons to be smug or whether he was merely stupid. At least he did not smell of spells and invocations, none woven into his clothes to mask his disgust. "I'm a bone witch. Of course I can."

"My father says bone witches are demon children," the boy persisted. "They curse the healthy and blight the sane. No other magic would touch them because they sell their hearts to the Dark. That's how they raise dead men, soulless as they are."

"Bone witches do not sell their hearts!"

The boy's eyes narrowed. "Because you have no hearts to give, the lot of you. So you take others for your own and bleed them dry. You grow the dead by the armies, and if we don't keep you in check, you will let them overrun us."

"That's not true." I grew angrier with every word. I had done nothing for the boy to single me out. "You hate us for nothing more than prejudice."

The boy pulled his cloak even tighter around himself. "I know your tricks. My father told me all about your kind. If you can't see my heartsglass, then you can't curse me."

"I don't want to curse you." That was only half the truth, because I was angry and did wish I knew how to shut him up.

From inside his hood, the boy's face hardened. "Your kind killed my mother," he snapped. He turned and fled back into the confines of the crowd but not before his heavy cloak shifted and I saw his heartsglass. It blazed back at me for an instant, a bright-tipped shimmering silver, and then it was gone, lost in the maze of people—and the boy along with it.

S HE HAD CHANGED HER HUA *in the interim. This time, it was of a deep blue, to mimic the depths of the sea. A pattern of waves made up half of the dress before tapering off as it drifted downward, speckled in areas with orange-colored carp and silver-backed trout. The dragon was again a prominent design here, but parts of its body remained hidden behind her waist wrap, which was tinted in turquoise and overlaid with peach and gray seashells, so only its head and front legs stuck out. Its eyes were made of black agate, and they peered out at me with its disproportioned snout raised, tusks on display. Its hind legs jutted out at the bottom of the thick wrap, tail ending in a long, sharp spike.*

To complement her hua, *she wore an assortment of jeweled pins on her hair commonly seen in royal courts. The gems dangled from long sticks pushed into her hair, braided and secured by silk bands and fashioned from aquamarine and fire-opal beads.*

"I have made twenty-eight visits to the Akyon oracle."

This announcement piqued my curiosity. I was aware of the Ankyo oracle's importance to the asha of the Willows, but the women are only required to visit her for the most important matters—when she begins a relationship with a patron, for example, or when she pledges service to a king or noble.

"The average asha makes only two visits to the temple during her

time as an apprentice," she said, sensing my next question. "The first to present herself when she comes to take up residence at the Willows, and the second when she is about to debut as a full-fledged asha. Until she finds a benefactor, she is no longer required to announce herself to the oracle.

"Unfortunately, the oracle had something very different in mind with me."

6

WHERE KNEAVE WAS A CLOSED city of shuttered trade, Ankyo, the capital of Kion, was a flourishing cornucopia of open spaces and color. It was a kingdom made up of other kingdoms, invaded by one or the other at different times in history before finally breaking away and achieving independence on its own terms. But such influences remained—from the severe-looking headscarves worn by some that were reminiscent of Drycht to the cylindrical top hats favored by men from the Yadosha city-states to the multiple inclined roofs of the houses here, distinctive in Arhen-Koshon and Daanorian architecture. The roads were wider, which I preferred, and most of the houses were simpler in design, no more than small square structures with white walls and angled roofs.

The Odalian capital was a colorful place, where people showed off their silks and jewelry, and many Kions made up for their simple homes with elaborate wardrobes. I didn't know how

I wasn't constantly tripping over cloths and hems, for the people favored heavier garments as much for fashion statements as for the colder seasons. Long trains of satin trailed behind the women, coupled with yards of sleeves of intricate designs that hung from their elbows or spilled down from their waists, imitating the asha's traditional *hua*. Headscarves were not as common in Ankyo as in Kneave, but every now and then, I spotted a covered head among the crowds. Many here chose to wear their hair loose or had elaborately coiffed hairstyles that sported as many as three or four gemstone ornaments. The men wore less than the women, but the designs stitched into their long tunics and overcoats covered every inch of space, elaborate to the point of fastidiousness. There was no surface on their clothes that did not have embroidery or patterns or motifs of paisley and crests in some way. Two or three layers of clothing appeared to be the standard, and Lady Mykaela's beautiful *hua* suited the Kion fashion perfectly.

And if the magic the Odalians wore had been enough to make my head spin, the spells here nearly forced me to my knees. Waves of it emanated from nearly every person we passed, and the world spun. I swayed in my saddle, and only Fox's quick thinking kept me from falling off my horse.

"Take these." Lady Mykaela was beside me in a moment, offering me two jeweled pins like the ones she wore in her hair. One was a curved accessory set with beautiful star sapphires, and the other was plainer, shaped like a strangely gnarled crescent moon, and wrapped in silver wire and amethyst. "Pin these to your hair."

The dizziness abated when I put both on. I could still feel the magic roaring around me, but it felt strangely muted and no longer hurt my eyes or my mind. "A countermeasure," the asha explained. "Do not let the simplicity of our city fool you. Kions take their love of magic to an even greater extreme than Odalians do."

"Is it always like this?" It seemed offensive to me somehow, how people wasted their magic this way, when the villagers in Murkwick struggle to make every runeberry patch count.

"There is a reason they call Ankyo the City of Plenty, Tea. Most Kions are rich, which also means they can't help themselves."

Kion castles were different in structure from Odalian castles. They were smaller in size but boasted multiple floors, each layer marked by a bowed rooftop—thinner than the ones in the kingdom of Daanoris but less ornate than those of Arhen-Kosho. The result was not unlike several tiers of sugared cake piled atop one another with pointed spires on every corner curling up into the sky. But this time, Lady Mykaela ignored the palace and turned to a small district nearby and into another world entirely.

The houses here were not as small and as square as most of the city but longer and more rectangular in form, the size of two or three average Ankyon houses. The walls facing the street were made of thick adobe and white brick, plain and devoid of any other design. "We call this the Willows," Lady Mykaela said, "home to the greatest asha in all the kingdoms."

"There aren't any willows," Fox said, who sometimes took things literally.

"Here is one." And Lady Mykaela placed a hand on my shoulder.

She led us to one house in particular. Only a peculiar symbol painted on a wooden sign out front distinguished it from several others along that same street. Beyond the initial doorway was a long strip of corridor that led into the inner rooms. The asha paused at a spot where the cobbled ground ended and the carefully tamped-down earthen floor I would learn was common in all asha-ka began. She took off her shoes and placed them in a small wooden cubicle built for that purpose and signaled for us to do the same.

The narrow passageway continued into an airy room that was both a reception hall and a transition place between the rest of the rooms and the street outside. Thick rugs of beautiful geometric designs lined the walls, and the floor was similarly covered with a thinner, less intricate carpet. The ceiling was higher than I had anticipated, with sloping curves that formed a hollowed out dome at its center. A small screen stood at the farthest end of the room, preventing visitors from seeing the inner chambers within, and a towering flower display was arranged on a table before it. A steel coal brazier lay in one corner, blazing merrily.

Two people rose to meet us as we entered. The first was a very old woman, her skin stretched so tautly over her bones that she looked nearly like a skeleton herself. Her hair was completely white and carefully set against the back of her skull in a severe bun. She reminded me of an aged *tamra* cat's, with her triangularly shaped face and pointed chin. Her cheeks were sunken in, but her eyes were a bright and intelligent green. She wore a *hua* even more elegant and elaborate than Lady Mykaela's; it was an abstract design of pale amber against a deep-brown background and an olive-green waist wrap with actual emeralds sewn into the gold-embroidered silk, matching the color of her eyes. She held a large, ornate fan with gold calligraphy that she kept snapping open and closed every few seconds.

Beside her was a round-faced girl wearing a simple peach robe over a gray tunic. Her dark hair was plaited into two braids, the ends of which traveled past her hips. She was remarkably pretty and looked curiously first at me and then at Fox.

But the older woman ignored us, addressing the asha instead. "And what is a man doing inside our asha-ka?" She had a high, penetrating voice that yowled out words rather than spoke them.

"It can't be helped, Mother. He comes with her."

The old woman refused to look at me. "Highly improper, highly improper. There are no rooms available for men here, whether they be wretched familiars or not. You know that, Mykaela."

"The Owajin boardinghouse is only a block away from the district, Mother. I can talk to the mistress there and set up lodgings for him."

"Do that, but do not arrange for anything more permanent. These wretchlings of yours come and fail so often that it would cost us more in the long run. Have you brought her to the oracle?"

"Not yet, Mother."

"I don't see why you bring these waifs here without consulting the oracle. If they do not pass the test, then they are not welcomed here."

"This one is different."

"Ha! You thought the same of those other wretchlings! What you consider 'different' matters little to me. Your unkempt charge might burn herself out soon enough, and then we would have to shoulder that expense on top of everything. Take her to the oracle, and then we shall see." She snapped her folding fan close one last time. "Come, Shadi."

The girl in the peach robe shot us an apologetic look but obeyed.

"That's your *mother*?" I whispered to the asha, aghast, as soon as the two had left the room.

Lady Mykaela chuckled. "I call her Mother, but we aren't related by blood. This is the House Valerian, my asha-ka, and she is Mistress Parmina, who runs it."

I was even more horrified. One of the books my father had bought for me dealt with the exploits of contemporary asha, and one of the warrior-maidens it told about was a woman named Parmina of the Fires. She had once served as the personal bodyguard to King Farnod, who also happened to be King Telemaine's father and Prince Kance's grandfather. The book talked in glorious detail of the many instances she had saved him from an assassin's blade before leaving to head her own asha-ka. Surely this could not be the same Parmina. The tale I remembered did not match that pinched face and that thin, reedy voice.

"She is one and the same. Do not let her appearance deceive you. She is still a powerful asha in her own right, and she is also one of Kion's best minds. She's a bit waspish now, because it is morning and she hates to have her sleep interrupted. Let us bring you to the oracle and prove her wrong."

"What did she mean about passing a test?" I asked once we were back out in the street. Instead of leaving the district, Lady Mykaela led us even deeper into its center. People stopped to bow low to Lady Mykaela before hurrying on. Some shot Fox and I inquisitive looks but did not linger to ask questions.

"It is a requirement for asha novices to be brought to the oracle but not to pass her test. Many who have failed the first time have gone on to become skilled spellbinders—apprentices must pass only their second tests, when they make their debut. Faceless insurgents have always been a problem, and the first test is simply our way of weeding them out."

"But if they do not pass—"

"For different reasons, and not because they are spies. Mother, unfortunately, is highly superstitious. If the oracle does not approve of a girl at their first meeting, Mother will not accept her into the Valerian. I believe it has something to do with what the oracle herself told Mother when she was an apprentice."

I didn't know what to say. A part of me balked at having traveled so far only to be turned away, but another part rejoiced at the possibility that they would return me to my family if I failed.

"There are many other asha-ka who are willing to take in those who Mother rejects," Lady Mykaela said, dispelling that last hope. "But do not worry yourself over it. I am certain you will succeed."

"But…why would she even consider letting bone witches into her asha-ka? Aren't we bad luck?"

"In Kion, we call ourselves Dark asha. 'Bone witch' is offensive here just as much as it is in Odalia, but all asha take offense at the term. And Dark asha are not necessarily a prerequisite to fail the oracle's test, little one. Mistress Simin, who was head of the Valerian before she died and Mother took over, was also a Dark asha." She smiled kindly at me. "Do not let the prejudices of a few people affect your place in the greater scheme of Kion. In the Willows, all asha are equally respected."

The oracle lived in a small shrine at the very center of town. It was small compared to the other asha-ka around it but looked more impressive. It had a double-domed roof, and I could see colorless smoke rising out of its top, like wayward clouds drifting back into the sky. A pillar of thin columns stretched across the entrance before large doors built of polished wood.

"I cannot join you inside," Lady Mykaela said quietly. "It is forbidden for more than one asha to enter at the same time, so Fox and I will wait here until you return."

"But what do I do?"

"The oracle will ask you for an item. Take the sapphire pin I had given you for this. Answer her honestly, little one. Asha also means 'truth,' and truth is the only weapon you need. The oracle sometimes speaks in riddles, but what she says must remain between the two of you." A small bell hung from one side. The asha rung it three times, the sound loud to my ears in the quiet. "Now go. She is waiting."

The entranceway led to a narrow passage not unlike the one we had entered the Valerian by, lit only by small torches on the walls. The path seemed to go on forever, and it constantly curved to the right like a snake winding around itself, leading into a large room devoid of furniture or decoration.

The first thing I saw when I stepped into the main chamber were the fires. They rose up from a large brazier at the center, but rather than breathe in soot and ash, I found myself taking in the smell of sandalwood. A small figure dressed in white was seated before it, and the train of her dress spread out around her like a pristine fan. A veil was drawn across her face, so I was unable to see her features, but when she lifted an arm, I saw her hand, smooth and unwrinkled.

"What is your sacrifice?" Her voice was like a mournful chorus that spoke as one, and it echoed across the bare room.

I fumbled at my hair and pulled at the pin I wore, the one made from star sapphires.

"Throw it into the fire."

I hesitated, shocked. Surely Lady Mykaela didn't mean to give me something so valuable only to be wasted in this manner? My hand wavered between the expensive blue gems and the less costly amethyst with its odd crescent.

The veiled woman made a swift, impatient gesture.

"Throw it into the fire, child."

It hurt to see those sapphires lost to the flames. The oracle remained unmoved, staring hard at the center of the fire, so close that I feared sparks would fall on her veil and clothes and burn her.

"Do you truly wish to return home, child?"

A yes hovered at my lips, but I hesitated. Lady Mykaela had told me to answer the oracle's question honestly. All throughout the journey, I had convinced myself that there was nothing I wanted more than to go back home to Knightscross. But then I recalled the hostility of the villagers, people I had long considered to be friends. In truth, I had thought much like them, but now that I was on the other side of that hate, I refused to go back to that way of thinking.

If I did return, I knew they would still treat me differently, even if I never drew the Dark for the rest of my life.

And then there was another reason.

The woman waited. Countless asha must have entered her sanctum, must have wrestled with the same choices I did.

"No." The word came out small and disbelieving. "I do not wish to return home."

"Why?"

I swallowed. "Because I like how the power to wield the magic feels."

The flames seemed to blaze brighter, as if the fire had heard my answer and approved.

"You will change Ankyo, for the good and also for the bad. You will change Kion. You will change the Eight Kingdoms. Return to me once you have entered a mind from where three heads sprout." And the woman turned away.

As I left the room, I saw her reach toward the fire. I saw the flames curling toward her outstretched hand, like a child would to his mother or a man would to his wife. And then a heavy gust swept through the room, dousing the fires in one swift motion, plunging the room into darkness. I looked over to where the white figure had stood, but she had disappeared with the wind. I was alone.

"Congratulations, Tea." Lady Mykaela was smiling as I stepped out of the temple. "I knew you could do it."

"How did you...?"

"The smoke changed," Fox said quietly. I turned to look and saw it rising out from the covered dome a light blue color, no longer the colorless wisps I'd seen when I entered. We had attracted a small crowd while I was inside, and people were already coming forward, proffering Lady Mykaela their congratulations. The Dark asha's face beamed; Fox's looked less enthusiastic.

Out of the corner of my eye, I caught someone staring at me. He was swathed in black from head to toe, the way Drychta women preferred their dress. The eyes were veiled, but I had the impression that they were staring straight at me, and it wasn't friendly.

I blinked, and the apparition was gone from view.

"Tea? Is something wrong?"

It's nothing.

"It's nothing," I echoed and turned away.

*T*HIS IS AN EVERFLOWING, AND this is a tamarisk." She touched first one flower and then another. "This one is colchicum. Amaryllis. Burdock. The language of flowers might seem a frivolous concept to most who live outside of our little part of Ankyo, but it's an important part of our lives. We asha are always expected to be on our most proper behavior, to never have so much as a hair out of turn. Asha do not cry or scream or make threats. When people cut us, we are expected to do only two things: smile and bleed."

She busied herself with the bouquet arrangement on the table, taking out a flower at one end, adding a few more in other places. Her finger grazed against the petal of a large pink blossom.

"Our houses are named after flowers for a reason. My house, Valerian, means 'of an accommodating nature.' Other asha-ka hold similar meanings. Hawkweed is for quick sightedness. Calla means 'magnificent beauty.'

"It was only after I learned the language of flowers that I learned how inappropriately my sisters were named. Lilac means 'the first stirrings of love'—and yet my sister Lilac was a spinster, more comfortable in her own company than in others. Marigold was a happy, bouncy girl, though her name meant 'despair.' Rose meant 'beauty,' but she was the homeliest of us sisters.

"And as for Daisy—"

The long, slim fingers stilled momentarily against the green leaves.

"There are many different kinds of daisies. A garden daisy means 'I share in your sentiment.' A wild daisy means 'I make no promises.' A Michaelmas daisy is to be an afterthought. And the common daisy means innocence.

"But Daisy died only a few years after I arrived at Kion."

Her hands moved again, pale against the vibrant flowers.

"In this regard," she said softly, "I'd like to believe she was quite common."

7

ISTEN HERE, GIRL. I DON'T need to know your name. I don't
want to know your name. So many girls flutter in and out
of this house, running away and getting married and dying and
leaving us in the red. You will begin work here as one of our maids.
If you last long enough to begin your formal lessons, then I will
finance your training to be asha. Until then, you will work at the
scullery and clean the rooms and do everything I say if you know
what's good for you."

This was how Mistress Parmina welcomed me into House
Valerian. This was how she welcomed every asha they took in, but I
felt that the old woman was more abrupt with me than she might have
been with the others. Lady Mykaela had brought half a dozen other
girls to Kion before she found me. The old woman refused to accept
any of them, certain they would fail their test with the oracle, and was
smug when proven right. That I was the exception annoyed her.

It took me several days to get used to the Valerian, and I was amazed at how big it truly was. The asha-ka was three houses joined together by a strip of corridor, with only the main house visible from the outside. The largest room was where Mistress Parmina received visitors, and the smaller rooms along the back were used for sleeping. Mistress Parmina had her own room, and Lady Mykaela and Lady Shadi had theirs as well, despite the long periods of time my mentor spent outside of Kion. A separate path led to the dining area and the scullery, where I and the two maids the asha-ka employed slept. Lady Mykaela also gave me permission to make use of her library whenever she was away, and what little personal time I had was spent reading my way through her impressive collection of books, returning frequently for second and third and seventeenth helpings.

The next was a guesthouse where visitors could spend the night, and that was composed of one large room with multiple screen partitions that could be added to or removed according to the resident's fancy. The smallest was a bathhouse made of wood. I learned much later that the water piped into the baths did so through a series of underground springs that traveled through the heart of the Willows and that supplied many of the asha-ka in this manner.

There was a courtyard garden within the house's walls, which contained a vegetable and herb garden. There was even a tiny pond filled with guppies and a few large turtles.

As the newest member of House Valerian, I was given many chores to do. I was one of the first to wake and spent most of my mornings watering the plants and tending to the vegetable garden, sweeping the floors and the street outside of the house, and cleaning the rooms. I was also given the task of cleaning the outhouses, which I hated most of all, though fortunately the maids and I took turns. Their names were Kana and Farhi, and both were seventeen years old.

Kana was amiable with a blushing, demure prettiness. Her family came from the small village of Belaryu in Southeast Kion, where her grandfather's ancestors had lived since Empress Undra's reign over a century ago. Her father sold pomegranates at the city market, and her mother looked after Kana's siblings, all three younger than she was. She was fond of pretty things and hoped to one day purchase a *sivar*, like those asha wore, from one of the many hairdressing establishments in the Willows. Mistress Parmina frowned on the maids wearing anything elaborate but allowed her a plain hairpin with a tiny faux ruby set on it, which she wore at all times.

Farhi came from different stock altogether. Her family moved to Kion from Adra-al when she was seven years old, but they continued to cling to their Drychta roots, wearing their traditional dress and veil, though her face was uncovered. To work in the Willows had not been her choice, but the job paid well. She looked on the asha's fancy *hua* and its ornaments with disapproval but otherwise kept to herself.

Both girls' families lived near Ankyo's market district, and whenever I heard them talk about visiting their parents or buying small toys from nearby shops to bring home to their siblings, I could not help feeling a small pang of homesickness. I would have to travel a longer way to see my family.

One other woman worked at the Valerian, named Ula. She served as Mistress Parmina's assistant and made an account of every transaction that went on inside the asha-ka—the household expenses, tabs incurred from shops, and all the fees asha earned from their parties and contracts. She also booked new engagements for them and kept track of all money changing hands, including any gifts and tips patrons may have presented to the asha.

I was surprised to learn that Lady Mykaela still went to the parties and dinner gatherings Ula arranged for her. I assumed that she had earned her independence and was free of such petty details. The asha herself explained to me that while she could take time off if she desired, these social meetings were her means of keeping track of the local politics of the day and to cement her influence with the powerful nobles who frequented such celebrations.

It took me awhile to learn more about the rest of the members of our little household, and they were fewer than I imagined. Mistress Parmina ran the asha-ka. Lady Mykaela was her adopted daughter and also her successor. Lady Shadi was the only apprentice asha, having arrived two years before I did, and was about to make her debut. She was nice, but she was always rushing out to attend lessons. With my chores taking up most of my days, we never had much time to talk. Like Mistress Parmina, she could not draw the Dark. While House Valerian was known for taking in Dark asha, it was not a requirement.

Lady Shadi was not expected to contribute to the household chores because she was busy enough with attending classes during the day and going out to entertain at night. These parties were the bread and butter of many Houses, where nobles and others who could afford it pay asha to bring life to what might otherwise be boring functions. Apprentices make their debut as young as fourteen or fifteen years old, and these parties were integral to their development as asha. While problems did come up—an asha apprentice had caused a scandal the year before when she ran away with a nobleman's son—most asha knew better than to jeopardize their chances of a good life.

I had always thought *hua* were made the same way: long, trailing sleeves, a waist wrap as thick as one's torso, a tunic-like front to display the detailed under robe underneath. That wasn't always the case. I saw asha wearing different variations of this wardrobe to mimic the fashion style popular in the kingdom they were born in or to put their own personal spin to the design. But asha policy required that they all wear the traditional *hua* when attending functions at an official capacity, including entertaining guests within Ankyo.

Lady Shadi often departed from the Valerian when I was waiting on Mistress Parmina, so I rarely saw her leave. But I caught a glimpse of her as she was stepping out of the house one evening. She wore a beautiful *hua* of a deep coral that made an elegant contrast against her dark skin. Blue-green bamboo swayed against swirling, silver cloud patterns on the rich cloth, and she had on a gray waist wrap with embroidered sparrows set in gold.

Heads turned to look at her as she made her way leisurely down the street, but Shadi must have been used to those admiring stares, for she never turned her head.

There were three other asha under Mistress Parmina, but they were contracted out to several nobles in other kingdoms at the time. Two of them were serving as bodyguards in the kingdoms of Istera and Arhen-Kosho, while one was at the Yadosha city-states. I must confess that despite the books I had about asha, I knew very little about the workings of the Willows until Lady Mykaela took me aside one day to explain it all to me.

The first asha-ka to come into existence was the House Imperial. It was founded by the legendary asha Vernasha of the Roses, also known as one of the Five Great Heroes, who made her home in Ankyo, in the then-newly-established kingdom of Kion. She was a noblewoman of the Tresean court and taught her novices the arts of dancing, singing, and etiquette. The most skilled of these she sent to work as entertainers at royal assemblies and by keeping an ear out for court intrigues was able to extend her influence into the other kingdoms.

Only a few asha proved to be skilled at the fighting arts. Of these, she offered the best to kings and nobles to serve as personal bodyguards. Once in these positions of power, they were able to affect kingdom policy, helping to cement a longer-lasting peace among the rulers. She was quite adamant, however, that all who wished to be asha be strong in the Runic magic, a law still enforced today.

"But why must I have to learn how to sing and dance?" I asked her, bewildered. "Isn't being a Dark asha enough?" It was true that the asha in many books I'd read were skilled musicians and dancers, but I had not known this was required of them.

"Being the most powerful asha there does not always mean you are the most influential or the most popular," Lady Mykaela explained. "In war, asha influence outcomes with their prowess in fighting, with their skills. But sometimes a beautiful voice can change a kingdom better than a sword ever could. Asha gifted in the arts are highly sought after in royal courts; quite a few go on to marry royalty. Defeat them in war and beguile them in peacetime—Vernasha believed both to be the way to stability."

She shrugged and added drily. "Over the years, however, asha-ka themselves have become quite political, more concerned with bringing prestige to their houses. Nevertheless, most follow the letter of the law that Vernasha has laid down, even if not always in spirit."

Word of the Willows spread, and women not just from Kion but from all over the lands flocked to Ankyo, wanting to be trained. Many did not possess the innate sense of magic Vernasha demanded in order to become asha, so she gave them other jobs—banquet masters and tearoom owners to cater to an asha-ka and their wealthy guests, ateliers to create the *hua*, hairdressers to fashion the hair ornaments important to an asha's wardrobe, and instructors to specialize in singing, in dancing, and in other softer arts.

The Willows attracted women from all kingdoms. There were dark-haired and dark-eyed Kion asha; blond-haired, blue-eyed asha from Tresea; and golden-skinned, angular-eyed asha from Daanoris. There were even asha as far away as the Drycht bluffs, fleeing from that kingdom to avoid persecution and finding refuge in Ankyo. A few still veiled themselves, though many forsook their traditions and embraced the customary Kion *hua*.

The thorn of my life was Mistress Parmina. The old woman frequently sent me out with a list of errands for special items— her medicines or the red bean cakes she was fond of or two dozen heavy *hua* to be laundered all at once—and punished me with double duty at the outhouses if I did not return within the hour. Because I had trouble finding my way around the city and because she wouldn't allow any of the other maids to accompany me, I was almost always saddled with these unwanted duties upon my return.

The old woman loved to bathe and insisted that I attend to her in the bathhouses in place of either Kana or Farhi. I spent many a night crouched on the cold, earthen floor, my knees numb and my hands gnarled from the moisture in the air, washing and soaping the old woman's back. Perhaps the most terrifying aspect of this for me was the mistress's naked body. It was hard for me to imagine her as having been a beautiful asha in her youth like Lady Mykaela claimed, because while she was as thin as a broomstick, her skin sagged and folded in the worst of ways, like yards of ungainly, sickly-yellow cloth that moved and breathed when she did.

She belched and passed gas whenever she felt like it, which was often. She demanded that I massage her feet every day, which were caked in old sores and pockmarks. I was commanded to prepare many of her favorite dishes, only for her to claim she had ordered no such thing when brought before her and then demand that the cost of these meals be deducted from the Valerian's investment of me. Because she was the head, everyone obeyed her, no matter how ridiculous or irrational her orders were.

I felt that Mistress Parmina acted like an overindulgent brat, as if her advanced age had regressed her to a spoiled child. Once, she ordered me to sit down on a chair propped up in one corner of the room. I obeyed, only to leap to my feet with a loud shriek that sent Lady Shadi and Kana running into the room. Mistress Parmina, on the other hand, was cackling. Half-hidden underneath the cushions was a small cactus.

I was not ashamed that I spent many a night coming up with different ways to kill that woman.

You would think that Lady Mykaela would rush to my defense, but she was strangely silent on the matter, content to look the other way every time the old woman would abuse her authority. Lady Shadi was kind but did the same. Kana and Farhi were powerless to do anything—the former was sympathetic, and since the latter looked at magic as a kind of sin, the mistress's actions were redundant. I felt like I had no one looking out for me at the Valerian, and I even began to resent Lady Mykaela for it.

Fox remained the one bright spot of my days. He would stand patiently in front of the Valerian for hours, if only to let me know he was close by. Sometimes he would explore the city, preferring this over staying at the lodgings Lady Mykaela had arranged for him. Whenever I was sent on another one of Mistress Parmina's errands, he would accompany me without anyone else knowing. He learned the lay of the city quicker than I had, taking time to roam the streets and commit many of the shops' locations to memory, so that we were never lost on our way to the same shop twice. After my initial frustration over the old asha's demands had faded, I realized I actually began looking forward to each trip. It was the only time I could spend with Fox.

"Are you mad at me?" I asked after one such errand to the sweetshop to pick up sugar cake. Sometimes when the list of things to do was overwhelming, Fox and I would divide up the tasks so we could return to the asha-ka with more than enough time to spare. Mistress Parmina had taken to falling asleep while she waited, and I knew from experience that to wake her was tantamount to suicide. I loitered outside the house with my brother instead, watching passersby. At this time of the afternoon, there were always people around, and I learned to distinguish between the maids doing errands for their own houses and the apprentice asha that bustled back and forth between lessons.

"Why would I be angry, Tea?" Fox sounded genuinely puzzled.

"Because I was afraid of you for a little bit." His death had always felt like a barrier between us, like it prevented the closeness we had once shared.

"I think that, given our situation, that's rather understandable, don't you think?"

"Not if this was all my fault to start with."

"I don't want you saying that ever again." Fox was firm. "You are not to blame here. And if you're staying in Kion solely for my sake—"

"No!" I said it more forcefully than I wanted to, and he

looked startled. "No, I don't want to leave Ankyo. I…I want to do this. I really do."

Fox eyed the entrance leading into the Valerian. "Even with the old prune inside?"

"Fox!"

"Isn't she? She looks like an old fruit left to dry out in the sun for so long that it grew hungry and tried eating its own face."

"*Fox!*" I was giggling. A novice hurrying past paused long enough to shoot us dirty looks, and I reeled in my laughter. "It's you I'm worried about, Fox. It must be so tiresome for you, having to follow me around—"

"I don't mind. I haven't been as idle as you think. If you want to stay, then I'll stay with you for as long as you want. And I'm sorry for making you afraid. This is new to me too."

"Are you trying to apologize for my apology?" I demanded. It was Fox's turn to laugh, and it was infectious. We stood there giggling until Mistress Parmina stuck her head out a window and yelled down at us to shut up.

"Y OU MUST THINK ME TOO *fastidious, listing an asha's* hua *in such detail every time I talk about one,"* she said. *"Some people assume that asha care only about their appearances, when that is the furthest thing from the truth. A* hua *collection is as personal and as private as toiletries or underclothes and as distinctive as a face or a voice. We can identify a particular asha simply by looking at her dress, for no one would think of wearing the same* hua. *To put on someone else's would be an invasion of her privacy, like stealing into her house or secretly assuming her identity. Lady Mykaela was born near the Swiftsea, and so she wears water motifs on her hua to remind her of home. Lady Shadi is fond of peach and coral, and her father raised birds for a living, hence her preference for doves and the like. Mistress Parmina wears fortune runes on hers for luck. And as for me—"*

The cauldron before us belched foul smoke. I stood downwind, but it did little to ease the fumes. She stoked the flames underneath it and added more wood to encourage the fires.

She ran a hand down her own dress, fingers stroking at the head of the dragon embroidered on her waist like it was a favored pet. Its body was still concealed underneath her waist wrap, but I fancied I could see the head of another dragon there.

She dipped a wooden ladle into the black concoction and spooned out the topaz-colored bezoar.

When she spoke again, her voice sounded far away.

"And that is why what I did was such a violation of Lady Shadi's trust."

8

OVER A YEAR AFTER I first arrived at the Valerian in Ankyo, nothing about my situation had changed, save that Lady Mykaela's visits to the asha-ka decreased over time, Mistress Parmina's petty indignities increased, and I was nearly fourteen. I was still an indentured servant, and the old woman made it clear I was to be that for some time. Lady Mykaela stayed only infrequently at the house, constantly rushing off to different parts of the kingdom. I suspected she was struggling with something important, but she never made mention of her troubles. I was at that time of my life where I felt both overworked and foolish, and I was too caught up in my own misery to inquire further.

The first inkling I had of her situation was a conversation I overheard by accident between her and Mistress Parmina. I was scrubbing furiously at the floors beside the old woman's room because she was fond of smoking *shisha* wherever she went. The soot and ashes left in her wake clung stubbornly to the ground, and it took several spongings for the black stains to disappear.

"Sakmeet died last week," Lady Mykaela said. "She had been ill for a number of months and could not attend to her duties. I had to put down the *zarich* in her stead. The Deathseekers still hunt for the *savul*."

"Losing Sakmeet is a heavy blow," Mistress Parmina agreed. "The Dark asha's numbers dwindle daily with little to replenish them. There is only you and the girl left. You are not strong enough to keep up this charade, and I do not like that you have very little time in between to heal."

"I *will* be strong enough, Mother."

"I would much rather you be weak and safe than strong and dead. There are reports that the people of the lie breed in Kion, and so we must be ever watchful. The King of Istera has sent me word; he has rooted out a sect of Faceless in his kingdom. But their leader, Aenah, is missing. His spies tell him that she may be in Ankyo."

"And what of the other two Faceless leaders?"

"Druj is rumored to be stirring up trouble in the Yadosha city-states; for the moment, he is their problem. Usij has declared war on Daanoris but remains holed up somewhere in their mountains, prepared to defend his stronghold there. I am thankful that none of them harbor much affection for the other; it would be much more difficult to stave them off should they pose a united front. Are you sure about the wretchling?"

"I have faith in her abilities, Mother."

"I dearly hope so, *daraem*. I have found her of little use so far: slovenly with the housework, slow to learn, but quite skilled at eavesdropping in matters that do not concern her." The old woman raised her voice. "I expect the outhouses to be clean by the end of the day, Tea. You'd best start immediately if you expect any dinner tonight."

I scrambled away as fast as I could, lugging my water bucket behind me. At the very least, I thought sourly, she had learned my name.

"Why can't you just resurrect her?" I asked Lady Mykaela sometime afterward. "Wouldn't it solve the problem?"

But the woman shook her head. "You forget, Tea, that Dark asha cannot raise those who share the same silver heartsglass as theirs. Whatever the advantages our abilities give, we cannot enjoy them in death."

"That doesn't seem fair."

"Neither is life, girl."

Already, I was restless. There seemed to be no end in sight as far as my servitude was concerned, and Lady Mykaela's library, extensive as it was, had no books about asha and Runic magic. Where was the training I was promised, the lessons I would learn to become asha? Sweeping floors and washing dishes may have taught me patience and determination, but unless I could defeat a daeva armed with a mop and bucket, Mistress Parmina was no more teaching me lessons than taking advantage of a free servant.

I wreaked my revenge in a hundred different, albeit petty, ways. Whenever I was sent to buy a box of sweetmeats for Mistress

Parmina, I took a piece for myself, and she never knew. On days when she was being particularly nasty, I would wipe the privy with her facecloth. I realize, looking back, how immature I was being, but it was the closest thing I had to rebellion at a time when I felt powerless.

Whenever I was at my lowest, I would pretend that I had a better future. I pictured myself as a powerful asha, slaying daeva and slowly earning the people's admiration. I imagined I was as Lilac had predicted, with jewels and gowns and a prince by my side, who resembled Prince Kance more and more with each passing day. From there my thoughts often drifted, and I wondered if I would see him again—or if he would even remember me.

Any good days I had were because I had spent them with Fox. He smuggled me small gifts when no one else was looking. Hair ribbons and new clothes Mistress Parmina was quick to notice, and they would have found their way into garbage bins. I was only allowed Lady Mykaela's crescent pin to wear in my hair, the amethyst ornament I would have rather consigned to the oracle's flames instead of my blue sapphires. Instead, Fox gave me things I could hide more easily: an occasional book he'd bought at the marketplace or some of my favorite snacks, like sweet, sticky mochi pastries, meat cutlets, and fried bread, to make up for the thin, watery soup, pickled radishes, rice, and runeberry fruit I was fed, offset only by grilled sardines twice a week.

At my suggestion, he gave these to Kana and Farhi as well. Kana received these "can'ts," as she called them—probably because these were things she wasn't allowed to have as a servant in the

THE BONE WITCH 87

asha-ka—with unfettered joy. Farhi was a little less welcoming, but the bland meals we were given soon wore down her resolve, though she would only accept the gifts if they came from my hand rather than from my brother's.

I had more chores than either girl, but soon both began pitching in when they could—Kana because she was grateful, and Farhi because she did not want to feel beholden to me. Often, they gave me early warning when Mistress Parmina woke, and we hid in the kitchens before she could find any one of us to scold. Kana giggled and cast shy, admiring glances at Fox when he visited, and I hadn't the heart to tell her he was already dead. Drychta custom dictated that Farhi couldn't associate with men who were not family, and so she kept a respectful, if aloof, distance whenever he was around.

I didn't know how Fox found the money to buy me food and books, but every time I badgered him about it, he refused to answer. He showed up one day with a slight limp, and my suspicions grew. "You're going to be an asha soon, Tea," he reminded me, "and that means you're expected to be truthful, so it would be for the best if you didn't know. I am not involved in anything illegal, if that eases your mind."

"If you aren't a part of anything illegal, then why won't you tell me?" I demanded. "And isn't this hypocritical of you to say that I be truthful when you've been smuggling foodstuffs to me for the better part of three months?"

"*Technically* not illegal," he amended. "And I said you had to be truthful, not starving." He never did answer my question.

One spring evening, when the leaves turned as green as the

fresh morning dew, I sat on the small veranda, watching the night sky. Mistress Parmina had just recently added one more chore to my already-busy schedule. Kana and Farhi took turns waiting up for Lady Shadi to return to the asha-ka after her functions, and the old woman had decreed that I share in this duty.

Oftentimes, the asha-in-training would return late, arriving only a few hours before dawn broke. We were responsible for letting her in and storing away the things she had brought with her to entertain, like her setar or her tonbak, two musical instruments she was particularly skilled at. Lady Shadi was still an apprentice, but she went to many functions like most regular asha in preparation for her upcoming debut. She had a sweet, finespun disposition and was a favorite among the guests. Mistress Parmina was very pleased with her progress.

The air was crisp and cool, and I must have dozed off for several minutes before I became aware of a knocking at our door. Thinking that Lady Shadi had come home earlier than expected, I stumbled to my feet, drawing back the bolt securing the door in place and tugging it open.

I didn't recognize the pretty girl standing before me, but I did recognize the simple brown robe she wore. Asha-ka were not the only buildings in the Willows. There were many shops there that catered specifically to them, such as the ateliers, the schools of the arts, and the apothecaries. Asha-ka were found nearer to the oracle's temple, while these shops were located closer to the entrances leading into the Willows. Some of them were the *cha-khana*, the "tea places," small teahouses where asha entertained their patrons. Women who served in the *cha-khana* wore brown robes much like the one the girl wore.

"Is this the Valerian?" she asked.

"That's what the sign on the walls say," I said, grumpy from being woken so suddenly. "What is it?"

"Are you Miss Tea? The one with that brother named Fox?"

My drowsiness disappeared. Save for the people living in the Valerian, I hadn't expected anyone else to know my name. "Who told you about me?" I blurted out, forgetting to be polite. I rarely talked to servants from the other houses, for we were often scolded when caught gossiping instead of working. I didn't know what punishment the others were given, but Mistress Parmina's was to withhold my twice-a-week grilled fish, and I was determined not to lose what little flavor I was afforded in my meals, Fox's smuggled treats notwithstanding. Lady Mykaela wasn't the kind of person to gossip, but I didn't think Lady Shadi was the type either. Kana was my best guess.

The girl only shrugged. She stank of magic and beauty. I guess even *cha-khana* assistants had their vanities. "Please bring a change of clothes for Lady Shadi—and her setar. And you'd better get to it too, or she'll be mad as hops!"

The Falling Leaf was one of the more well-known teahouses in the district, and it was not uncommon for some of their staff to call on houses. Asha normally visited two or three *cha-khana* a night, sometimes more if she was popular. Occasionally they would send word to their asha-ka and ask for a fresh set of *hua* or an instrument they could play if their guests wanted a performance. Asha usually select what to wear based on how appropriate the design is for the season and often laid them out in their rooms before heading out in case a change of clothes was required in the course of the night. I had gone on similar errands in the past. But no one from any of the tearooms had ever called for me by name before.

Because it was springtime, Lady Shadi had left for the night wearing a beautiful olive-green *hua* with doves embroidered along her voluminous sleeves and a waist wrap of deep plum with silver-stitched outlines of chrysanthemums. The *hua* she had laid out before leaving was golden in color, with white puffs of dandelions billowing out along its edges, paired with a light-gray waist wrap with turquoise leaves. Her setar lay across her bed, slightly worn and scuffed from age and constant use. I wrapped both up carefully with delicate paper and followed the girl outside.

Like most tearooms, the Falling Leaf looks deceptively simple from the outside. One entered it by walking up through a domed doorway, with a large folding screen made of carved wood and embossed in intricate metal designs preventing anyone from looking in on the festivities within. Past this screen lay a large garden common in every *cha-khana* in Ankyo. Fishes swam in small ponds, with trellises serving as shade. A large fountain statue in the likeness of the Great Hero Anahita stood at the center, water flowing down a jar she was pouring into one of the many streams below. A series of rooms on a raised platform surrounded this garden, separated by wooden dividers and drawing screens, ensuring that anyone who might want to leave the party for a few minutes to wander among the trees and flowers can do so easily and with all the privacy they desired.

The girl bade me to wait at the entrance but was back in less than a minute, gesturing for me to follow. Soft strains of laughter reached our ears as we approached one of the rooms. The girl tapped lightly against the screen, and it was pulled back almost immediately. A moon-faced asha stared back at us before turning back and announcing to the party inside, "The bone witchling is here!"

A long, slim hand shot out and grabbed me by the sleeve, tugging me into the room before the door slammed shut before the startled attendant's face.

There were no guests inside, only asha. They circled me, giggling, and their silver heartsglass glinted in the candlelight. I sat on the floor, confused and suddenly dizzy, still hugging Lady Shadi's clothes and setar to my chest.

"Why, she's smaller than I expected!" said the asha who'd dragged me inside. She was easily one of the most beautiful girls I had ever seen, with flowing, brown hair artfully arranged in complicated coils at the nape of her neck. Strands of multicolored gemstones hung from her hair and dangled on either side of her face, accentuating her light-brown skin. Her *hua* was a buttercup yellow, with blue-tinged butterflies fluttering at her lengthy sleeves. "I thought Dark asha would be more imposing, like Mykaela of the Hollows or like the Pincher."

The rest of the girls collapsed into laughter. "If Lady Parmina hears you call her that, Zoya, she would have your hide!" one of them proclaimed. She wore a gray veil covering her head and chest and a salmon-colored *hua* of a wisteria design.

"Then let her, Tami," Zoya retorted. "I'm not afraid of an old crone who spends her days picking her nose more often than she picks *hua*!" The laughter grew in volume because that was, in fact, one of Mistress Parmina's unfortunate habits.

"Where is Lady Shadi?" I asked, my voice quavering, trying to quell the pounding on the side of my head.

"If Lady Shadi were here, then that would take the fun out of everything, wouldn't it?" Zoya's blue eyes were bright with glee, "but she did happen to mention that your name was Tea. How unusual! Shadi must be feeling so left out, being the only asha in a sea of darklings!"

I turned toward the door, but a couple of asha blocked my exit.

"You came here to explore the *cha-khana*, didn't you? It would be a shame to let you leave so early," said another asha. Her long braids were coiled around her head, and the long pins in her hair made tinkling sounds every time she moved.

"Don't worry, Brijette. The fun's only beginning. Open the package! Let's see what's inside!" Zoya's fingers danced, and I saw the telltale glow of an unfamiliar rune in the air before the *hua* I carried was snatched out of my hands, floating toward her. Another flick of her hand, and the setar followed, one of the other asha catching it in midair.

"Why, look! It's Shadi's! Naughty little servling!"

"Hurry!" Tami urged. "The boys are waiting!"

The girls converged on me, and any screams I made were cut off as the Wind rune's spells wove themselves around the room, preventing anyone outside from hearing me. I remembered a tangle of arms and faces, felt myself being physically disrobed and forced to lie on the floor while the asha began to dress me in Lady Shadi's *hua*.

"Let's see how she looks!"

I was tugged back into a sitting position, my head spinning. Zoya assessed me carefully. "I suppose she will do nicely, given such short notice to prepare. Place the setar on her lap, Brijette."

The girl with the braids complied.

Zoya pursed her lips. "Something's missing." She reached down and plucked the crescent amethyst clasp from my hair. "Sveta, lend me your opal pin."

A yellow-haired asha lifted her hand up to her hair in horror. "Why take mine? Take one of Tami's. She's got more than any of us here."

"*Hand it over*, Sveta."

Grumbling, Sveta took the exquisite, purple-jeweled pin from her hair and tossed it at the other girl.

Zoya gathered up one side of my hair and pushed the pin through it. I winced when the sharp point jabbed at my scalp. "There you go. She looks rather like an impoverished asha with only two *zivars* to her name"—she poked at my crescent pin with disdain—"but with this she can pass as one of us, if barely! We're giving you a promotion, little Tea. Imagine—from lowly maid to full-fledged asha in the space of an hour!"

The others found this especially funny.

· "What do you want?" Now that I was sure they had no real intentions of harming me, I was growing angrier by the second despite the strange buzzing in my head. "Why are you doing this to me?"

"Consider this a small life lesson. Your Lady Shadi took the role I wanted in the *darashi oyun*, and I've been meaning to find some way to return the favor." She smiled at me. "I didn't ask you to come here, little girl. But you played the truant, so you're in trouble anyway, regardless of what you do. You'd best play along to make things easier on your house. You're wearing Lady Shadi's *hua*, and you have her setar. I'm sure you know what that means."

I froze. She was right. I may not be an asha yet, but Lady Shadi and I were members of House Valerian. Everything I did in her clothes would be done in her name, on Mistress Parmina and Lady Mykaela's names, and on the Valerian's name, and it did not matter one whit that I had been forced into it.

"I have to go," I burst out, struggling, but more hands held me in place. My headache refused to go away, and I wasn't even sure I could stand on my own even if I had wanted to.

"And how can I let you leave," the pretty asha said, "after you've stolen my good friend Shadi's *hua* and her favorite instrument? I ought to alert the mistress of the Falling Leaf and have you thrown out in full view of all the other paying guests."

I knew what she was telling me. If I tried to leave, she would make sure that the Valerian's reputation would suffer. And while I didn't care about how Mistress Parmina would react, the last thing I wanted to do was disappoint Lady Mykaela.

"That's better." Zoya grinned when I relaxed. "Don't worry.

Keep a smile on your face and do everything I instruct you to, and you'll be free to leave once the party is over."

The party? But the other girls were already forcing me to my feet, and I was still too dazed to put up much of a struggle.

They led me across the garden to another room, where the murmur of voices within told me that guests were already in attendance. Grinning, the braided asha named Brijette drew the door open.

And I found myself staring into the eyes of Prince Kance.

*H*AVE YOU EVER BEEN IN *love?" the asha asked.*

She was up before dawn. I found her by the grave again, looking up at the jaws of yet another skeletal horror. Salt water and sand swooped into the open, gaping mouth, egged on by the rising tides, to bleach its lower mandible a brittle white. Her fingers weaved through the air beside the beast, sampling at the breeze. She carried a small vial in her other hand, filled with the nauseating potion she had boiled the day before.

I did not expect the question. I stammered, "Well, there was this girl I've known all my life. We grew up together—our parents hoped we would marry when we came of age—"

"And did your banishment from Drycht put an end to that engagement?"

"There was no engagement to speak of. She valued my friendship, but that was all. She—she liked someone else."

"Did her parents approve of that match?"

"No. She was in love with a young bricklayer her father hired. But I'm not important. I want to know more about you and the prince."

"My relationship with the prince had always been very complicated." She smiled, amused, and looked up at the bones. "They say monsters like these were common during the First Days, before the

Five Great Heroes slew the daeva. But as imposing as they are, it is futile to raise them from the dead; they have no limbs to walk out of water onto shallow shores. Daeva are a different story." She tapped at her heartsglass. "You stare at this when you think I do not see. Speak your mind."

"Our heartsglass, Mistress Tea. Heartforgers bear silver hearts. So do asha and Deathseekers. The lesser of them have purple, while the common folk have red. I have never seen black heartsglass before."

"It is because few do what I have done. Not since the False Prince. Not since his followers. Black heartsglass is a punishment meted out to those who commit certain atrocities that asha find repugnant. No one with a black heartsglass should be able to sense the Runes, much less wield them. It is why they gave me exile instead of death." She smiled grimly. "They were wrong, of course. I have found black heartsglass to be useful in ways they never could have imagined."

She held out her hand to show me a bezoar that glittered gold in the light. "This is the bezoar extracted from the taurvi. It rampaged through the old world for thirteen days and thirteen nights before the great hero Mithra slew it. It rises from its grave every ten years since. This glows bright in the presence of all poisons—essential for kings and noblemen wary of those who prepare their food and drink. I harvested it three weeks ago."

"But, Mistress Tea, if your Lady Mykaela harvested the bezoar when you were only twelve, and if it rises every ten years—"

"Then it would not have been potent for many more years, yes. But I could not wait that long."

I waited for her to explain further. Instead, she changed the subject.

"You wanted to ask me about my loves and my romances? Prince Kance started out as a simple infatuation. Back then, I had no inkling how much of my life he would change. But when you are younger and know no better, an infatuation can lead all the world to burn." She lifted the vial to her lips and, without pause, drank down the potion.

9

H E HAD GROWN A FEW more inches since I'd last seen him, and his hair was longer now, curled at the nape of his neck. But his eyes were still the same bright emeralds, and his face still maintained that solemn bearing even as he stood, smiling, to greet us. His heartsglass was just as I remembered, its encasing engraved with his royal seal and still that pristine, flawless rose red.

He was not alone. Another boy lounged at the end of the table, and three girls sat around him, settled among the cushions. One of them had a hand on Prince Kance's arm, which she relinquished with some reluctance when he stood. She was tall and willowy, fair where the other two girls were dark. She wore a lovely chiffon gown that highlighted her heartsglass, which looked to be made from inlaid gold and pink alexandrite. Her eyes were a vivid blue, though the look she sent our way was as hard as diamonds.

"I hope we haven't kept you waiting, Your Majesty," Zoya apologized, playful and coy. She glided in to take the empty seat beside his.

"I'm sorry, but I have the strangest feeling that we've met before." Prince Kance was staring at me with a puzzled smile. The blue-eyed girl had reestablished her hold on his arm, ignoring Zoya.

"Why, Your Majesty," one of the asha declared, fluttering her eyelashes at him, "what a thing to say! Here we are, and yet you barely spare the rest of us a glance or even a word of greeting!"

"I mean no disrespect, Yonca, but I don't think I've met her at any of the *cha-khana* here before, which makes her familiarity even more puzzling."

"One asha is the same as all the others," said the blue-eyed girl with the death grip on his hand, her obvious disinterest a visible fog that clung to her shoulders. "Why even bother with learning their names, Kance? There'll be a new set next week with the same faces and dresses!"

The smiles of the other asha broadened. Zoya's even managed to look pitying. "To understand asha is a mark of one's understanding of foreign affairs." The sincerity and gentleness in her voice nearly fooled me. "I would be happy to help you improve your education on such matters if you'd like, Princess Maeve."

The girl scowled. Prince Kance snapped his fingers. "I remember! Weren't you in Kneave last spring with Lady Mykaela, during our heartsglass ceremony? Tea, isn't it? I'm quite sure of it."

He remembered my name!

"You're welcome, Your Majesty," Zoya said demurely. At his puzzled expression, she continued, "I heard that the newest recruit of the Valerian was from Odalia, and since you are friends with Lady Mykaela, I thought it would be nice for you to see a familiar face from home while you are staying in Kion."

"Why, you're the little bone witch!" Princess Maeve exclaimed, suddenly gleeful. "Tea? An odd name surely. You look nothing like they say at all—just a little thing in black weeds and dirty shoes! There's nothing scones and crumpets about you." The other girls giggled. Emboldened, the pretty girl continued. "Maybe it's true. You're younger than my mother said you should be. You're Mykaela's get, I suppose? Bone witches oughtn't breed. Rats have better reasons to."

"Your manners, Maeve," one of her companions remonstrated, a pretty, doe-eyed girl.

The yellow-haired princess laughed. "Why should I, Lia? Nasty gits, bone witches. The older one is who they call Mykaela, isn't she? You look too young to be anything, though I suppose even witches were young once."

"Lady Tea was a new apprentice when she left Kneave. I may not know much about the Willows, but I know not even your finest asha could have risen through the ranks so quickly." The prince gestured at me to sit, and I did so with relief, afraid that my shaking knees might give me away. My headache had only increased since stepping into the room. "Tell me the truth, Lady Tea. Are these girls playing a trick on you?"

I tried to work through the logic in my head. I could appeal to the prince for help, but that would put me in more trouble in the long run. The last thing I wanted was punishment worse than cleaning the outhouses.

"My sisters were kind enough to make an exception for me for this one night, as a favor to Your Majesty," I said, hoping I sounded meek enough for Zoya's satisfaction. The room tilted, and I shut my eyes briefly. Lady Shadi was slimmer than I was, and her hua must have been tighter than I had thought.

A snort sounded from one end of the room. Prince Kance's lone male companion didn't bother to rise from his seat to greet us when the prince did. He was a year or so older than him, was dressed in a somber black from head to toe, and still gave off the impression of wearing chain mail despite being garbed in expensive silk. His brown eyes regarded me with suspicion. "Knowing what I know about Lady Zoya, I think that unlikely."

Zoya lifted a hand to her chest, pretending a show of dismay. "Oh, Lord Kalen! I'm distraught by your low opinion of me. But as you and Prince Kance seek our companionship whenever you stay in Ankyo, perhaps you do not dislike me *too* much?"

The man snorted again. "Prince Kance makes the arrangements. I'm only along to keep an eye on him." He made no protest, however, when the other asha crowded around him, laughing, and he accepted a glass filled with an amber-colored drink that one of the girls poured.

Prince Kance smiled at me. "I hope they haven't been teasing you. They're nice girls, for the most part."

"They've been teaching me a lot about what it's like to be an asha," I said softly, because that was true enough. "What brings Your Highness to Ankyo?"

"Politics, for the most part. My father is visiting Empress Alyx for a few weeks, to bolster a new trade agreement between Odalia and Kion."

Another snort from the other boy. "That's an odd way to describe your impending engagement with Alyx's daughter, Kance."

"Do not joke so, Kalen," Princess Maeve said tartly. "My mother would have known of any such arrangements. And why would anyone be affianced to that Kion strumpet?"

"Princess," Prince Kance chided.

I felt deflated. Arranged marriages are common among royalty, but I hadn't thought that applied to Prince Kance for some reason. "But you're not that much older than I am!"

"Kance isn't engaged," the boy in black drawled. "But they do marry Odalian princes young. All the easier to indoctrinate."

"This is my cousin, Kalen," Prince Kance told me. "You'll have to forgive him. We've been visiting *cha-khana* since we were eight years old, but he's never been one for good manners."

I could barely concentrate on what he was saying. I kept my gaze on my lap, trying to focus. This felt wrong. I had never felt so lightheaded before. Had Zoya or one of her friends done something to me?

"I don't see the importance of good manners the way asha seem to," Kalen said. "People respond to a show of force, not to etiquette. You asha are powerful in your own right. I don't see why you have to wrap it up in pretty clothes and dancing. People don't kowtow to me because I know what type of spoon to use with my stew."

"You're a man, Kalen," Zoya laughed. "Or, rather, you are the type of man who has little patience for intrigue, and so you dismiss it and think others should do the same. We women prefer to have more subtlety. No one should ever need to feel offended just because we're getting what we want—less of a mess on the furniture, for instance."

"You're right about one thing," Kalen said. "I have no stomach for schemes. Tell me what you think of me to my face so we can have it out once and for all; that's *my* kind of etiquette."

"With all due respect, Lord Kalen," Sveta purred, "I think that's exactly why people prefer subtlety—to avoid a confrontation, not least of all with a Deathseeker like yourself."

"Girls!" Zoya exclaimed. "We're here for our guests to relax and unwind, not talk about the petty politics between Odalia and Kion. Their food has arrived, so I propose we play some songs while they eat! We've been practicing hard for the upcoming *darashi oyun*. Would you like a preview?"

Prince Kance nodded with some eagerness, and Kalen straightened up in his seat, setting his now-empty glass down on the table. Even Princess Maeve could not feign boredom.

One of the other Falling Leaf attendants arrived, laden with trays of food: five kinds of soft cheeses, fresh flatbreads, stuffed vegetables steeped in spicy sauces, a fancy legume stew called *āsh*, and *sabzi polo* rice with chopped herbs and trout. They all smelled good, but I was too distracted to appreciate them.

Zoya, as usual, took the lead. She glided before the two noblemen, her hand lifted in the air, and waited for some unspoken signal. Four other girls took their positions behind her, copying her movements. Two more asha took up a corner of the room, strumming at setars. As one, they began to play a slow, almost mournful melody.

Zoya moved. Her sleeves lifted and fell as she pivoted on one heel and began a series of complex moves, and I felt my breath catch in my throat, the pain in my head forgotten for the moment. There was something haunting about the way she turned her head, as if she were filled with an inconceivable sadness that lent gravity and a sense of genuine melancholy to her dancing. She pivoted across the room, and the long robes that clung to her became less of an impediment and more of an emphasis, a weapon by which she could direct her energy, and every step she took appeared effortless. As much as I disliked the asha, I felt like I could forgive her in those minutes when she danced, if only for the chance she gave me to see something so magnificent.

It was only when they were halfway through the routine did I notice the spell she was weaving. Zoya was expertly sketching out a rune in the air without taking a break from her dancing, so that the act of drawing the rune looked like a natural part and parcel of her choreography. It blazed out before us, the symbol perfect and flawless and so heavy in size that it stood as big as she was.

Zoya's fingers made a minute, almost inconsequential flick, and one by one, tiny flames sputtered up from nothing, dancing

in the air in silent accompaniment. I clapped a hand to my mouth
to swallow my gasp. Everyone else had left their food untouched
on their plates, mesmerized by the asha's performance. A mixture
of grudging appreciation and envy painted the girls' faces. Kalen
leaned forward, eyes intent, and Prince Kance... The admiring
way he looked at Zoya made my heartsglass flicker in pained
response.

I wanted to dance like her. I was captivated by her grace,
by her fluid movements, by the way a series of small steps and
hand gestures can make someone look so beautiful. And I too
was selfish: I wanted Prince Kance to look at me the way he was
looking at the dancing asha.

Zoya ended with a graceful flourish—one hand raised, the
hem of her dress swishing forward as she performed her final steps.
She held the pose for a few seconds and then giggled, breaking the
silence. She clapped her hands, and the asha behind her bowed.
Prince Kance and his friends applauded. Princess Maeve scowled
again. My headache returned.

"That was breathtaking, Zoya," Kalen said, reluctant
admiration in his voice.

"I have to agree," Prince Kance added. "I have seen asha
perform many times, but yours put many of them to shame."

The asha smiled at him. "Thank you, Your Highness. And I
sense, Lord Kalen, that for all your distaste of the subtle, this is the
one exception about asha that you do appreciate. You must try the
sabzi polo, milords. It's the Falling Leaf's specialty, and the cook
will be disappointed if it goes untasted."

"It's almost a wonder that they did not give you the role of Dancing Wind in the *darashi oyun*." Honey dripped from Princess Maeve's voice.

Zoya's smile disappeared abruptly. "How did you know that?"

"My mother is an avid fan of the performances, and she makes it a point to attend every year." Maeve shrugged. "The role you are to play is—let's see, that of Falling Tears, isn't it? A subordinate role to the main lead. An adequate performance, but it must be shocking to know that there are better dancers than you. Let me recall—why, it's Lady Shadi of the Valerian cast as Dancing Wind! She must be brilliant if she can beat even full-fledged asha for the role even before her official debut!"

"Unfortunately, to be the most accomplished dancer does not guarantee one a starring role in the *darashi oyun*. There is more of the subtle politics at play here that Lord Kalen despises. And the houses have decided on Shadi." Zoya shot me a nasty grin. "Isn't that right, Tea? The Valerian is known for its dancers, isn't it? Would you like to see how my dancing fares with House Valerian, Lord Kalen?"

"Lady Shadi isn't here."

"I'm sure her apprentice would be more than adequate for the task."

I felt cold all over. Zoya gestured toward me, her lips wide and her eyes glittering.

"But isn't Tea still a novice?" Prince Kance protested.

"Oh, I'm afraid dancing is still a bit over her head. I've never seen an asha with such two left feet! No, she'll play a simple enough song on her setar called the 'River Dance,' which is the first song we learn. All novitiates know that melody by heart. She would not be worth her salt as a budding asha if she makes a mess of even that."

Some of her friends looked less certain. It was one thing to dress up in *hua* and pretend to be an asha, and it was another to force one to prove it.

"I'm not so sure about this, Zoya," Sveta said uneasily.

"I am very sure," Zoya snapped. "Come on, Tea. It wouldn't do to embarrass me in front of your noble guests, would it? She came prepared enough to bring an instrument to play!"

Grabbing my arm, she led me, stumbling and still clutching Lady Shadi's setar, to sit in front of all the guests. I sank down onto the floor and tried to fold my legs underneath me. My mind was a blank, the pounding in my head had worsened, and I was no longer sure it was because Lady Shadi's *hua* was too tight on me.

"Well?" Zoya urged. "What are you waiting for?"

"Lady Zoya," I mumbled. "I don't feel well."

"She doesn't look very good, Zoya," Prince Kance said. "I think we ought to let her rest."

"Absolutely not," the asha said firmly. "We are taught to perform even when it greatly inconveniences us. If she doesn't learn how to get through a little sickness, then she won't be of much good as an asha. Come on, Tea. Here, let me help you."

She sat down beside me and tried to guide my fingers to the strings. She was having difficulty because I was shaking. The pressure in my head increased, a hideous buzzing in my ears so loud that I could barely hear anything else. *Let go*, I thought I heard something whisper.

"What a disappointment you must be for your mother," Princess Maeve said. "And I thought Lady Mykaela's get would be more impressive."

"She isn't Lady Mykaela's daughter," Prince Kance reminded her.

"Mum says the Odalian bone witch has no heartsglass," one of the other girls interjected.

"But why not?" another asked.

The princess laughed. "Because she gave her heart away. Take a bone witch's heart and you take most of her powers. That's what happened to the Odalian witch. Gave her heart and paid for it, crying and bleeding, in the dust."

"Don't you dare talk about Lady Mykaela that way!" Sudden anger seized me, and the fury pulled and prodded at the growing pain in my head, like someone had taken a hammer to my skull. I felt my heartsglass change to the color of soured milk.

"Why not? It's what happened," the girl taunted. "It was a scandal, it was. Even Princess Nercella knows it, and her kingdom's all the way up Stranger's Peak. Your mother gave her heart away, and King Vanor took her powers just as she deserved. She can't raise the dead the way she used to anymore or curse people even. The more daeva she summons, the faster she'll die. She'll spend the rest of her days drawing hearts for children's amusement and be good for nothing else until the day she falls into her own grave."

Her words whirled around me like a hurricane. It explained

so many things—the king's easy acceptance of Mykaela and his insistence that we be treated well. Bone witches weren't welcomed in many kingdoms. But if they grew weaker with every Dark rune they drew because they no longer had a heartsglass to draw strength from, then people could afford to be magnanimous.

And Lady Mykaela had kept it hidden from me all these months. They all had.

"I'm bored with all this dancing and setar playing. Witch's get or not, she would have powers of her own, wouldn't she? Do you, little girl? Come, show us your stuff."

"Your Highness," Yonca spoke up, alarmed. "I don't think that's such a good idea."

"And why not? Surely the queen of this decrepit little kingdom won't go so far as to allow bone witches to slum at her doors when they can entertain with their magic. King Telemaine's only soft on her because she reminds him of his dead brother!"

"You mustn't talk that way, Maeve!"

I clutched at my head, the blood roaring through.

"Please..." I gasped, fingernails digging at my temples. There was an unbelievable pressure there, an elephant settled onto the weight of my brain, demanding escape.

Prince Kance was on the ground beside me in an instant, holding my shoulders. "Are you all right, Tea? What's wrong?"

Let go.

With a strength I didn't know I possessed, I pushed at the immensity of that crushing force with my mind. I let go.

Something snapped inside me, a coiled spring finding release.

The girls paused in their bickering to stare at a large crack that appeared on the wall, the lines zigzagging and growing as they watched. It crumbled—and hordes of skeletal rats came scampering out, the bony, tail-flicking mass filling the room and overrunning the carpet.

Screaming, the girls stumbled over each other to get out of their way. Several more, Princess Maeve included, fled. I felt a pair of arms encircling me, as both Prince Kance and Lord Kalen dragged me up onto the table, out of the rodents' path.

And then the floor splintered, and a thin, bony hand reached up from beneath. The figure that pulled itself up through the hole was nothing more than a skeleton with rags that clung to bits of its frame, the always-grinning skull leering up at us. The sight of that and of the other smaller, gleaming skulls scuttling out into the corridor, where more screams and shouts greeted the swarm, were the last things I remembered.

S HE PAUSED. BONES CREAKED IN *the wind above us.*

"I thought I would be expelled from the Willows for that. To put on another's hua was reprehensible enough; to attend to important guests pretending to be an asha is even worse. But to release a horde of undead from one of the most popular cha-khana *in Ankyo? Other people had been thrown in prison for lesser offenses."*

This time, her movements were deliberate. She circled the massive skeleton, heedless of the mud and wet sand that swirled around her ankles and the hem of her hua. *I could not see the runes she made in the air with her fingers, but her gestures suggested they were larger than the beast's jaws. A chill settled around us.*

"Rise," the girl commanded. The topaz-colored bezoar in her hand broke apart in response, dissolving.

And the skeleton moved. I staggered back, horrified, as something unseen wrapped around the desiccated limbs and took form, muscles and tendons and skin forming around the joints before my very eyes. The creature shuddered and sighed and rose from the sand. At first it resembled a gigantic, skinless animal, and I could see the blood bubbling through its veins. But the spell continued its curse, and skin formed up along those pink sinews to become a rough, leathery hide. The daeva shook itself free and rumbled. Its tongue unfurled, saliva dripping onto the ground, the sand it landed on dissolving like acid. Its red-and-silver-striped eyes look back at me, and it crooned.

The girl lifted her hand, and I saw something swirl into focus before her. The magic congealed and sprouted a shape—it was a heart without a heartsglass, as black as shadows, as bright as stars. It solidified enough that she could reach out and take it from the air, though it continued to shift and twist, never staying in one shape for long. She plucked that shining jewel from the air and pushed it into her own heartsglass.

The light blinded me, and I had to shield my eyes from the sudden glare. The girl remained steady on her feet, the taurvi by her side. Her waist wrap had shifted, and on her hua's *embroidery, I saw a second dragon's head look out from where it had previously been hidden, followed by another.*

"Don't worry. It won't bite."

I scrambled back anyway. The girl placed a hand against its muzzle, and the creature actually purred. It regarded me with interest, with curiosity—but with neither hate nor hostility.

"When your heartsglass is black and steeped in the spells of the Dark," the girl said, smiling, "you find that there is no need to wait five more years to raise daeva."

IO

IT WAS DAWN WHEN I woke, judging from the light trailing in through a window. For several moments, I was confused, because the Falling Leaf had small, oblong frames that look out into their central garden, while this had a view of the oracle's temple, pale smoke still rising out from somewhere underneath its polished dome roof. Lady Mykaela stood before the glass pane, one hand lifted to brush back a curtain. She was staring at something in the distance.

"Do you know of King Randrall the Quiet?" she asked without turning around.

"I think so." My head felt better, the unwanted pressure gone. I had read about him in one of Lady Mykaela's books. "He ruled Odalia during the Plantenorth Dynasty but disappeared during his eighty-third naming day celebrations. What happened to him has always been a mystery."

"He disappeared during his trip to Kion; this is a very important detail because the history books will need rewriting. King Randrall the Quiet briefly rose from the dead. Whoever his assassins were is not certain, but we now know they buried him underneath Falling Leaf, whose gardens and flowers have greatly benefited from his royal compost ever since. Randrall had a very prominent nose, mind, and they were still able to identify the king from the impressive amount of flesh and muscle you brought back along with him."

I shot out of bed, fear gripping my insides. The colony of rats. The grinning skeleton that had broken through the floor. The inexplicable pain I felt that cut at me like knives. The unexpected release and relief, the sudden weakness that followed—and then remembering nothing after that.

"King Randrall the Quiet proved the lie to his name," Lady Mykaela continued serenely. "For a corpse, he was quite emphatic. He declared that the then-crown prince was not his son at all but came about as a result of his wife's liaison with General Bosven, the commander of his army, and if there is one thing constant about the dead, it is that they cannot lie. It would seem that King Telemaine cannot claim to be a descendant after all, though his son still shares the man's lineage from his mother's side of the family, centuries of royal intermarriages being what they are."

"Did I...?"

Lady Mykaela turned to look at me, and I read the answer in her gaze.

"How...how many did I—"

"King Randrall and a little over half of the Ankyon cemetery. You also resurrected some dead rats, a dozen cats and dogs, and disrupted a funeral in progress. There was a small stampede when they realized the guest of honor was clawing his way out of his coffin, but fortunately no one was hurt—much. You have a habit for interrupting burials, don't you?"

I gulped. "When am I to be executed?"

Surprise bloomed on Mykaela's face, and she actually laughed. "Executed! Don't you worry your young head about it, child. No one shall be executing anybody. A term of imprisonment was more likely, but the good thing about being bone witches is that people fear to keep us even in castle dungeons. Prince Kance and I convinced the empress that it was an accident—yes, Prince Kance spoke on your behalf, so you have at least one ally in Odalia. You may be punished by the asha council, however, but they have no desire to expel you from the Willows. I trust this to mean they are still interested in continuing your training. For the present at least. The long-term effects can be far-flung, but it is something we shall have to accept as unavoidable. Even as I speak, Fox is guarding the door outside, ready to defend your honor if necessary."

"Fox?"

"He brought you here. We discourage people from loitering around the teahouses when they have no business there, but in this instance, I am glad he is quite a stubborn man. He sensed you leaving the Valerian and thought to follow, just in case."

"I'm sorry." I couldn't stop crying. Tears spilled from my eyes, dousing the sheets and blankets in salty rain. I hunched over, hiccupping, and Lady Mykaela left her perch by the window to wrap her arms around me.

"It's called a seeking stone," she said softly once the violence of my sobbing had abated. "It finds those with the strongest capacity for magic and amplifies their abilities at the cost of their strength. Draw far more than what you can handle, and there is a danger of burning yourself out, even fatally. It is particularly potent for Dark asha, who by nature draw the strongest spells innately, which explains how it ignored the other asha and drew on you. I found it hidden behind one of the stone pillars outside the room you sat in with Zoya and her friends. All unbound corpses should have fallen the instant you lost consciousness, but the seeking stone kept them sentient and moving, which was how I was able to guess its presence. It is not your fault, Tea. It seems that some people are not satisfied with despising us from afar."

"But why?" The idea that I could have been killed made me want to throw up again. "What do they want?"

"There are many reasons to despise us bone witches. It may be that they seek revenge against some other bone witch or perhaps one who conspired with a kingdom that cost them their own in ages past. Sometimes it can be no more than listening to the tale of Blade that Soars and Dancing Wind to be inflamed by self-righteousness. More likely, it is a Faceless who entered the Willows undetected and sought to ferment discord. Ankyo would be a good place to start for that, and few people can get their hands on one so rare as a seeking stone. We shall lay low for a while, until people remember to forget again, so if this was their purpose, they have succeeded—for now. You need some time to recuperate from what the stone drained from you, and that means bed rest and no unnecessary work. Mother agrees with me."

"But whoever attacked me—"

"Shall be dealt with at the first opportunity. Your health is more important than even that."

"But I feel so helpless."

"That is usually the rule when you are taken advantage of. You can be the most powerful witch in the land, but you will always have a weakness, and that will always make you believe you have no power when someone exploits it. There is no greater strength than the ability to understand and accept your own flaws."

"Are we still welcomed in the palace?"

"The empress has always been a staunch ally of ours, and King Telemaine and I are old friends. We've known each other for a long time. We met back when he was still a skinny child with a loud, squeaky voice."

"One of the princesses—Maeve, I think—said something about you." I didn't want to upset Mykaela but felt I had an obligation to inform her of anyone who bore a grudge, in light of everything. "She said that you don't have a heart because— because you've given it away, and that King Telemaine only allows you here to honor his brother's memory."

For several seconds, Lady Mykaela remained immobile, smooth and alabaster as a statue against the morning light. And then she breathed again and resumed flesh and blood.

"I think you should know," she said, "the more people you meet in the city, the greater the possibility of you learning of my past, and I would rather you hear it from my own lips, as much as it pains me, than from someone else. I would make myself to be a liar and a hypocrite otherwise, after all my talk about knowing your flaws to learn your strength."

Mykaela settled herself into a more comfortable position beside me on the bed.

"It happened when I was young—not as young as you and surely old enough to have known better. I tell you often not to give your heart away because my own mentor taught me so, as did her teacher before her. It is a warning passed down from teacher to student and one that I paid little heed to. For I broke the rules and gave mine away. I fell in love, you see."

My face must have looked funny, for she smiled. "Yes, sometimes it's that simple. Princess Maeve must have heard about it from her mother. Queen Lynoria rules the kingdom of Arhen-Kosho to the west, and she was my rival for his heart. I'm not surprised her daughter would inherit her hatred of me. It was Telemaine's older brother, King Vanor." Her voice changed; it grew softer, a faint tremor in her usually strident tones. Her eyes returned to the window, but they gazed at something farther away.

"It didn't matter that I was a bone witch and he was the successor to the throne. He wanted to marry me, was willing to give up everything. His father threatened to disown him, which suited him just fine. But I refused. King Telemaine is a just and able ruler now, but he was only sixteen years old then, too young to rule. Vanor was brilliant. He built schools for the poor and spearheaded runeberry farming as one of the kingdom's chief exports. Odalia only had Murkwick's runeberry patch to go by, but he learned how to import runeberries the world over, to package them into high-quality wine and spin the fibers into cloth good enough to rival Drycht's. I could not take him and his achievements away from the people.

"He refused to marry anyone else; that was his only stipulation to remaining on the throne. That did not stop his father from forbidding us to see each other, but it was too late. Vanor gave me his heart, and I gave him mine, like we were bound by marriage, and you know that you cannot give your heartsglass away unless you give your consent. But a bone witch needed her heart for her magic, or she would be much diminished. It didn't matter to me at that time. I had his heart, and that was the only thing I wanted."

Mykaela sighed, and the rising sun cast small shadows across her ageless face. "I do not know what made him change. Perhaps he was beginning to realize that I was a millstone around his neck, that his relationship with me forever colored how other people judged him and made his state affairs all the more difficult. He began to pull away. It was the little things at first. He would put off days we'd planned on spending together, citing meetings and other unavoidable duties. I knew I was insignificant in comparison to his other royal responsibilities and went along with his requests, until the day came when he stopped visiting altogether and refused to see me when I came. The heart that he had entrusted to my keeping began to fade over time. I watched it shrink, little by little, eaten up by the neglect and the worry and my tears, until one morning when there was nothing left.

"But my heart remained with him. Isn't it funny, these little ironies? He could take back his heart because he grew indifferent, but I could not take back mine because I loved him no matter what he did. He never used it to harm me; more likely, he tucked it away someplace he wouldn't need to see and forgot about it in time. Even today, I can still feel it grieving.

"And then he died. It was one of those little insurgencies that crop up from time to time in Odalia. Vanor's grandfather was too free with titles, and as a consequence, there were too many nobles and too much greed for more land and property to go around than there actually was. He was ambushed on his way to meet with Emperor Undol of Daanoris, to conclude a peace treaty. I never found my heart.

"The sadness can eat you up sometimes, remembering what could have been, what you should have done. Perhaps my presence would have averted the tragedy, and he would still be alive. Or perhaps my being there would have made no difference, because he had my heart and with it most of my magic. We can endure any amount of sadness for the people we love.

"I have told you many things, Tea, and this is the most important of them all. Never give your heartsglass away to anyone. Anyone else versed in magic can do you harm with it. People will never be what you make of them, but at least your own heart stays yours and true."

And Mykaela squeezed my hand; her own was warm, with only a touch of the early frost.

T HINK OF IT AS A pet," she suggested when it became clear that I would not grow accustomed to the daeva. It tried to lay its head on her lap like it was a puppy, though its snout was as large as all of her. She stroked its ridged head, and it closed its eyes in bliss. It paid little attention to me, and I was thankful.

"With all due respect, Mistress, few people would take the undead for a pet."

"And why not? They're not as bad as you think. They like to play, and they do not attack unless they feel threatened. But stray too close to their lair—well, that is a different story. They only wish to be left alone. I share that much in common with them."

"Do you control them?" I asked. The girl had found a rock as large as my hand, perfectly round and polished smooth from the waves. It sailed through the air to land some distance away. The daeva let out a playful bark. Soon it was scampering across the sands in eager pursuit.

"Of course," she said. "I know everything it feels. To a lesser extent, it knows everything I sense. That's how I know that it means no harm. It has a mind like a child's."

"But its grave was in Odalia, near Murkwick."

"Where it lies buried is no longer of any importance. All it requires is its bezoar and a spellshifted heartsglass. The bones of the *dead creatures on this beach are enough to suit my purpose, to bend and form into a daeva's shape. It is easier to weave the spells this way, quicker than to start from nothing."*

"It is no magic I have ever heard of before."

"It is not magic most asha know, one that even the Faceless only recently discovered."

"Then why did you kill that first daeva the day I met you?"

"I would not have been able to control it completely the way I can this taurvi. I must first build it up myself, with the proper rituals, as I have done here."

"But why? Why are you raising it from the dead? Why won't you return it to its grave, like the other daeva you killed?"

The taurvi trotted proudly back to us with its prize. Its sharp teeth scored ridges against the sides of the rock. Its purr was strangely compelling.

She smiled. "Because daeva make for good armies."

I I

"WHEN ASHA FIGHT, THEY PAINT their faces, array themselves in jewels, and call it war." It's an old saying I found appropriate at that moment as I sat in Mistress Parmina's room and watched her prepare for the day, wishing I could disappear. I tried to curl up and make myself as small as I could but knew it was only a matter of time before she directed her attention to me.

I had no way of assessing the damage I had done when I had raised the dead because I had been exiled to the room I shared with Kana and Farhi for four days since that night. I was ordered to do the chores that didn't require me to leave the Valerian, and Kana and Farhi were commanded not to talk to me. I could sense Fox's presence close at hand, but because of the way the asha-ka was built, even he could not find any other way inside to reach me. I felt miserable, certain that despite whatever Lady Mykaela had promised, I would be seeing the inside of a dungeon soon enough.

When Kana and Farhi were told to bring me to Mistress Parmina's room, I was certain that time had come. The side glances the Drychta maid threw my way as we approached Mistress Parmina's room were accusatory and seemed to confirm my worst fears.

Kana filled me in on what she could along the way. "I'm all poked up with fright," Kana whispered, more excited than afraid. "They've cleaned up the market, but the graveyard is in chaos. They said you did it all. Did you?"

"I think so."

Kana looked puzzled by that but squeezed my arm comfortingly and hurried off with Farhi.

The old woman had dressed before summoning me, which I was grateful for. What I hadn't expected was the richness of the *hua* she wore. The length of its train took up nearly a quarter of the room and was black in color. Strips of red ceremonial incense paper, folded into doves to symbolize auspiciousness, were hand-painted into the rich silk with meticulous detail, and yellow coltsfoot flowers dotted the edges of her sleeves. Her waist wrap was magnificent to behold; it was made of pure golden silk, with the embossed House Valerian symbol stitched in silver thread on its edges.

A collection of creams, color sticks, powders, and oils crowded Mistress Parmina's bed stand. I watched, curious in spite of myself at first, and then with slowly growing horror, as she applied liberal doses of a varied selection onto her face: beige face cream against her sagging neck, dark ink on the edges of her eyelids, pink rouge on her cheekbones. Despite my misgivings, the magic in those ointments worked. The lines around her eyes decreased; her face firmed up and lost a greater part of her excess skin. Mistress Parmina still looked old and crass and angry, and men were more likely to cross the street to avoid her than stop to admire—but now they might hesitate. She looked a little less forbidding, leaning toward seventy instead of ninety years old, which I thought was as much of an improvement as was possible for her.

Next, the old asha opened a wardrobe beside her bed, revealing drawers filled to the brim with jewel ornaments of every size, shape, and color. I believe anyone could live off the proceeds of such a collection not only for the rest of her life but also for the rest of her children's and grandchildren's. She selected a slim hairpin shaped like a heart and made of solid gold, with yellow and orange silk coltsfoot flowers to match her *hua*, and twin hairpins with fluttered crepe paper and red coral. She took her time weaving them through her long, white hair and finally turned to me. She looked—I would be lying if I said she looked beautiful or enchanting—powerful. I had never seen anyone who dripped energy and willpower and magic the way she did.

"So," she said, voice clipped. "I suppose it is time for your punishment. Come with me. Hold the edges of my train. Dirty or damage it in any way, and I shall take the money for its repair from selling your hide if need be."

Confused, I followed her out, careful not to trip over the yards of cloth trailing in her wake. Kana had been lounging out in the garden but quickly sprung to her feet at the sound of our footsteps and was furiously sweeping the entrance when we passed. The old woman paused to slip on her sandals, and the maid shot me a worried look. I could manage nothing more than a weak smile her way before Mistress Parmina picked up the pace, walking swiftly forward like the rest of her clothes weighed no more than a small bag of feathers.

Fox stood in front of the asha-ka. The expression on his face never changed, but I thought I sensed a quick flare of relief from somewhere inside my head before he fell into step behind us, careful to keep his distance from the asha and her yards-long robes. Mistress Parmina didn't acknowledge my brother nor did she tell him to leave. We made an odd trio as we continued down the lane: the old woman at the head of the line, with her head thrown back in cool arrogance; me, trying to carry her voluminous train and walk at the same time; and Fox guarding the rear, favoring his leg a little but still looking every inch the soldier.

Everyone around us must have had the same thought; they all did their best to get out of the old asha's way. Maids took one look at the woman stomping down the road and bolted. Apprentices bowed so low to her that their foreheads nearly hit their knees before they too went scurrying past. One asha strolling down the street in casual robes instead of her *hua* was more confident in her manners. She gave Mistress Parmina a graceful curtsy, but I saw her shoulders slump down in relief once she was safely past. They paid no attention to the girl on the other end of Mistress Parmina's *hua*, and I was grateful for their inattention. If my last encounter with people in the Willows had told me anything, it was that I would much rather remain undetected in the shadows than saunter out into the light, with my flaws out for all to see.

We turned onto a street I had never been on before; there were no buildings here other than a long row of atelier shops, each boasting beautiful and expensive-looking *hua* in their storefronts. A few apprentices gathered beside a few of the boutiques, admiring the clothes on display. Mistress Parmina led me away from even these, toward the smallest shop at the farthest end of the street. Unlike the others, there was no *hua* for show. It looked like a private residence that had somehow gotten itself lost on the clothes-makers' lane.

Mistress Parmina didn't knock. She simply marched up to the front door and slid it back with little ceremony. "I'm here!" she announced. "Rahim! Where are you, you old rascal? Rahim!"

I found myself standing in the messiest, most disorderly room I have ever been in—and I have seen the worst my own brothers' rooms had to offer. Strips of fabric lay scattered in such heaps and piles that I could barely see what color the floor was. Bolts of cloth were propped against the walls, and people dressed in white were rushing back and forth, carrying more. Despite their air of diligence, they all stopped to bow low to Mistress Parmina before they hurried on and somehow still managed to jostle into me as they did. Fox sidestepped them with little effort and looked around with interest.

"Parmina?" It wasn't a voice; it was a roar that could have rattled glass, though none of the people running around so much as blinked. The largest and hairiest man I had ever seen in my life stepped into view. He was so tall that the top of his hair grazed the ceiling, and his arms looked as if a brown bear had mated with the

THE BONE WITCH   129

fuzziest carpet in the land and produced twins. I could barely see his face, for his beard started somewhere near his eyebrows and ended at a carefully trimmed point several inches away from his chin, at the center of his chest. He wore a thick, knee-length jacket made of bright-silver silk and several gold rings bearing different cuts of diamonds on his fingers. His curly hair was pulled back from his face in a long ponytail, and his right ear was pierced with a crystal stud. In contrast, his heartsglass was unadorned and purple hued.

"Ah, Parminchka! How good to see you!" He reached us in three long strides and scooped Mistress Parmina up in his arms, swinging her around. This was a difficult feat, but the men and women around us simply ducked out of the way. I didn't know if I was allowed to drop the asha's train but decided at the last minute not to; when the man snatched the old woman up, he nearly jerked my arms off its sockets. "Ah, what should I do for you? I see you wear my most elaborate of *hua* today! Do you wish another? More *dragotsennosti* for you? More gold?"

I feared Mistress Parmina would slap him and was shocked when she threw her head back and laughed. "Put me down, you large buffoon! I have not come here to add to my collection, my *milaya*. I have come here to help this wretchling start hers."

The man she called Rahim set her down, his attention now riveted on me. "Ah! Is this your new *uchenik*? Is she the little novice I have heard so much about, raising the corpses and causing damage to the Falling Leaf? Ah!" He clucked his tongue, a strangely matronly sound coming from someone who looked anything but. "But she is strong, ya? I can tell that much. As Dark as an asha can be. You will be my latest challenge, little *uchenik*, and your Mother Parminchka will thank me for performing yet another miracle on the Valerian. Agata! Pavel!"

A boy and a girl disengaged themselves from the rest of the people bustling about and hurried forward. The girl held a piece of parchment and a small quill, while the boy moved toward me, holding a curled piece of measuring tape.

"You will stay there and not move for the better part of an hour until I am done with you." Rahim instructed me. "Stretch out your arms on either side of your body, like so."

I obeyed dumbly. I thought I was on my way to be punished, not to be measured for…for what? "Mistress Parmina?" I asked weakly.

"Silence, girl." The old woman kicked away a pile of doublets on a chair and settled herself comfortably on it. On cue, two more assistants appeared beside her. One carried an elegant crystal goblet with wine, and the other a footstool and a pile of cushions. The old asha lifted her feet, and the girl slid the footstool underneath them with practiced skill. Fox quietly retreated from the whirlwind of activity that was starting up around me, moving instead toward one of the tables laden with rough sketches of motifs and patterns. "You will only speak when spoken to. Do you understand me?"

She gave no indication that she was going to explain any further, so I said nothing, only listened in a kind of daze while Rahim continued his one-sided conversation. He prowled around me, eyeing me the way a tiger might eye a young deer, while Agata took furious notes and Pavel measured me from all angles with his tape. "There is some promise in you, little *uchenik*. Skin between beige and barley, midnight eyes. Gold for accents only then, but you wrap yourself around as much silver as you want and still shine. Pavel! Under her arms and three inches below her bust." The measuring tape dipped down to comply. "Thirty-four *dyuymov*, two and three-quarters. How do you like this sherwani, little girl?"

"Excuse me?" I was losing track of when he was talking to me, to his assistants, or to himself.

"I said, how do you like this sherwani?" Rahim tapped at the long coat he wore. "Popular for the men in Kion but not for the men in Tresea. Agata, take note. Eighteen inches down and across, three and a half in the waist. In Tresea, the men wear fur, but not in the fashionable ways. We kill the bears, the possums, the beavers, and then we stick them on the head, like so." He gestured. "Boring and unappealing. So I move here to Kion, where the clothes have shape and the hats do not stare back, and your mistress, she has the heart of gold and took pity on the little downtrodden boy from the cold north. I start my shop with her support, and now we flourish. We flourish very much. Rahim Arrakan is now the best word in *hua*."

"I think the correct phrase would be 'the last word in *hua*,'" Fox murmured.

Rahim frowned. "No, we are the *best* word. I would prefer death than being last. Agata! Fourteen inches, twelve on each side. Don't move, little *uchenik*. I must see how big your breasts are."

I turned bright red and instinctively tried to cover myself.

"No, no, *uchenik*! We are all girls here." He laughed uproariously at his own joke, and then large, burly hands enveloped my smaller ones, holding me still. "Except the handsome brother, of course. Pavel, line it up a *santimetr* to the right; we must accentuate her form like so...yes. Agata, twenty-one, twenty-seven, twenty-two."

"Well, Rahim?" Mistress Parmina spoke up.

"Very nice, Parminchka. She has a nice form and will do very well in silks. Long legs and a high waist. Small or large, her breasts will be works of art in my gowns."

I blushed harder. No one paid me any attention.

"But not the dark gold for this one, no. No oranges and peaches and brown leaves, and I shall know the day you hate me if it is the same day you let her wear all shades of pink, Parminchka. The embers are already in her skin in abundance, and she will have no need of their colors in her *hua*. The tasteful, bright-gold etchings, maybe. But mostly blues and greens and grays for this one. Do not touch that, boy!"

Fox, who was in the middle of reaching for one of the sketches on the worktable, paused.

"They're spellholders, boy! A little smudge and they can go..." Rahim's beefy hands began to raise but then lowered again. "Well, they will be hard to remake."

"I will require a dozen official hua for her, my *milaya*. Two of each color you think best for her. And then half a dozen more in every kingdom's style to start."

"A dozen official *hua*?" I echoed.

Rahim looked kindly down at me.

"You still do not know, little *uchenik*? You are to debut as an apprentice in two months' time, and it will not do to have no collection of your own. It will not be seeming to borrow one from another asha, for they might believe my Parminchka thinks cheaply of you."

I stared, dumbfounded, back at Mistress Parmina.

"We shall need to leave in an hour's time, Rahim *milaya*. We have an appointment with Chesh."

Rahim beamed. "Excellent! She will pair her *zivars* nicely with my *hua*. Agata! Take down the blue swatches from the inner room and bring them here. Pavel, take the green and purple from Anabel." He spun me around like I was a wooden ballerina doll and deftly wrapped my waist around a bolt of silver cloth before I had time to react. "See there, little apprentice? You look lovely in silver."

I stared at the mirror, at my image with the beautiful and expensive fabrics wrapped around me. *I'm not going to be punished*, I thought numbly. *Or is being an asha apprentice to be my punishment?*

"And the purple drapes nicely here!" Rahim thrust a piece of paper under my nose. It had a rough but stunning sketch of a purple and bright-gold sunset overlooking a gray sea. "I had been saving this up for a special occasion, and you will be it. We will show you to the world in this two months from now. Isn't that lovely? Now where are my girls with the cloths? Agata! Pavel! You there—you look like you have nice muscles for carrying. Come with me!"

He bustled off, dragging a confused Fox off with him. I looked away from the mirror and met Mistress Parmina's steady gaze.

"Yes, Tea," she said calmly. "I could have punished you and turned you out with nothing but the clothes on your back and your tail between your legs. You have caused more chaos among the asha-ka than has been seen in my lifetime, and that is a very long time indeed. But if there is one thing I will forgive for the mess you have made, no matter how indirectly your responsibility in it lies, it is that you are the strongest asha I have seen in recent times, and I will not have you loose on the population outside these walls, where you are likely to wreak even more havoc. You are strong in the Dark; I think that is punishment enough, as you will learn in your own time. What matters now is that you must be taught as soon as possible, so that the Dark will not have the better of you. Mykaela is rather fond of you, and I owe her that much at least. Do we understand each other, Tea?"

"You made my life difficult," I said.

The old woman burst into laughter again. "If you think running errands and doing chores are difficult, child, then you are not ready to be an asha. But for all the indignities I heaped on you, you have held your head and done what was expected of you. And after your accident, I no longer see any reason to delay." She drained the contents of her goblet. "You must, of course, earn your keep well. You will have to pay back the costs of these *hua* after you make your debut. It is the only proper thing to do."

I am going to be an asha. I am going to be an asha.

"Yes," I said weakly as Rahim and Fox returned, armed to the teeth with fabrics. The huge man looked triumphant, and Fox resigned. "It's only proper."

*I*T TOOK ME TWO DAYS *to grow accustomed to the monster that roamed outside. Two days to be convinced that it would not come and eat me while I slept. The girl refused to answer any more questions about the beast's purpose in between tales about her hints of war. I tossed and turned in my sleep; every time I dreamed, I saw the blue moon looking down on me, blinding me with its brightness, and I woke up sweating.*

"You're aware of the circumstances of my exile," she said to me while the daeva dozed outside, unaffected by the hot sun baking down overhead. "You wouldn't have sought me out otherwise."

"I know that they accused you of conspiracy and of treason."

"They accused me of many things. Of killing a king and an asha. Of being one of the Faceless. Of betraying the kingdoms. But I am only guilty of one of those."

"But was it wrong for them to believe you capable of these things?"

"That is not quite true; I am more than capable." She smiled wryly. "But the last time I tried to explain myself, I was cast out and banished for my troubles. I will let them sort out what I did and did not do when this is all over. My work is not yet complete."

She showed me her collection of tiny bottles, all glass and different colors. It was a curious luxury, given her surroundings, but she disagreed. "This is our beauty secret," she laughed and picked up a small vial that held a red liquid. She pressed the tip of her finger against the opening and upended the bottle, so that the liquid inside coated the skin but prevented more from spilling out. She dabbed her finger against the sides of her neck. I caught a whiff of jasmine and flowers.

"These are my potions," she explained, selecting another bottle that contained a thick, yellow concoction. "The cheapest of these spells are sold in the market commons all around the world. The more expensive spells are those that cater to each specific individual, made to draw out their strengths and hide their weaknesses. I have a blunt personality, more likely to say what I mean instead of sparing someone's feelings. This will not temper my words, but it will help those who listen to me accept them with lesser offense. Of course, if one is strong in the magic themselves, this may not work on them. Or one might wear another spell that cancels out this magic. You cannot put on too many of the stronger spells all at once, for they muddle together and make themselves ineffective. Choosing which spells to wear is like playing a game, except you are forced to decide your moves without knowing what your opponent might bring to the fight."

She selected a color stick next and gently daubed her cheekbones with it. "This is more for me than for show," she admitted to me. "It keeps my strength up." The rest she left on the table, and she drew the divider back to hide them once more from view. "I don't wear them as much as I used to. Nowadays it's easier to face people as myself instead of looking through a mask." She looked around and added wryly, "Though the amount of visitors in the three months I have been here leave something to be desired."

She turned back to me, and the changes became apparent. She looked softer somehow, more graceful as she stood. Her dainty feet moved over the uneven ground, and she lifted the hem of her dress to step over the threshold that separated the cave from the rest of the sandy shore. The stained, muddied fabric only further highlighted to me the difference between who she once was and the sympathetic state she was now in. She walked with her head bowed, and I admired the way she carried herself—even in exile, she remained dignified.

It didn't feel right for her to be here, forced to take up house in a nameless cave on a sea of skulls bordering on the edge of the world. It didn't feel right that she be forced to live on this lonely beach like a nomad. It didn't feel right to see her so sad, and it angered me that so many misunderstood.

The taurvi *approached to lick at her hand, and a fog cleared from my mind. The rush of affinity I felt for her diminished. My sympathy remained, but it was no longer racked by the growing, passionate force that seized me when she first rose from her vanity table.*

"That's been another problem with these spells," she said. "A taurvi *diminishes magic the way its bezoar does, and only the Dark runes are most effective on it. That is why most rely on Dark asha to put it back into the ground."*

I stared at her. She only shrugged.

"You knew; still you were affected by the charms I wear. Now imagine the subtlety it can wreak on an unsuspecting world."

12

THE DAWNSEED APOTHECA HAD THE most peculiar fragrance, smelling like everything and nothing at once. Scents of orange and thyme and sandalwood warred with durian and dried herring and coal, fighting for supremacy. Dried herbs were stacked on the shelves, and clumps of plants grew in pots overhead, foliage spilling down the walls. Its proprietress, a middle-aged woman named Salika who still managed to look youthful, scrutinized the list of items Rahim had written out, bustled off, and soon came hustling back with a basket full of oddly shaped glass vials and containers. They all held liquids of varying colors. Behind her, an assistant stirred a large cauldron bubbling over a clay oven. It was filled with something too thick to be water.

"Here, Lady Tea. Tell me what you think of this." I bent my head to take a cautious sniff of one of the bottles Salika offered me, but I could barely get a whiff of the scent before the woman yanked it back, stoppering the lid. "No, this might be better for you." I leaned forward again, but all too quickly, she had rescinded the offer, picking up yet another vial.

"I think this one would be more to your liking." This time, she held it long enough for me to inhale a heady scent of straw-berries and rosemary. This bottle she set down on an empty tray while she found another. For the next hour, I did nothing but take in smell after smell, and we went through almost a hundred bottles in this manner before the apothecary was satisfied. Of these potions, she set aside only twenty-three on the side tray.

"She is a mix of both Water and Metal and a faint touch of Fire," she told Mistress Parmina. "Determined and highly intel-ligent. This is good. She will strive for perfection, and she has a strong sense of righteousness. She accepts change quicker than others might, but she will always be questioning herself and her abilities, no matter how far her training takes her. That is not necessarily a good thing."

I didn't know how she could say that much about me by shoving vials under my nose, but because I was "highly intelli-gent," I knew enough to keep my mouth shut.

"She must look after her lungs and her stomach, for she is weaker to poisons taken through the air. I will prescribe her gingerroot tea, taken every morning for as long as she is able to. She will not require any further modifications when it comes to the lesser spells, but she will need some extensive changes for several of the stronger ones to take hold. It will take some time to make and may be expensive."

I was expecting Mistress Parmina to grow angry over this new expense, but she looked pleased. "Which ones?"

"The strengthening spells, for one thing. Commonplace magic will have little effect on her. She will get the usual headaches, but she shall see through them easily enough." She moved across the room, and the jars she selected this time were tinier in size, holding no more than a few ounces of liquid or several grams of powder in each. Finally, she stepped toward the boiling cauldron.

"Dusk mushrooms," she pronounced, tapping a few of the contents of one vial into the bubbling liquid. "Quickroot," she said next, sprinkling bits of a green substance into the water. "Eyetails," she said next, and I cringed at the name. But my fears were unfounded; she added two pieces of pale petals into the mix and watched as they sank to the bottom.

"And finally." Salika reached into an ornate-looking jar and slowly took out a small gray pebble. I thought for a moment that it was an ant of some sort, because I could have sworn it wriggled between her two fingers. But the woman added it into the cauldron, and it dissolved the instant it hit the hot surface.

"Yes," she said. "It is part of the bezoar of the *taurvi* that Lady Mykaela very kindly offered for my collection. It is not a requirement for the potions, but it is an extremely potent addition that will greatly enhance her skills."

"But why?" I wasn't sure I wanted one of the daeva anywhere on my person.

"Bezoars help to enhance a Dark asha's magic, Lady Tea. You're quite lucky; none of the other apothecaries have had bezoars in such a long time. Kings claim the right to take the bezoars of daeva whose graves fall within their kingdoms."

"King Telemaine is a good man," Mistress Parmina said. "This is an honor, Lady Salika. No one has taken a bezoar in their potions since a *nanghait* was presented to my predecessor, Simika."

"Because of Lady Mykaela's generosity, I add this free of charge for you. But I cannot say the same for the other ingredients, which, though a little easier to come by, are nonetheless costly."

"Well." Mistress Parmina leaned forward, her green eyes sparkling. "Why don't we talk about that?"

I sidled closer to Fox while the two women quibbled over price. My brother was inspecting the cauldron, which had turned a bubbling brown after Salika had added the last ingredient. "What's a *nanghait*?" I whispered.

"It's another daeva. I'm told that it's got a tongue as long as a street." He turned to look more closely at me. "Are you all right, Tea?"

"I am now." I looked back at the two women. I could not stop my lower lip from trembling. "Fox, they say I'm to be an asha."

"I would say that much was obvious, Tea. Isn't that what you wanted?"

"But I don't understand. I caused a lot of grief and damage to the teahouse and to many parts of the city. That's what Lady Mykaela told me, because I hadn't been allowed outside the Valerian until today. Why would they do this?"

"Think about it, Tea. Given the power you've displayed, I would think turning you out with all this magic at your command is the last thing they would want to do." Fox's expression softened.

"Just say the word, Tea. I'll throw a few bottles through the displays to distract them, and we can make for the forest outside the city."

"No." Leaving was the last thing I wanted to do. I recalled the strength surging through me when I had summoned the rats, the panic I had caused. What would happen to me if I left Kion untrained? How many more people would I inadvertently harm? Leaving now would be the most irresponsible I could do, and it would justify the hatred people had for bone witches.

But talk of the *taurvi* and the *nanghait* had stirred up another memory. "I don't think this is only about me. I think there's something wrong with Lady Mykaela."

"About her heartsglass?"

"Not just about that. I overheard a conversation between her and Mistress Parmina not too long ago." I tried to swallow the lump I could feel lodged in my throat. "Fox, I think she might be dying."

Behind us, the two women chortled their agreement and finalized their deal with a lengthy handshake.

•• ⧄⧉ ••

The *zivar* shop was less chaotic than Rahim's atelier workshop but was almost every bit as colorful. Long, traditional hairpins were mounted on different stands as we entered, decorated in every kind of motif imaginable. There were paper-crepe flowers, silk paper fashioned to represent seasonal scenes, lacquered combs, and fan-shaped metal streamers. I saw a few simple designs, such as a long, silver stick unadorned save for a small, ceramic rose at the end of its chain and extremely elaborate works of art, such as a tortoiseshell comb depicting a long bouquet of paper goldfish and silk flowers woven along its length, so large and cumbersome that I wondered how anyone could walk around balancing such a heavy display on their heads.

The store proprietress was a sunny-faced young woman named Chesh who talked a mile a minute as we browsed and never once came up for air that I could tell. She knew the details of every pin and comb in her store and had admitted to crafting most. "People want what everyone has nowadays." Chesh wore eight or nine of her own pins in her hair. Jewels and flowers dangled down on either side of her face, before her ears. She shook her head, and the bright jewels swung back and forth as a counterpoint. Fifteen boys and girls worked for her, but unlike Rahim's workshop, hers was neater, with lesser suggestions of constant chaos. "Last year, everyone wanted rubies carved in the shape of twin hearts offset by white clovers. The year before that, it was yellow lilies in green jade, mounted in white streamers. Only a few weeks ago, we were inundated with people asking for pink jasmines and silk rabbits on emerald-studded leaves, just because they saw Princess Inessa wearing them at a dance." She wrinkled her nose. "Don't they understand that the point is to cater to *your* personality and not others you see wearing *zivar*?"

I couldn't say that I understood the point of *zivar* yet either, so I just nodded, still somewhat awestruck. Fox, overwhelmed by all the beauty and femininity inside, had opted to wait outside the store.

"I'll help you find what kinds of *zivar* appeal to your tastes," Chesh promised. "And knowing Mistress Parmina, I would be more than happy to come up with one-of-a-kind designs for you, as I have always done for the Valerian. I will talk to Rahim and Mistress Salika with regard to the color patterns and spells Mistress Parmina has decided for you. In the meantime, please feel free to look around and tell me anything that you might find appealing."

I had already decided that there was no way I could wear some of the larger designs, out of a small fear they would somehow dislodge themselves and tumble to the floor, taking most of my hair with them. Instead, I idled by the simpler hairpins and combs and found that I enjoyed looking through them. Quite a few caught my eye, but I hesitated, not sure how many I could choose. I would have been satisfied with two or three, but Mistress Parmina would have none of that.

"Why are you concerning yourselves with these cheap trinkets?" she demanded, uncaring that Chesh was within hearing range. "Do you think people will look up to the Valerian if their asha walk around with things in their hair that you would need a magnifying lens to see?" She was about to say more had Chesh not smoothly intervened.

"We have a new supply of gold combs like the ones you prefer, Mistress Parmina, and I want you to look through the collection before I put them up for display. I have made the silver silk doves you've been asking for, but there is the matter of selecting which comb to pair them with…"

"A new supply, you say?" Interest piqued, the old woman

turned to her, and I took the opportunity to get out of the way, retreating to a display stand where I exhaled noisily.

"You shouldn't bother yourself too much about her," someone said. "We're all used to Mistress Parmina, and we don't see her all the time. You live in the same house, so why aren't you?"

He was easily one of the loveliest boys I have ever met, a few years younger than I was. I knew it was a strange thing to say, but "lovely" suited him well. He was clad in the simple frock that all the other shop assistants wore, and he had long lashes and a gently rounded face. He also had eyes of the brightest blue, a magnificent complement to his tanned skin. He bowed low, and his heartsglass spilled out over his shirt. The boy looked younger than I was, but Lady Mykaela had said that those who worked in the Willows were allowed to receive their heartsglass earlier if they wanted. His was a rich-red color, but there was something strange to it, something I couldn't quite place at the moment.

The boy slipped his heartsglass back inside his robe, then held a silver hairpin out to me. It was shaped like a wing, with blue sapphires embedded along intervals on its metal feathers. It reminded me of the sapphire pin I had to sacrifice to the oracle when I first arrived at Ankyo.

"It's beautiful," I gasped. "But how did you know…?"

The boy shrugged shyly. He had long hair tied neatly back in a small ponytail, and he tugged at its end. "I just thought it suited you."

"I love it," I told him, smiling. "My name's Tea."

"Mine's Likh."

"Well, Likh, thank you. You're really good at this."

Instead of beaming back, the boy looked a little sad. "That's what Chesh says too. Do you want me to help you pick out some more pins? I know a few other things that you might like."

"That would be good because I don't even know what I like yet."

He grinned. "This place seems intimidating, especially if you're new to *zivar*. The whole of the Willows seems intimidating, really. The trick is to remember that we're all here to make you look prettier, so it can't be that bad a thing."

We laughed, and he led me to a few more display stands.

I spent most of the day happily occupied and found enough items to sate even Mistress Parmina's need to show me off. She settled the bill, Chesh promised to deliver them to the Valerian as soon as she finished them, and Likh waved at us as we left. "This is enough for one day," Mistress Parmina announced.

I expected us to return to the Valerian. We didn't, and I started to break out into a fresh sweat when I realized where she was taking us.

The Falling Leaf had seen better days. The garden had escaped mostly unscathed, save for a few disturbances in the soil. But the roof above the room Zoya and the other asha had entertained Prince Kance and his friends had collapsed, and the door leading in had been ripped out. Some attempt had been made to clean the area, but I could still see bits of broken wood and debris. The smell of sawdust clung to the air. Though it was the only room that looked to have been severely damaged by my mishap, there was a small sign by the entranceway announcing that, while the

Falling Leaf would be closed until repairs were finished, visitors were still free to come and enjoy their gardens.

I was horrified—had I done all that? How had the rest of Ankyo looked?

I knew who the owner of the tearoom was: a short and stocky woman of middling age was supervising some of the cleaning and was deep in conversation with a few men whom I assumed were carpenters come to assess the damage. I understood immediately what Mistress Parmina wanted me to do. I hurried forward, my cheeks scarlet and my hands trembling, and stood before the woman, waiting for her to acknowledge me.

Once she did, I knelt forward and bowed until my forehead lay pressed against the earthen floor. I had once seen an apprentice do this to a mistress from a neighboring asha-ka for carelessly ruining one of her expensive *hua*. She had remained in that position for the better part of the afternoon, out in the street for all to see, until the mistress had determined she had been humiliated long enough.

"Oh, you don't need to do that," the Falling Leaf's mistress exclaimed when she saw me. Oddly enough, it was she who was embarrassed. "It was an accident. It couldn't be helped, I'm sure."

"Nevertheless," Mistress Parmina said, "my apprentice was somewhere she was not supposed to be, and your *cha-khana* suffered as a result. House Valerian pledges to pay for any damages made during her visit."

"That is very kind of you, Lady Parmina," the woman said, "but House Imperial has already offered the same thing."

"I understand that Zoya had an important role in all of this and must share the blame. But," the old woman added firmly, "as my apprentice was guilty of at least the physical consequences of this incident, I insist we assume the financial responsibility. And because you receive no profit while the Falling Leaf remains closed, please also accept a small daily stipend from us as well, until you are ready to reopen."

The teahouse owner paused and finally nodded, if a little nervously. "I hope Mistress Hestia will understand…"

"Mistress Hestia shall," Mistress Parmina assured her. "I will personally inform her of my decision."

The other woman seemed to wilt in relief. "Thank you for your kind generosity, Mistress."

"Get up, Tea." Mistress Parmina told me, and I scrambled to my feet. "We will take our leave, Mistress Peg, and thank you for your clemency."

"Wait." If I was to beg forgiveness from the *cha-khana* mistress, I may as well ask forgiveness from everyone. "I would like to apologize to the girl who brought me to the Falling Leaf that night."

"A girl?" The woman look astounded. "I sent no girls out that night."

"But one came to the asha-ka and asked me to bring Lady Shadi's *hua* and her instrument…"

"All my girls bring such matters to my attention before I send them out. I do not remember any of them doing so that night."

"My charge must have been mistaken," Mistress Parmina said smoothly. "Thank you again for your consideration, Mistress."

Confused, I bowed low again before we departed, keeping my eyes glued to the floor until we had put the Falling Leaf some distance behind us. Before we entered the Valerian, Fox squeezed my hand reassuringly. "I will be nearby," he promised, slipping away before Mistress Parmina could command him to leave.

The old asha had other things planned. "You will begin your lessons tomorrow. Lady Shadi and I will accompany you to your classes. In the meantime, I find it insulting how gracelessly you stood after Mistress Peg accepted your apology. That is not the way asha should stand, and fortunately, she was aware of your situation and did not take offense. But tonight, you will practice until I am satisfied with your performance. Kneel as you did in the tearoom."

I hurried to comply, pressing my forehead against the soft bamboo mats that covered the floor of her room.

"Too slapdash, too quick. It looks as if you want it to be over. Do it again."

She made me practice this throughout the night, always finding fault with the way I moved. By the time I returned to my bed, it was night and the candles had burned low, and I was exhausted. I reached out to Fox's reassuring presence in my mind, finding comfort there. I felt him respond—and with it the faintest of images: Fox's hands clenched into fists, bandaged but not from injury. There was another man in front of him, hands also raised, with a shock of red hair and a tattoo on his neck shaped like a bird—and then the image disappeared.

Cautious, I prodded at his presence in my head. After a

moment's pause, I felt his thoughts drift back to mine. *Go to sleep, Tea.*

Easy for you to say, I thought grouchily just before I drifted off. *If today was any indication of how my lessons shall fare, I might not last the week.*

*T*HE DANCE WAS AS OLD *as time. They performed it every year at the* darashi oyun, *a beautiful solo that singled out the most accomplished asha dancer of the season, the most distinguished award she could be presented with. Winning the role could have dramatic effects on an asha's success.*

They performed it on rare occasions in Drycht, in the cool summer palaces of King Aadil. They performed it in the Yadosha city-states, where men in loud voices and women with tobacco in hand paid exorbitant prices to watch them onstage, like these dancers were exotic species of a human menagerie. They even performed it in cold Istera, where the muffled cloaks and fur did nothing to hide the sway of bodies and grace of form.

But here, before the lonely grave, the girl performed the ritual of the Dancing Wind, and the waves jumped around her and applauded. The taurvi *moved on instinct, circling as the girl did, leaping and bowing so that it rose when she rose and fell as she did, and with them, the world spun.*

The dance wound down, drew to a close. The girl's eyes were a mystery. The taurvi *drew closer and licked her face like a faithful dog might greet its owner, and her laughter echoed across the waters, a sound of joy.*

13

ESPITE MY EXHAUSTION, I WOKE up early the next day out of habit, while everyone else in the Valerian still slept. Careful not to wake the sleeping maids, I tiptoed out into the asha-ka's entrance armed with my broom, prepared to do my morning chores. Fox was waiting as usual, leaning against the wooden stand that displayed the asha-ka's name and crest.

"Who were you fighting with last night?" I asked as I began sweeping the sidewalks.

"Fighting?"

"I saw you. You were with some guy with a bird tattoo."

"Oh, him." He dismissed my question with a wave of his hand. "I've only just realized my army training in Odalia was woefully inept, so I've been asking some of the soldiers for some tips on fighting. That's how I learned that something's been happening at the palace."

"Isn't there always something happening at the palace?"

"There's an army of Deathseekers preparing to leave the city."

I stopped. Like the asha, Ankyo was the Deathseekers' main headquarters, and most served the Kion empress. "What? But why?"

"I'm not sure." For once, Fox's uncanny ability to know the city gossip had failed him. "I think it has something to do with the *savul*. The Dark asha in charge of raising it died sometime ago, but no one knew about her death until after mine."

"Yes. Her name was Sakmeet, I think." I still wasn't used to Fox treating his demise so casually. "I hope they find it before you do. That is not something you should be holding a grudge against."

"Can't hurt to try. I've acquired certain advantages since then."

"I don't know much about Deathseekers. I've only met one so far, and he didn't have much to say."

"They do pretty much what asha do. Except they're not as pretty to look at, and I don't think they dance very well. Little boys are taken away to be trained as soon as their heartsglass change color. Not the best childhood to have, but as a fighting force, they're pretty effective. I intend to find out more about where they're going or if they have an inkling of where the *savul* is hiding."

"Fox, please don't tell me you're planning on infiltrating the palace just to assuage a curiosity."

"OK." My brother shot me a grin, gently nudging the broom out from my grasp. "I won't tell you, then."

"I'm serious. You could get in trouble." I scooped out some water from a small metal bucket on the side of the gate, dousing the walkway with its contents. He stepped out of my way, limping a bit, and continued to sweep. "I'm already in trouble, so I think I've made the quota for us for this year alone."

"It doesn't look like you're in trouble right now. Has the old lady been punishing you again?"

"Unless you count buying up half the stores in the district for my upcoming wardrobe as punishment."

"They're afraid of you, you know."

"Me?"

"What you did at the Falling Leaf wasn't something any other asha could do. The mistress of the Imperial was in an ugly mood yesterday. She wanted to pay for the Falling Leaf's damages. She was livid when Parmina convinced the tearoom lady otherwise."

"And how do you know all this?" I asked, suspicious.

"The Imperial's maids like to talk." He shrugged. "Two of them were at the sweetshop, trying to stay out of their mistress's way. I'm not entirely sure why those old women were vying to pay for repairs though. Most people would do the opposite."

"It's less about feeling sorry for the Falling Leaf's proprietress and more about showing off." I dunked a rough sponge into the bucket, scrubbed at the white walls with it. "It's about power and how much influence you can sway on behalf of your House. The one waving the most money around commands the greater amount of respect. More importantly, people get to see how influential they are."

"Looks like you did learn something from your time here after all." Fox leaned the broom against the now-clean wall and found another sponge. "Are you certain you want to step into this kind of world? I don't think the cut-throatedness of this business is good for you."

"I'm already in it too deep for me to get out. When I raised those rats and those"—I hesitated, not sure if calling them corpses would be respectful or appropriate, then forged on anyway— "corpses, it was both terrifying and exhilarating all at once. I was scared stiff. I felt like a part of me was being swept away, and I didn't know how to get that back. But it also felt good."

This time, Fox stopped, looking at me. "It felt good?"

I nodded. "Every time I draw in the Dark, it feels like I could keep drawing on it forever. Lady Mykaela promised to help me keep it under control. And it's in Mistress Parmina's best interests to protect me, no matter how much more she puts me in debt."

Fox no longer drew in breath to sigh, but the noise he did make sounded empty, troubled. "I'll stand by whatever you think is best, but don't expect this conversation to be over. I still think there's another way."

"Tea!" Mistress Parmina's shrill voice scared a flock of doves into flight. "Where are you? What are you doing outside? Scrubbing the walls! What would an asha apprentice be doing with the chores of the hired help? Come in at once and take your breakfast. Your first lesson starts in an hour! Do not keep Shadi waiting—no, no, your brother can stay and do the chores until Kana comes. I have no need of him. Rahim has brought over some apprentice robes for you. Get out of those cheap tunics before the rest of the world sees you in such rags!"

"Become an asha if you must," Fox whispered to me, voice

tinged with amusement, "and should you ever get to run the Valerian, promise me you won't inherit that screeching voice and prune face."

·· ≥⫯⫰ ··

The robe laid out for me to wear the day I began my apprenticeship was of light chartreuse. It was nothing like an asha's *hua* collection, but it was still a cut above most of what I'd seen novices wear. It was a soft green attractive to the eyes and an ivory waist wrap smaller than what asha wear, only a third of its size, so that it served more like a belt than as a form-fitting adornment. I was also given a small silk bag that contained a plain folding fan, a headscarf, and several pieces of sweetmeat and bread wrapped in fine paper to eat in between lessons.

I was used to dressing hurriedly and was already done half an hour before the others came down. Lady Shadi arrived first, in a very becoming beige and olive-green *hua* that highlighted her eyes. She smiled at me. "You're early. That's a very good skill to have for your training."

"Thank you, Lady Shadi." The beautiful asha still made me nervous, even after all these months. We never had the opportunity to talk to each other before, and it felt strange to realize there were two kinds of worlds in the asha-ka. In one of those worlds, asha ruled with their odd secrets and curious customs. The other was the more mundane, everyday world occupied by everyone else, where maids cleaned and cooked and scrubbed and ran errands but still thought and functioned in the same way most people in the city did. And I was leaving this second world that I was more comfortable with in order to join the first, which I still knew very little about.

"A word of warning about Mother: she can be a miser when it comes to money, and she has a lot of bad habits, as I'm sure you know. But she will always work for the best of the Valerian, which means she will work to make you popular. And after what happened at the Falling Leaf, we all have very high hopes for you. Don't let her intimidate you, and be confident. We will be visiting many people today for your first lessons. Bow when we do—as low as you can, for you are the junior of everyone we will meet—and stay quiet unless you are spoken to. Do you understand?"

I nodded. Mistress Parmina bustled in, looking hideously regal in red and gold. "What are you two dawdling for? Come! We are wasting time, and Lady Yasmin is expecting us."

Fox, as usual, brought up the rear, and once again, Mistress Parmina neither forbade nor acknowledged his presence. Unless they had a pressing engagement, few asha were out at this time of day, so we only encountered servants rushing out on errands and other apprentices hurrying for their lessons. Just as before, many stopped to pay their respects first to Mistress Parmina and then to Lady Shadi and then rushed ahead.

It took us several minutes of walking to reach the studio of my first instructor, a smaller bungalow carefully hidden behind a large tower of trees growing at the entrance of the lane. With Fox resuming guard outside, we were ushered into a small, cozy-looking room. I was surprised by the age of the instructor who rose to her feet to greet us; Lady Yasmin was as tall, as slim, and as pretty as my sister Daisy, but the similarities ended there. Instructor Yasmin's green eyes were fringed by long, dark lashes, with freckles scattered across the bridge of her nose. She was dressed in long, flowing robes dyed a soft lavender, and her reddish-gold hair was tied back in a loose ponytail that reached her thighs.

This was the first time I had ever seen Mistress Parmina bow to anyone. "Lady Yasmin," the old asha said formally. "I am pleased to introduce a new jewel from House Valerian. Please instruct her to the best of her abilities, and we ask that you take extraordinary care of her, that she may flourish under your tutelage."

Lady Yasmin returned her bow. "I am honored, Mistress Parmina. Shall we retire to the inner chamber, Miss Tea?"

I was glad that Mistress Parmina wouldn't be on hand to witness my first lesson. The last thing I wanted was her scrutinizing every mistake I made.

"Let us begin, Tea." Mistress Yasmin raised her hand above her head and extended her right leg out so that only the tips of her toes touched the floor. "Do as I do. Good. Keeping your leg straight and without lifting it off the ground, move it in a half circle away from you, and end by touching it to your left heel. Extend your left leg this time, and do the same, brushing your toe against your right heel. Now for your arms. Raise both over your head and keep them steady. Every time you move your leg, bring the arm on the same side down and extend it as far away as you can until it runs a straight line from your shoulder. Now left heel and left arm. Right heel and right arm. Repeat."

And just like that, my dancing lessons began.

"She has potential," Lady Yasmin said an hour later, after we returned from the inner chamber. Lady Shadi and Mistress Parmina had been waiting for us the whole time I had my first lesson, enjoying tea and scones served to them by Lady Yasmin's assistants. "She takes to instructions well and has an ear for music. With time, she can be more than adequate."

This seemed to be what Mistress Parmina wanted to hear. She rose, and we bowed again. "We are delighted," the old asha said, "that you have accepted her as your student."

The next studio we visited was similar in size, with different musical instruments framed against the walls, some weathered with age. My instructor was a dark-skinned woman named Teti, but Mistress Parmina gave the same speech, I bowed just as I was told to, and Lady Teti brought me to another inner chamber as Lady Yasmin had. Once we were settled in, she handed me a wooden setar, and my face burned. It was a reminder of the trouble Zoya had put me in.

"First, I will teach you how to position your fingers over the struts and the different techniques you can use to strum at the strings. Hold the neck of the setar loosely in the palm of your right hand, letting your fingers hover above the strings. Settle the base of the setar on your lap, with your other hand cradling its underside, like this. That is good. But why is your hand trembling? Don't be nervous, Tea."

I couldn't help it. I tried to stop my tremors, but although I managed to place my fingers the way she had instructed, the setar in my hands quivered.

We practiced for close to an hour, and she gave me more

instruments to practice on: a pair of drums with treated sheepskin stretched over their surfaces; a thin, reedlike cylinder with seven holes carved into its body and a mouthpiece on one end; and an unusually shaped bow made of wood that produced a range of powerful sounds when scratched. I found my rhythm easily on the first, could produce no sound at all on the second, and could only manage scraping noises on the third. Finally, I managed one long note on the setar, the closest thing that sounded like music that I could manage. "It will get easier with a little more time and practice, of course." Lady Teti promised me. "But you already learn quickly. That is good."

She said as much to Mistress Parmina when we returned. "She is doing well on the setar. I believe she will have a similar aptitude for the sahrud, though I do not think she will fare well with the mey. I will help her find her footing and see which shall appeal to her most."

Mistress Parmina looked pleased again.

We visited four more small studios that day: one for singing; one for general instruction, mostly about history and politics; one for meditation; and one for flower arrangement and etiquette. The fifth place I was brought to was bigger than the others; it consisted only of a large hall as big as three or four *cha-khana* put together and loosely sectioned off by thin dividers to shield some areas from view. Yells and shouts of pain came through some of these partitions, alongside heavy thumps, as if something had hit a hard object at great speed. Asha and asha apprentices milled about, but they were all dressed in long, plain white robes and breeches.

The instructor here was a Lady Hami. She was petite and slim, only an inch or two taller than I was then, and with her hair in multiple braids like asha Brijette. Mistress Parmina gave the same introductions and then took several steps back. So did Lady Shadi. I was unaware of the reasons why and was wondering if I should follow their lead, until I was literally knocked off my feet.

The floor was lined with thick bamboo mats that cushioned most of my fall, but that didn't stop it from knocking the wind out of me. I lay there for a few seconds, stunned. Lady Hami took the opportunity to drag me back to my feet. She lifted her hand, and I was down on the floor again, though she never touched me. It felt like a great gust of wind had picked me up and slammed me onto the ground.

"You are a Dark asha, aren't you?" She circled around me, while I gasped for breath. "That means you will never be able to command the runes we can: Fire, Water, Earth, Forest, Metal, Wind. Unfortunately, that doesn't matter. Get up."

I struggled to my feet, my dress greatly restricting my movements, and was knocked down again for my efforts.

"You will be taught to defend yourself. You will be taught to fight back. That you start off at a disadvantage does not excuse you from losing. Get up." It took me longer this time, but another push of air sent me on my back while I was still on my knees. "This will not be like your other lessons, where you are taught finery and flowers. Get up. You will be taught to hone your body like a weapon, to understand the strengths and weaknesses of each rune so that you can learn to counter its effects. Get up. Understandably, it will be difficult for one who cannot harness their use, but that does not make you completely vulnerable. Get up. The Dark rune has its own advantages, but it will take work on your part to master. Get up. I will reassess your progress in two months and determine whether or not I will continue with you as a student or send you away. Not every asha can do this, and I will not waste my time with those who cannot cope with the demands of the training. *I told you to get up, novice!*"

I scrambled up, heart pounding, and fought to get my breath back.

Lady Hami surveyed me critically for a few seconds. "Return here tomorrow wearing the plain white robes you see and none of your ornamentations. Your mistress will be familiar with my other requirements."

There was a commotion outside of the room and a surprised cry. At the same time, I could feel Fox's presence draw closer, and from our link, I felt something much like consternation on his end.

Lady Hami led me outside. A group of asha circled a figure on the ground. It was my brother.

"Incidentally," Lady Hami continued mildly as Fox pushed himself back up, "your familiar will be allowed to stay and watch during your lessons but will be discouraged from interrupting, as you see here. I understand that the rapport you share means that he feels your distress and would want to act accordingly, but I will not have your training disrupted by these attempts. Do I make myself clear, my good sir?"

"As crystal." Had blood still been running through his veins, I was sure Fox would have blushed.

S IX BEZOARS REMAINED ON THE *table, identical in every way but their colors.*

"What do you intend to do with them?" I asked.

"I would think it obvious, considering my experiment with the taurvi. *This is a bezoar retrieved from the head of an hawklike daeva called the* indar.*" She picked up a bezoar the color of sapphires; up close, it resembled a fossilized ostrich's egg. "See how it glitters so? It can detect truth from the lies its holder tells." She moved down the line, touching each piece as she went. "This emerald stone was taken from a* nanghait *and can make anything grow on barren soil, exempting only runeberries. This peach-colored bezoar once belonged to a* zarich; *it can ease hunger and give back strength. Mix the bezoar of a* savul *into any metal and it will be impenetrable to most weapons. An aeshma's bezoar is said to heal even mortal wounds. And I'm sure this will be familiar; it is from the same* taurvi *Lady Mykaela once slew." The yellow stone glinted its venom at me, promising malice.*

"And this is my greatest achievement." She held up a large stone, plain and milky white. "The strongest of the daeva, one who can transport you from one place to another faster than even the wind. Its bezoar protects against all runes but the Dark. Such is the power of the azi.

"Do you want to know what I intend to do with them all?

I have seen the toll these creatures have taken on Lady Mykaela through the years. I have seen the deaths they cause, the grief they bring. Whenever a Dark asha raises one from the dead and banishes them to the grave, they only give the land a few years' peace. They only delay the inevitable. It is a matter of time before there will be too few Dark asha to carry out these tasks. This is what the enemy wants, but few people are willing to change such traditions." She stepped back to survey her collection.

"*After all,*" she mused, "*who would deliberately break all eight kingdoms only to save the lives of Dark asha?*"

14

THIS WAS HOW A TYPICAL day went during my time as an apprentice in the Willows of Ankyo:

I woke up at the same time I had as a maid in the Valerian, when the tower bells rang at six, mostly from habit. Breakfast would not be served until half-past seven, but I took the opportunity to practice the dances I had learned the previous day or study the books I was given to read for my history lessons. Sometimes, if I had nothing else to do, I would sneak downstairs and help either Kana or Farsi with their chores. I knew Mistress Parmina disapproved, but she was never an early riser, and if Lady Shadi knew, she never told. If there was one thing about my new position that I was thankful for, it was the food—instead of the gruel that marked my servant days, I was given Lavash bread and cheese, with jam specially prepared for us by a nearby confectionery. Some days it was marmalade or fig or sour cherry, but my favorite was always quince. I had sweet gooseberry tea with my meal and two runeberry slices.

Mistress Parmina often woke when I was done, and together with Lady Shadi, we would make a small offering of water and bread to a small shrine set up in the main room we received our guests in before two abstract idols that symbolized Blade that Soars and his lover, Dancing Wind. Mistress Parmina had never shown any inclination for the old gods or for the Great World Spirit or for any of the other major devotions in the months I lived at the Valerian. Lady Shadi explained to me that this was done at every asha-ka regardless of their affiliation, out of tradition and respect for Vernasha, the Willows founder, who had also been a devotee of Dancing Wind.

After the offering, we went our separate ways. Ula usually arrived after breakfast, and she and Mistress Parmina would retire to her room to sort out the asha-ka's financial accounts and tally up any expenses and earnings House Valerian took in from the day before. Lady Shadi would leave for the dancing hall to rehearse for upcoming dances. Sometimes she would accompany me to one of the studios whenever she had her own lessons to attend. "We never stop learning," she said, "and to dance or sing or play an instrument, we must always seek to improve and be better, never too stagnate. Asha will continue to take lessons from instructors throughout the course of their careers, until they become masters themselves or retire. There is always something new to discover every day, no matter how skilled you are."

Lady Shadi would know. Though she never boasted of her

own merits, she was one of the best dancers in Ankyo and was frequently asked to star in one of the several performances always taking place in the Willows, especially during the spring and early summer when they were common. She was guaranteed a role in the upcoming *darashi oyun*, the most popular dance in Ankyo, performed during the spring equinox, which is around the same time most kingdoms conduct their heartsglass ceremonies. This was also the dance that Zoya had been envious of Lady Shadi for, the reason she had used me to cause embarrassment to the Valerian.

My first lesson for the day was my meditation class, where Instructor Kaa taught me breathing exercises designed to soothe any volatile thoughts and focus my mind for the day ahead. She even taught me to temporarily block out Fox's presence in my head, giving me my first real privacy since raising him. The first time I succeeded, Fox came hammering at the doors of the studio, alarmed, demanding to know if I was all right.

After my meditation sessions ended, I visited Instructor Merina, who taught me the more refined arts. These included flower arrangements, reading and composing poetry, color coordination, and formal court etiquette.

My singing lessons came next, which I was terrible at. While my teachers have praised my ear for music, nothing I did helped me modulate my voice to follow the melody I did hear. Instructor Mina was understandably disappointed in me and soon deemed me unsuitable for important singing engagements. But the lessons were a requirement of asha training, and I had to attend her classes anyway. Fortunately, she placed me in a class with other apprentices and made us all sing in chorus, and so my poor attempts at warbling were not as noticeable.

I returned home for lunch, the heaviest meal of the day. The Valerian had no cooks, and so a nearby restaurant prepared food catered to our tastes. A typical fare may include a savory eggplant and tomato stew they call the *bademjan* or slices of grilled lamb and beef garnished with onions, lemon juice, and saffron or pomegranate-walnut soup. They were almost always accompanied by rice—sour-lime *biryani* one day, perhaps fried basmati *tahdig* or jeweled rice at another—served with nuts and an herb salad. Asha and apprentices do not normally eat large suppers—they believe the feeling of fullness that comes after makes one languid and unable to entertain visitors in their best capacity. I felt bad for Kana and Farhi, who still had to make do with gruel and a bit of fish. But as Lady Shadi ate very little, I secretly gave them what she'd left untouched. I knew what it was like to go hungry. Farhi sometimes refused her portions; I think she didn't want to be constantly beholden to a group of people her devotion disapproved of. The food never went to waste, for Kana was only too eager to dispose of what Farhi turned down.

My musical training continued after lunch, where Instructor Teti taught me how to play the setar, the most basic of the stringed instruments and the most popular choice among asha. I fared better at this than I did at singing and could play the simplest songs after only a month. I also showed some promise with the tar, a drum you held in one hand while beating it with the other.

My combat training was next, and that was easily the most

difficult part of my day. Instructor Hami was a hard taskmaster and gave me no quarter despite my lack of experience. She put me through the most grueling exercises. I had to run the length of the hall several times, made to jump with heavy stones chained to my feet, and pulled myself up thin metal bars that connected one wall to the one across from it. Soon I had a wooden practice sword to call my own, though I wound up getting hit more often than I hit opponents.

Sometimes Instructor Hami trained us in a group, where we went through a series of fighting forms at her command. It was hard work, and I always felt as limp as a rag when my lessons ended, but I would often stay behind after classes and watch the more experienced novices perform. Dark asha could not use any other runes, but most asha have no limits selecting the kinds of elements they were good at and specializing accordingly.

Many of the mock fights that took place were educational to watch and almost always entertaining. To the untrained eye, it resembled dancing; some students drew runes with large, overarching gestures; a few kept their movements close to their body, sketching out the symbols in the air in quick succession; some did a combination of both. Fire runes appeared to be the easiest to call among the apprentices, and many a session was interrupted because of a few stray fireballs. Once, an overly enthusiastic student set the whole room on fire, but before anyone else could panic, Instructor Hami whipped up a hand, crooked a finger, and sent a huge wall of water cascading down onto the flames, leaving everyone but her soaked to the bone.

Despite all the mishaps, I could not help but feel envious. It looked like so much fun!

My history lessons gave me a short respite from all the hard training. With a dozen other apprentices, I learned more about the geography and politics of not only the eight major kingdoms but also of the city-states of Yadosha and the major cultures and prominent rulers of each. I learned of how the kingdom of Yadosha had once comprised the entire continent, and that bickering among the royal descendants led dissenters to form Odalia and, eventually, Kion. I learned of the Five Great Heroes, the first warriors to confront and successfully defeat daeva. I also learned the Runic language, to recognize the two hundred kinds of runes that asha used for combat and magic.

Next came my dancing lessons, and they quickly became my favorite part of the day.

Mistress Parmina had enrolled me in what was called the Vahista school, and Instructor Yasmin was its current head. The Vahista was the first among many already-prestigious academies in Ankyo that specialized in training asha to dance; while some schools did teach outsiders, the Vahista taught only those who could draw runes.

That I would love dancing was something I never expected. There were slow dances, where every movement was made with exaggerated gravity and every gesture had to be placed just right. There were fast dances, where I had to be agile on my feet, spinning and leaping despite the heaviness of my *hua*. Most asha learned about two or three hundred dances, while those who sought to master the craft learned at least seven hundred. I loved the way the silk of my robes whispered and rustled every time I moved, the sense of proud accomplishment whenever I finished a difficult routine.

I loved dancing and fighting, but I didn't always have the patience I was expected to have when it came to my other lessons. I didn't always practice and consequently started to let some of my setar playing slide. I was restless when a history lesson went slower than I wanted, and I didn't pay as much attention to learning the language of flowers. I was able to skip classes once, after a dozen more students had been added to my instructor's class and my absence was easier to overlook. I used the extra time to practice my sword fighting with Fox, who nonetheless disapproved of my skipping class and told me rather pointedly not to do that again.

"I'm here to fight daeva. Why do I need to learn everything else?" I demanded.

"Duty means doing something not because you like it but because you're supposed to," he reminded me. "You chose to be an asha. That means doing everything that comes with it."

It was hard to argue with Fox; the disappointment I could feel through our bond was enough to make me cry.

Before arriving home from my lessons, I would always take a walk with my brother, and I would tell him about my day. We would first visit Chesh's *zivar* shop and browse, also an excuse to visit Likh, with whom I had quickly formed a close friendship. Then we would take a walk around the marketplace in Ankyo, and we would purchase a few snacks to eat, such as feta cheese drizzled in a spicy sauce or salty watermelon seeds or crunchy carrot and zucchini slices we could eat with chickpea dip. Fox was evasive when I asked him about his day and would only say that Instructor Hami had been assisting him in training as well. But when he showed up one day sporting fresh cuts on his arms, I couldn't wait.

"Have you been getting into fights?" I demanded. "Are you doing something illegal? Don't make me look into that stubborn head of yours!"

Fox laughed and raised his hands. "I'm not doing anything the asha haven't approved. It's combat training with army soldiers, Tea. You can't expect me to get out of every fight blemish free."

"But your wounds aren't healing!"

"I don't feel the pain, and I don't bleed. Another perk of being dead."

My brother wasn't taking it seriously, so I tried appealing to Lady Mykaela. "There is a remedy for Fox's physical injuries," she told me gently, "but you are both not yet ready for it. When the time comes, I will teach you myself. Trust me, Tea."

I did, so I grudgingly acquiesced.

It was a foolish thing to hope for and unrealistic given my circumstances, but I always kept hoping to run into Prince Kance, though I never did. I had not seen him since my mishap at the Falling Leaf, and I'd been wanting to find him and apologize, even if I knew I was using this as an excuse for something else. But the prince did not return to Kion, and I forced myself to abandon such unreasonable hopes.

It was late in the afternoon by the time I arrived back home, and I would often lock myself in my room and practice the dances I had learned that day until supper was ready—usually a savory stew and bread and some yogurt sweetened with honey. I studied my lessons, practiced both my combat and dance training, and went to bed early to begin the cycle all over again the next day.

•• ⫶⁄⫶ ••

"Out with it, Likh."

"What do you mean?" Fox and I had brought along some sweetly chilled *paloodeh* as a gift for Likh. Clients were few at this time of day, and Chesh was kind enough to give him a half-hour break. We three made a strange sight, sitting on the side stairway, watching the long row of stores and the different customers who trooped in and out of the shops, browsing and bargaining. Likh looked tired. He was noticeably thinner and only picked at his food.

"There's something wrong with this." I reached over and tapped at his heartsglass, which stuttered between red and pink.

"I don't understand what you're saying."

"I may not be an asha yet, but I know heartsglass. I am good at reading heartsglass, even when you do your best to hide it under your shirt whenever we meet. And yours don't make sense."

Now he looked nervous. "I have the same heartsglass as everyone else."

"No you don't, and that's my point. I thought there was something unusual when we first met, but I didn't think much about it. But your heartsglass repeats that same rhythm over and over again regardless of what you're really feeling. It's not natural. No other human heartsglass does that. What is it?"

"Tea," Fox interjected. "This is a personal matter."

"No, it isn't. You don't have a life-threatening condition I'm aware of. You're nervous and worried, but your heartsglass never changes color to reflect that. I don't know how else to explain it—unless you're not human at all."

"I'm as human as you and Fox! Well, maybe not Fox…"

"Thanks," my brother said.

"Then what's wrong? Likh, you know you can trust us."

"Fine." The boy took a deep breath. "I'll tell you." He turned so that his back faced the street and removed one of the pins in his hair. His heartsglass changed immediately—into a brilliant silver sheen.

"Likh!" I gaped. "You're a—you're a—"

"I can draw runes," Likh said bitterly. "And you know what that means. Nobody knows because no one really looks at a shop's assistant, but when my Heartsrune day arrives next year, they'll find out. I'll be forced to become a Deathseeker."

"You can't," Fox said, alarmed. "It's a hard life. You're lucky they haven't found you yet, or you'd be at a training camp by now."

"I don't have a choice."

"Does Mistress Chesh know?"

"Yes, this was her idea. But she can't do anything about it. It's the rules."

"Why not be an asha?"

"I'd want that more than anything." Tears rolled down his face. "But you know I can't be one. I'm the wrong—well, I'm the wrong *everything* for it. Just not where it counts most."

I felt terrible for him. Likh was easily more beautiful than many other asha I'd seen. He was light on his feet and graceful. I also knew that he would not be able to survive Deathseeker training. He would make an exceptional dancer if only...

"Why not?"

It was Likh's turn to stare at me. "Why not what?"

"Why not be an asha for a little while?"

"You're teasing me. In what way can I—"

"The *darashi oyun* is coming up. The performances are not all strictly for asha. In the hours leading up to the main dance, the stage is open for all who'd like to participate. It's what makes the *darashi oyun* special—they encourage people to take part, to experience being a part of the ceremony for themselves. It gives those who've been taking lessons a chance to join in, if informally."

"But only children perform there," the boy protested. "It's a chance for parents to show off their daughters, and the association encourages it. It's easier to find gifted dancers that way, and I'm not."

"You're forgetting that you're barely thirteen and still a child yourself. And I can tell you're lying. You can dance, can't you?" I shot a pointed glance at his heartsglass, which was now peppered with blue ripples across the surface. "Have you been taking dancing lessons?" His heartsglass turned a beautiful cobalt blue, and my eyes widened. "Likh! You've been taking lessons?"

"Some schools don't require you to be asha to take them," he said defensively.

"I'm pretty sure they require you to be female though," Fox said.

"You didn't!" I gasped as his heartsglass flowered into a deeper indigo.

Likh grinned sheepishly. "I wore a few spells to disguise myself. Most of the students use them, so no one gave me a second look."

"I know that look she's got on," Fox said, watching my face. "You may not be in trouble right now, Likh, but I have a feeling Tea will gladly volunteer you for it."

"It's not illegal," I said. "And I'm helping out a friend. How much trouble could that be?"

Fox saw it before I did. He leaped to his feet, and I caught a quick glance of the robed figure before it turned a corner and disappeared from view.

"Stop!"

My brother took off after it, and we abandoned our *paloodeh* to give chase. By the time we had caught up to him, the robed stranger had vanished from view.

"Did you see him?" Fox demanded of a passing maid.

"I saw nothing," the girl said, thoroughly confused.

"But you must have! He passed right by you!"

"I'm sorry, milord, but I didn't see anything."

"What's going on?" Likh demanded.

"Did you see him?"

"I didn't see anything."

"You saw him too?" I asked Fox.

"Of course I did. I could sense it stalking us. It was looking at you, Tea."

I felt cold. "How could you tell? It was—it was dressed all in black, and it had a mask on."

"I'm not sure. I just know."

"I didn't see anyone fitting that description," Likh said. "Lots of people here wear Drychta clothing. What makes you think there was something wrong with this one?"

"Because we shared one thing in common, at least," Fox said grimly. "It had no shadow."

I KNEW IT WAS FOOLISH TO *make Likh something that he was not, but I never did understand why the role of an asha was restricted to women alone. In the course of my wanderings, I have seen men who could be just as graceful as women. Men who, with the constant training we have had to endure, could perhaps rival even the likes of Lady Shadi. Are there any male dancers in Drycht?"*

"The royal court seemed to prefer the women more," I said.

"In a court of men, it is likely. But males are not the only people who can rule a realm. If women are encouraged to fight and draw runes and strive to be a man's equal in those regard, then why can't a man be encouraged to sing and dance and entertain as we do?"

"In Drycht," I admitted, "men consider such trivialities beneath them. The performing arts are not a show of strength. They are a sign of weakness."

"Then perhaps we should carve a world one day where the strength lies in who you are rather than in what they expect you to be."

15

I HEARD THAT THE HEARTFORGER WAS in the Willows almost by accident. Chesh mentioned it only in passing when I visited her and Likh at the *zivar* shop. "The asha are abuzz with the news," she told me, pinning a new selection of dovetail combs into my hair while Likh looked on. "They say he's taking up lodgings for a couple of nights at the Snow Pyre, since he's a close friend of its owner."

I was no stranger to the Heartforger's work by then. Some of Lady Mykaela's books talk about him in detail, including stunning illustrations of the heartsglass he forged over the years. He had discovered a cure for smallpox and spotted fever and was notorious for charging the wealthy exorbitant prices for his wares while giving them away to the poor at practically no cost. The book also went on to say that the Heartforger, like most heartforgers before him, had close ties to Dark asha, though they were never specific on the hows and whys of the relationship.

"How long do you think he'll be staying?" I asked, keeping my voice casual.

Chesh shrugged. "No one knows. Perhaps a week but probably no longer than that. I don't think he stays for too long in the Willows."

"I wonder what he plans to do here," Likh mused, weaving gem-studded ribbons through my hair. "He hasn't been to Kion in years. He dislikes both royalty and asha, and Ankyo has both in spades."

I didn't know either, but I wanted to find out.

.. ≥⟋≤ ..

I was in a rebellious mood all that week; Mistress Parmina had grown impatient with my lack of progress with my singing skills and had decided banning sweets and cold drinks was the answer, to protect my throat. Looking back, it was probably a ridiculous excuse to break my curfew, but deprived of my favorite *paloodeh*, I was looking for a way to get back at Mistress Parmina. And I was curious: if heartforgers maintained close ties with Dark asha, I reasoned, then sneaking out to meet him was merely preemptively establishing the friendship.

I wished I could say that Fox did his best to stop me, but he was just as curious about the Heartforger as I was. Mistress Parmina was already asleep, and everyone else had gone out. Only Kana had been taken into my confidence.

"People tell me that this current heartforger is something

of a recluse," my brother said as we crept toward the Snow Pyre, making sure we didn't meet anyone who would recognize us on the way. The night was warm, but I carried a paper umbrella behind me, which was perfect for shielding my face when people walked by. Fox had found a top hat, much to my amusement, and wore it over his eyes for the same reason. "He used to be friends with King Vanor, I believe—I think he even encouraged his romance with Lady Mykaela—but after the king shunned her, the Forger turned his back on the king too."

"Maybe he knows more about what went on between the king and Lady Mykaela."

"Are you going to ask?"

I thought that over. "No. I think Lady Mykaela explained everything that she wanted me to know. I shouldn't be nosy."

We turned a corner and nearly walked into Lord Kalen, who was standing by the entrance to the Snow Pyre. He didn't look happy to see us. "What are you doing here?"

"Ah—" I had been hoping to sneak in undetected. "We heard—we heard that the Heartforger was staying here."

"You can't see him."

"And why not?"

"He's busy. Kance is with him."

I started. The prince is here too?

"You may speak for your cousin," Fox pointed out calmly, "but I don't think you speak for the Forger. We're perfectly willing to wait until their meeting ends if need be."

"And I'm perfectly willing to bet that you are once again

sneaking out of your asha-ka without permission. Should I alert Mistress Parmina to your whereabouts?"

"Good luck." I managed to say this cheerfully, hiding my worry that he would make good on his threat. "She's fast asleep at the Valerian. Once her eyes close, a parade marching through her room can't wake her."

"Kalen? Is everything all right?" The door to one of the rooms slid open, and Prince Kance peered out. "Lady Tea?"

It was one thing to stand up to Kalen, but it was another thing to have to explain myself to the prince. I faltered again. "Your Majesty, I was—"

"Lady Tea?" I heard someone call out from inside the room. "Is it that Dark asha I keep hearing about? Send her in!"

Kalen scowled but obeyed. Without another word, he ushered us into the room where Prince Kance was. Two others were with him, garbed in black cloaks that hid their faces, and I felt Fox tense up.

Prince Kance smiled at me. "I'm glad we have the opportunity to meet again, Lady Tea. Good evening, Sir Fox."

"I am s-so sorry," I stammered. "The last time we met— I was—"

"No apologies are necessary. Lady Mykaela explained everything to me. I'm glad to see you have fully recovered. This is the Heartforger, Lady Tea. We've just been talking about you as a matter of fact."

The shorter of the two robed men took off his hood. He was easily the oldest man I had ever seen, even older than Mistress Parmina. He had a face like a shriveled monkey that had been shorn of all hair, and he did not appear to have any eyebrows at all. He took off the rest of his cloak, and his heartsglass caught my eye. It swung free, a bright, shiny silver.

"Well," he said, "His Highness here is an old friend, and with his help, I was able to get inside the Willows without the customary fanfare they like to play to announce my presence. Seems you don't like playing by the rules either, little girl. I was going to send for you anyway, but no time like the present, eh? You're scrawnier than I thought you would be."

I gaped at him and then at his companion, who was also removing his cloak. He was a younger boy my age, with sleepy, gray eyes, nearly colorless hair as to appear white, and a silver-colored heartsglass similar to the Forger. He lifted a hand up to smooth his hair back and accidentally knocked off his spectacles. "Sorry," he apologized to the table. I couldn't shake off the suspicion that I'd seen him somewhere before.

"They said you despise royalty," Fox said.

"Not all of them, no. But I hope they believe it. I started the rumors myself."

"But why?"

The Heartforger coughed and spent several minutes clearing his throat. Kalen looked away, and even Prince Kance looked a little nervous, his heartsglass flicking from red to cornflower blue. Only the Forger's assistant remained serene, sipping at his tea.

"Circumstances permit me to be more favorable toward the Odalian royal house," the Heartforger finally said. "They are my patrons of a sort."

"You were going to send for me?" I managed.

"I make it a point to meet every Dark asha they find. I don't know how much Lady Mykaela has told you about us, but we share what you might call a mutually beneficial relationship." He peered up at Fox. "Not every day I get to see a familiar either. Few Dark asha keep them—need strength to have 'em. You don't feel lightheaded, Tea?"

"I feel fine," I said.

The younger boy looked interested, hopping up to circle Fox, studying him carefully. Fox bore the scrutiny with quiet good humor.

"She told me that you despised asha too," I continued.

"We can despise someone and still maintain a mutually beneficial relationship. Mutual beneficence, you see, usually trumps everything else. But I take an exception when it comes to bone witches. It is only fair to have some empathy for a class that is despised even more than your own. This boy here is my assistant and successor, for lack of better options."

"Hello," the boy said. "I hope you don't mind, Mister Fox, but can I examine your chest for a moment?"

"What?"

"It's where the wound is, isn't it?"

After a moment's pause, Fox shrugged and pulled up his shirt, where the *savul*'s claws had done their work. The boy rubbed his chin. "It's not healed yet."

"My body hasn't been in a condition to heal for a long time," Fox said.

"You haven't been blooded yet?"

"What's that?"

"Is there something wrong with Fox, er…" I remembered belatedly that heartforgers no longer took personal names of their own.

"Call him Junior. Someone has to." The Forger looked me over. "Your mentor, Lady Mykaela, serves as one of the main suppliers of my craft, and as thanks, I try to get to know her charges better. You are her first and only longstanding apprentice, and so I am forced to make good on my promise."

The Forger produced a few small bottles from a bag around his waist. They all appeared empty. "Choose one."

Hesitant, I selected a green one.

"Remove the stopper. Carefully."

—the sounds of children laughing and at play, the sensation of running through grass—

The Forger's gnarled fingers closed over mine, shifting the stopper back into place.

"What was that?" I sputtered.

"Happiness." The Forger tapped at the bottle and took a small sniff to ensure it was sealed again. "At least, how happiness is defined if you're a young mother with three small children. I collect memories like these in the course of my work."

"But why?"

"I am called the Heartforger for a reason, girl. To make a heart, you need memories. There are many people who trade them in for a little cash to spare. Try this one—"

Watching a tiny casket lower into the grave, weeping as the first shovelful of dirt is poured into the grave—

"Sadness is a popular commodity to sell," the Forger said, stoppering the bottle again. "And it is a common ingredient in my work, so fortunately the supply rarely outstrips the demand. People are more willing to forget what makes them sad instead of what makes them happy. But happiness? Happiness pays very well. If it's a strong enough memory, it comes back over time—several years on average. But few people are willing to part with it, despite the financial compensation. It is not something you can easily put a price on. And then there are certain kinds of memories I require from asha, from those with silver heartsglass. Dark asha are especially strong and potent. That's where you come in. Will you?"

"Will I what?"

"Supply me with memories?" He grinned at the face I made. "I never grow tired of seeing that look on your faces when I ask. You don't forget them, of course. We've got silver heartsglass for a reason. Our hearts can rarely be replaced, but the upside is keeping our memories intact, no matter how much of them I draw out. We don't forget. Can't tell if that's a blessing or a curse most days. You'll feel a bit out of sorts for a week, but you'll be all right. In exchange, I give you information. My customers make up the bulk of the city, all cities."

"I would be honored to do all I can to help you. But what kind of hearts do you make?"

"Difficult hearts, of course. The money I earn from forging one heart can keep me fed and clothed for a couple of years. The nobles can afford it. All the backstabbing and politics and scheming, I imagine, having their hearts taken away by some rivals and such. They'll want a new heart quick for that before they go completely in someone else's power. Once I get a new heart ready, the old heart stops working, you see, becomes worthless in enemy hands. I've got hearts in reserve, primed for the day some nobleman loses his heart to someone out for his blood and needs an immediate replacement. They lead very exhilarating lives is all I can say."

"But can't you do the same thing for Lady Mykaela?"

"Ah, yes. Missing her own heart too, isn't she? Dark asha hearts are more complicated than your commonplace weaselly backward politician. Too many rare ingredients to find, too expensive. There's still three or four key things missing from your mentor, and she's been hunting for years. Memories from breaking free of a possession—that's difficult enough to find. Memories of a False follower, a Faceless committing—well, committing False follower atrocities—that's even more difficult, considering how secretive they are, how they'd rather die than be taken alive, and how you'd still require their permission. No, Tea, I think Mykaela will have to resign herself to a lack of heartsglass. She's been doing well without one so far. As no one knows where King Vanor had it hidden, I suppose it's a good compromise, even if it isn't the compromise she wanted." The Forger cuffed Junior lightly on the back of his head. "Say something, idiot."

"I'm making a heart for an old man," the boy said amiably. "Growing dementia."

"I'll try to make as many visits here as I can," the Forger said. "But usually Junior here does the extracting for me. I won't be around when you're older, given my age—don't give me that vile 'but you'll live to be a hundred' speech," he added when I opened my mouth. "I *am* a hundred. I won't be here forever, and Junior's slow on the uptake but good enough with his hands to work the forge. You'll be the primary Dark asha when I pass on the title to him, so I expect you to keep him out of trouble. Damn fool's got a bleeding heart of his own, would build hearts for anyone who asked if they cried hard enough."

"But is that necessarily a bad thing?" Prince Kance asked.

"In this business, it is."

"That doesn't strike me as a fair trade," Fox pointed out. "You get her memories, and all she gets is information?"

"True enough." The Heartforger reached into the folds of his robe and produced a polished white stone no bigger than my thumb. "Lady Mykaela turned over to me a certain seeking stone used one summer night a few months ago. I destroyed the parts I didn't need, wove my brand of magic on what remained, and feel it only appropriate for you to receive this."

"Why?"

"I've bespelled it with a young soldier's determination and an old woman's stubbornness. Wear this on your person at all times, and anyone else seeking to control your mind will find it an uphill battle." He waved a finger. "Whether they eventually succeed though, depends entirely on your own resolve. Take this as a show of goodwill on my part, I suppose."

"Then let me return the favor," I said, closing my hand over the small stone. "What memory would you like me to provide?"

The Heartforger was surprised but pleased, though he tried to hide it. "Any memory?"

"Whatever you need." I didn't think I had any experiences too traumatic for me to relive over again, and I assumed the memory he would try to take was when I first raised Fox from the dead.

"I usually wait until the second meeting to provide a list of my demands. But if you insist, there *is* one thing I've been hoping to finish tonight…"

He reached over and traced something in the center of my forehead.

I felt an odd sensation, a sudden influx of memories bubbling to the surface, like the Heartforger was rifling through the pages of my mind.

"Ah, this one should do nicely." There was no pain, but I felt my thoughts being gently prodded toward—

"Fire and calm, these two; water and flash. Much like my sons. This is Prince Kance."

The boy smiled at me, and I felt my cheeks prickle with heat. "It is my honor to meet you, asha." He bowed.

"That will do." His hand left my forehead, but with it trailed a little sliver of mist that wrapped around his finger. He guided it into his heartsglass, and we watched it disappear into its bright depths. I was still red. I knew Kance and Kalen saw nothing, but that made no difference to my embarrassment.

The Heartforger rose with a grunt, joints creaking. His apprentice abandoned his study of Fox and rushed over to assist his master.

"I've got a long night's work ahead of me still," the old man said. "Never a moment's rest. You have my gratitude in indulging an old man's curiosity, Lady Tea, you and your familiar. Good night, Your Highness, Lord Kalen."

"That was the first time I've ever watched him at work," Prince Kance said once the two had left. "Though I must confess I didn't see anything out of the ordinary. Did you, Kalen?"

Kalen only shrugged.

It was difficult to be in the same room with the boy who your first memory of had just been handed over to be measured and processed like medicine.

Fox's face was devoid of expression when he looked at Prince Kance, but I could practically *feel* his grin. So it came as a surprise when he merely said, "I don't believe I was able to thank either of you for taking care of Tea that night at the *cha-khana*."

Prince Kance smiled at him. "That won't be necessary. If anything, Kalen and I should be in your debt. To be a Dark asha is no easy life, and I know the sacrifices you all make to keep our kingdoms safe. I hope we didn't inconvenience you too much tonight? The Heartforger can be persistent."

"Oh, no—I had nothing to do today. I mean, I had my classes and practice but not at night, which I'm sure Your Highness knows—not that I had no plans tonight, just that there are no classes for asha at night—"

Kalen cleared his throat. "I am going to step out for some air for a bit."

"I'll join you," Fox said, to my relief.

"That's Kalen's way of saying he's off to patrol the area," Prince Kance said after they had left. "He takes his duties as my bodyguard very seriously."

"I know the feeling." With my brother gone, my anxiety diminished, if only a little. "Fox has always been protective of me."

"How has he been adjusting?"

"Surprisingly well. Nothing really bothers him for long. Even this."

"Isn't it difficult to be sharing each other's thoughts all the time?"

"I can't read his thoughts unless he's under some extreme emotion, and the same holds true for me. It's not as invasive as you might think. In many ways, he's a comfort."

I soon found myself telling the prince about my childhood in Knightscross, and he, in turn, told me a little about his own life. His mother had died when he was only five years old, and his father, while kind, was too engrossed with the kingdom's affairs to have much time for him.

"That sounds lonely," I sympathized.

"I can't complain. I have good teachers and mentors. I know I can always count on friends and family like Kalen. I can't blame my father either. He wasn't expecting to be king."

I remembered. "Your father had an older brother, didn't he?"

"Yes, King Vanor. My father never liked the way my uncle

treated Lady Mykaela, and he always felt guilty about that. He spent a month searching the palace from top to bottom, hunting for her heartsglass. It was his idea for me to check up on you during my stay in Ankyo, though I'm glad he did." He made a face. "We don't have long. We only have this room for an hour, and Empress Alyx gets worried if Kalen and I are gone for too long. Has Mistress Parmina given you leave to attend parties at the *cha-khana*?"

I shook my head, not trusting my words.

He smiled. "I hope we can continue to meet like this once you've obtained her permission—not just because my father requested it."

I felt like my smile could stand independent from my face. "I would like that very much. How long do you intend to stay in Kion?"

"For the next year, possibly longer. Kion is our closest ally among the kingdoms, and Father thinks it would be educational for me here." He reached across the table and squeezed my hand. "Thank you, Lady Tea. After days spent overseeing my father's affairs in Kion, it feels nice to relax and talk about other matters."

"How did the first date go?" Fox asked after we had left the Snow Pyre. "Has he asked for your hand in marriage yet, or should we have stayed longer?"

I was grateful no one else was around to see a young asha apprentice chasing her brother down the lane leading back to the Valerian, their laughter riding on the wind.

*T*HE GIRL SHOWED ME THE *polished stone she wore on another thin chain around her neck, bright and smooth. It was easy enough to overlook when set beside her heartsglass.*

"I wear the seeking stone all the time," she said. "It has saved my life on countless occasions. I will always be grateful to the Heartforger, for it was backbreaking work to change a seeking stone into one of protection. It was a precious gem worth more than my own weight in gold, yet he gave it to me without asking for compensation. Do not let the stories about him intimidate you. He is a hard man to understand because he is a man capable of strong feelings. He hides them underneath heavy layers of indifference and distrust and hopes no one else notices. He is a wise man but often sad—though I have found that both frequently go hand in hand."

16

Rahim beamed at us as we entered—Fox and I and also Likh. "Ah, my little *uchenik* and her brother! What will it be for you today? Does Parminchka require a new frock? Or do you allow me to design you an original *hua* for the day you make your debut? It is never too late to start too early."

I had been to Rahim's establishment many times since that first meeting, but it was easy to feel intimidated by the man's affectionate demeanor and his booming voice. "Actually, I was wondering if you could design something for my friend here."

"Your brother? Yes, we can make more than *hua* here. The dark and somber colors he wears will not do. He shall have the most appealing of red, scarlet like a woman's lips, so that the ladies they are encouraged to use theirs on—"

"It isn't for Fox," I interrupted while my brother grinned. "It's for Likh."

"Likh? Ah, you wish to splurge? I will give you the bargains, because Chesh has been so kind to me. The best sherminas for you, the—"

"We don't want a shermina. We'd like a *hua* for him."

Rahim looked at us. He stroked his massive beard. "A *hua*? But why so?"

"We—we were hoping you could make something for Likh for the *darashi oyun*, when the gates open for those who would like to dance before the asha's performance."

"Well," the man said. "Well, well, well."

He took a step back and gestured at us to follow him into a smaller room, away from the bustle of activity taking place outside. Nervously, we sat down on a few chairs he pulled out for us. Rahim perched on a tall stool and stared at Likh.

"You do understand," he said slowly, his Tresean accent less pronounced, "that some asha consider this an affront, a joke made in poor taste. The association of elders surely will."

"And that's why I was hoping *you* could make it," I said eagerly. "Everyone knows you would never make a *hua* just for the jest of it. Then perhaps they will take him seriously when he dances."

"The elders would censure lesser-known ateliers for this. Even with my influence, they may still do so. What makes you think I am willing to take such chances?"

"Because you have taken such risks before," Likh said softly. "Chesh told me your story, of when you first arrived at Kion. You were a refugee fleeing from a place that punished people like us. When you opened your own workshop, people looked at you and laughed and said a bear could not possibly know how to hold a needle, much less sew. You ignored them because you knew you could do better than the clothes they made, the designs they created. You set up shop along the smelting district because that was the only place you could afford. But you were brilliant. Everything you made was a work of art, and people noticed. You made a living by not compromising who you are. I…I want to do the same—to prove to people that I can and to prove to myself that I can."

Rahim sighed, a rumbling sound.

"That is a pretty speech. But there is a difference between a bear who wants to sew clothes like an atelier and a boy who wishes to dance like a girl, and the difference is there are no traditions that says a bear cannot sew."

Likh's shoulder slumped.

"I'm the last person in this room to know anything about asha tradition," Fox said quietly, "but I believe there's nothing that explicitly prevents Likh from dancing either. Tea and I read all the books we could find about asha conduct."

Rahim thought it over. "Likh, dance."

The boy's head shot up. "What?"

"I want you to dance. Show me what I am staking my reputation for." The man gestured at a spot at the center of the room. "Go on. Here is as good a place to perform as any. Do you know the songs the asha play?"

"I know about a hundred in their repertoire."

"Really?" I hadn't known that either.

Rahim grinned. "Your dedication is admirable, but so must your dancing be. Begin whenever you feel ready."

I recognized the dance Likh started with—a complicated piece called "Good-bye," about a woman from Drycht to be executed for dishonoring her family when she fled with a disreputable lover. It was a popular song used as propaganda against that kingdom in the olden days, though few people nowadays think of it as anything more than a tragic ballad. I was stunned. There was a heaviness to Likh's body, a weariness that translated beautifully into his movements, and I could almost imagine him as a woman who was putting everything she had into one final dance, a heartbreaking eulogy.

"That was excellent, Likh," Fox said when he'd finished. My brother wore an expression close to amazement on his face.

The image of that solemn, weeping woman disappeared, and Likh was back, fidgeting and nervous. "Was that OK? I'm told it's difficult to do well—"

"It is a dance that must be as successful at conveying emotion as it is with performing its intricate steps," Rahim said. "And a dance where the latter means nothing if you cannot accomplish the former. It looks like I have no choice but to design a *hua* for you."

He closed the distance between them and clapped both hands on Likh's shoulders. The boy staggered. "Agata and Patel must know, of course, but the others will gossip and the word will spread, and so everyone else must be kept in the dark. I shall say it is a fine *hua* commissioned by a connoisseur from Yadosha, and no one shall be any wiser. We will arrange the bustline like this so that you will give the impression of breasts, and then alter the hips so that you can sway and fill out like a woman. Green and lavender! Your skin is light enough for winter but not too coarse for summer fashion. And ravens! A motif of ravens to suggest your hair. Agata! Patel! Come and measure!"

"Don't worry," I called out to Likh as Rahim dragged the poor boy out of the room. "This is part of being an asha too!"

·· ＼|／ ··

During the days that Likh was being subjected to Rahim's enthusiasm for *hua*, I was not without my own tribulations. My dance lessons proceeded as normal, but Lady Hami had decreed that I could now rise up one tier in my combat training. Now, no longer content to have me jump through obstacles and swing my way through bars, she made me swim underwater with weights attached to my feet, got me to claw my way through swamp underneath streams of Fire other asha shot out in my direction, and had me face off against several opponents at once. Other apprentices simply parted the waters so they could walk or hardened the earth underneath them to avoid the mud or used Wind as a shield to prevent their opponents from attacking. I had no such weapons at my disposal.

Mistress Parmina had also decided that it was time for me to start attending parties with Lady Shadi, and this I looked forward to.

The night I was due to make my first appearance, Rahim and Chesh arrived at the Valerian to help me prepare. Rahim told me rather gleefully that he had just made his first *hua* for Likh and was pleased with how things were progressing. "Guaranteed, no one will look at him and see a boy," he promised me.

"I'm still not sure how the elders are going to react," Chesh fretted. Likh had felt compelled to inform his guardian about his plans, and she harbored some understandable misgivings.

"Our little *uchenik*'s brother is correct when he says it is not against the rules for Likh to dance," Rahim pointed out. "I do not think your charge will last very long with Deathseeker training. This may be his best hope."

"The worst we can do is fail," Fox pointed out. "They'd still force Likh to join the Deathseekers. I don't think they're going to sanction either of you, and I don't really care what they decide to do with me—the most they can do is send me back to the grave, which isn't much of a threat. It's Tea I'm worried about."

"I don't think they're going to punish me," I said slowly. "They'll stick chores on me, humiliate me a little—but I don't think they'll expel me. They think I'm too important for that."

Chesh glanced at me and smiled faintly. "I also think you're smarter than they give you credit for."

The *hua* was of a modest design—tiny butterflies climbed up its sides, white against a cornflower-blue background interspersed with small lilies. Rahim showed me how to tuck the waist wrap around me to prevent any folds and ungainly creases in the robe. A small elegance spell made from some of the vials prepared for me by the Dawnseed apothecary had been woven in, but try as I might, I could not detect their magic—only a faint sense of them but nothing else.

"Of course," Rahim snorted when I asked, "they would not be worth their price if anyone could!"

Chesh showed me the kinds of hairpins and combs that went well with the dress. Tonight I wore a tortoiseshell comb adorned with tiny diamonds that would help inspire gaiety and a hairpin with white flutters and an aquamarine gem set on top, which has a soothing spell. As always, I wore my crescent pin. Then she began to paint my face, showing me how to use my color sticks and pigments to properly contour my face.

"I think you're ready," she said, stepping back.

I glanced at the mirror and my mouth fell open. I looked amazing!

"We didn't come here to help you prepare and expect different results, child," Chesh laughed. "You'd best get going. We wouldn't want you to be late!"

They waved at Lady Shadi, Fox, and I as we left the house. This time, other apprentices hurrying past stopped to bow to me as well as to Lady Shadi, and I felt very grown-up in my new outfit. Unlike that night at the Falling Leaf, my *hua* fit me perfectly.

The *cha-khana* was looking better than when I saw it last. Parts of the garden that had caved in during the undead rodents' rampage had been fully restored, and some of the rooms gleamed, shiny in their repaired newness. I still could not quite get over the guilt that I felt for destroying it in the first place, but Mistress Peg was most forgiving. In fact, she was ecstatic.

"We're booked solid until winter," she informed me, nearly

giddy in her joy. She pressed something into my hands—it was a small envelope customarily used for giving tips. I had never heard of a tearoom mistress handing one out to an asha before a party began. I started to protest.

"Mistress Peg, surely I can't—"

"Don't think about it," she assured me, still all smiles. "Here's one for you too, Lady Shadi, for all the help you have given Lady Tea here. Now hurry up. Your guests are waiting for you."

I didn't know what to do, but Lady Shadi tucked the envelope inside her waist wrap and bowed, and so I did the same. "Good luck," Fox said to us before resuming his post outside the tearoom.

Mistress Peg led me to the exact same room where Zoya had made me entertain Prince Kance and his friends all those months ago, and I was sure she could hear how hard my heart was pounding.

When she slid the door back, I was almost disappointed. Prince Kance was not inside the room. But Kalen was. With him were other boys his age, also clad in the black he was so fond of wearing. To my chagrin, Zoya was also present, and two of her friends—Yonca and Brijette, I remembered.

"If it isn't the Valerian girls!" one of the boys hooted, rising to his feet and extending both hands to us with a large grin. He was tall and muscular, built for a fight. "And it's the Dark asha too! Come join us, pretty ladies. We don't bite!"

That set off a chain of laughter among the rest, and for an instant, I thought about fleeing. I knew the necessary etiquette when it came to dealing with people, but as Mistress Parmina had pointed out already, the theory paled when it came to practice. To my relief, Lady Shadi took charge.

"Don't tease her, Ostry," she scolded him. "This is her first party, and we should be making her feel at home. Come sit between me and Kalen, Tea, and I'll introduce you to the boys. You've already met the duke, haven't you?"

"*The duke?*"

Kalen shrugged, still glaring at me; he had not displayed such hostility before. He addressed Lady Shadi instead and did not look back in my direction. "I never told her. We're not in the immediate line for the crown, so we tend to be glossed over in your history lessons."

"Kalen is the son of a duke," Ostry said. "The Duke of Holsrath to be more specific—King Telemaine's own brother." He scratched at his unruly red hair. "Unfortunately, the rest of us come from humbler origins. I am Ostry of Mireth. My father runs a pig farm there, so perhaps you can refer to me as the Duke of Hog."

"Ignore their idiocy," Lady Shadi said, but she was smiling. "They leave Kion tomorrow, so they're trying their best to get drunk before then."

"Idiocy? Lady Shadi, you slay me." One of the boys grabbed at his heartsglass in mock pain.

"You're all leaving tomorrow?"

"Except Kalen, that lucky bastard. He's manning the fort here while we go chase after daeva," Ostry said, gulping down his drink. "And who better to hunt it down than a roomful of Deathseekers? But I'd much rather be here, drinking on Empress Alyx's tab and being entertained by pretty ladies."

"Not the best attitude to have before leaving to fight daeva," Kalen said with stiff disapproval.

"Oh, lighten up, Your Lordship. We've got one last night. Where's the attendant? We need some of those *alut* they like so much in Yadosha. This wine is not doing much to get me drunk quickly enough."

"Aren't you one of Tea's friends?" another man asked Zoya. "You were together when that accident here happened, right?"

"I suppose so."

"'I suppose so'? That's an odd answer. Are you or aren't you?"

"Little Tea here has friends who think shielding her from all sorts of harm is the best way to teach her how to be an asha. I don't believe in such nonsense. If she wants to tread the waters of the Willows, then the best way to teach is to throw her into the river. There is no better way to learn to swim than when you are struggling to keep your head above water."

"That's a harsh way of putting things, Lady Zoya."

"Isn't being a Deathseeker the same way? And yet you do not mind."

"I suppose it pains me to see beautiful women placed in such difficult situations."

"We are not paper flowers that easily rend and tear in the wind, Alsron."

"You must try to be nicer to Tea, Zoya," Lady Shadi chided.

"That's none of your concern, Shadi." Zoya flashed me an artificial smile. "Some wine, Lord Alsron?"

Lord Alsron did want some wine, as did most of the others. Yonca pulled back the door to summon a passing attendant.

"Would you like me to refill your bowl, Your Highness?" I asked Kalen.

"No, thank you." Kalen only looked irritated.

"Now that we have the celebrated asha apprentice in our midst," Ostry continued, and I felt embarrassed when all eyes turned to me again. "We must know—what did happen at the Falling Leaf that night? We deserve a firsthand account, don't you think?"

"Zoya was there," Kalen said. "She could probably tell it better."

"But she has! Now we want the story from the girl herself!" A chorus of agreement met Ostry's words. "Well, Lady Tea?"

I decided not to delay what was inevitable. I cleared my throat. "I don't understand it myself. Everything happened so quickly that it's hard to know where to begin."

"How did you come to be at the Falling Leaf in the first place?" someone interrupted. "Lady Zoya says that you'd snuck into their party without anyone knowing."

Instructor Kaa taught me several breathing techniques to control my temper. I employed one of them because the alternative was to rise to my feet and attempt to strangle Zoya. "I was an idiot. I was barely a novice, and I didn't know the rules. I worked at the Valerian as a servant far longer than most apprentices had, and I found the rules constricting. I'm sure you know Mistress Parmina. She is a hard taskmaster."

"We've had the misfortune," Ostry said, and the room roared.

"She's not as bad as you think," I said once the laughter died down. "She likes a clean house though and was always sending me out on errands. One night, I was determined to see how asha worked in the evenings—I wanted to see if all my hard work would be worth being an asha. So I did sneak out. I still feel guilty, thinking about it now."

"Don't be," a boy they called Mavren said. "We've all done that—playing truant and sneaking out into the city when the master of arms isn't looking."

"Lady Zoya, Lady Yonca, and Lady Brijette here were at that party—it was in this very room, in fact! Sir Kalen should remember; he was here with Prince Kance and the Princess of Arhen-Kosho." I smiled at Zoya. "Lady Zoya was kind enough to let me join them. There were too many guests about, and she knew I would be caught if I snuck back out on my own. They lent me a *hua* and made me up to look like an asha."

I saw the asha trade looks with her friends, but no one else noticed.

"But then something happened—"

"It was a seeking stone, wasn't it?" Alsron broke in. "We'd spent hours searching for it in all the rubble. It was Lady Mykaela who found it underneath the floorboards."

"I felt sick," I continued. "Dizzy. It was shortly after Lady Zoya danced for us. I remember someone asking me what was wrong, but I couldn't respond. And then something in my head burst"—I made a gesture—"and before I knew it, there were dead rats streaming in through one of the walls and a skeleton climbing out of a hole in the ground! Prince Kance yanked me on top of one of the tables, and I must have passed out shortly after—"

"And what a sight to see that was," Brijette countered. "The Prince of Odalia, holding you up by the legs like that! Why, we could see your shift—"

"Impossible," Lady Shadi said firmly. "Our waist wraps hold our robes securely in place. Was Tea's waist wrap dislodged in any way?"

"Well, er—yes," the asha floundered. "I suppose so—"

"I was there, as was pointed out," Kalen said, "and excepting the fact that she was unconscious, there was nothing wrong with the girl's clothes."

Zoya gave her friend a warning look.

"I must have been mistaken," Brijette withdrew. "It was so hard to keep track of all that was going on."

"But what happened next?" Ostry demanded.

"Prince Kance lifted Tea onto the table," Zoya said, "and we got to work trying to stave off as many of those rodents as we could. The skeleton was easier—it was Prince Kance's own ancestor, imagine that!—but it was a difficult job; we were worried we might accidentally burn down the tearoom if we drew in Fire, and the ground was beginning to cave in. And little miss asha-in-training here slept through it all with a smile on her face!"

"I think you asha exaggerate many parts of the story," Alsron said, already drunker than the rest. "The length of leg you can display while wearing the standard *hua*, for instance. I am more interested in investigating that matter further. What if Lady Brijette was right and it is possible to see one's shift despite the waist wrap?"

Lady Shadi rose demurely to her feet. She tugged lightly at her waist wrap, gathering the cloth from underneath that kept it securely in place, and then lifted her dress to display a pretty ankle. "See how difficult it is just to show you men that much?"

Every male eye in the room was immediately drawn to her. Brijette and Yonca eyed her with thinly disguised scorn, but for a few beats, Zoya's heartsglass pulsed a deep scarlet.

This was a new side to Lady Shadi that I had never seen before. There was a reason, I realized, why she was popular—and very clever. My story was quickly forgotten.

"Let's make that a challenge!" Ostry proposed, taking another swig of his drink. "How about we play a round of worm-frog-snake and test Lady Shadi's claims?"

A round of approval met his words, and I watched, a little bemused, as Ostry started off against the asha, the other boys yelling out, "Worm! Frog! Snake!" in the background like they were eight-year-olds in a schoolyard. Worm beat frog, and soon Ostry was shucking off his shirt amid catcalls. They tried again, but Lady Shadi was either skilled or very lucky, and soon Ostry had to take off his belt. "I surrender," he said. "I respect Lady Shadi's skill too much to be losing my pants over it!"

Fortunately, the wine ran out, and since none of the attendants were in sight, I elected, being the most junior of the asha present, to run out and get more. Relieved, I slipped out of the room, pausing at the gardens to gather myself. The Falling Leaf had made some improvements; two more statues were added to that of Anahita's, this time of Dancing Wind and another Great Hero, Ashi the Swift. I paused for a moment to stare up at the three, taking in the crisp night air to calm myself.

There was a movement to my left, and I saw a dark figure emerge from the gardens. It was clad in black, and its face was obscured by a heavy mask.

We stared at each other. I swore I could feel a presence settle in the corner of my mind that wasn't Fox—odd feelings of caution and expectation as it tested for a way in, and a telltale trail of annoyance at finding the entrance blocked. The Heartforger's stone felt hot against my chest.

Without looking away, I bent down and picked up a small garden shovel that had been carefully set behind a large quarry stone.

It fled, and I followed without thinking.

The figure barreled through the carefully trimmed bushes and out the *cha-khana*'s gates. It moved quickly, but I kept pace behind it, thankful for once for Lady Hami and her leg weights.

"Tea!" I heard my brother call out from somewhere behind me, heard him chasing after me, but I did not stop.

I should go back, I thought.

But another part of me, irritated and annoyed by all the restrictions being placed on my daily life, shrugged off the suggestion and ran faster. I raced into a dark alley, and I felt a surge of exultation upon realizing it was a dead end, with nothing there to hide behind. The figure had stopped, standing motionless before the blank wall. A small lantern hung overhead, and I saw it had no shadow.

"Who are you?" I shouted.

It turned to face me. With deliberate slowness, it reached up and pulled the veil off its head.

What stared back at me was a skeleton, bleached and polished so that no trace of flesh remained. The gaping mouth grinned malice at me; from within the depths of those empty eye sockets, something glinted. The skeleton gave me no time to recover but lunged at me, moving faster in the fifty yards that separated us than it had when I chased it.

My training took over, and I dove to the ground as its bony fingers swiped past, missing me by a few inches. Still on my knees, I swung with the shovel and felt it connect. The skeleton's legs gave out underneath it, knocking one knee joint loose as it tried to maintain its balance. It lifted its hand again, and I saw its fingers against the moonlight, the bones on each end honed and sharpened like knives.

And then Fox's sword cleaved the skeleton's hand, cutting it off at the wrist. The fingers hit the ground with a disturbing rattle, but Fox did not stop, angling his sword so that his next stroke took its head cleanly off its shoulders. The rest of the body disintegrated before his blade could complete its arc, the skeleton's ashes sending small clouds of dust around us.

"What in a daeva's teeth is that?" Fox demanded, staring at the skull's remains.

"This is what's been following us!" I scrambled to my feet,

kicking at the discarded veil and black robes and feeling sick. "I knew it wasn't human, but I wasn't expecting this!"

There was no one else in the alley. Fox insisted on checking, but the street we stood on was deserted.

"We'll have to tell Lady Mykaela when she returns," he said grimly.

"Only after she returns," I agreed quickly, "and no one else." I could only imagine the restrictions Mistress Parmina would place on me if she knew.

"This is more serious than I thought, Tea."

"I know." There was someone else in Ankyo who could channel the Dark. And whoever it was, was after me.

•• ⟩∖⟨ ••

"I'm sorry I'm late," I apologized as the door slid open. Faint traces of laughter wafting out told me that the party was still in full progress, that I had not been missed. Fox had already slipped away, still intent on searching the neighborhood for the skeleton's summoner.

Kalen stepped out through the door and took the heavy tray of drinks out of my hands.

"Thank you, milord. Was there anything else you wanted me to—"

"Stay away from Kance, asha."

The air felt colder, a strong chilly wind sweeping through the gardens unannounced.

"I—I don't know what you—"

"Stay away from him, Tea. And if you do not, then I will make sure you do." He stepped back inside, and the door slid shut.

I remained there a little longer, until Mistress Peg found me. It wouldn't do to keep my guests waiting, she scolded, and I would have all the time to rest when the party had ended and my visitors had gone home. I nodded dumbly, barely listening. Kalen disliked me—because I was a danger to the prince or because he disliked bone witches? And after tonight, I couldn't even say he was wrong.

I slipped in quietly and resumed my seat. For the rest of the evening, Kalen said nothing, though his silver heartsglass pulsed red.

*I*T PAINS ME TO SEE *these put to use in this way," she said, studying the bezoars. "We could cure the world with these, heal almost every known ailment. But I have no choice. The dozens we could save today pales in comparison to the thousands and millions we could save tomorrow."*

But I could not imagine how raising an army of daeva could save so many people; I feared the opposite held true and said as much.

"Imagine a world filled with daeva like my friend over there." The taurvi *basked happily in the sun, tongue lolling over the black sand. "Imagine the lives potentially lost by their rampages, by the people's fear."*

She lifted up a ruby-red bezoar from the akvan *she had slain only days before. "Now imagine that these daeva can be tamed. Imagine how, under a benevolent ruler, they could right everything wrong in all the kingdoms. We could use the daeva to rid ourselves of the Faceless once and for all. We could fill the world with runeberries, see that no one would go hungry or thirsty ever again. We could punish the tyrants of Drychta for your grief. Where would you like to begin?"*

"I am more concerned," I said, "of knowing where it will end."

She laughed, a mirthless sound. "Where it always ends, Bard. With me."

17

Lady Mykaela returned a week later, and I was shocked by how much she had aged in the interim. Her hair had lost some of its luster, and dark circles lurked underneath her eyes. She had arrived sometime the night before, but I found her already at the breakfast table. She gave me a wan smile as I entered, but as she lifted the bowl to her lips, I saw her hand shake, a little of the tea sloshing over the brim.

"What happened to you?" I rushed to her side. She looked so thin and frail that I feared she might topple over at the first sign of wind.

"It's good to see you again, Tea." Her laughter reassured me; it was still every bit as warm. "You're looking very well. I'm afraid I've been feeling a little under the weather and so can't say the same about me."

"A little under the weather, my ungainly behind," said someone by the door. "Would a ten-year war be a minor inconvenience for you, Mykaela? Would a devastating hurricane be an errant breeze?"

Two asha stood at the entrance, slipping out of their wooden sandals. The bright morning light shone behind them, so that at first I only saw their outlines silhouetted against the rising sun and thought for a moment that they were my sisters Rose and Lilac come to visit. But one was a plump woman with bright-red hair half-hidden behind a gauzy veil and large spectacles. Her maroon-colored *hua* had one of the most unusual motifs I had ever seen—light green cantaloupes were painted at the bottom of her robes, interspersed with holly sprigs and small white butterflies. The other was almost a head taller, with dark hair cut short above her neck—a style rare among asha, most of whom preferred to wear their hair long—and pale-gray eyes. Her *hua* was a bright yellow, in a simple buttercup pattern.

"The *nanghait* took more out of you than we wanted, but it is not good of you to trivialize your health in this manner," the tall brunette continued, her voice slightly accented.

"I am fine, Polaire."

"Not from where I stand." The brunette turned her attention to me. "You must be the asha apprentice people are so terrified of these days. Aren't you going to invite us in?"

"Terrified?"

"Ignore Polaire," the plumper girl chimed in. "Where Mykaela likes to understate, she is fond of exaggeration."

"But not by much." Without waiting for my reply, Polaire entered and settled herself on the table beside Lady Mykaela. She placed a heavy bag containing large twigs beside her. "I bought a bag of forkroot at Maseli's. That *salope* of a woman charged me an extra three shekels because it was fresh, handpicked just this morning. She wanted five, but I would have none of that. It should get your strength up, at least."

"When people gift others with fresh herbal tea, they grind it into powder first," the other asha murmured, "not present it with the leaves still on their branches."

"I could never figure out how to prepare these things," Polaire said. "If the recipe calls for half a pound of butter and a dash of nutmeg, I would probably forget and take half a pound of nutmeg and a dash of butter and kill somebody in the process. I simply take the ingredients and shove them on to someone more knowledgeable than me. It's healthier that way. You're good at potions, Althy. Why don't you whip up some tea for Mykaela here—and for me too while you're at it."

Althy shook her head sadly at her companion but picked up the bag and moved toward the scullery.

"You'll have to forgive me, I'm sure," Polaire said to me. "We are old friends of Mykaela here. Tea is your name, isn't it? How odd, since Althy has just repaired to the kitchen with your namesake. But I am not one to make fun of odd names, having one myself."

"Polaire is known to speak her mind," Lady Mykaela said, smiling.

"Oh, I'm the life of the party," Polaire said. "They ask for me all the time. And if anyone gets too forward, Althy will take care of them. Althy doesn't look it, but she can floor a man in the time it takes to raise an eyebrow. That's why she's Princess Inessa's bodyguard. But we took time off to accompany our Mykaela here to Istera. Gloomy *la épave* of a place, is Istera. Have you been? Aren't you going to give me some breakfast?"

I slid a large platter of Lavash bread and some quince jam across the table. She fell on it with gusto.

"Mmm, much better. Not much of a vacationing spot, Istera. Good only for its runeberry wine, elk antlers, and burly men— exactly in that order. Stranger's Peak always has good vintage, but it's a terrible place to live—snow piles eight feet tall and everyone up to their ears in mufflers and fur. If you thought Tresea was cold, wait till you've been to Istera. You will, eventually. Mykaela can't take much of this any longer."

"Polaire," Lady Mykaela warned her.

"But it's true, Mykkie. You can't hide that from Tea forever. In two years, the *nanghait* will rise again, and if you're in no shape to deal with it now, then think about how much of a headache it will be when you're weaker."

"Weaker?" I echoed.

"Mykaela's health is fading," Althy said, returning from the kitchen with a bowl of the freshly pounded forkroot and a kettle full of steaming water. She added the powder to the pot, then poured its contents into four bowls. Steam and a faint scent of spice rose up. "A lifetime spent raising daeva from their graves and sending them back would take a toll on anyone, and there aren't enough Dark asha to go around anymore."

"Sakmeet died a few months ago, and Mykkie had to take

up her duties as well," Polaire said. "Nasty bit of goods, Sakmeet. Was fond of beans and thought she could pass wind and get away with it. Nastier bit of goods, the *nanghait*. Took more tricks to get it back into the ground than it used to. That's your last daeva, Mykkie."

"I can still do it," Lady Mykaela protested.

"Not for as long as I breathe, you silly idiot. I thought for sure you were dead when you passed out like that, and if Althy wasn't there, I wouldn't have known how to bring you back."

"*Passed out?*"

"See? Your apprentice agrees with me." Polaire wagged a finger in Lady Mykaela's direction. "Permanent bed rest from now until the end of the winter solstice. We can pick up the slack until this one makes her debut. It might take longer, but we've got something you don't." And she tapped at her heartsglass on its silver chain around her neck.

I felt cold all over.

"Don't worry your head about it," Polaire said, catching the expression on my face. "Only Mykkie is arrogant enough to go about raising daeva on her own. You're both rare enough breeds that whole armies would accompany you if you asked nicely enough." The asha scowled. "They never accompany me though."

"You're not nice enough, Polaire," Althy said mildly.

"Shut up. What were we doing here again? Oh, yes—we're here to watch Mykkie drink that horrible forkroot concoction that hideous *salope* at the apothecary overcharged me for, and then we're going to force her to lie down for the rest of the month."

"I'm *fine*, Polaire."

"Your hand's shaking, Mykkie, and there're two of us against you. Three, because I'm recruiting your Tea too. One bowl, and then it's up to bed, Mykkie."

It took nearly a half hour to convince Lady Mykaela to do so, and only after Polaire threatened to draw a rune on her. She and the other asha traded respectful bows with Mistress Parmina along the corridor, and the old woman allowed the women to drag Lady Mykaela to her room, the latter's voice raised in counterpoint to the others' determination. I remained in the dining hall and stared at my bowl until my drink grew cold.

•• ⅍ ••

"Have you given some thought to her sisters?" Polaire asked Mistress Parmina after Lady Mykaela was fast asleep. Both asha had stayed on for lunch. "Surely there are some names that come to mind."

"It's too early," Mistress Parmina demurred. "Tea has only begun her apprenticeship."

"It's never too early to consider her sisters. Dark asha need more preparation than others, and Tea would need more training than Shadi… Where is she, by the way?"

"She is practicing for the *darashi oyun* at the training hall."

"Elegant girl. Nabbed the main role again, didn't she? I turned my ankles enough times during my dance lessons that Yasmin used to order me home ten minutes in."

"Are you volunteering, Polaire?" The old woman sounded interested.

"Of course I am. Why else would I bring this up? I know all the people who matter, and I'll teach her to liven up a party. And Althy can teach her the other boring stuff, turning lizards into powder or something."

"Medicine is a strictly vegetarian affair," Althy murmured. "Daeva notwithstanding."

Polaire pursed her lips. "I know Mykkie would normally be the best candidate for a third sister, Auntie. But I'm worried she may not have the strength for it."

"Tea will need someone to teach her the Dark runes, Polaire."

"Mykaela can teach her when it becomes necessary but not in her current condition. Frankly, Auntie, I'm worried. The *nanghait* took a lot out of her. She can't do much more of this. I don't know about you, but I would give a good deal of what I own to raise Vanor from the dead and beat the life back out of him again."

"Why can't you?" I asked before I could stop myself.

"Why can't I what?"

"Why can't you raise the king from the dead and demand Lady Mykaela's heartsglass? I mean," I added, somewhat flustered now that all three asha were giving me their full attention, "wouldn't he know?"

Polaire grinned. "She thinks. That shows promise. But she thinks without thinking her way through, so probably not. Don't you think we've tried? We have had Dark asha summon the king until they were blue in the face, and still he refuses to speak. You cannot compel the dead to obey you when they have no intentions of doing so. Hate and anger can linger long after death; it is a powerful emotion that is harder to let go than life. The dead have a reputation, and it is not for their amiability. They feel no pain, which is a shame."

"Polaire caused quite a scandal back then," Althy said. "It's not every day that you get to see an asha punching royalty in the face, even if it's dead royalty."

"It felt more satisfying to use my fists," Polaire said. "And I was always better at my combat training than I was at my dance lessons. I was hoping you could find someone else to serve as Tea's third sister, Auntie. I know that Mykkie would insist, and I want to head her off while I can. She needs to concentrate on healing. There will be enough time to teach Tea. Perhaps Shadi might consider it?"

"Shadi is newly pledged, with a busy schedule. I would like to get her settled in before I start putting little sisters her way." Mistress Parmina sat still for a few minutes. A small smile stole across her lips. "I do have a suitable candidate in mind," she said. "Let me talk to a few other mistresses and see if she would happen to be available."

"There is a formal ceremony for such things," Althy explained to me. "In older times, most asha used to have only one sister to guide them through their apprenticeship until they make their debut. There aren't as many of us as there used to be, however, and there is not always time to attend to a novice, especially when you serve as a bodyguard or have a patron several kingdoms away. The three-sisters system was developed for this. Lady Mykaela, Lady Polaire, and I often mentored girls together in this way."

"But since Mykkie is indisposed, you will be one of those rare apprentices with four sisters sharing the responsibilities," Polaire chimed in.

"We shall schedule the ceremony in a week," Mistress Parmina decided. "You are right, Polaire. We shouldn't wait."

After the meal, I snuck away to look in on Lady Mykaela, who was still asleep. I watched her tired face, looked at her empty heartsglass. I looked down on my own and touched the glass with a finger. It rippled for a few moments, blue and yellow heart-beats that soon faded into its usual silver. In the excitement, I had forgotten to tell Lady Mykaela about the attack—but whenever I tried to, a voice in my head would rise up, insistent. It told me that Parmina would curtail my freedom and ban me from leaving the asha-ka ever again, and I knew in my heart that it spoke the truth. And so I held my tongue. Lady Mykaela had other more important concerns to worry about.

Lady Shadi made her debut a month later, throwing the Valerian into chaos. I was not allowed to take part in all the preparations, as I still had to prioritize my lessons and the rest of my training, but for three days before her official coming out, there was a constant flux of people rushing in and out of the asha-ka. Kana and Farhi spent a whole day cleaning the house from top to bottom. Rahim popped in and out at all hours of the day and brought three of his assistants whenever he visited, all armed to the teeth with piles of cloth and patterns. Chesh was also a regular guest during those days, her hands full of hairpins and combs, and sometimes she brought Likh with her, who watched the proceedings with wide eyes. "This is only the third asha-ka I've ever been to," he admitted to me, envious. "It's a different experience every time."

"It doesn't sound like you've been punished much," Lady Mykaela told me, laughing as we watched the preparations from the safety of her room. She sat up on her bed, still looking tired but noticeably perkier.

"I've been wondering about that. Why wasn't I? I must have caused so much damage—"

"Don't think about it," she interrupted. "And don't feel bad either. When you live in a district full of asha, most Ankyons learn to shrug things off. Reparations have been made, and if anything, you've actually bolstered ours among the people. Mother would only have punished you if she hadn't gotten some substantial profit from what you've done. Why do you think she decided to speed up your novitiate?"

Other visitors came and went. There were people from gift shops, some of the subordinate mistresses from the dance and musical schools, an elder asha representing the Willows association, people from dry goods stores and specialty food shops, and vendors from the Ankyon market.

Anoush, the owner of the Dawnbreak, the tearoom that the Valerian did the most business with, also called on Mistress

Parmina. I woke up one morning and walked into the dining hall where Polaire and Althy already sat only to trip over a trio of ducks that had been wandering around the table. One of them, taking offense, promptly bit me. My screams and Polaire's laughter brought him and Lady Shadi running.

"My apologies, Lady Tea," Anoush apologized, scooping up the ducks. "Mistress Parmina wanted to have a look at the ingredients we will be using for the party."

"The party?"

Lady Shadi smiled at me. "After my debut, the Valerian will be hosting a party at the Dawnbreak later that night, and close to three hundred guests will be invited. There wouldn't be enough room here to accommodate everyone."

"But why would Mistress Parmina need to see what she'll be eating?" I scooted as far away from the fowls as I could.

"She likes to stick her nose in everything in the belief it makes things run more smoothly." Polaire licked the *panir* off her fingers before taking another bite of bread. "Still, without the meddling on her part, I would not have been made privy to such marvelous entertainment so early in the morning."

"You have cheese on your cheek," I told her sourly. Both asha had been staying at the guesthouse so they could check up on Lady Mykaela, who was more or less confined to her room and forbidden to take part.

"Are you all right, dear?" Althy asked me. "I could put some flyjelly on the bite to ease the pain if you'd like."

"No thank you." I stalked out of the room with my appetite

gone, my hand over my rear end, and Polaire's laughter still ringing in my ears.

Even though I was a member of the Valerian household, apprentices were not allowed to attend a new asha's debut, so I remained at home with Kana and Farhi while the others were at the Dawnbreak to celebrate. For once, Lady Mykaela was allowed to leave the house, though kept under close watch by Polaire and Althy. Farhi still refused to speak to me and tried to stay away when she could. I couldn't really blame her. Kana was friendlier, though sometimes I caught her looking at me expectantly, like she was waiting for me to raise a dead bird or rat. Fox had business to attend to, though he wouldn't say what it was. His limping had grown pronounced as of late, but he always grinned in response and told me not to worry too much.

With the Valerian almost empty and Fox away, I felt lonely. I kept to my room and practiced the day's lesson and then the other previous days' lessons when I grew tired of repeating the same dance over and over again. The rest of the party wouldn't return until early in the morning, and the only highlight of the night was when some of the Dawnbreak's attendants arrived to give us some of the leftovers. The maids were delighted at the change of cuisine and ate as much as they could. I sat and stared at the head of a roasted duck, not feeling very hungry. It was probably the same duck that had bitten me, but for some reason, it didn't feel like retribution at all.

*T*HEY WERE THE BEST SISTERS *I could ever ask for." The girl had put the fires out, thankfully. The stench remained but at a fraction of its vigor. Steam rose from the heavy pots, hissing. She began to boil the six remaining bezoars again at daybreak, each in separate cauldrons. Once they were steeped to her satisfaction, she poured a generous amount into their own vials, each liquid darker than the other. Even the daeva thought the smell was terrible. It took a whiff of one of the cauldrons and hurried away, sticking its snout into the sand and blowing noisily.*

"Polaire should have made a terrible asha. She was lazy and inept when it came to her lessons. She sang worse than I did, had no patience with the refined arts, and was too impatient for meditation. She had terrible coordination, which meant she was barely adequate when it came to dancing. She was fond of insults, swore a lot, and had a high opinion of herself. But she was popular. She was the most popular asha in the Willow district for two years before she scaled back her schedule. She was also highly skilled with runes—one of the best.

"Althy was different. She was every inch an asha—a whiz when it came to herbs and potions, skilled in both dancing and fighting. The problem was that she looked more like a jovial fisherman's wife than anything else. She used that often to her advantage. I miss them both, though I don't think they miss me."

"*Are you going to make more potions out of these, milady?*" I gestured at the pots.

"*Why else would I stand all this stink? But I'm not looking forward to drinking them.*" She stoppered the bottles and placed them on a small wooden tray with the rest.

"*Milady, you talked of two of your sisters. Lady Mykaela was the third. Who was the fourth?*"

She smiled wryly. "*Who else?*"

18

"How long has he been dead?" Polaire wanted to know.

"Who?" They called it the *khahar-de*, old Runic for the "sisters' ceremony," and mine was set to take place only a week after Lady Shadi had made her debut. The party at the Dawnbreak would be smaller, with only the residents of the Valerian and my would-be sisters in attendance. Chesh, Likh, and Rahim appeared at intervals, taking more measurements from me and discussing colors and motifs with Mistress Parmina and Lady Mykaela. Polaire and Althy still made their daily visits, with Althy happily moving on to the kitchens to cook, despite Lady Mykaela's protests that she was a guest. Polaire simply lounged around and did as little as she could get away with.

"That man who often waits outside the Valerian whenever Althy and I come to visit. I am told that he is your brother. No, that's not right. I am told that he is your *deceased* brother."

"He's my *brother*," I corrected her, offended on his behalf.

"Still looks dead to me, and I've seen a lot of corpses. He's getting pale and raggedy around the edges. I'm assuming you haven't blooded him yet."

"I haven't *what*?"

"Has no one been teaching you?" Polaire sank back against the cushions and frowned. "No use keeping you in the dark like this, girl, no puns intended. Most Dark asha make their debut first before they get to keep their familiars, but it would appear that you are not most Dark asha." Polaire took a drink from her bowl and then marched out of the door, returning momentarily with a piece of twig. She threw herself back down on the pillows. "See this?" With deliberate quickness, she broke it in half. "This is your familiar as he is at the moment. He receives no strength other than the rapport you share with him, and he is denied sustenance through the usual means, like food and drink. But this." She picked up her table fork and tried to bend it in the same way she had the twig. "See how it does not break? Now, tell me why this is so."

"Because the fork is made of metal, and the twig is not."

"Excellent. Our blood is made up of a certain kind of metal—I am hazy on the details; Althy will tell you more about it if you're interested—that also works the same way with familiars. If you give him a bit of your blood, he will better simulate life. He will look like he breathes, blinks, has normal digestive tendencies without needing any of them to work. And when he hurts himself, he will heal almost instantaneously with blooding. One of the many advantages the dead have over us."

I remembered Fox's limp, an injury that had never went away. "Can I do that now?"

"I see why they have neglected to tell you." Polaire waved a bread roll at my face. "He has all his limbs intact, so whatever aches and pains you think he has should wait until your own debut. There are repercussions to drawing runes you have no business drawing yet, as you should do well to remember every time you walk past the Falling Leaf." The asha snapped her fingers, and the twig was immediately enveloped in Fire, reduced to ashes in the time it took me to jump back in shock. Polaire rubbed the soot off her fingers and then did the same to the fork. It sparked briefly, and its tips glowed a cherry red before fading again.

"Just as your familiar will break like a twig until he is blooded, so will you be reduced to embers if you draw in too much of the Dark. Wait until the time you are trained so you can glow like the iron in this fork." Polaire leaned back and smiled. "Tea of the Embers. That's a nice name, don't you think? I'll be sure to suggest that to the association should that time ever come. Ah—Farhi, isn't it? And with Althy's special *haleem*! You ought to try it, Tea. Althy stays up late the night before preparing, and the turkey melts like butter in your mouth… Incidentally, Farhi, would you be so kind as to bring in the Fox boy who waits outside?"

Farhi looked horrified by the command, but Polaire raised an eyebrow. The maid quickly left.

"Mistress Parmina forbids men from entering the Valerian," I said.

"I've seen Rahim traipsing in and out of here at all times,"

Polaire said. "For lack of a better word to describe him, 'man' works. Familiars follow different rules. Mistress Parmina won't make changes until you petition her to. The old woman's a shrewd player, though stingy as the seven hells. I've been told you've visited the Heartforger and were given a gift."

I slipped the small stone over my head and handed it to her for scrutiny.

"I'm surprised he would give you something so precious at first meeting. You must have made quite an impression on the Heartforger and His Majesty."

"His Majesty?"

"Didn't you know? The Heartforger's successor is Prince Kance's older brother. Kance holds some sway over the old man, though that coot won't admit it."

I froze. I remembered the sense of tension in the room, Prince Kance's and Kalen's reactions. I now understood why Junior's face had looked so familiar—behind his spectacles he had the king's eyes and the same high cheekbones as the prince.

"Of course, when you're in line to be the Heartforger, you're expected to renounce all claims to your royal house. Must be hard on the brothers, but I know Kance has been doing his best to stay close. He's always been the unflappable of the two—it's Khalad who's the hothead."

Farhi hurried back into the room, followed shortly by my brother, puzzled and wary.

"Do you know who I am, Sir Fox?" Polaire asked.

He thought carefully before replying. "Yes. You're Lady

Polaire from House Hawkweed. I've seen you and Lady Altaecia of House Yarrow around here often."

"You're observant, which is a plus. And from the way you're toying with that dagger you've got hidden up your sleeve, protective, which is even better. You've obviously done your research on us, so your brains haven't deteriorated since dying, which is something to be thankful for. If I had a shekel for every corpse who'd literally allowed their heads to rot… Today is Tea's *khahar-de*. Later tonight, I want you to join the procession heading for the Dawnbreak. I know you'll do that anyway, but this time, I want you walking with us out in the open instead of stealthily as you often do." She grinned at the faint start he made. "See? I can do my research too."

"And what do you intend to accomplish with this?"

"Dark asha may not be looked on with disfavor in Ankyo when compared to other kingdoms, but they are nonetheless treated differently, even inside the Willows." Polaire's heartsglass blazed brightly, not with anger but with faint disgust. "Many view people like you and Mykkie as a necessary if unwanted means to an end, a way to take credit for keeping the lands secure from daeva while distancing themselves from the hatred the commons have for them. Dark asha never stay in the spotlight long enough to enjoy the adulation they deserve, and I mean to change that with your sister. I've seen Mykkie wither and age under the heavy burden of her responsibilities, Tea. I will not see you follow the same path. And I'm sure neither will your brother. Mistress Parmina might be against it now, but if I put it in a different, more financially rewarding light, I'm sure she can be persuaded to relax her rules. What do you say, Sir Fox? Do you want to officially be part of the Valerian?"

Fox considered it. A slow smile spread across his face. "It beats having to skulk about, with the old woman pretending I'm no better than shadows on the ground," he said. "And I say this as one without a shadow."

"There's something I want you to know," I began hesitantly, addressing Polaire.

"What is it?"

But already I felt ridiculous. I had thought to tell her of the strange figure I'd seen flitting around the Willows, the shadow at the Falling Leaf and at Chesh's, but I couldn't manage the words.

Oh, it's nothing.

"Oh, it's nothing," I said.

$$\cdot\cdot \; \geqslant\!\!\mid\!\!\swarrow \; \cdot\cdot$$

Khahar-de is considered a private affair between a young novice and her sisters. Only the most important people in her life are invited, which is apparently more than even I had thought. I had shyly asked if Kana, Farhi, and Likh could come along. Farhi turned down my invitation, as I had expected. Kana and Likh both accepted eagerly.

Cha-khanas' most distinguishing feature are their gardens, and the Dawnbreak's most arresting character was its miniature, interconnected waterfalls that flowed down into the center of the enclosure. Master Anoush was already waiting in the Dawnbreak's biggest guest room. My three soon-to-be sisters sat among the cushions in a half circle around a low table, which held a flagon of runeberry wine and four simple, ceramic bowls to drink. The others took up seats against the adjoining wall. I don't know what Polaire had told Mistress Parmina to allow her to include Fox, but it worked, though the old woman still ignored him.

"Where is she?" Polaire complained. "Did our fourth sister back out so soon?"

"She will come." Mistress Parmina made it sound like an ultimatum.

The door to the room slid back. Zoya stood there, not looking happy at all.

Neither was I. "What's she doing here?" I whispered to Lady Mykaela in a near panic.

"She's going to be your sister, Tea."

"I don't want her to!"

"What's done is done, Tea," Mistress Parmina said sharply. "I would expect more courtesy from a novice of the Valerian."

I swallowed hard but kept my silence. Zoya sank into the empty spot beside the old woman. "If it makes you feel any better," she hissed under her breath, low enough for me to hear, "I would rather scald myself with hot water than be here, had I a choice."

It was an awkward session. A generous amount of runeberry wine was poured into each of our bowls, which we sipped from time to time. The whole purpose of this ritual was for my new sisters and I get to know each other and for me to listen to any advice they doled out. Polaire took up most of the conversation, chattering cheerfully away, with Lady Mykaela and Althy chiming in. Rahim was never the type to stay quiet for long, and soon he was regaling us with tales of his home in Tresea. Zoya refused to talk, more interested in her bowl than in any of us. When Lady Shadi rose to her feet though, Zoya's head snapped forward in the pretty asha's direction.

"I've stayed for as long as I'm able to," the pretty asha said regretfully. "Sir Ballard and his family requested for me at the Green Bough."

"That's all right then." Not even a *khahar-de* could interfere with Mistress Parmina's desire for money. "You go ahead and tell Chester Ballard that I send him greetings."

"Yes, Mother. I'll see you all back home. Congratulations again, Tea." Lady Shadi left amid a chorus of good-byes.

Zoya watched her leave, then reached for her bowl, drained her wine, and set it back down with a noisy thump. "Well then," she said with a small snort, "let's get this over with. What exactly is the kind of advice you seek from your betters, novice?"

"It would be best to teach them how not to get into trouble, Zoya." Mistress Parmina may have chosen her to be my sister, but Polaire was just as much opposed to it as I was.

"Did she not benefit from our little accident at the Falling Leaf? And I've heard stories of you as a novice, Lady Polaire. You are the last person to tell me to stay out of trouble." Zoya looked at me and smirked. "It looks like I am saddled with you, novice. What other mischief shall we get into, hmm?"

"Surely not the mischief you had planned when you summoned Tea to the Falling Leaf when her novitiate had yet to begin," Althy murmured.

"Has the little girl been telling lies so early into her apprenticeship? I summoned no one to the Falling Leaf that night. If she chooses to sneak out and explore the Willows on her own time, it would not do to have her blaming others for her trouble. And imagine—in no time at all, you shall take Lady Mykaela's place, putting daeva back into the ground, sapping away inches of your life with every summon!"

"Zoya," Mistress Parmina said, and the girl shut up. For the rest of the evening, she sulked, nursing her wine, and stared at Lady Shadi's empty seat.

I HAD ALWAYS THOUGHT ASHA WERE *sorted according to the elemental magic they wielded—there would be Fire asha and Water asha, who would specialize in Fire and Water magic, respectively. Books called Taki of the Silk a Fire asha because she had set fire to the beard of a man who had insulted her in King Marrus's royal court at Highgaard, for example.*

"But that wasn't the case at all. Most asha are well-versed in different kinds of elemental magic, so to call one a Wind asha would be misleading, for they can use Earth and Water and Fire and Wood magic just as well."

The girl was hard at work, emptying the contents of the cauldrons now that she had taken samples of each in her phials. The tauvri *drew close, prodded at one of the discarded pots with a clawed paw, and shuddered.*

"There were asha who could dance and sing but whose command of the runes were minimal enough that they would be useless in a real fight. Lady Shadi fell into this category. I don't think anyone would have expected her to go out and do battle. They often earn the most money for their asha-ka, and they are the most likely to have patrons outside of the Willows who would further finance their careers in the arts. It's not unusual for them to wind up being wives of powerful rulers and noblemen. This ensured that those in power would always look favorably on asha.

"*There were asha who were known for their expertise in battle rather than onstage. Althy was this type. She could wield the runes with ease, and I have seen her win a match against three Deathseekers at once.*

"*What few people know of are the asha who are highly skilled in politics, in management. They often wind up managing their own asha-ka, and they have the most influence. Mistress Parmina is one and—though she would never admit it—so is Polaire. And then there are those who can sense magic, though not enough to command them. They often become ateliers and apothecaries and hairdressers instead, easily discernible by their purple hearts.*

"*Dark asha are the grunts of the system. We do the most import-ant work—raising and banishing daeva—but we rarely receive acclaim for it. We are more likely to be known for our mistakes than our successes. Lady Mykaela had summoned and put down daeva for the greater part of a decade, and yet she will always be known as the bone witch who had bespelled a king, one who had her heart taken as punishment.*"

She upended the last of the large pots. We watched it mix with the waves, the seawater diluting its colors until we could no longer distinguish it from the rest of the surf.

"*And then there's me,*" *she added.*

19

L IFE AFTER MY *KHAHAR-DE* CHANGED. Aside from my usual
lessons, I was now also obliged to attend some of the
parties the asha went to at least twice or thrice a week, which gave
me even less time to myself. I didn't see Fox as often, and I grew
to rely on his steady presence in my mind, because it was better
than nothing at all. I was encouraged by Lady Mykaela to call her
and the others "sister," although my dislike for Zoya prevented
me from ever saying this to her face. I was also encouraged to call
Mistress Parmina "Mother," but I found that equally difficult and
never did so unless she prompted me to.

Although I could not draw other kinds of runes, Lady
Hami began to teach me the combat stances asha used—I had to
recognize and understand the movements they made when they
drew in their magic, even though I couldn't use them.

"Tell me everything you know about runes," she demanded

as I stood shivering in the cold. We were outside Ankyo, in an open field used for Runic training, to minimize the injuries and damages that came with the territory. I was clad only in a short tunic and very thin pants my instructor called a *sirwal*, which did nothing to keep out the chill of the morning. Lady Hami was dressed no better than I was but ignored the morning cold.

"There are three thousand characters in the Runic language," I narrated, my teeth chattering. "But only five hundred runes of the old language are known today. Of these, only two hundred runes are used for magic—no one yet knows how to make use of the other three hundred. There are ten words associated with meditation and healing, thirty for Fire magic, thirty-five for Water, thirty-seven for Wind, twenty-nine for Wood, thirty-one for Earth, twenty-five for Metal, and three for Dark magic. The more complicated the rune drawn, the more powerful a spell it can—"

"That's enough. You've been paying attention to your lessons, but theory is useless without practical applications." With one finger, Lady Hami sketched out the rune for *Wither* in the air, an aspect of Wood magic. It was roughly the size of her head, and it dissolved easily as soon as she directed her will downward.

The grass around us started to decay. It spread out like a disease, until we stood in a brown circle roughly a yard across.

"Now spot the difference." Lady Hami flung her arms out above her as high as she could and then brought them back down. She drew the *Wither* rune in this manner, so that this time, the symbol was as large as she was, shining a bright, sickly green light.

The circle of decay around us spread farther, five times the size of the original.

"The bigger you draw the rune, the more damage it can cause," she said. "You would expect, then, that bigger runes are always better when in battle, yes? But that is not always the case." She whipped out an arm, punching at the air for a few seconds, and three small holes popped up, one after the other, alongside the large decayed circle, so that from above, it resembled a dog's paw.

"Or perhaps this." She gestured, this time drawing the *Rot* rune, and the circle around us sank to a lower level than the rest of the ground. She sketched out *Rot* and *Mud* next, weaving both runes together, and a large patch of land beside me turned into sticky quicksand. She did it again, rushing her movements so that the runes were poorly drawn, like bad handwriting. Another area of the ground roughly the same size as the quicksand appeared, more solid than the first—a fact Lady Hami demonstrated by deliberately stepping onto it. Her boot sank an inch or so but went no deeper.

"There is no point in drawing so large a rune when someone could get off three smaller runes and incapacitate you before you can complete the spell. But there is no point in attacking with three smaller runes if they do little damage and allow your opponent to finish. There is also no point in writing your runes poorly, as slovenly written runes to make quicksand will not make it quicksand. Some runes do more damage but take longer to create. Every fight is unique. There is no blueprint for opponents, and you must learn to decide quickly in the course of a battle—or you will be dead."

"But I c-can't do any of these."

"On the contrary, you know three Dark runes and then ten more."

I stared at her. "But those runes are for healing and for meditation. I don't know how—"

"Ah, so now you know better than I which runes to use in a fight, little chitterling? You have suddenly mastered the craft after only half a lesson?"

I clamped my mouth shut and shook my head.

"Support magic is almost always forgotten when one refers to spellbinding. It can be just as deadly as combat magic if you know how. There is a reason why Instructor Kaa teaches you these exercises. Many people do not remember that while Dark asha cannot use the more popular elemental magic, they can still invoke support magic as well as their own runes. That is why ateliers and hairdressers, who cannot use Fire runes or Water runes, can use potions and weave support spells into their fashion. Only a rare few know how to turn this into offensive magic, and that is what you are here for. Attack me."

I was at the fourth tier in my combat training, still at the second-lowest level, but was competent enough to be further along than many apprentices who started at the same time I did. But I hesitated.

Lady Hami's fingers moved, and I was down on the ground. My mind had been suddenly overwhelmed by unexpected and irrational fright.

"You were afraid, weren't you?" Lady Hami extended her

hand, helped me to my feet. "See what a little support spell can do? Attack me again."

Her fingers moved, and immediately I was overcome by anger. I rushed at the asha but was stopped in my tracks by a sudden barrage of doubt. *What was I doing?*

"You can use emotions to win a fight without taking a step," Lady Hami said, and both the anger and doubt disappeared. "The first thing an asha is taught is how to recognize emotions that are outside of their own and nullify them before they take over. Veteran asha will not be affected by these spells—unless you are subtle enough that it passes beneath their notice."

She held out the Heartforger's protection stone that I had entrusted to her before the practice began. "You have an advantage, but you cannot always rely on this stone to protect you. I will first teach you how to defend these attacks. In time, I will teach you more. And perhaps I will even teach your brother, so that he needs not hide behind trees to watch his sister at practice."

There was an injured silence from a cluster of oak trees a few meters away before Fox walked out. "I felt her distress," he said, like this alone was reason enough for his presence.

"Yes, you do. And that is why you will accompany Tea from now on to most of her training unless I say otherwise. It would be a waste of time to teach you both separately."

"If that is an offer, Lady Hami, I am honored."

"It is not an offer," the woman told him. "It is an order. You are Tea's familiar, and it will do you both good to learn to control your emotions together. If Tea is to profit from her training, then it is important that you learn the same things she does. But not today. You are not fully her familiar yet, and there are certain requirements that must be in place before I accept you as another student. For now, you will watch, and you will learn when the time comes."

I was grateful when Mistress Parmina decided to end my singing lessons. I had improved to the point where I no longer sounded like a dying frog and could pass off a reasonable warble. But both she and Instructor Teti decided that to give me more lessons was a waste of time—I would never be asked to sing in any official capacity. This was not a blow to the Valerian's honor, though it was certainly a disappointment. Lady Shadi, for instance, excelled in singing, dancing, and all the refined arts but was only an average student in combat training. Her movements were too refined, without the quickness and speed necessary to make her effective.

The dissolving of my singing lessons gave me more time to pursue my combat lessons with Lady Hami, and I admit that I enjoyed those lessons more, though I frequently lost. My dancing classes continued, where I made better progress. I loved to dance, and I loved my fighting classes—they were compatible skills. I breezed through many of the easier songs and learned two new dances a week on average. I was soon promoted to the fourth tier of dance, the same week I was also promoted to the third tier in my combat lessons. Instructor Yasmin and Lady Hami were pleased, so I supposed Mistress Parmina was too.

Matches became part of my regular schedule. I sparred every day as often as I could. The week after I received my third tier, I walked into the training hall, still basking in my accomplishment. It was early enough in the day that there were few students about, but I saw Lord Kalen was present, already geared up for sparring. My steps faltered.

"What are you waiting for, Tea?" Lady Hami called out, and I hurried to comply.

Kalen frowned when he saw me approach. "I suppose there's a reason she's here."

"Tea is one of my most promising students, Kalen. Her training is going splendidly."

"I find that hard to believe."

"Would you like to see for yourself? Tea, stand at the ready." The instructor tossed me a wooden stick.

I caught it. "Against *him*? But, Lady Hami, I'm only a student. I haven't even warmed up—"

"Only a student, yes. But if you participate only in fights where your opponent is either evenly matched or weaker—or where you have been sufficiently warmed up—then you have already lost. Stand at the ready, Tea."

I obeyed. Kalen stood on the other end of the mat, flexing his fingers. A few other pupils drew nearer, attracted to the discrepancies in our skill. "Begin," Lady Hami said, and any hope I'd had that the Deathseeker would go easy on me was dashed when he sprung forward, striking a blow to my shoulder before I had a chance to gather my wits.

"Point to Lord Kalen," my instructor said. "Begin."

Kalen leaped again, but I managed to counter his next attack. The wooden stick whirled and blurred, and it took all my concentration to keep him from striking another hit. For the next ten minutes, it was a one-sided affair where he kept up the offense, until he scored another blow to my leg.

"Point to Lord Kalen. Begin."

His blows are weaker when they come from his right side, Fox's voice said from inside my head, and I nearly tripped. *Use the room to your advantage. Circle him from your left and wait for an opening.*

I followed his instructions and dodged to the left. He spun to confront me.

Now!

I dropped to my knees, and the stick flew above my head. I struck out at the same time and managed a glancing blow off his hip.

"Point to Tea. Begin."

"No," Kalen interrupted. "I'm satisfied with her progress." He looked down at me, still sitting on the mat and struggling for breath. "You're pretty good," he said, placing his hand on his side and wincing, "as much as it pains me to admit it."

"Thank you, milord." I spotted Fox strolling aimlessly along the side of the room, grinning.

"I was hoping you would be so kind as to help me train Tea," Lady Hami told Kalen. "I think you have much to show her."

"I'm not sure I would have the time to—"

"You said only yesterday that your post here at Ankyo hasn't given you much to do," the woman pointed out. "And you offered to help me instruct some of my students."

The colors in Kalen's heartsglass flickered. "I…did say that."

"Excellent." Lady Hami was brisk. "Tea here takes her lessons in the afternoon. I think between us, she will be quite proficient."

Kalen turned to me with a brittle smile, and I stopped myself from outwardly flinching. "I think so too."

•• ゝⅠ⁄ ••

Lord Kalen poured his resentment into our training sessions and made Lady Hami's seem like child's play by comparison. I frequently came home bruised and tired, with little energy for anything else. But I made no protest; he could have used them to justify how I wasn't strong enough for his training, and he would have been wrong.

And as hard as he worked me, he was making me better. I started winning more matches against others in my class, sometimes outclassing those above my tier. Lady Hami still trounced me often, but I was lasting longer with each fight.

I don't know what kind of arrangement had sprung up between Fox and Kalen, but I walked in on them sparring on several occasions, with Fox holding his own exceedingly well.

"Why doesn't he like me but has no problems with you?" I asked my brother once in a burst of frustration.

"He's fairly protective of the prince and views you as a source of danger to him," Fox pointed out, carefully wrapping his hands in thick strips of gauze. "And there's an advantage to teaching you, even if he doesn't want to. On the off chance that you're with the prince when something attacks, you'd be more adept at fighting them off and protecting him. I reckon it's also why he's sparring with *me*."

"But I don't want him angry with me."

"You've got a choice, Tea. You can choose to distance yourself from the prince and possibly earn Kalen's friendship, or continue your meetings and retain his bodyguard's ire."

Fox looked at my face and sighed. "I thought so."

I HAVE ENTERTAINED MANY PEOPLE IN *the course of my short time as an asha. It is believed that asha only accepted discerning nobles of exemplary tastes and good standing within the community as patrons. The truth was that many who went to those parties could be just as crass and rude as the next person on the street. Being a noble didn't exempt you from being fool born. Some of my favorite guests came from humble beginnings. Some of my worst guests came from the highest of positions. Breeding isn't what you were born as; breeding is what you grow to be. You were born a man of Drychta, Bard; you didn't choose the kingdom of your birth. But you chose to protest against the injustices you did see, even as they drove you out. You are a good man.*

"And as for me…"

She held out her hands, and the daeva flocked to her, nuzzling at her palms like a newborn puppy fresh from the litter, yearning for its mother.

"I don't know if I can claim to be good and principled," she said softly, "but I know exactly what I need to do."

20

N O MATTER HOW TIRED I was and no matter how many bruises I earned during my training, I never turned down the prince's requests to join him for an evening meal at the Snow Pyre. Sometimes Kalen accompanied him, though he preferred to remain outside the room, ostensibly to keep guard. My practice sessions with the Deathseeker continued. When not criticizing my techniques and form, he ignored me. His dislike still made me nervous, and I frequently made mistakes I would not have with a different teacher.

I never told His Highness about Kalen's disapproval. It was obvious that Prince Kance didn't know.

"Is Lord Kalen always this…serious?" I asked him hesitantly one time. "He never seems to take any days off."

"Kalen's always kept to himself, even when he was younger," the prince admitted. "His childhood wasn't always easy. His father, my uncle, is in prison."

My history lessons had glossed over this. "What?"

"My uncle had ties with many nobles in Odalia who tried to rebel against my father ten years ago."

"Daar's Rebellion," I remembered.

"The farmers claimed poor treatment, but some of the gentry used it as fodder to declare war against Odalia. A daeva had attacked the city previously, and many citizens perished, my mother and Kalen's mother among them." He paused, then added sadly, "We all took their losses hard."

"I am so sorry, Your Highness."

"There were a few who believed that Dark asha had somehow conjured the daeva and that my father conspired with them against his own kingdom. The Duke of Holsrath was one of those ambitious gentry who believed in these lies. There was some evidence to prove he instigated the rebellion, but my father chose imprisonment for him over the hangman's noose. I know Kalen harbors guilt over his father's actions, and he can be very single-minded when it comes to my safety. He has trained with the sword ever since he was a child, intending to right his father's wrongs. His heartsglass only turned silver recently—not very long after my first meeting with you in Kneave, in fact. But he has continued to remain devoted to my family. I trust him like a brother."

"And what about your older brother, Khalad? If you don't mind my asking," I added quickly, worried that I was being too inquisitive.

"Most people pretend that my older brother doesn't exist. It's refreshing for someone to be upfront about him." He smiled sadly. "He was supposed to take over the reins of the kingdom after my father. But his heartsglass turned silver three years ago. At first, we feared he would be conscripted to the Deathseekers, but much to our surprise, the Heartforger asked to take him in."

"As a favor?"

"No, the Heartforger would never choose anyone out of sympathy. He has never had an assistant; he said he never found the right one. Khalad was very angry about it at first."

"He didn't seem angry to me," I said, recalling the smiling, if vague, young man sitting beside the Heartforger.

"Khalad always liked helping people. Being king would have suited him well. But he soon realized he could help people just as much in this way. Forging new hearts for the sick, helping people start anew in life—he was very good at it. Except he started using his own memories for ingredients, more than what he ought to. Khalad always liked to test boundaries." He sighed. "Sometimes I wish I had the silver heartsglass instead of him. Some days I feel like I don't have the right temperament to take the throne."

"But you do," I said, driven to his defense. "It would be a shame for Odalia not to have you as its king."

I stopped, flushing a little because I hadn't intended to sound so passionate. But the prince laughed.

"Thank you for your confidence. I have talked many times to Khalad since then, and he has also been supportive. I suppose that's what brothers are for. But I don't think I have to tell you that. You and Fox have had your share of troubles."

"I took his death hard," I confessed, still embarrassed by my previous outburst. "I knew nothing then of Dark asha. I thought I had raised him from the dead through sheer force of will alone."

"And now he's both an asha's familiar and a third lieutenant."

I stopped. "Third lieutenant?"

Prince Kance looked surprised. "Didn't he tell you?"

"He's in the army?"

"He's conscripted, but his duty is only to protect you. My father made him a third lieutenant, with financial compensation guaranteed for your family. Sir Fox has been taking part in Kion's military exercises and has performed admirably enough to be ranked in so short a time."

"And how long has this been going on?"

"Shortly after you became an apprentice. I'm sorry, Lady Tea, I assumed he'd told you."

"Don't be, Your Highness." I wasn't mad, not really. It explained Fox's bruises, his limp. If anything, I felt glad that he wasn't involved in anything shady. But that didn't mean I was going to let him off that easily.

•• ⧗ ••

I'd never had reason to visit the Ankyon palace before, but most of the courtiers and servants took one look at my apprentice robe and left me alone. I concentrated on keeping my presence hidden from my brother until the last possible minute, but I soon saw that this wasn't necessary; Fox was distracted, judging from the irritation I could feel coming from him.

A large man in a general's uniform passed me, confirming my suspicions. There was a large tattoo of a bird on his neck—he was the same man I had seen in my previous vision of Fox.

I peered into an inner courtyard and found him with his arms crossed, staring stonily down at a younger woman dressed like an asha. I'd come at the tail end of their argument; the woman threw her hands up in disgust and marched away. Fox was too busy watching her leave to notice me.

"A lover's spat?"

"Tea! What are you doing here?" My brother was wearing a soldier's uniform: plain tan breeches and a long-sleeved shirt.

I pointed at a star insignia on his shoulder, a symbol of his soldier's rank. "I could ask you the same question," I countered.

He coughed. "I'm getting my official papers at the end of the week. I planned on telling you then."

"Was all this your idea?"

"No. Your Mistress Parmina's." My mouth fell open. "The Odalian army doesn't have the intensive training Kion's does. She wanted to make sure I could protect you if it came down to it."

"I'm surprised she paid attention to you long enough to suggest that."

"Lady Mykaela's doing, I'm sure." He scanned my face worriedly. "I'm sorry, Tea. I should have told you sooner."

"I can't say I'm pleased by all this planning behind my back—but honestly, I'm relieved. I thought you'd be involved in something illegal."

"Thanks."

"Make it up to me. Tell me who that girl was. A girlfriend? She knows you're dead, right?"

He winced. "No! She's…she's not very happy to find a corpse wandering around the castle. She's dead set against them, in fact. That's another reason I agreed to join the army. I may be a corpse like she claims, but I'm not useless."

It was easy for me to forget that my brother was dead, easy for me to forget that he wouldn't forget it. "You're not useless, Fox. And I'll beat up the next asha to say otherwise."

"She's not…" He trailed off and then hugged me. "Thanks, Tea." He sounded amused for some reason, and I didn't understand why until much later.

·· ≥⟋⟋⟋ ··

I had one other patron who frequently requested my presence at parties. Councilor Ludvig of Istera was an old man with a pinched face, prone to going into rants about how things were better in his time, because for many years he served as King Nodvik's most senior political advisor and guided the small winter kingdom into a robust economy and into one of its most peaceful eras. He retired a few years ago, but his mind remained as sharp as ever. He had no patience for flattery and always called things the way he saw them, regardless of whose feelings were hurt in the process. I enjoyed conversations with him immensely.

When I first met him, he was in a horrible mood. Another round of Deathseekers from the kingdoms had been dispatched to hunt for the still-elusive *savul*, and he was opposed to the idea.

There were already other asha in the room when I entered, trying to steer him away from the gravity of the discussion. Other guests were also present, all close friends of Councilor Ludvig and used to his ways.

"Do the kings today have nothing but empty space between their ears?" he demanded, ignoring my entrance. "Have they done nothing but be coddled by their mothers for the first thirty years of their lives? To take out most of the Deathseekers in the kingdoms is tantamount to suicide. They are inviting open conquest of their own kingdoms. If I were a jackanape with a large enough force and a command of the runes, I could conquer Tresea in three days before any word could reach the bulk of your men, Vorkon! A standing army will not last long when there is magic involved."

"We are at peacetime, my lord councilor," one of his friends pointed out. "And there are no standing enmities among the kingdoms. Even your Istera and Tresea have a treaty, and historically, you have always been enemies."

"And you are an idiot for letting peacetime lull you into a false sense of security," Councilor Ludvig raged at him. "Can you not see that there is no need for treaties to one who might be biding their time?"

"Now you're being paranoid, Ludvig," the first diplomat to the Yadosha city-states rejoined good-humoredly. "No one can control the daeva. That is the point. Not even the Dark asha can do so, as Lady Tea can attest to. None of the Faceless have been strong enough to do more than—"

"And what enemy would choose to show their strength? It is not enough to fight off attacks as they happen—it is important to predict how and when they occur to prevent them from happening to begin with!"

"My apologies," Vorkon, the Councilor to Tresea, said to us in a near whisper. "He hasn't always been this angry. He was the most brilliant man I'd ever met as a young man, despite our kingdoms' animosity. Quite a mind."

"Now, now, Councilor," a pretty, brown-haired asha named Bryndis interjected. "We shouldn't be talking about such serious things at a party. Come, why don't you tell us about the many achievements you have had? It is not every day that we have as our guest of honor one who has forged such a successful path for the kingdom of Istera! King Rendorvik must owe a lot to you!"

"If only his son had his father's guts," Councilor Ludvig snorted, unswayed.

"Councilor Ludvig! Such a thing to say about your king!"

"He'll live. I have said worse things to his face."

"Oh, let's not talk about such worrying things," Caddie, one of the other asha, begged. "It all sounds so frightening to me!"

The conversation drifted to other matters, and soon the other politicians began lecturing the asha on the history of their countries. Our history lessons had included such matters, but we nodded our heads like we have never heard them before.

Councilor Ludvig leaned back while the others talked, scowling into his tea. The others were occupied, so I angled closer to him. "What makes you think that some of the kingdoms could be invaded in the near future?" I asked.

He started—I don't think he remembered I was even in the room. He eyed me suspiciously at first, but my sincerity must have shown on my face.

"Peacetime does not excuse the reality that there are numerous factions there out for blood. For as long as the problem of the daeva exist, the Faceless will use them to breed fear and terror among the people."

"What should the kings do instead?"

"Send all available spies and scouts out to gather intelligence as to the daeva's whereabouts first. Once located, gather all Dark asha—well, you and Lady Mykaela—add a few more asha and Deathseekers for additional firepower, and strike out. To have every able Deathseeker scouring the lands hoping to stumble into a *savul* by accident is a waste of time and ability. It doesn't matter that the people clamor for a show of force. Pomp and fanfare for so few results will not help defend a kingdom, only expose its weaknesses to the unseen enemy."

"That sounds logical, but why won't they listen to you?"

The old man snorted again. "Because they think they know better. Kings nowadays play more to the politics than to any real strategies. Kion is more welcoming when it comes to Dark asha like you, my dear, but other kingdoms aren't as open-minded. Bone witches passing through their territories does not make kings popular. Deathseekers guarding their borders satisfies their need for security, however false it may be."

I felt disheartened. I had nurtured the foolish thought that being an official asha meant that people would be more inclined to look favorably on me, even if Lady Mykaela's reception had been anything but.

"Don't worry your pretty head over it, my dear," the old man said kindly. "You Dark asha have my respect and my trust, and I wish that counted as much as it used to. Tell me more about your lessons. How many runes of the Dark have they taught you?"

Councilor Ludvig started coming more often to the *cha-khana* after that. Despite my busy workload, I always did my best to spend at least an hour with him. Because he usually only asked for me, our meetings were less of a party and more like my lessons. He instructed me on politics, geography, and military history and taught me more about strategy than any instructor I had.

"But why can't you flush out all the other Faceless?" I asked him at one time. "If you know where their strongholds are, shouldn't it be only a matter of time?"

"It's not as easy as that," Councilor Ludvig said. "It's easy to imagine them concentrated within one small area instead of being dispersed over a population of people who have little idea of whom they are truly fraternizing with. They do not build their defenses with high walls and fortifications, Tea. Even Druj conceals his fortress well in his mountains, and it would be difficult to lay siege. As for Aenah and Usij, they build their defenses with a population of innocents for a shield, which is a considerably more difficult hurdle to overcome. It took us twenty years to cobble together a comprehensive report to capture Aenah's men, and still that witch escapes us! I have always advocated for King Rendorvik to train more spies. He acquiesced occasionally, though he always considered it a dishonorable trade. Dishonorable!" Councilor Ludvig snorted. "There is no dishonor to winning a war!"

Once or twice a month, the Heartforger's assistant would ask for my presence at the Snow Pyre. A Dark asha's heartsglass was in high demand, and many ingredients could be gleaned from its depths. The old Heartforger himself, the boy said, was frequently away on trips; his services were constantly sought after even outside of Kion.

I was willing to provide what his assistant needed, but I also felt awkward around him. Now that I knew his true identity, I didn't know what name to refer him by. I could no longer call him by his royal honorific, so should I call him Lord Khalad instead? Or Junior, as the Heartforger had called him?

"Khalad would do," he said calmly. "The forger calls me Junior as a means to distance myself from the royal house, but sometimes I think I need to remember who I was to have an idea of who I should be."

"How did you...?"

Khalad smiled, nodded at my heartsglass. "You asha do not have the monopoly on reading them."

"But not to that degree of specificity."

"You mean you can't do that?" He sounded surprised. "My master said I was unusually perceptive, but I always assumed it wasn't uncommon. Take a deep breath."

He touched my heartsglass and I felt a quick twinge, like someone had pricked me with a tiny needle made from ice.

—the gaping mouth grinned malice at me; from within the depths of those empty eye sockets, something glinted. The skeleton gave me no time to recover but lunged—

When he took his hand away, I saw a wispy thread of smoke winding around his knuckles, disappearing into his own heartsglass when he pressed his fingers against it.

I was shaking. For a moment, it felt real, like I was confronting the skeleton all over again.

"Thank you. True fear is harder to find than you might think," he said conversationally, patting my hand. "I visit the army for most of that." He'd pulled a lot of memories from me these last few months—memories of seeing my brother rise up from the grave, memories of Lady Mykaela summoning the *taurvi*, memories of meeting the oracle.

"You've never asked me about them."

"About what?"

"About the skeleton? Or my brother or the *taurvi*? You see my memories as well as I can every time you take them out."

"I do, but your memories are only important to me in forging hearts. Their importance to you is your own business and no one else's. I do not ask, and I share them with no one else." He flexed his fingers. "I'll need one more, and then that's enough for today."

"You impose limitations on how many you can draw from me, but you don't do the same for yourself."

He smiled sheepishly. "Too many hearts, not enough memories. Master says I overexert myself, but maybe it's for the better. I have something of a temper. This will only take a—"

From inside his hood, the boy's face hardened. "Your kind killed my mother," he snapped. He turned and fled back into the confines of the crowd but not before his heavy cloak shifted and I saw his—

Khalad stopped. He leaned back.

"Well," he said.

"Is something wrong?" I asked nervously.

"Nothing's wrong." He rose and bowed to me. "I think I have all that I need. Thank you again, Lady Tea."

It was only after he left that I realized he had not taken my memories of the boy in the hooded cloak.

*E*VERYONE IS BELIEVED TO HAVE *two faces—one they show to the public and one they wear in private. The first face is their* shaxsiat, *or their honor. The second face is their* ehteram, *their dignity. It is a concept practiced more commonly in Odalia but also adopted by the asha-ka in Ankyo. It is important for a person to interact with others in such a way as to enhance their* shaxsiat *while still maintaining their* ehteram—*to increase others' estimation of them while remaining true to one's self. It is harder than it sounds. Many actions that elevate people's opinion of you are not necessarily what you truly wish to do. It is a matter of balancing both faces so you can do what is expected of you and at the same time pursue your personal goals."*

"I did not fare very well with my shaxsiat, *then," I said, bitter. Our meal that night was composed of Odalian delicacies: fried rice soaked in saffron and caramel, called* tahdig; *kabab koobideh, flavored with turmeric and set on sticks hewn from more driftwood; and* doogh, *a flavored, sour yogurt. I had not seen her prepare the meals, did not think she was capable of cooking them in such a short time.*

"You considered your dignity to be greater than what the royal courts demanded of you, and this imbalance is the reason why they cast you out of Drycht. In the same way, I considered my dignity to be more important than the rules and restrictions that clog the traditions of the

Willows, and that is why I find myself in the Sea of Skulls, foraging for bones. But would you do it again, given the chance? Would you sacrifice your shaxsiat *to retain your* ehteram?*"*

"*Yes,*" *I said without hesitation.*

She smiled at me. "Then we are not so different after all."

21

Y ASHA SISTER ALTAECIA WAS a lot like my sister Rose. She was round and quiet and keen on gardening. She was also Ankyo's foremost expert on herbs and medicine and was a consultant to many apothecaries operating in Ankyo. She made the best *dizi* I had ever tasted, and her *ghormeh sabzi* could silence even Polaire. Unsurprisingly, her ingredients were always fresh, and she was in the know with most of the vendors in the marketplace, so that her roasted lamb, seasoned and cooked for three hours to perfection, went unbelievably well with her sautéd kale, chickpeas, and parsley stew, along with anything else she chose to cook.

Every other week, I would accompany her on what was a typical morning for my sister-asha. Most people visit the market-place at dawn to find the choicest seafood and cuts of meat, but much of the preparations took place long before the sun rose. Altaecia was hard on vendors who sold rotten food, and it was an easy way to go out of business. Meek and mild mannered for the most part, she changed into a no-nonsense, uncompromising taskmaster when it came to food standards.

We didn't always visit the Ankyon market. When she brought me to a tall, white building at the edge of the city for the first time, the smell of dirty linen assailed my nose the moment we entered. People dressed in gray frocks rushed past us, carrying an armful of sheets or complicated-looking metal instruments. Patients lay on pallets on the floor, as many as a dozen in every room we passed.

"There is one skill people often overlook in an asha," she said as she stooped over an old man swaddled in blankets, fast asleep. "And that is the precision by which we can perceive color. Tell me the color of his heartsglass."

"Green."

"No. It is octarine."

"But isn't octarine just another shade of green?"

"And therein lies all the difference. Ailments give very specific tints, Tea. Green only tells me that the illness is a physical one. Hues, heart rhythms, brightness—they show me the specifics of a disease. I will teach you how to observe and keep track of these differences. You there, Cecely!" She snapped at a woman built like a broomstick. "Didn't I tell you to change the patients' bedsheets every day?"

"But, Lady Altaecia, Mistress Mal made it clear that we could only—"

"I don't care what that *khar* has made clear!" Althy raged, a veiled tigress. "Tell her that Lady Altaecia demands clean sheets and linen for every patient, and if that happens to cut into her profit, then so be it! Perhaps she needs to be reminded one more time of the cow?"

The woman paled. "I will see to it, Lady Altaecia."

Many also came to Althy for ailments that normal physicians and apothecaries could not heal, and they were as complex as they were varied. She taught me to prepare ointments and medicine. I pounded pescilla seeds and groundroot for smallworm antidotes or mixed dragon fruit pulp and stingberry juice for high fevers. The variations among the heartsglass colors were difficult to distinguish, and I made many mistakes. But each day I improved.

Two months after we began, Althy regretfully informed me in the middle of our cooking lesson that she would be leaving. We were preparing chicken *fesenjan* with yellow rice, which also happened to be Polaire's favorite meal. As was common during these lessons, Altaecia would grill me about the kinds of herbs we used. "You must learn to make this by the end of the day," she explained, "for I will have very little time to teach you when the week is out. Now, do you remember what nuts we top the stew with?"

"Ground walnuts," I replied, "paired with pomegranate sauce. What do you mean, 'you have very little time'?"

"I will be returning to my duties as Princess Inessa's bodyguard in five days' time, and so ends my stay in the Willows. What other sicknesses do walnuts treat?"

"Canker sores and bright fever. Unless the patient is allergic to nuts, which means we substitute saffron and twisted barley.

You're to be Princess Inessa's bodyguard?" It was hard to imagine her as anyone's bodyguard, with her broad face and glasses and the circle motifs in her *hua* that only emphasized her roundness. It also occurred to me that I have never once seen her fight.

Althy smiled at me. "I have always been her bodyguard; I merely asked for leave to care for Mykkie and oversee your education. I will still be in the city. The castle is a stone's throw away, and the princess has always been accommodating when other asha come to visit. Besides, you'll have your other sisters here to take care of you."

"But none who cook as well as you do." I was crestfallen. As much as I was fond of her cooking, I was even more fond of Altaecia herself.

The redhead laughed. "I am sure there will be more than enough to do here to occupy your time. Now—what are the three illnesses that ingesting applecrut and figberry syrup will help alleviate?"

"Stone fevers, diarrhea, and indigestion. Althy, when we visited that charity house a while back, you threatened the mistress with a cow."

"Mistress Mal owns that charity house, and she once told me she would pay more for her clean linen when cows fly."

Althy went back to chopping more onions, and I had to prompt her again. "But you eventually came to an agreement?"

"Only after I punched a new hole in her house, using one of two wooden cows I had commissioned at the carpenter's. It went through her wall like a plunger through churned butter. I built it to size, so I expected such results." Althy continued to chop serenely, paying no attention to my shock. "I paid for the wall, of course, but I also paid to have the second cow erected on the field across from her place. Mistress Mal has been getting on in years, but I've found it to be a most effective way to jog her memory. Now, what color would gingivitis look on someone's heartsglass?"

•• ⅀⎮⅂ ••

When Altaecia finally left to take up her duties in the castle, my time was claimed by Polaire. Because of my lessons and my training, the evenings were one of the few times I had for myself. Polaire soon usurped even that.

There were two sides to Polaire as well. She scrutinized me as I entered the small tearoom at the Gentle Oak, her lips pursed. "That's a horrible outfit," she said.

"What?" I was wearing the prettiest *hua* I had. It was a deep maroon, with golden butterflies fluttering halfway up its skirt, and a waist wrap of soft beige with outlines of brown leaves embroidered along its edges.

"We're meeting the envoy to Drycht, you dummy. He's an old and cranky stick-in-the-mud, and he wouldn't approve of women wearing such bold colors." She gestured at herself, at her lavender *hua* with tiny lilies painted in large clumps along the bottom of her gown. She shook her veil at me. "Didn't I tell you to do your research? It's a little too late to go back and change—he chafes at delays. Let's see what we can salvage."

She was right; the envoy was a yellow-faced old man with cheeks pulled down like a bulldog's, and he drew back a little when he saw my *hua*. "Do asha-ka take in courtesans now?" he sputtered, scandalized. "Women were not so bold in my day, least of all asha apprentices!" His heartsglass actually bristled, the colors palpitating between turgid yellow and green.

"Forgive us, Envoy Mu'awwan." I never knew Polaire could gush so. "I told Tea here to come in her most outrageous *hua*, so you can point out all that is wrong with it, to teach her. Who is the authority on all manners of propriety and custom, I asked myself, and thought of you."

"Well." The man relaxed, mollified. "Quite, quite clever of you. Unlike some of my countrymen, I am not one to deny progress and women's rights—my views are known to be liberal." I stared at him in consternation. "But with all these indecent girls nowadays showing off legs and ankles without so much as family to accompany them, they wind up in all sorts of trouble. It's important to cover up, to prevent men from indecent thoughts. Why, the stories I could tell you—if you knew the shamelessness of such women!"

We didn't want to know, but he regaled us with them anyway. Afterward, he told me the fifty-seven things wrong with my hua, and my dislike for him grew with every justification.

"We're wearing practically the same thing!" I hissed at Polaire when Envoy Mu'awwan excused himself to go to the bathroom. "How can he find fifty-seven things wrong with mine but not with yours?"

"The Drychta are a conservative people. Most would consider us terribly underdressed, and they avoid the Willows altogether. Envoy Mu'awwan is a diplomat and a progressive man in comparison, but what you consider similar is to him a world of difference. Red on a female implies that she flouts tradition and is therefore a loose woman. You wear the color on your clothes and in the jewels in your hair. Drychta men prefer that their women dress simply, without any ostentatious gems. Your *hua* has a slit on your side and exposes a part of your leg, while mine has none."

"Maybe he just doesn't like the color red."

"That is no excuse, Tea." Polaire was stern. "Know the people you entertain. If they are offended, you not only bring dishonor to the Valerian but also to the tearoom you stay at and me by association as your sister. Our opinions do not matter, and if you have to swallow your pride to keep them happy, then so be it. Now, stop slouching. I can hear him coming back."

We attended a larger party the next night, with a group of wealthy merchants from both the kingdom of Arhen-Kosho and the Yadosha city-states. This time, Polaire was dressed like a princess, in silver and gold, and it brought out the gray in her eyes. The style of her *hua* was bolder, more brazen; her hair was skillfully piled up on top of her head and kept in place by half a dozen hairpins, where bright diamonds dangled, and long ringlets of brown hair framed her face. I had done my research and had once again donned my maroon *hua* but had not made myself up to the extent that she did.

The group of men greeted our arrival with cheers and

guffaws, the noise loud in the usually quiet tearoom of the Golden Bough. It was early in the evening, and most were already drunk or at least well on their way to being drunk.

"Ah, Polaire! We were wondering where you were! And who is this pretty little thing?" One of the men bounded over, the tallest I've ever met. His hair and beard were golden, his face a healthy pink and white, but the hand that enveloped both of mine in a hearty handshake was brown and weather-beaten and twice my size.

"Don't be so free with my little sister, Aden!" Polaire scolded, slapping his hand away. "Didn't I tell you to behave this time around or will I have to stick your head into the pond outside again?"

Rather than be outraged, the men laughed harder. "She got you there, Aden!" one called out, shorter and wirier than the bearded merchant, with a thicker accent. "The last time you shook a *flannin* with Lady Polaire, she sent you headfirst into the fountain!"

"I remember her chasing Balfour around with that pole they clean the garden's fishponds with. Mad as hops she was—"

"I was tipsy!" the red-haired man with darker skin protested.

"You were tipsy all right—tipped right into the stream!"

The group roared again. A tearoom attendant hurried in briefly, setting large tankards of a foamy golden drink on the table, and hurried out. I was ushered into a place among the cushions between Polaire and a dark-skinned man who was younger than his silver hair suggested.

"Your younger sister, you say?" Aden continued. "What's your name?"

"It's Tea, milord."

"Milord?" Another one of the men guffawed. "No need for formalities. We're all friends here. Tey-uh? What an odd name."

"It's spelled like the drink, Isamu," Polaire explained.

"How strange to name someone after a drink! Where are you from, Tey-uh? Kion?"

"Her skin's too dark for Kion, Isamu," someone said. "She looks Odalian if anything. Or perhaps even Drychta."

"I'm Odalian, milo—I mean, sir."

"I'm Jolyon." The man bowed. Unlike Aden, his beard was black, carefully trimmed and shaped so they were thin lines that crisscrossed his face.

"It's hard to tell who the locals are in Ankyo," Isamu protested. "Look at Knox here. He's as black as night, but he comes from Yadosha like the rest of you."

"Yadosha is also a melting pot," Jolyon observed. "Not like you people in Arhen-Kosho. You all look the same."

"That is not true!" One of Isamu's countrymen extended his arm out, palms facing upward. "See? My skin is darker than Isamu's!"

"I can't tell the difference!" Aden complained. "Isamu, hold out your arm alongside Eito's."

Fairly soon, all the men in the room—all respected merchants, all rough-and-tumble men of influential standing—had their arms out, comparing skin tones. I had no idea what was going on.

"Aden's arm is much darker than his face, see? He doesn't even have the same color on himself!"

"I work outside! My face isn't covered the way my arms are!"

"Polaire, what about you?"

"I think I will go and dunk myself in the spring outside if the lady asha is darker than mine—"

"Maybe only in the places that count," Eito said slyly. That was enough to set the men off again.

"We apologize," Knox said to me. "We have known each other for years."

"I remember now," Aden said. "Isn't Tea the Dark asha who nearly obliterated the Falling Leaf tearoom?"

I winced. "I'm sorry."

"Now, now," Jolyon said. "That wasn't her fault. And no one blames you, little miss. In fact, people have been asking for you, wanting to know if asha novices can be invited to the *cha-khana* regularly. I'd say you'll have mistresses of the other tearooms knocking at your door, demanding that you wreck theirs too!" He laughed when I turned red. "Ah, don't mind me. I say these things just to make the pretty girls blush. Here, have some *alut*."

"I'm afraid Tea is still too young for your horrible drinks, gentlemen," Polaire said primly. To my horror, she went and smacked the man lightly on the nose when he tried to hand me a glass, anyway. "You Yadoshans! Always looking for any excuse to get drunk!"

"But that's why you like us, Polaire," Aden said childishly. "Jolyon is offering to pay for all our meals, so let's grub up some *cants* that the ladies might like—would that be apology enough, Lady Polaire?"

Polaire's response was to tap him playfully on the cheek, and the men laughed again.

"Yadoshans like to fight and argue," she explained to me after the party ended and we were walking back home. "Arhen-Kosho tend to be more reserved as a people—until they get drunk. You cannot treat everyone in the same way when you entertain them, Tea. Yadoshans sulk and get bored easily when you do not share in their revelry. Treseans are superstitious and like to get straight to the point in discussions but drink even harder than the Yadoshans. Drychta are—well, I'm sure you can already imagine what the Drychta are. There will be a few exceptions, but this is the general rule. What can you say about your own fellow Odalians?"

I thought. "Hardworking for the most part but very concerned with money. They're suspicious of outsiders and of magic. No—they're only suspicious of magic that other people use but not when they do."

"Exactly. Would you say that your family too or your friends in Knightscross can be described in this manner?"

"But my family are nothing like that at all! The people in Knightscross aren't—" and then I paused. I thought about their distrust of bone witches, their hostility toward me. Were they any different, after all, than the cold treatment Lady Mykaela and I received from strangers in Kneave?

She nodded at my growing understanding. "That's right.

Over the course of your life, you will meet many, many people. The trick an asha must learn is to read people accurately. So if a Tresean comes in and consumes a stupid amount of *kolscheya* and grunts at everyone in the room, then he is a typical Tresean to whom small talk will have no effect, and if you understand Treseans, you will wait patiently until he finally chooses to speak. But if he is a Tresean who is fond of chatter and has an eye for fashion, then you must ask Rahim what he is doing at such a party."

I giggled. Polaire flicked her dark hair over one shoulder, the diamonds in it twinkling in the twilight. "Everyone is a puzzle, Tea, made of interlocking tiles you must piece together to form a picture of their souls. But to successfully build them, you must have an idea of their strengths as well as their weaknesses. We all have them," she said, adding almost as an afterthought, "even me."

*S*HE CARRIED ANOTHER VIAL IN *her hands. Black liquid sloshed inside from one of the many cauldrons that had gutted the landscape with its smoke and odors the last couple of days. We stood before the hulking carcass of a mastodon-like beast. Only its rib cage remained intact, wide enough for us to pass through. Two brown tusks lay nearby; the ends of one lay broken, the other buried so deep underneath the sand that only its tip gleamed out at us through the muddied churning of seawater.*

The girl lifted the bottle to her lips and drank until there was nothing left. When she was done, she let it fall from her grasp, and before it hit the ground, she was already moving, performing the same ritual as she had with the taurvi.

Something that resembled lightning lanced through the bones, circled the massive ribs, and struck at the barely visible tusk. And then the skeleton moved. It struggled to stand, and the tusks rose, attracted to the rest of its body like a magnet. It settled atop the bony jaws. One by one, like a life-sized puzzle, it built and took form. Femurs attached themselves to pelvic bones and tibia, vertebrae lining up to collarbone and neck spurs. What it could not find, it created out of thin air.

And throughout it all, the girl never stopped. Her fingers danced and her feet moved, and she circled her creation like a parent

awaiting the birth of her child until the massive being rose before her,
whole and complete, magic spun into flesh.

"Imagine if you had the power to control daeva like these.
Imagine the kingdoms that would quake and tremble before you.
With such a threat at their borders, how quickly do you think they
would mend their ways? Would more people fall under King Aadil of
Drycht's iron grip? Would he look out from the windows of his castle
and see us at his gates and still send innocents to the headsman's
block? Would he still exile those like you who strive for a truth he does
not wish to see? Would murderers in his kingdom still go unpunished
for killing their daughters?

"And if I turned my taurvi *and my* akvan *southward, to cross*
the rolling plains of Odalia to enter the kingdom of Kion, would the
asha of Ankyo regret what they did to the man I loved?"

The akvan *shook the sand and water from its hide and bayed at*
the rising moon. Its black heart shone, suspended in the breeze, until
the girl reached out and plucked it from the air.

"Do they not understand," the girl asked, her voice so very soft,
"that they are nothing more than playthings in the eyes of daeva?"

22

Lady Mykaela was finally allowed out of bed a month after my *khahar-de*, though restricted to the immediate vicinity of the Willows. Mistress Parmina had banned her from taking up any new requests outside of Ankyo and dismissed all her protests to the contrary.

"You are more important than anything they might ask of you," she informed her firmly. "The next daeva to require raising will not be for another year. You will stay here and attend to your younger sister until I have deemed you fit enough to work, and that is all there is to say about the matter."

My sister still tired easily and always excused herself early in the evening, much to my worry. "She will get better," Polaire told me often, though occasionally I would detect minute changes in her heartsglass as she spoke—a brief spatter of blue, too quick for anyone else to notice.

Lady Mykaela asked me one day to accompany her out into the fields outside of Ankyo, the same ones asha used for training practice. She had also asked Fox to join us. My brother still limped, and his face looked more drawn than I was accustomed to, but he was otherwise unchanged. I felt guilty. My free time had been gradually taken up by the lessons my new sisters had begun to teach me, and I had been seeing less and less of him, taking for granted the bond we shared as an excuse that he was doing well, that the army took his time from me as much as my lessons took me from him.

"I told you once that death would make the better of us, and that holds true for your brother, at least." Mykaela looked especially lovely today, some of the color returned to her cheeks. Instead of her *hua*, she wore a flowing dress that was pleated at the knees and tightened around the waist by a long belt made of shiny blue silk. Her hair was unadorned. "Hold out your finger. This may sting a little."

I had barely held it out when Lady Mykaela moved, and a sliver of a blade sliced through my skin. Small drops of blood trickled down the wound, but I stood stock-still, not moving despite that tiny blush of pain. I had seen the asha do this when she had raised that *taurvi* nearly two years ago—how long ago that was to me!

"Now, draw the Heartsrune for me again."

I stared at her, finger dripping red, confusion unmistakable. To draw the Heartsrune was the last thing I expected her to make me do.

She laughed and laid a hand on Fox's shoulder. Only then did I see the new heartsglass case that hung around his neck. It was simpler than Lady Mykaela's and mine, bound by a small white chain instead of gold embellishments. "I would have thought it obvious."

"But he can't!"

"He can. Not for the usual things we use them for, no. Not to exchange wedding vows with or to delve for illnesses. His heart will be silver marked and identical in every way to yours. No one who knows the magic will mistake him for anything but what he is: a bone witch's familiar. But even the dead have uses for a heart, even one they're given instead of the one they were born with. Go ahead."

Fox said nothing, only waited.

With shaking fingers, I drew the Heartsrune in the space between us. The red flowed from my finger and followed the path my hand took, staining the breeze with every movement, so that when I was done, the symbol stood before me, written in my own blood. I felt that welcome rush of relief and elation as the magic filled me up, infused itself into the rune.

The heartsglass rippled once, twice, took hold. Mist filled the tiny case, swirling into every nook and corner. At the same time, Fox opened his mouth, took a breath, and exhaled noisily, his first since his death. His face no longer looked wan and sallow. Color leeched back into his face, a healthy pink from neck and chin to cheeks and forehead, and it warmed every feature it touched.

"He will be stronger," Lady Mykaela said. "Faster than when he was living. Tougher. Unkillable by normal means. He will need blooding for every half and full moon, and only your blood will take. He will never be fully alive, but this is the closest to living that the dead can know. It is, naturally, your brother's choice."

Fox examined his hand, flexed his fingers. They no longer creaked like old bones.

"I would like to stay for as long as Tea wants me to," he said. His eyes were brighter, smiling at the corners, like he had found more reasons to laugh at the world.

"Then stay," I said, and my hands shook. "If I can make you stronger and if I can help you live the life you ought to have had, then stay. For as long as you want and for as long as I can."

Fox watched me fidget and shiver, and when I felt the tears welling up in my eyes, he opened his arms. I ran into them without another word. For the first time since his death, Fox was warm and smelled of home.

·· ☼ ··

The graveyard lay on the outskirts of the city, a sensible distance for citizens to pay their respects to the dead without intruding on their territory. I looked around, wondering what traces remained of the damage I had caused, but the masons and bricklayers of Ankyo were efficient workers, and the only things out of place were the few new headstones whose polished brightness stood out among the weather-beaten graves like bad notes. But I was uneasy. This cemetery was divided into two fields: one allotted for more recent burials, the other for graves dating back centuries. We stood in the latter.

"Heartsglass were not originally created for courtship nor were they crafted for business," Mykaela said as we stood among the rows of dead. "In the olden days, asha were employed in battle-fields, and so noblemen and others of royal blood took to wearing heartsglass in battle, because even there, they were granted special privileges. If they fared badly in their wars, bone witches from the opposing side could take their heartsglass instead of their lives. Better a prisoner than dead, apparently. Over time, other soldiers protested this treatment and began wearing heartsglass of their own, until the asha could no longer distinguish between commoner and royal."

"As things should be," Fox noted.

Lady Mykaela drew another symbol in the air. "This is the Rune of Raising. I'm sure you recognize this."

I nodded. It was the rune I had raised Fox with, a feat I could not recreate no matter how many times I tried on my own. Once, without anyone's knowledge save Fox's, in the quiet still-ness of the night, I crept out of the Valerian and tried to recreate the summon Lady Mykaela had performed on the *taurvi* on the carcass of a rotting beetle.

"You knew I'd fail," I accused my brother when nothing happened. Even with only him to see, I could not hide my embar-rassment. He had thought it a terrible idea but had done little to dissuade me.

"And so did you," he returned. I couldn't find a wittier response, had slunk back inside.

"And this is why you were given slices of runeberries for the better part of your training," my sister explained. "The Dark takes more from you than you might think, and every casting can make you weaker, more vulnerable. The berries make up the difference and will keep your strength up. Follow exactly as I do, and direct it toward this grave."

Lady Mykaela drew the rune again, and I copied her movements, the blood from my cut hand floating around me, settling into its shape. This time, I felt the tingling along the length of my arm when my fingers drew at the air, sparking at the tips. As she instructed, I guided the thriving energy down to one of the stones, at the bones I could feel lying underneath.

There was a shifting in the soil, and the ground before us caved in.

Something clawed its way out of the small hole that appeared. It had lain dormant for so long that any remaining bits of skin hung like rags around its bones, its skull shorn of all hair. I could see a string of pure energy that wound along my raised finger, attached to what was left of its waist. The corpse fixed an eyeless gaze on us and rattled. Its form was almost skeletal, but its voice was clear as spring in my mind.

I will never tell you! The words snapped at us, shrill and angry. *He's my child, and nothing else matters!*

"Ask for her consent," Lady Mykaela said.

I gritted my teeth. The corpse's stench turned my stomach,

but I persevered. *Do you accept me?* I directed that thought toward the rotting apparition.

I will never tell you his father's name! The corpse rattled. *I'll carry his secret to my grave!*

"It's not working." A peculiar buzzing began in my head, and it began hurting. Whether it was because of the dead woman's ferocity or the strength it was taking to maintain contact with her, I wasn't sure. "She's not listening."

"Try to command her."

Never! You will never taint my family name with your vile lies!

"I can't!" The noise grew worse. I clutched at my head.

"Let her go!" Mykaela ordered. "Cut through the string that binds you both!"

I forced my will through the rope of energy between us, severing our connection. Immediately the corpse sagged, bereft of life once more, and toppled back into the open grave.

"That was Lady Liset," Lady Mykaela said, "a former Odalian duchess. King Telemaine's many-times-great-aunt and King Randrall's wife, buried here instead of at the royal tombs because of her fall from grace for reasons we now know since you raised the old king. The dead cannot lie, but they can withhold the truth. That is the first rule of the Dark: you cannot compel the dead if they are not willing. The duchess is a benign corpse and harmless enough for our purpose. Other dead will not be as gentle. If they do not consent, deprive them of their movements quickly. They will use your own strength to attack you for as long as your bond remains."

She had me practice this rune for a month—on graves Lady Mykaela herself had raised in her youth, taught to her by other Dark asha that came before her, or on the bones of small animals. Unlike their human counterparts, the animals did not need consent, and I soon learned to distinguish between the corpses who were willing and those who were not almost as soon as they rose from their mounds. But Mykaela had me return the dead, human or animal, compliant or not, to their rest every time, because to maintain Fox, she said, was difficult enough for a young asha-in-training. "Besides," she added, "I have something else in mind for you."

The stallion was of a sturdy breed, born and raised in the Gorvekan steppes of Istera. The short, bandy-legged tribes that called that barren veldt their home bred this steed for war and territory but were ill at ease in Ankyo. They were an unusual sight to see, and people turned to stare at the two men, tall and covered in fur save for their bare legs sticking out underneath, armed with crude swords and pushing a makeshift wheelbarrow that contained two lifeless stallions through the streets of the Willows. The Gorvekai were an unsmiling tribe whose men and women shaved their heads and wore fur that draped loosely about their persons, yet also muffled the contours of their bodies at the same time. At least three hundred leagues lay between Istera and Kion, and I could not imagine how they had accomplished the journey the way they had and with two dead beasts in tow.

Lady Mykaela awaited them at the entrance to the Valerian. As the crowd watched, the two men lifted the corpses with unusual care, with a gentleness that belied their fierce, bearded faces. Once the horses were laid out on the ground, they took a step back. One of them addressed the asha in a harsh, nearly guttural language, and I was shocked to hear her respond in kind.

She approached the dead animals, cutting her hand as she did. Several drops of blood spilled onto one of the horses, and in no time at all, it stirred and stood up on all fours, whinnying and stamping its feet. A few people gasped, and most of our audience retreated when it turned and regarded them with bright eyes, like it meant to attack. Lady Mykaela extended a hand out. "*Come here*," she said.

It tossed its head at the watchers one last time and approached her. It nuzzled at her fingers like a puppy might.

"There are two horses," Lady Mykaela called out to me. "Would you care for the other?"

I very much did. I walked forward eagerly, saw Fox keeping in step beside me. More blood, and soon the second horse was up, trotting across the street with its head proudly raised.

The Gorvekai made no sound, only bowed to Mykaela three times, and left without another word, their empty wagon creaking behind them. "A favor for a favor," Mykaela explained but said nothing more.

The horses themselves were magnificent, and their love of duty and honor showed in their bones. They held their heads high, were docile in their rest, and did not require feeding. Mykaela was delighted and named her mount Kismet. Mine was half a tail smaller in size, but I called him Chief. They took to us, and they also took to Fox, who found a nearby stable, paid its owner twice as much to keep them away from the curious public, and cared for them whenever we were busy. Dark called to Dark, he said, and the horses called to him as strongly as he called to them.

"How do you feel?" Lady Mykaela asked me a day later. I was riding astride Chief, exploring the streets of Ankyo for the first time on horseback, and she was on Kismet.

"Stronger." I'd thought an additional familiar would make things more exhausting for me, but the opposite was true.

"The Gorvekai have a special connection with their horses; the bond draws and provides strength for both. It is not magic, nothing that even asha understand. Only bone witches can do the same as them with Gorvekan steeds and only in death." She watched me for a long moment, then sighed and nudged Kismet forward, and I followed.

•• ⌇⼁⼂ ••

"What was it like to be dead?" I asked one early summer evening while I watched my brother at practice. They had given him leave to stay at the Valerian if he wanted to—or, rather, Fox, taking Lady Hami's suggestion, began to visit more regularly and for longer periods, and Mistress Parmina gave no protest. But Fox rarely entered the asha-ka, preferring instead to remain outside. It was a rare outing for us; Althy was at the Ankyo palace, still serving as Princess Inessa's bodyguard, and Polaire was at the Flowing Waters *cha-khana*, entertaining at an important function that frowned on mere novices. Lady Mykaela and Mistress Parmina napped inside the asha-ka. I was astride Chief again. My mouth was occupied with smoked ham; I ate in small bites and constant meals nowadays, because blood and runes took strength and gave back appetite.

"Nothing and everything at once," Fox replied and swiped with his blade at a falling leaf. It folded itself into two halves at his feet. The leaves cast a shadow on the ground, and I cast a shadow too, but though he looked more alive than he had before, Fox and Chief had none. "Colder, without feeling; grayer, without seeing. Alive but without aim. Hunger without flavor."

I watched him batter at a bare trunk with a plain sword, glinting steel against dead bark. The pallor had long since left his face, and his legs no longer creaked and spasmed. Some days it was easier to believe that I was not a bone witch watching my creation but just a sister watching a sibling at swordplay. I closed my eyes; the bond between us was stronger than ever, and I could pinpoint with near accuracy just how far away he was from me without seeing him. I also sensed Chief below me, impatient at remaining still.

"As it should be with your familiars," Lady Mykaela had told me. "It is the same on their end, and their instinct will always be to seek you out to protect you at the first signs of danger. That he is your brother makes the chains between you even harder to break."

"Canter," I told Chief. The horse whinnied and began. He

pranced across the street, encircling the large oak tree that stood across from the asha-ka and then returning. I had brushed his white coat beforehand until it gleamed. Chief knew he was the best-looking horse in Ankyo and was not afraid to let everyone else know it.

"Did it hurt?" I had never asked Fox this before. Heartless Fox had been quiet and distant, always watchful and concerned. He could sound angry and sad and worried and happy, but never would his expression change to suit the emotion. Heartful Fox was different, more prone to show with his face and his eyes what his words meant, more of the brother I remembered and less of the shade that had remained.

Fox paused to think about it. "It did at first. We were patrolling the swamps that separated Odalia from Kion. News reached the king of some strange creature lurking there, feasting on nearby villages. There were bodies, half-eaten and ruined beyond recognition. Another regiment brought one to camp the day before, and I threw up the small army rations I had for breakfast all over my new boots."

He made a face at the memory, then flicked at the small half leaf, turned it over. "I was the first one to die, I think. I was scouting ahead of my group, because I was quiet on my feet and never one to talk much, and I counted on that to see things before they see me. It didn't matter though, because the creature was like a shadow and made no sound at all. I managed to shout out a warning before it jumped me. One swipe of the claw, shock and pain. And then nothing."

He paused and then lifted up his shirt, and I saw the claw marks knifed across his body in three red streaks, half-healed and no longer the gaping wound it had been that night at the Snow Pyre.

"That's horrible." I shuddered and turned my head away, not wanting to look at the fatal injury that had claimed his life.

Fox only looked thoughtful. "I would like to face it again, for my pride if nothing else. There are days now when I can make no sound either." He held out his arm and made a quick shallow cut at the back of his hand with the sword. A small wound gaped back, but for all his pink-faced, alive-seeming countenance, Fox did not bleed.

I slid off Chief's back and moved toward him.

"It's only a small cut, Tea. You don't need to."

"But I need the practice too. There's a reason I've been eating those runeberries, as terrible as they taste." I cut my finger with my knife, a new gift from Lady Mykaela for this purpose. I allowed the blood to drip onto his palms. The brown of my skin was paler now due to my frequent bloodletting, because after that first lesson, there had been many more for Lady Mykaela to teach, many more still to learn.

The blood spread across my brother's skin, seeped into the flesh. He turned his hand over, and the wound was gone. The marks he wore on his chest retreated but did not diminish completely and remained red stained and angry.

"One day," Fox said, and Chief neighed in agreement.

*T*HE **TAURVI** *WAS SUSPICIOUS AT first. The other daeva was larger and more ungainly on its feet, and it tottered as it walked until time smoothed out its stride. They moved in a circle, sniffing each other warily. The girl said nothing and watched them with an old smile on her young face.*

Finally, the taurvi *raised its head and let out a bellow. The* akvan *did the same, its tusks twitching.*

With a growl, the taurvi *sprung onto the akvan. They grappled for several seconds, rolling in the sand. Finally, the* akvan *let out a gleeful cry, and I realized they were playing.*

The taurvi *disengaged, shook itself free. It returned to smelling the other creature's hide. The* akvan *butted it affectionately on the stomach, and the monster flopped onto its side, purring again.*

"If the rest of us could only get along so well," the girl mused.

23

THE *DARASHI OYUN* TOOK PLACE one cool evening just three months after my *khahar-de*. The intricacy of the scenery— from the gold leaves scattered about to mimic a forest clearing to the sparks of silver diamonds hanging above us to resemble stars—took my breath away. I plumbed the air for traces of the spells made to enhance our surroundings, to instill a sense of awe and wonder in those less attuned to the magic, but found none. Asha take the *darashi oyun* seriously, and to resort to such tricks cheapens the performances.

But many of those who attended did not hold themselves to such standards, and the magic they wore on their clothes and hair was nauseating to my senses. The crescent amethyst hairpin in my hair was sufficient enough to ward off the worst of those spells, but I could feel them all the same.

The first of the *hua* Rahim made for me had arrived the

previous day, and I was dumbstruck by his skill. It was of a beautiful emerald green, with silver leaves in fan-shaped patterns around my waist and down one side. It complemented my dark-gray under robe and my white waist wrap, which had embossed outlines of doves at play. Lady Mykaela told me it was a typical *hua* that apprentices wore; I would have more control of the designs I preferred after my debut. Besides the crescent pin, I wore a dark-green tortoiseshell comb in my hair and one of the silver hairpins Likh had first picked out for me, a jade design with a tail of tiny, white streamers that brushed against the side of my cheek.

Seeing royalty in the audience was a common sight at the *darashi oyun*. Nobles have been honored guests at these dances for hundreds of years—since the time Vernasha of the Roses performed for Mushan, the then-emperor of Kion. Being subordinate asha apprentices, we occupied seats in the middle row. The nobles occupied the front, while asha not participating in the dances took the seats behind them. The rest of the populace, those who could afford to splurge on money to attend, took up the rear. I spotted my sisters Mykaela and Polaire on my left, with Lady Shadi a seat behind them, and saw Zoya's friends on the far right. Althy sat with Empress Alyx farther up front. Some of the older asha were seated together with the nobles, conversing with them like old friends.

My history lessons served me well here—I recognized Czar Kamulus of Tresea and his queen. I saw the regal King Rendorvik of Istera and his three sons; five representatives of the Yadosha city-states, led by First Minister Stefan; and the Queen of Arhen-Kosho and her daughter, the Princess Maeve, who had talked cruelly about Lady Mykaela at the Falling Leaf. Mistress Parmina was seated next to one of the Yadosha representatives, and something he said made her chuckle out loud.

I was nervous. As was tradition, the stage was open to all who might wish to dance before the program commenced. Already several children had taken command of the stage, pirouetting and giggling in their best gowns. Few people in the audience paid them much attention.

My heart beat faster when I caught sight of a familiar dark head as he sat two seats away from Empress Alyx and the unmistakable figure of his father, King Telemaine, a row before him, whose loud voice could be heard wherever you sat. Beside the king was his nephew, Kalen, still dressed in black as before.

"What's wrong?" Fox asked when I gripped his arm. An exception had been given for my brother, and he was allowed to sit beside me at the very end of the row.

"Prince Kance is here!" I said happily.

"Of course he is. Even the czar of Tresea has come to watch—if that really is the czar. I can't tell underneath all that fur."

I opened my mouth, but my witty rejoinder died at the sight of Prince Kance engaged in deep conversation with Princess Maeve, whose laughter was unmistakable despite the noisy chatter around us. She placed a hand on his arm and drew closer so that her head hovered over his shoulder.

I forced myself to look away and stared hard at the stage where an old woman was performing the *Rise of the Sea Foam* in jerky, half-remembered steps.

"I met a girl once when I was in the army," Fox said. "Her name was Gisabelle, and she was from Tresea. She was the prettiest girl I've ever seen, with the lightest yellow hair and the most fetching blue eyes. Her brother was a fellow soldier in the same regiment I was in, and because we were stationed for three months in Batlovo, their hometown, she visited us often. It took me two weeks to work up the nerve to ask her out. I finally made up my mind one day and bought flowers from the local florist—only to come across her kissing Maharven—another fellow soldier but someone I had disliked long before. I was depressed for weeks—"

"Fox, your romances with Tresean girls are the last thing I want to think about."

"But you should. It was difficult to see them together, especially when Gisabelle had no idea how I felt. Especially because Maharven was a rot, you see. Drank too much and could be nasty to the locals if he thought they were beneath him—he had some royal Daanorian blood on his mother's side, or so he claimed. But I couldn't. I had a motive for seeing them apart, and she would know it if I broke them up, however good my reason would be."

I watched Fox out of the corner of my eye. He too stared straight ahead, at the now-empty stage.

"It got better when we had to leave, and I didn't see her as much. But from time to time, Maharven would get a letter from her, and I would feel jealous all the same. Just because I didn't see her as often didn't mean I didn't forget."

"But it's difficult all the same."

"It wouldn't be natural if it wasn't difficult." He reached

over and tapped at my heartsglass. "Just remember what Lilac had always told us, what Lady Mykaela always tells you." And then his eyes widened, and he bit back a curse.

I turned to follow his gaze and spotted a familiar-looking girl now seated between Prince Kance and Empress Alyx. Prince Kance immediately turned to her, and it was obvious that Princess Maeve was not pleased. It took me a moment to remember where I first saw her, another second more to realize who she was. While I was taught to recognize the semireclusive Empress Alyx by face, my lessons did not provide as much emphasis on her children.

"The girl you were arguing with at the castle." I gasped. "You've been fighting with *Princess Inessa?*"

Fox blushed for the first time since we entered Kion. "It's complicated. I didn't realize who she was. I thought she was just another—"

"*Didn't realize?* Fox, are you hearing yourself?"

"It was a misunderstanding. I was hoping she wouldn't be here—"

"Of course she is," I said, echoing his previous words. "Even the czar of Tresea has come to watch—if that really is the czar. I can't tell underneath all that fur."

Fox glared at me, but the drumming began. The rhythm was not a part of the main asha performance. People craned their heads to look, puzzled. And it was then that Likh danced into view.

Rahim and Chesh had outdone themselves. The young boy wore a black *hua* with white roses that had gold-rimmed petals, and a modest copper-colored wrap. A crown of white roses circled his head, weaving into his long tresses. Likh was dancing the Fox Spirit's Song, where a beautiful fox demon was caught by hunters and forced to dance in order to gain her release. It was a second-tier piece I had watched other asha rehearse several times before but was not yet cleared to do myself. How had Likh learned this?

The boy pirouetted and extended out a hand. Fire sprung to life, settled against his palm. The audience gasped and Likh withdrew, leaving it suspended on nothing, and drew another Fire rune at the next corner, repeating the movements until he was surrounded by balls of steady flames, licking at the air like candlelight.

"Likh didn't tell us he was going to do that," I muttered. It was one thing to dance like an asha, but to show them you could draw runes too was inviting trouble. They were going to seek him out afterward, and the boy knew it.

"Now you know how we feel every time you do something you neglect to tell us." Fox was amused, to my irritation.

A hush fell over the audience as Likh completed the dance, balancing himself on one leg while the other remained poised in the air on his left. When he finally sank down to the ground, extinguishing the balls of fire as he did, the applause was deafening. Likh's solemn demeanor disappeared, and he turned red. Chesh was already hurrying forward, her face beaming, to help the boy off the stage.

"I have a good feeling about this," I whispered gleefully to Fox.

"I hope you're right," my brother whispered back. "They might like him now, but opinions may shift later."

"You're a spoilsport, you know that?" I would have added

more, but the torches flickering around the stage dimmed—the play was about to begin.

For the dance, the asha wore floor-length sleeves and full-body overcoats that opened at the front to expose silky inner garments, accentuated by hints of bosom. Asha played both male and female roles; the former's clothes were not as ornate, with scarves around their necks as long as the women's sleeves but with shorter coats and trousers. The magic emanating from them was overpowering—my hairpins, created to withstand the worst of what the city could offer, tingled from the surplus. And with every additional garment the asha wore, the greater the potential for higher magic stitched into the cloth.

The dance itself was as old as the lands, as ancient as people remembered time. The villagers of Knightscross knew the story, acted it out in simple plays during the winter solstice. But paper masks and sticks were nothing against art in its fullest flavor, under the watchful eyes of rich patrons.

The asha chorus had soft voices, but their words carried effortlessly.

"In the beginning, Blade that Soars. In the beginning, Dancing Wind."

Two people danced into the center of the room; Lady Shadi wore an eye mask of unparalleled beauty, with tiny diamonds that encircled her eyes and golden agates that rounded out the corners of the cloth, set in stone along a profusion of sapphires and rubies. But the greatest of her treasures was a brilliant diamond around her neck, set inside a heartsglass case. Black onyx lined the man's mask, deepening the hollows of his cheeks and smoothing out the sternness of his chin. The woman tilted her hand up, a coquettish movement, and the man accepted.

"They ruled the sky as far as the wind took breath, the lands as wide as the ground held sand and soil, the seas as fathomless as their darkest depths. The god cloaked his lover in moonlight and wove stars into her hair. He gave her the brightest and most beautiful of gemstones, worn on her graceful neck. Magic flourished in abundance, runeberries plump and primed."

Two more dancers entered. The second man wore an eye mask of midnight black; rubies and sunstones painted his brow. The second woman wore a strange combination of moonstones and black pearl. While Lady Shadi wore a magnificent array of colors, Zoya's was a muted enterprise of black and gray.

"But not all creatures were happy. The god's brother was Hollow Knife; the god's beloved, a sister named Little Tears. Hollow Knife resented his brother, for the people loved Blade that Soars, and the younger sibling desired his influence. Little Tears too loved Blade that Soars and hated her sister." The newcomers began their own dance—fierce, angry gestures.

"Hollow Knife came to Blade that Soars and said, 'Brother, keeper of the winds and crown of the world, we are of one blood and of one purpose, with no secrets between us. I ask, where does your heart keep?'"

The asha in the rubies-and-sunstone mask minced around the onyx-gilded dancer, a crafty satyr encircling his unwitting prey.

"And Blade that Soars told him, 'Inside the egg of a nest in the highest tree in the peak of the highest mountain, guarded by twelve rocs and twelve eagles as large as the sun and as swift as the fastest rivers. It is there, and only there, I keep my heart.'

"And so Hollow Knife traveled to the mountain. He slew a dozen rocs and a dozen eagles, but when he reached into the nest to claim its prize, he saw it was only a normal egg, round and black speckled.

"And Blade that Soars berated him, saying, 'Why do you seek to unman me, Brother? My fields I have given freely, and my waters you can drink your fill. Do not seek what is not yours to take, for the world will suffer.'

"'Forgive me, my brother,' Hollow Knife groveled." And the dancer bent gracefully on one foot, her body straight as an arrow, muscles straining against her weight. "'I only meant to see for myself that it was true, all the better to protect you from harm. But it is not right to lie to your own kin, I, who have only your best interests in mind.' And so Blade that Soars relented and forgave him his treachery.

"After some time had passed, Hollow Knife came once more to Blade that Soars and said, 'Brother, bearer of light and eye of the storm. We are of one blood and of one purpose, with no secrets between us. I ask, where does your heart keep?'

"And Blade that Soars told him, 'Inside the belly of a fish swimming in the lowest reaches of the deepest sea, guarded by twelve sharks and twelve kraken as large as the moon and as fierce as the hottest fires. It is there, and only there, I keep my heart.'

"And so Hollow Knife traveled to the nethermost sea. He

slew a dozen sharks and a dozen kraken, but when he took the fish to claim his prize, he saw that it was only a normal fish, small and white tailed.

"And Blade that Soars berated him, saying, 'Why do you seek to unman me, Brother? My crops I have harvested for your care, and my animals I sacrifice for your meat. Do not seek what is not yours to take, for the world will suffer.'

"'Forgive me, my brother,' Hollow Knife groveled. 'I only meant to see for myself that it was true, all the better to protect you from harm. But it is not right to lie to your own kin, I, who have only your best interests in mind.' And again Blade that Soars relented and forgave him his treachery.

"More time passed, and Hollow Knife came to Blade that Soars one final time. 'Brother, guardian of man and soul of the heavens, we are of one blood and of one purpose, and with no secrets between us. I ask, where does your heart keep?'

"And Blade that Soars told him, 'We are of one blood and of one purpose; there are no secrets between us. On the pendant that hangs around Dancing Wind's neck, from where shines the brightest light of the world. It is there, and only there, I keep my heart.'

"And so Hollow Knife sought out Little Tears and told her, 'If you wish to own my brother's heart, then you must do as I say. It lies within the heartsglass your sister wears. You must take it from her in the dead of night when she lies sleeping, when they are weak and unaware.'

"And so Little Tears, driven by jealousy, did as he ordered. In the thick of darkness, with only the light of the moon to guide her, she stole into the tent where her sister lay fast asleep. With deft fingers, she took the heartsglass and drew it over her head, and Dancing Wind, oblivious, slept soundly on.

"But Hollow Knife lay in wait, and when Little Tears emerged from the tent with the precious heart in her hand, he knocked her down and claimed the jewel for his own. With great and terrible force, he dashed the heart into the ground, and the beautiful gem shattered into countless pieces.

"A cry came from every creature in the land, for they felt their creator die and their hearts along with him. Dancing Wind woke, but she was too late, for her lover lay dead beside her, and Hollow Knife's betrayal was complete."

The dancer with the diamond-encrusted mask sank to her knees beside her partner's unmoving form, and the next dance she performed was slow and heavy with sorrow but no less graceful for it.

"Hollow Knife wrested control. He gathered followers and infected them with his taint. He gave to himself instead of giving back to the sea and sky and lands, and the world suffered. He joined his heartsglass with the remains of Blade that Soars and crafted a new, beautiful heartsglass that was as dark as shadows and ruin. With it, he created the daeva, worst of beasts; monsters whose grotesque forms mirrored his own heart. They blotted out the sun and turned the world into endless night, and the people wailed in terror and anguish. Among them, Hollow Knife ruled, laughing, as the False Prince.

"But Dancing Wind was unbroken. 'Help me, Little Tears,' she implored her sister. 'Help me gather Blade that Soars' heart so I can make him whole.'

"'It is an impossible task' was her cruel reply. 'There are more pieces of his heart than there are stars in the sky and grains of sand on the ground—that is one. To repair it, you must give of yourself that which had been lost—that is another. And if you restore his heart, he will return only to you. I would rather we both spend eternity alone and grieving than to watch another instant of him in arms that are not mine. That is the last.'

"And so it was Dancing Wind who hid herself in the caves and, alone, began her task. Slowly and carefully, she pieced together the remains of Blade that Soars. But the heart was only half its original size, for Hollow Knife had usurped the rest. And so she gave half of her own heart to its making, so that the light inside flared once more, and Blade that Soars opened his eyes again, newly resurrected. Dancing Wind's sacrifice had made their heartsglass like one, so that Blade that Soars wore hers and she wore his.

"And so the god rose from his grave and smote that false prince, Hollow Knife, and took back his lands and his seas and his skies."

The man in the black onyx mask stood and began a series of complicated dances with the woman in diamonds, moving faster until the sleeves of their robes were a blur, their steps light and quick despite the heaviness of their *hua*. The man in the sunstone mask reeled back with every spin, retreating into the shadows of the stage. As one, Blade that Soars and Dancing Wind struck out at him, and a very real puff of fire erupted from their fingers. The stage erupted into flames. There were gasps from the onlookers.

But just as quickly, the fire was doused, and among the rising smoke, we could see that Hollow Knife was gone.

"But the False Prince cursed the world. Now none of the fields could seed magic. Now all the world's creatures lay stricken with death and disease. His followers hid, swearing their vengeance against the god who had so smote their master. And all were lessened as a consequence.

"And so Blade that Soars took his heart, strengthened by the love of Dancing Wind, and broke it into three parts. The first he buried in the soil, so that the fields could once more grow with magic. But because it was only a third of his heart, not all the land took hold, and so runeberries grew with lesser abundance.

"The second he gave to his creatures to heal their sickness. But because it was only a third of his heart, death and pestilence could not be cured completely, and so they shall always remain afflicted.

"The third he kept for himself. And it was here that Blade that Soars became the first of the heartforgers.

"But despite his treachery, he could not find it in his heart to kill his brother. Instead, he banished Hollow Knife to the underworld, where he was to wander among the ruins of the dead for all eternity.

"And Little Tears fell to her knees before Dancing Wind. 'Forgive me, dear sister,' she moaned. 'It was Hollow Knife who bewitched my mind against you. I would not go against you for all the world.'

"And Dancing Wind's heart was heavy when she replied, 'You mocked me and sent me away. You are no better than Hollow

Knife, and given the chance to do harm to me and Blade that Soars, you shall do so again. I will not banish you from the world as Hollow Knife has been banished, but no longer will you be able to use life's magic for your own—that is one. You preferred Blade that Soars dead in your arms than alive to my touch; henceforth, your influence shall be limited to the ways of the Dark and of the dead—that is another. And you will never be able to give your heart away, like I joined mine to his, without taking most of your strength and your power. In this way, you will learn what it is like to be completely and utterly alone. That is the last.'"

The asha dancer in her gown of white and gray, with her mask of moonstones and black pearls, cowered back from her sister, swept a hand up to shield her face, and crept away from the stage.

"And Little Tears, the first Dark asha, fled but never could she escape her sister's curse."

There was a long pause. All the actors onstage remained still, and a nervous titter ran through the crowd.

"What's going on?" a novice on my right whispered, puzzled.

"Lady Brijette was supposed to enter," another girl hissed, clearly a veteran. "She's missed her cue!"

"Silence!" One of the older asha thundered at us, though it was no use. People began to murmur among themselves. The other dancers onstage, trained not to react when mistakes were made, waited patiently for one of their own that never came.

Instead, a loud keening shrillness ripped through the air, and a daeva of gigantic proportions burst through the ground before us, inches away from the stage.

*T*HE ASHA PAUSED. ABOVE US, *bones of dead monsters creaked in the wind.*

"I learned one important thing at the darashi oyun. *I learned that there was more to me than they first thought, that there was more to me than even I thought."*

She drank from two more vials and raised two more daeva. From the bones, she called forth the long-tongued nanghait *and the many-eyed* zarich. *The first was an abstract form given life, with a torso composed primarily of humps and legs. Its head was made of two faces, one forever looking forward and the other forever looking back, and it had a horned back, webbed feet, and bloodshot eyes. The second was a reptilian satyr that stood on its hind legs. Five horns sprung up from its forehead, but its face was elongated and furred, with a snout like those they call a "crocodile" that slither up and down the swamps of Yadosha but certainly horrifying to see in the cloven beast before me.*

As before, the girl took their hearts, and I watched them disappear into the depths of her heartsglass.

They all flocked eagerly to her, like trained dogs.

"What do you intend to do with them?" I mustered enough courage to ask, though I feared the answer.

She cast her gaze toward the east. "Daanoris would be a good place to start," she said thoughtfully, selecting a kingdom like it was a dress to wear on the morrow.

24

I DIDN'T REMEMBER MUCH. I HEARD the sounds of people screaming, felt my world turn upside down as a mad dash commenced, upending my seat in the process. Fox was on me in an instant, rolling me out of the way from the stampede before anyone could trample over us. Lady Hami would have been critical of my reflexes; only then did my training take over, and I pushed away enough of my shock to scramble to my feet.

It was complete chaos. The bulk of the audience had fled, but the asha remained. I could see the sparks of magic knifing through the air at the creature that had clawed its way out from the floor, leaving a hole on the stage the size of an asha-ka. It was a hideous serpentlike thing with three heads, each with a long snout and teeth that were the stuff of nightmares: there were two on each mouth, curved cruelly upward along the sides of their jaws, like a boar's. Their long necks ended in a scaled body the size of a large farm, with wings the span of two horses and a large tail that ended in a spike. Its unblinking, yellow eyes blazed at me from underneath hooded, scaled ridges of brow.

My heartsglass quickened. It was a black dragon.

It screamed again, and I saw fire leap into the air and fall in an arc toward the creature, bathing its stomach in flames. Smoke curled up from Althy's clenched fist, arm still raised toward the beast. It had little effect; the beast reared its head up, and its tail whipped forward, destroying the stage in one blow. Many of the apprentices had fled; some remained rooted to the spot, staring up in horror.

"Tea!" I heard Polaire roar over the din. "Take as many of the novices as you can and get them out!"

I hesitated. I was a Dark asha—a Dark asha-in-*training*—and it was a daeva, but there must be some way I could help—

"*Now, Tea!*"

Fox made the decision for me, grabbing my hand and steering me away. With his other arm, he grabbed a frightened apprentice around her waist, lifted her up, and ran. I stumbled after him, following other asha guiding the rest to safety, away from the Willow district and toward the Ankyon market. "Make for the castle!" I heard someone scream behind me. "Their walls are the strongest in the city!"

I didn't think those walls, strongest or otherwise, would stand up to a three-headed monster of that size, but we all turned obediently toward it, knowing nowhere else to go. Groups of people were already running past the palace gates, soldiers stationed in places to herd them inside like frightened sheep to make room for others still pouring in.

"I have to go back," I told Fox, stopping just short of the gates.

"Don't be stupid, Tea!"

"Fox, I have to go back! Lady Mykaela won't be able to face that thing alone!" I was desperate, as frightened as I had ever been. But I also knew that I would never forgive myself if I ran while Lady Mykaela stayed behind.

"Keep behind me." An advantage of our bond was his knowing any more attempts to convince me otherwise wouldn't work. We deposited the rest of the novices with the asha who had taken charge of the refugees, then pushed against the tide of people fighting to enter, back toward the training hall.

The battle had not been without its casualties. I saw a few bodies huddled up in crumpled heaps at the corner of my eye but refused to look. I forged ahead, matching Fox's pace.

"I told you to get to safety!" Polaire's *hua* was torn in several places, and she had a small cut across her cheek. I was too wound up to speak and could only shake my head. I saw a row of asha with their hands extended out to the dragon, *Shield* runes glittering above their raised palms. Every time the beast lashed toward us with its tail or whenever one of the heads tried to snap at the nearest asha with its teeth, it encountered that wall of air, preventing it from drawing too close. Another group of asha formed behind the first, and here, different Runes gleamed—*Burn, Storm, Lightning*. There were two dozen Deathseekers, all clad in black, also slashing runes in the air.

But none of the magic seemed able to hurt it. The dragon

only shook off the worst of their attacks, and the asha flinched when it rammed into their wall.

"It's an *azi*," Lady Seta, one of the asha reinforcing the *Shield*, muttered. "The books say it is the daeva most impervious to Rune forms. We can't keep this up for much longer."

I looked around frantically for Lady Mykaela, just in time to see her step through the line of asha and walk toward the beast. I leaped forward, but arms wrapped around my waist and held me back.

"Don't even think about it!" Fox's voice was loud against my ear. "Do you want to get yourself killed?"

"I can help!" I struggled, but he was too strong for me.

"Don't think you can do what she does after raising only dead mice and old duchesses and brothers, Tea! She knows what she's doing!"

Grimly, Lady Mykaela raised her hands up. The dragon's three heads focused themselves on her. I watched her draw the Dark, looked on as I felt the magic lift up and around the *azi*, the Dark trails winding around it like rope.

The huge creature struggled, and I felt a wild glimmer of hope. "*Stop*," Lady Mykaela commanded.

It ignored her and continued to struggle.

"*Stop*," the Dark asha repeated, her voice louder.

The dragon screeched, and the wall of Wind began to shake. One of its heads lunged toward Lady Mykaela, its mouth open, and my screams were lost over the sound of its roaring.

A small string of Wind wrapped around Lady Mykaela and

yanked her back, and the *azi*'s teeth missed her by mere inches. Panting, Polaire lowered her arms, and the Wind around Lady Mykaela fizzled out. The dragon growled, shook all three heads, and stepped forward to try again.

"Let me go, Fox!"

"I'm not going to let you—"

"*Let me go.*"

He dropped his arms, and I was free, tearing past the wall and toward the asha. I heard Polaire yelling after me, but I paid her no attention, punching at the air to draw a *Compulsion* rune of my own. I aimed it at one of the heads snapping dangerously close and focused.

No amount of training can prepare you for stepping inside a monster's head. There was nothing there to cobble any logical thought together, nothing close to reason. But there were emotions running rampantly through, anger and rage and fear and hunger, all unfiltered by any semblance of a mind—only a monstrous, terrible awareness.

I didn't remember much. I remembered the feeling of being in two places at once, of staring up at the three-headed dragon and at the same time staring back down at myself from a much greater height. I felt a sudden need to destroy and maim, coupled with a towering rage of such proportions that it almost felt like a separate entity. *Kill*, that rage whispered, its intentions spiraling out toward Lady Mykaela, who remained still on the ground, unmoving.

NO. I put everything I had into that one word and turned it into a command. The being hesitated, and I repeated it again, pulling at the remainder of the magic around me from the runes the other asha wielded.

NO. I wrapped the magic around me like it was a cloak and then like it was the strongest armor ever forged.

NO. Lady Mykaela did not protest when I drew the rune away from her, added it to bolster my own. In that moment, despite the disorientation and the feeling of wrongness, I felt powerful and complete, and more importantly, I knew that the beast knew this.

NO!

The creature backed away from us and spread its wings to prepare for flight.

"Kill it, Tea!" I could hear Polaire screaming at me. "Kill it!"

But I hesitated. As strong as I felt I was, I could not bring myself to say those fatal words. I was trapped between two minds, and at that moment, I was a part of the creature just as it was a part of me.

My hesitation was all it needed. I was assailed by a sudden image: a vast, serene lake, glittering. The creature's thoughts reached for those waters, yearning.

With one final scream of fury, the dragon hurtled itself through the air, flying at such great speeds that soon it was nothing but a speck in the distance, heading toward the fullness of the moon. A few seconds later, it was gone, and the only thing left to remember it by was the carnage around me, the moans of the injured and the dying.

My legs gave out from underneath me, but Fox caught me before I could hit the floor. "You stupid, absolute, unbelievable idiot!" I heard him say. My eyes were trained on Lady Mykaela, who had not moved at all. Polaire and two other asha were already by her side, talking urgently among themselves. There was a faint whiff of something metallic; looking down, I was surprised to see that the front of my clothes was drenched in blood.

I must have fainted after that.

.. ⅀⅂⅃ ..

My brother was sitting by my side, scowling, inside my room at the Valerian. Fox never had a good bedside manner to begin with, and he was in a foul mood long before I'd opened my eyes.

"Whatever possessed you to do something so dangerous?" he all but exploded as soon as he saw I was awake. "Of all the foolish ideas—did you know how easily you could have been killed?"

"But I wasn't killed." The excuse sounded weak, even to me.

"Out of sheer luck! How many times have you faced down a dragon before, Tea? And don't try arguing with me! I was in your head when it all happened! I felt that daeva in my head as thoroughly as you did! It could have killed you just as easily as it killed so many others!"

"Can I at least get some rest before you scold me?" My head was pounding. I felt like I'd just been pushed down a cliff and had hit every stone and branch on the way down. My mind was free and clear, but there was something curled somewhere in the recesses of my mind that Fox did not seem aware of—something not even I could reach.

There was a long silence before he sighed. Taking great care not to put pressure on the bandages wrapped around my leg, Fox leaned over and wrapped me in a fierce hug. "Did you know how scared you made me?" His voice was muffled against my hair. "Did you know how close I came to losing you?"

That would be ridiculous, was what I wanted to say in an effort to lighten the mood. *If I'd died, you wouldn't have had time to miss me, because you would have died too…*

A choking sound rose up from the back of my throat, and I burst into tears without trying. He hugged me again. "Idiot," I heard him say, but this time with none of the heat.

Someone cleared her throat. Mistress Parmina stood by the doorway, accompanied by Polaire and Althy. None of them looked happy.

"If I had my way," the old woman said before either of us could speak, "you would be cleaning the outhouses in perpetuity. Banned from the rest of your lessons for at least two more years. Forbidden to so much as raise your hand as draw in the Dark. Massage my feet until you are older and grayer and hopefully wiser. I can think of many other such chastisements. In fact, I *will* punish you regardless of what the other elders say."

She pointed at a small tray on a table beside me that contained several slices of runeberries. "Eat them quickly; you will need your strength. The elders require your presence later this afternoon. They will want their turns at yelling at you for your insolence."

I knew better than to argue with Mistress Parmina at this point though and dutifully picked up a piece.

The mistress of the Valerian sighed, turning toward the other two asha and speaking like I was no longer in the room. "Did I not tell Mykaela that she was going to be trouble? And yet I have no right to be so surprised. Mykaela was just as unruly in her younger days."

"Mykaela is one of our best asha, Mistress," Althy murmured. "In time, Tea here might prove the same."

"In time, but not today." Mistress Parmina shot me one last look, sighed again, and left.

"If she could condescend to listen to us every now and then." Polaire gave me a scowl. "Whatever possessed you to run out like that, Tea? Do you know how easily the *azi* could have killed you?"

"I was afraid it was going to hurt Lady Mykaela," I mumbled. "Is she...?"

"Resting comfortably, thanks to you—although I am still very angry. You are never to do that again, do you hear me?"

"Yes, ma'am."

She snorted. "Said so easily and ignored just as quickly too!" She sat down on the bed beside me. "Oh, Tea," she sighed. "What are we to do with you? If you'd been my own child, I would have given you such a throttling! Unfortunately, the elders do not think so."

"The elders?"

"The asha-ka association wants to speed up your novitiate," Althy said. "You will be made an asha by the end of the year and sent off to tame your first daeva."

Cold fear gripped me. Polaire nodded knowingly.

"Since you are this eager to confront daeva, they are doing

their best to quicken the process. We will accompany you, of course. As will a Deathseeker—and Zoya too, unfortunately. She is skilled in the runes, and the disadvantage of having her for a sister has come back to bite us in our behinds. Fortunately, you will be kept too busy to get into too much mischief."

"What about Likh?"

"Likh is fine. The elders have not yet called on him. Worrying about it now will not change anything." Polaire snorted. "There is some trickery at work here, and I suspect these elusive Faceless have been busy. If they have found some way to control the *azi*, then we're in trouble. Which of the three do you think did it? As far as I know, Usij is still shackled at his Daanorian fortress, but it would be easy enough to sneak out when no one is looking. There have been no sightings of Druj in the last few weeks, and no one's quite sure if he's still in Yadosha. Similarly, there has been no word of Aenah in Istera, though the bulk of her sect has been imprisoned."

"Quite disturbing," Althy agreed.

"Can I see Lady Mykaela?" I asked.

Polaire looked at my empty plate, at the rinds that were all that was left of the runeberries. She looked back at Althy, who nodded.

Lady Mykaela was sleeping in her bed, her face white against the pillows piled up around her. Her lips were bloodless, and the dark circles around her eyes were more pronounced. My heart broke for her.

"You are not as quiet as you think you are," she said, opening her eyes. But she smiled, and a bit of color returned to her cheeks.

"I'm so sorry." The tears began before I'd reached her bedside, and they wouldn't stop. Every fear and small terror I had felt during the play, the growing dread of knowing they would farm me out the way they had farmed Lady Mykaela out to the daeva, like cattle led toward a high cliff, bubbled to the surface, and I wept. I looked at Lady Mykaela and I saw my future, and I knew then that I did not want to lie in her bed, wearing her stretched skin and her sunken eyes.

Thin hands enveloped me. "It would appear that I owe you my life," Lady Mykaela whispered in my ear. "I hope they did not go hard on you, even so."

I made her promise to never draw the raising Dark again, but it rung as hollow as the vow I had given Polaire so many minutes ago. And in my mind, the Darkness curled at that strange corner, waiting—but for what, I didn't know.

*T*HE STRANGER CAME AS A *surprise. I woke at dawn to find him wandering the beach, staring up with dread at a massive skull. He started upon seeing me. "I didn't think there would be anyone else here," he explained, speaking in Daanorian.*

I took an immediate dislike to him. He wore too many rings on his fingers, his heartsglass nearly hidden by the copious glitter of jeweled embellishments that littered his neck. He stank of magic; even I, who have had no training, could smell it on his person. My Drychta upbringing rose to the surface as much as I tried to stem its ascent; like Istera, Drychta have no love for Daanorian folk.

"Are those things real?" he asked, staring up at the hideous bones that stuck out from the sand. His heartsglass glittered, more green than gold. I did not need to be an asha to read what was written there.

"As real as you or I," I responded shortly.

"To find such a skeleton intact is a rare treat," the man marveled. "Is it daeva? Imagine how many millions of li it could sell for at the black markets! It is just what she told me!"

"She?"

"The woman in my dream. I followed the blue moon over twenty hills in twenty days and found her standing underneath the bones of a great beast. She spoke of valuable cargo that I must deliver and promised the most precious of rewards if I obeyed."

I began to tremble. "What is her name?"

"I do not know. But she has soft brown skin and dark hair, and a dragon lines her robes. Her eyes—" And he too shuddered.

"You are Lu Ren of Daanoris. A governor of the Santiang province."

Neither of us heard her approach. The man recoiled at the sight of her, with her hideous pet taurvi *trotting by her side.*

"A daeva!" He stumbled and fell onto the sand but continued to scramble away.

"Stay," the girl said gently. Lu Ren stopped. He turned in compliance to her wishes, his face a mask of anguish.

"In three days' time, Daanoris will be overrun by daeva, and Santiang will be among the first to fall. They will scorch your lands and destroy all that they see. They will enter the capital of Tuadan, and nothing will remain of your houses nor of the palaces of your emperor and his royal court."

The merchant swayed on his feet, wringing his hands. "But why?" he cried.

"Because it is necessary," the girl told him sadly. "Because the man who sits on your throne is a cruel emperor and an obstacle in my path. And that is why you are to return to Santiang immediately, to warn your people of what is to come. You will order them to flee the cities and to take refuge in the mountains. Save as many as you are able. Spread the word to other towns, and encourage them to do the same. In five days, Daanoris will fall—do not let your people fall with it."

The man recoiled, but even in the face of such tragedy, his avarice struggled for dominion. "And my reward, Mistress?" he asked. "The most precious of rewards that you promised?"

"*You leave with your life intact, good merchant,*" the girl replied, and the taurvi *raised its head and meowed at the terrified Daanori.* "*Surely that is the most precious of rewards? Now, go.*"

And so the merchant turned with a cry of despair and began his trek back toward Santiang, leaving nothing but his footprints behind.

25

T HE ASSOCIATION OF ASHA HAD thirty members, half of whom were mistresses of asha-ka. A quarter of them were chosen delegates among owners of the *cha-khana*, and the rest represented the numerous florists, ateliers, apothecaries, and hairdressers within the vicinity of the Willows. I couldn't see much of a distinction then; all were gray-haired women of an age between seventy and eighty-five, with elegant, flowing robes wrapped about their wizened persons, and their hair sorted into appropriate buns. I don't know whether they were selected because of their similarities or if their similarities became apparent after they were chosen, but I could only tell them apart from the *hua* they wore. All looked hostile.

I stood before them, hoping I could somehow melt through the floors, away from their accusing gazes. Did they look on every asha aspirant with this kind of bitterness, I wondered, or did they reserve this kind of special hate for asha like me, who caused so much trouble even before they made their debut?

I was nearly fifteen. It had only been a week since the *darashi oyun*, and Mistress Parmina was true to her word. Aside from a temporary suspension of all my lessons, I was forbidden to attend parties for another month. I had to turn down both Councilor Ludvig's and Prince Kance's offers, though Lady Shadi told me that the prince inquired frequently about me at the *cha-khana*.

I had to clean the outhouses. I was made to kneel on the street before the elders' association and remain there, unmoving, from noon until four in the afternoon. These were still not the worst sanctions the mistress could have meted out to me, and I suspected Lady Mykaela had convinced her to moderate my punishments.

"You are here because Mistress Parmina has petitioned you for the rank of asha," said one.

Should I speak up, or should I simply nod? Lady Mykaela had said nothing about this. I inclined my head, not trusting my voice at that moment.

"This is an unusual matter. Apprentices require at least another year of mastery. What skills do you believe you possess that makes you believe you deserve exemption?"

I was sure now that they were going through the motions, falling back on questions they gave other novices since time immemorial, because the whole city by now knew what skills I possessed, not all of them necessarily welcomed.

"I am well versed in all my current lessons, miladies. I can dance songs at a grade above my level, and I hold a third tier in combat. I am familiar with the culture of all Eight Kingdoms, including those from the Yadosha city-states and from Drycht. I am fluent in the language of flowers. I can treat wounds and read heartsglass. I have attended over fifty parties under the watchful eyes of my sisters and have always strove to obey my elders." That last part was a bit of a stretch, but none of the mistresses batted an eye. I don't think anyone had blinked since I began speaking.

"Very well. You may begin the first part of your test. The piece we have chosen for you is "Waves at the Shore." You may begin."

I bowed and positioned my hands and feet accordingly. Somewhere behind the women's seats, someone began to play, and I moved across the floor, letting the music seep into my skin, my mind blank as I focused on nothing but the song and my response to it.

I allowed all the worries and fear that had plagued me in the days leading up to this moment to melt away, to block Fox's constant presence in my mind the way I was taught to, until little remained but me and the music.

I danced, and for those several minutes, I was nothing more than a crest in the sea, a swell among the tides that crashed into the rocky seashores of my mind, leaving pain as I rolled and ebbed against the sand, aimless against the vastness of ocean and at peace.

The dancing hall was quiet when I finished and bowed again. The mistresses held themselves too rigidly for me to guess at what went on in their heads.

"Sing 'A Village Feast,'" one of them instructed.

I was on less confident territory here, despite it being one of the simpler songs in the repertoire, but I sang nonetheless. Instructor Teti had given me enough training to learn how to modulate my voice, to pitch it in the same range as the instruments to maintain the harmony, but unlike my dancing, I knew there was nothing special about it. Once that was over, I bowed again, awaiting the next set of instructions.

"Name me the eight types of surgical procedures available to us."

"Incision, bloodletting, stitching, probing, cutting, scraping, puncturing…" For a moment, I panicked, the last answer not immediately coming to mind. *Breathe*, I told myself, relying on the meditation Instructor Kaa had taught me and the techniques I had come to rely on to calm myself. "…and excision."

"Name me five uses of enderroot."

"To treat gout, to congeal blood on open wounds, to relieve the pain from bonesmelt disease, to alleviate symptoms of stone cough, and as a remedy during the initial stages of progressive blindness."

"Give me the names of five nobles whose lineages descended from the Great Heroes."

"Prince Kance of Odalia, Duke Maurion of Tresea, Prince Yesta of Daanoris, Baron Selan of Istera, and Second Minister Kisling of the Yadosha city-states."

"You mention the prince of Odalia but not his father, who is the king. Why is that so?"

I cleared my throat, hoping my cheeks had not reddened as I replied, "Ah…given the testimony of King Randrall the Quiet, whose corpse was recovered due to…unexpected circumstances, it was shown that King Parthan, King Telemaine's own father, was not King Randrall's descendant at all but a descendant of Queen Liset and Commander Bosven of the royal army. He therefore cannot claim descent from Koshti, one of the Five Great Heroes. However, Prince Kance *is* a descendant of Koshti from his mother's family, whose ancestor married into the Latvell family."

"Ah." The woman shuffled a few papers in her hand. "I see. History that has only recently come to light…very well. Twenty feet above your head, there hangs a silver hoop five inches in diameter, attached to a piece of string. Use any one of the runes at your disposal to bring it down."

I paused, stunned. No one had told me about this part of the test. Had I been any of the other asha, it could have been easily accomplished—a Fire rune to burn through the string, a strong enough gust of Wind to snap at the line…

Hastily, I drew in the Dark and cast my mind below us, at the ground. I found nothing. No taste of bone and decay, no hint of death. I threw my mind lower, burrowing through.

Impossible. There was always a dead mouse or insect, some decomposing animal no matter how little or unimportant, that I could reach out to with my thoughts and find contact.

Faces watched me, knowing. Their heartsglass gleamed silver in the gloom.

They had planned for this. I could not wield any other rune but the Dark, and so they had made painstakingly sure that it would not be easy for me. I could tunnel through the ground for years until my ears bleed and still find nothing. And that left me with only one last recourse.

"I can't do it." The words echoed throughout the hall, the finality of them ringing in my ears. "I'm sorry, but I can't do it."

"Is that the answer you would like to submit?" The old woman's voice sounded mocking.

I swallowed. "Yes. I can't."

"The test has concluded. Return to the next room to await our decision."

Fox, Mistress Parmina, and Lady Mykaela still waited for me, and they were now joined by Polaire and Althy, which only made things worse.

Polaire jumped up when she saw me enter. "Well?" she demanded eagerly. "How was it? Did you pass? Did you allow those old geezers to intimidate you?"

"Polaire," Althy remonstrated, "let her speak."

"I failed." I could not help but feel miserable. I felt like I had let everyone down.

"What do you mean 'failed'? Did they tell you?"

"No, but I'm almost sure I did."

"Let's see what the association has to say," Lady Mykaela said optimistically. "I'm certain you're wrong."

I didn't want to get her hopes up but didn't know what else to say. I only nodded, my head bowed. It seemed like a waste of time to wait for my results, but my melancholy didn't put a damper on the others' spirits.

It felt like ages before one of the women entered the room.

I kept my eyes on the floor, not wanting to see the expressions on everyone's faces when she revealed the truth.

"Thank you for waiting, Mistress Parmina. I am pleased to report that Tea has passed her test at the highest level. She is now free to make her debut at your choosing. Congratulations again."

And then I saw nothing but skin and arms because Polaire had dragged me to my feet and enveloped me in a jubilant hug. "You passed—and at the first level! Ha! And you so ridiculously modest, thinking you'd failed—"

"I am so proud of you, Tea!" Lady Mykaela laughed, and Polaire scooped her up, adding her to the embrace. "This is very good news for us!"

"We will stage your debut in a few days," Mistress Parmina announced. "I see no reason to delay. The Valerian will need cleaning. Rahim and Chesh must be notified—"

"But—but I don't understand." I was confused. "I failed the last test. How could I pass at the highest level?"

Lady Mykaela gently disentangled us from a still-enthusiastic Polaire, who made up for the lapse by latching onto Althy instead. "What test was this?"

"The rune test. They asked me to take down a silver hoop they'd hung from the ceiling, and I refused."

"Why?"

"There was nothing for me to raise. Not even a speck of ant."

"That was deliberate, Tea. The asha do a ritual cleaning of the halls before any asha test, and they are very thorough. I encountered the very same thing during my exams."

"But how did you pass?"

"I did the same thing you did—I refused."

I stared at her, more puzzled than ever.

"Think about it, Tea. You have no need to display your proficiency with the Dark. If they were not convinced when you raised half the town's dead during your stay at the Falling Leaf, they would have believed when you chased away the *azi*. As you were unable to use the *Raising* rune, what other options did you have?"

"I could have used *Compulsion*," I said, "to force one of the women to take it down for me. I didn't think they would have liked it."

"Yes. And now do you understand the reason you passed?"

She left me to mull that over as Fox approached. "Are you happy?" Now that I was no longer shielded from him, I felt his thoughts mirroring my own.

"I think I am," I said, ignoring the little Darkness in the corner of my head. I was getting used to compartmentalizing my mind whenever someone new was added to my roster of familiars— Fox had his own space, and then Chief, and they both, to some extent, were dimly aware of the other through the link I shared, and each accommodated for the other's presence. But something else lurked at the farthest reaches of my head, something that neither of them knew of. Being told that I was now an asha had unlocked something within it, like a sleeping giant roused from an ages-long slumber and was now ready to begin the hunt.

Don't worry. It's not important.

With some effort, I pushed it away for another time.

"Then that's all I ask." And my brother hugged me in turn, smiling. "Congratulations, Sis."

I smiled back. It was the only thing I could do. For the first time since raising him, it occurred to me that while Fox was privy to some of my thoughts, he wasn't privy to them all.

•• ⚘ ••

Likh's testing had not been as smooth. Once more we confronted the asha association, but where I had faced them alone, Likh stood with me, Polaire, and Lady Mykaela.

"It has never been done before," one of the old women said firmly. "It breaks with our tradition, and tradition must be honored above everything else."

"It is an archaic tradition," I argued, more vehement and less apprehensive than I had been at my own test. "I don't see why men who can sing and dance and draw runes should be prevented from becoming asha if they meet all other requirements."

"It is an insult to our profession!" another old lady thundered. "It's nearly as ridiculous as a woman joining the Deathseekers!"

"Well, now, that's a very good idea, Mistress," Polaire drawled. "This is Kion, miladies, not Drycht. We are at an age where men and women stand together on equal footing, unlike our barbarian brothers to the south. Why shouldn't a woman petition to join the Deathseekers any more than a man can petition to join asha?"

"Do you not understand the complications that arise from such thinking?" a particularly weaselly old woman at the end of the table snapped. "It is highly unnatural for men and women to fraternize in this manner!"

"Unless you wish to purchase the *hua* they make, of course." I couldn't help myself. I was familiar enough with many of Rahim's work to know that what the crone wore was an Arrakan design.

"Perhaps," Lady Mykaela said gently, "Likh would like to make his case."

Swallowing hard, Likh stepped forward. Unlike us, he wore his plain gray robes.

"When I was three years old, I knew I was not like other boys." His voice carried, soft and gentle, across the hall. "I did not enjoy rough play or making games with wooden soldiers and other such toys. I loved dolls and dresses. I saw my first *darashi oyun* during my sixth summer and liked to pretend I was an asha myself. I am standing before you today to tell you that I have never been so sure of anything else in my life.

"I am also here to plead for my life." His voice shook. "I will not survive Deathseeker training. I know it. The only role I can hope to fulfill for the black brothers is as a fresh corpse on the plains. I will be nothing more than another victim, be it of daeva, of Faceless, or of brigands. I can do so much more here in the Willows, and you will have no reason to regret it. I ask you to give me three months to prove my worth, and you can see at its end whether I should stay or go. It is only three months of your life, but it will decide all of mine."

It was not until the next day that the association announced their verdict.

"It is not for us to determine whether the supplicant can withstand the rigors of Deathseeker training or whether he is more suitable to the way of the asha. We are here to uphold the laws and customs of the Willows to ensure that they are followed to the letter. With this in mind, we reject the supplicant's appeal, but we are willing to leave this up again for reassessment after his Heartsrune day."

•• ⟩⟨ ••

The funerals were held two days later. Three asha had perished in the battle against the *azi*, and the whole community turned up to pay their respects. I stood along the street and watched as they drove the coffins past, which were draped in heavy black ermine. Lady Seleni of the Hawkweed. Lady Brijette of the Imperial. Lady Deanna of the Larkspur. I wondered about Polaire; she had lost an asha-ka sister in Hawkweed, possibly a friend. Those with silver heartsglass can't be raised from the dead, Lady Mykaela said. It felt wrong somehow, for Dark asha to grant others a second chance at life, but not to her asha-sisters and Deathseeker brothers. I remembered Brijette from the Falling Leaf. Though my time with her had not been pleasant, I felt sorry to see her gone. Zoya gave nothing away; her head held high, she marched beside the coffin that held her friend, and I watched them until they turned a corner and were gone from view.

The mood within the Willows was somber, but Mistress Parmina had decided not to delay my debut. The preparations were even worse than the one for Lady Shadi's, and my being in the center of the maelstrom only made it worse. A constant stream of people traipsed in and out of the Valerian, most entering my room and catching me in differing stages of undress, because I was once again being measured and dressed for new *hua*. "Can't they announce themselves before coming in?" I wailed, clutching a discarded robe against my chest. A group of men had just left after a lengthy consultation about the banquet to take place later that evening, heedless of the fact that I was clad only in undergarments when they had first entered.

"I'm a boy too," Likh said, grinning at me. Although Chesh served as my official hairdresser, she knew of our close friendship and had appointed him to be her assistant every time the Valerian required her services.

"But I know you. You're different." I scowled at him. He was taking his rejection by the asha association better than I had. "I'm not going to do this anymore."

"Do what?"

"They want me to be an asha, don't they? What if I refuse and hold everything up until they reverse their decision?"

"I'm not going to let you do that for me." Likh piled my long hair up one side of my head and began to pin several beautiful rhinestone combs into it.

"Hold still," Rahim grunted, holding out another robe for me to slip into. As was the custom, I wore a *hua* that highlighted the Valerian crest, in blue and sea green, and a waist wrap with patterns mimicking the waves of the ocean. There were silver seashells along the edges of my sleeve. "This is the traditional dress you must wear for the one and only time. After that, I shall make the designs of your choosing. Still, this blue is beautiful and of your color. If I had the smoothness of your complexion…" He kissed his fingers with a smacking sound. "*Krasivyy!* Agata, tuck this piece in here, and we shall see about the waist wrap."

I squirmed free from Rahim's hold. "I'm serious."

"Thank you," Likh smiled sadly. "But as much as you think otherwise, an asha's debut isn't about the asha. It's about the asha-ka. Remember that refusing will dishonor the Valerian and all who live in it."

"It isn't fair," I complained. "You act more like an asha than I do!"

"We have time. That they're willing to reconsider after my Heartsrune day gives me hope. I wasn't expecting that." Likh smiled shyly. "You look beautiful."

"I wish I could do more. But I'm glad that you are here with me for this."

"The asha, they are *ostoró nyj*," Rahim scoffed, tugging at my wrap. "Hypocrites. The sentiments and the emotions they will not be deterred by. They are the greedy lot, *uchenik*. The best approach to sway them is to give them what they want. The association, they said no to me too. Then I come with my *hua* and the gowns they desire, and now they say yes."

"Are we not yet done?" Mistress Parmina poked her head in, looking irritated. "It's time, and I do not want to be late. There are crowds of people outside already."

"Crowds of people?" I exclaimed.

"As much as you might dislike it, you're a phenomenon, Tea." Lady Mykaela had convinced Mistress Parmina that she was well enough to leave her bed. She sat beside me as Likh and Rahim gave the finishing touches. "After everything that's happened, you can't be surprised that you're famous in Ankyo. Enjoy it while you can. It's not every day that one can hold a debut such as yours."

I was dubious. Truth to tell, it wasn't the upcoming procession I was dreading, even if it meant I had to be in the public eye. It was the destination that I feared more.

Mistress Parmina was not exaggerating; the crowd broke into a loud, raucous cheer the instant I stepped outside, and their jubilant shouts followed me throughout the rest of the walk. I think that after everything that had happened, they were only too happy to find something to celebrate.

But the sight of the crowd angered me all of a sudden. *You don't understand!* I wanted to shout at them. *You care nothing about me! All you see are the magic and the pretty clothes and the dances! When this is all over, most of you won't even remember my face!*

As usual, Fox took a spot beside me without asking anyone for permission. He placed a hand on my shoulder, and I could feel his presence like a balm on my mind. *I know, Tea,* he whispered, *and I agree. But you know this is not the place or time for it.*

Mistress Parmina, as the second guest of honor, walked at the front with her head thrown back, beaming like this whole parade was for her benefit. Lady Mykaela, Polaire, and Althy took up positions behind me, with Zoya following closely behind.

From time to time, I would sneak a look behind me, but it was hard to tell what the asha was thinking. Her expression was too serene and her heartsglass too calm to be genuine.

Our journey ended before the temple. White smoke still billowed out from the dome, and Lady Mykaela dutifully rang the bell that was the prelude to entering. It was hard enough with everyone watching, but I did my best to slide the door back and step inside, shutting it behind me with some relief, glad that there were still some things in an asha's life that warranted some privacy.

The oracle hadn't changed; she was still heavily veiled and draped in silk, still tending to the large fires that burned in the metal brazier. The fire leaped and blazed up along the hearth like it was a live creature, but it gentled whenever her hand drew near.

"What is your sacrifice?"

I had come prepared this time. From my hair I drew the metal hairpin I had so loved, the one Likh had first picked for me. The sapphires sparkled in the gloom, bright against the darkness.

"Throw it into the fire."

Sadly, I watched as the fire wrapped itself around the jewel until it disappeared from my sight.

The oracle stirred, her head inclined toward my direction. "You saw the dragon," she said. "A mind from which three heads sprout."

"Yes." I wondered if she would ask me why I had not come sooner, but she did not.

"They believe that you turned it away. They believe that you have sent it fleeing from Ankyo."

"Yes."

"You did not."

It was a difficult question to answer, seeing that it wasn't phrased as a question at all. "No, I did not."

"Why?"

I lifted my head. "Because my mentor is dying. She has never told me this, but I know she is. She has spent her whole life chasing these demons and has nothing to show for it but her failing health. She will not stop, and she has resigned herself to an early death. She refuses to protest her fate, so I am doing it on her behalf. If there is another way to tame these creatures without Dark asha giving up our body and soul, raising and killing daeva for the rest of our lifetimes while the years tick by, then I will do it. Not just for her sake but for mine and for every other Dark asha that will pass through these chambers. I believe that the *azi* is the key to her salvation and to mine. If I keep it close, then I might learn how."

I felt chastened by my outburst almost as soon as I said it. For all I knew, the oracle might tell the association everything I said. But for one instant, through the sheerness of her veil, I could have sworn she smiled.

"Come back to me when you have taken two familiars," she said. "One that lives and another who has never known life. You may leave."

The crowd cheered again when I stepped back outside, the blue smoke behind me testament to my success, and for their sakes, I tried to smile.

*T*HERE IS SOMETHING YOU WANT *to ask me," she said.*

"You lied." The taurvi *frolicked among the waves, ignoring us. "You sent me that dream on purpose. You summoned me here."*

"I did not lie. You only assumed what you wanted to see."

"But why? I have never met you before in my life. Why did you call for me?"

"Because your reputation precedes you, Bard. Because you once had a girl you loved, who loved a bricklayer."

I felt cold. "What does she have to do with anything?"

"More than you think. You know what it feels like to be betrayed by the law, to be betrayed by a society that was supposed to protect you from harm, not a society responsible for your grief. She died, didn't she?"

"Yes."

"By her father's own hand."

"Yes." Waves crashed against the shore, the remains of the water pooling around my feet, gathering dust and sand before sweeping them back out into sea.

"Why?"

"He said she dishonored him by running away. The only way he could salvage his honor was to kill her because every day that she lived was only a reminder of her betrayal." The sun baked us with its

heat, and still I shook. "He killed her, and they said it was lawful and justified—and they let him go."

The girl laid a comforting hand on my shoulder. "I chose you," she said quietly, "because you know what it feels like to want revenge when they kill the person you love. So do I."

26

To my mortification and to Mistress Parmina's delight, I found that I had been booked solid for three straight months the day after I had made my debut.

Ula showed me the books she had been working on at my request, not very happily. "I never make mistakes," she said stiffly. "And if that's what you're implying…"

I hastened to mollify her. "Absolutely not. You've been Mistress Parmina's accountant for years, and I trust you. But I'm a new asha. How could I have no free evenings until early winter?"

Ula shrugged. "I only do what the mistress tells me. You should be happy, Lady Tea. Not all asha are requested for as frequently as you have been. At this rate, you'll be number one for the next few months."

When entertaining at functions, an asha is charged for every hour that she spends with her guests. The mistresses of the tearooms keep track of the asha who arrive every night as well as the length of time they stay in an official ledger. The next morning, a representative from the asha association visited each tearoom and took these tallies. Accountants like Ula would then note down how much an asha had made that previous night and then send a bill to the *cha-khana* they visited. The asha-ka then takes a hefty commission after that—more, if they had invested heavily in her, like Mistress Parmina had done with me—and the remainder becomes the asha's wages.

But unless the asha was away from Ankyo for a lengthy period of time, the asha-ka traditionally held their money for them and managed their tabs with shops in the city, so the latter could charge them for any purchases their asha made. At the end of the month, the association would announce who had earned the most money for their asha-ka, to encourage competition.

I was glad that people took an interest in me—it would go a long way toward paying what I owed the Valerian, and the quicker I could work off the debt, the better—but I was appalled by the idea that I would have no rest for the better part of nearly four months. The only consolation was that my dinners with Prince Kance and Councilor Ludvig were unaffected by my new schedule, Mistress Parmina being clever enough not to distance the Valerian from either noble.

"This is a very good start to your career, Tea," the old woman said almost dreamily as she looked through Ula's records. "I don't see how you can complain."

"But I'm already overworked! I'm not sure I can juggle

my lessons and go to these functions at night and still keep my health! I think I should be scaling back on meeting any more guests after—"

"Oh, really?" Mistress Parmina's voice took on a flintier edge. "Are you saying that your history lessons are all you need to know about the world? That you are too good to meet with royalty and people of all kinds and learn more about their culture, their kingdoms, through their own words and habits? That you think you would be able to go out into the world and interact with no more than the books you've read instead of the people you've met? To go to parties may seem like an odd fancy to you, little girl. Oh, I am sure that you will enjoy yourself from time to time—I have seen my share of parties when I was your age and had my fun—but if you think an asha can live by lessons alone, without the support of the powerful kingdoms that surround Kion, then perhaps you should return to your novice lessons until you think otherwise."

I opened my mouth, closed it.

She smiled at me, a large, gumless grin. "Now go and prepare for your party, and no more back talk." She browsed through Ula's books again, a beatific expression on her face. "Didn't I tell Mykaela that she would be such an asset to the Valerian?" she asked Ula, and I was almost sure she believed her own words.

•• ⌇ ••

It was surprising to find how easily things fell into patterns, how a schedule that had at first overwhelmed me could become a matter of course in just a few weeks. I worried that I would be too exhausted to manage, but I wound up adjusting better than I had thought.

Life also had a way of balancing out. I now met with Instructor Kaa only four times a month for my meditation class. Some of my other lessons had also been scaled back. I still had singing lessons once a week to keep my voice from getting rusty. I was expected to do my own research when it came to the guests I met in the evenings but no longer needed history lessons. My dance classes and fight training remained as grueling as ever, but cutting back on the other lessons helped me focus on them better. I was approaching second tier in combat, and everyone seemed happy at how things were progressing.

Lady Mykaela tired easily, and when she couldn't teach me as often as she wanted when it came to my rune lessons, Instructor Hami took over. While she couldn't draw the Dark, she had mentored enough Dark asha to know enough to guide me, and her sense of magic was strong enough that she could pinpoint any mistakes I made.

I wasn't allowed to take part in Runic exhibitions with the other asha because I couldn't wield elemental runes, but I could now participate in standard combat sessions with those more skilled than I. My first opponent was a lithe young girl named Tella, who was as deadly as she was pretty. Five seconds into my fight, I found myself knocked to the ground by a well-placed kick that left me stunned for several minutes. I never even saw her move.

"Always strive to do the unexpected," she told me kindly, extending a hand out to me to help me up.

"I think it's a bit difficult for me to be unexpectedly half a foot shorter, weigh no more than ninety pounds, and have a mean right sweep," I said, and she laughed.

Tella was first tier as it turned out and, despite her youthful good looks, also ten years my senior. I could beat most of my other fellow combatants, but I knew almost as soon as my name and hers were paired up that I was in for a hard time. Instructor Hami knew this; she called our names together frequently.

I had the same trouble with Kalen. I received more bruises from him than from all other opponents put together, including Tella, but he still never once offered any word of encouragement and only pointed out my mistakes. He never made small talk and left as soon as our sparring had finished, always leaving me feeling both irritated and useless.

There was one match where I caught him off guard. I was tired and cranky after nearly an hour of nonstop sparring, but he was unrelenting. "Is this the best you can do?" He taunted, delivering a swift blow to my shins, forcing me down on one knee. "You're not good enough, Tea. You won't be good enough. You're only going to get the prince killed."

He'd never used the prince to insult me before, and that triggered a sudden spurt of rage and, with it, a rush of energy.

I ducked to avoid the wooden blade about to strike my shoulders, dove to my left, and threw my sword at him. He was quick enough to deflect the blow but didn't expect me to tackle him about the knees, sending us both to the floor.

I rolled to my left and scrambled to my feet. He did the same. From across the bamboo mat, we stared at each other.

"I won't," I said once I had recovered my breath. "I'll be good enough."

He looked at me, and for a moment, I thought he might say something. But he only gestured at me to begin again, and the fight resumed like it had never stopped.

Fox came to watch and often competed in his own matches against other asha and also against a few soldiers of Empress Alyx's army. I was amazed at his skill, at how quickly he could take down his opponents.

"I need to be strong enough to protect you," Fox said simply after I had pointed this out. "I knew you weren't going to like me fighting, especially on your behalf. That's why I didn't tell you I joined the army. It's not just about me owing you my life. It's about being a brother. You're not going to cry, are you? Your eyes are getting misty."

"Shut up," I said and hugged him. "Your match's starting. Go beat the crap out of that other guy."

"Yes, ma'am."

I laughed, ignoring the guilt bubbling up. I was keeping secrets from Fox. And though I knew it was for his best interests, I didn't like it one bit.

.. ﹈ ..

"I promised you information, didn't I? Let me run through my list. There's been a nasty spate of sleeping spells in Tresea—it's gotten hold of a few of the nobility, so I assume it's not natural, politicking being a cutthroat business everywhere. But that's not something you'd be interested in, I suppose. There have been sightings of the *azi* at the Odalian border. The man I got that information from claimed he'd seen it rise from the lake. Hightailed it out of there as fast as he could, considering he's eighty if he's a day and stricken with gout."

We were at one of the smaller rooms of the Snow Pyre, and the quiet Darkness lodged within my head stirred with discomfort. "Is there any way he was mistaken?"

The Heartforger glared at me. "I can read heartsglass better than you."

"I'm sorry. It's just that the Deathseekers have been looking all over for it—"

The forger cackled. "The average Odalian won't talk to authority, much less Deathseekers. They're just as much afraid of them as they are of the *azi*. Not one for asha and magic, the typical Odalian. Got too many things to hide themselves. More than likely you won't be believed. Your old asha are as stubborn as they come, and they will never believe that you know better than they do. They dislike me even more to give credence to any news I bring. But your three-headed dragon's hiding in Lake Strypnyk in Odalia. I'd stake my reputation on it."

I PLANNED MY ESCAPE THAT NIGHT; *in my quest to listen to her tale, I had neglected to realize my own danger. A lifetime of stories was not enough payment for what I knew she would ask me to witness, for the only reason she would raise such monsters from their graves stood out to me as plain as the sky was dark.*

The beasts slept outside the cave, black, misshapen outlines against the heavy twilight. There was no sound save that of waves lapping at the shore, the rush of tides as they ebbed and flowed back into the black, unforgiving sea. I was terrified at first, fearful that one may wake without the influence of their mistress, but I wrapped what bravery I had left into my soul and walked on, making no sound as I made my way through the sand, away from the Dark asha and her creatures.

She found me a mile away from where I began. She sat beside the grave, its polished stone bright despite the dim. Fear gripped me and I stood stock-still, waiting, certain she would kill me for my betrayal.

"You misjudge me," she said before I could say a word. "I compelled you to come here, with the blue moon as your guide. I admit to that." She carried something under her arm; it was the sapphire-hued bezoar of the indar, *the bezoar that discerned truth from lies. "But I swear on this grave that you were never under any obligation to remain. You only needed to ask, and I would have granted you safe passage anywhere you desired."*

The three-headed dragon on her hua gleamed at me, their

bright eyes remonstrating. The blue bezoar shone radiant and true as she spoke.

The girl pointed toward the east. "When you reach the end of the beach, you will find a path leading out into the plains. Follow the road you see there, and it will take you to the borders of Tresea twenty leagues out. Or take the road on the left, and several days will find you in Santiang, though I would advise you not to linger."

"How do I know that this is not a trick?" I dared to ask. "What proof do I have that what I choose to do is not from your Compulsion?"

"This is how you know."

The strange blue moon blazed to life above us, as bright and as magnificent as the day. At the same time, I felt my feet move through no desire of my own, forcing me back to where the girl sat staring out onto the sea.

"Stop."

I stopped.

The girl drew out a small pin from her hair and pressed it into my hand. It gleamed like ivory, plain save for its strange silver sheen. The peculiar pressure in my head eased, and the blue moon faded from view.

"One of the strongest spells is woven into this hairpin. It will prevent anyone else from directing your thoughts. Keep it close by you at all times and not even I can command your actions. If you still wish to leave, then you are free to do so. If you wish to stay, then I will tell you more. Look at this bezoar I carry and see that I do not speak false." And she held out that blue stone, which continued to glitter like gems, proving the truth to her words.

"*Thank you for the company,*" *she said gently.*

The girl walked back in the direction of her cave, leaving me to make my decision alone.

The daeva woke before the sun rose again the next morning. I watched them frolic among the waters like children at play. The girl sat atop the taurvi *and smiled at me when I approached, wearing her pin on my shirt.*

"*I am glad,*" *she said.*

27

T HE LOSS OF TWENTY DEATHSEEKERS came as a blow. We learned of this two weeks later, long before the royal messengers came trickling into Ankyo, armed with grief. We learned of it when the silk merchants arrived, pale and trembling, speaking of the heavy, black smoke that moved across the Odalian landscape like an angry storm. We learned of it when the wagons returned from Kneave, from refugees fleeing the carnage that ravaged the small towns littering the borders of Kion.

We learned of it when the Heartforger and Khalad returned to the Snow Pyre *cha-khana*, both grim and sober. "It caught them unawares," the old man said. "Went through the troop like butter—they died before they knew what was happening to them, a blessing if you can call such a death by that word. Looks to me like you've been made asha at the right time, Tea. If there is no more fortunate time to draw in the Dark, it is now."

I remembered it again when an old woman came through the doors of the Valerian and begged me to raise her son from the dead.

"He's barely twenty, milady," she wept. "Fresh off his training, only to be sent off to die. You can raise him from the dead, can't you, milady? That is what they say. I have no other sons for my old age. I beg you!"

I could only stand there, numb, as she was gently guided away, still sobbing, by two of the many soldiers that took to roaming the city for a sense of security that no one believed, with the whole of Ankyo tensed in expectation of a war they did not know for sure would ever come. Not for the first time, I plumbed the depths of my mind, seeking for answers in the strange presence curling up at the furthest corners. I had sensed nothing wrong until the horrible news had come, and I was desperate, wondering if I should have investigated further. But the *azi*'s mind slipped easily away from me, and all I could find was darkness.

I looked at Fox, and we did not need our bond to know what he was feeling or for him to know what I was feeling.

I found Polaire waiting for me among the ruins of the graveyard sometime later, where twenty new headstones now stood out among the older tombs with their pathetic shininess. "No," she said.

"I didn't say anything."

"But I know what you plan. When Lady Mykaela was as young as you were, she thought to do the same thing. It will kill you, child. Raising twenty men at once is not the same as raising one brother. You do not have a seeking stone this time to amplify your powers."

"But I do!" My hand went to the small stone I still wore around my neck, beside my heartsglass. I was grief-stricken. I was angry.

"The Forger shaped it to protect you, no longer to draw strength from. And even if you could, you will draw in too much and take in the darkrot, and we will have to put you down all the same. The seeking stone is gone—it is too dangerous in anyone's possession. Mykkie has done all she could to save your life. Do not repay her by dying for the sake of twenty men."

Later that, day a new contingent of Deathseekers, Kalen among them, left Kion to join their surviving brethren in Odalia.

"You have barely served your three months as an official asha, and now you seek to know better?" Mistress Parmina was in full fighting form, less about my safety and more about my inability to take in money if I were to take a leave of absence. "Asha who have been at it far longer than you are frequently denied leave. What makes you think you would be any different?"

"I know where the *azi* is."

I said it quietly, but the effect was immediate. Mistress Parmina sat up straighter among the cushions and Lady Mykaela, recuperating in bed, opened her eyes.

"Are you sure about this, Tea?" my sister asked me gravely.

I chose my words carefully, for my heartsglass could have betrayed me. "When I first confronted that dragon during the *darashi oyun*, I saw into its mind. I could sense how it felt, and all it knew was a desire to go home. And home for it was a boundless lake of black salt."

"That's a good description of Lake Strypnyk," Polaire conceded from her perch beside Lady Mykaela. "But you could be mistaken."

"The Forger confirms it." The old man had permitted me to inform the mistress of the Valerian of his assistance, but I thought both Althy and Polaire counted as honorary members, if nothing else. "His sources also report that it hides inside Lake Strypnyk."

"Even if he is right," Lady Mykaela pointed out, "and he often is—what makes you think you would fare better than a squad of Deathseekers?"

"Because Dark runes are weak against it. Because I have a better chance at taking it down than twenty Deathseekers. Remember the *darashi oyun*. Nearly all the asha in Ankyo present, and still it escaped us. You're throwing away a lot of lives when you don't need to, when all it would take is one of me."

Lady Mykaela took a deep breath. "That is dangerous thinking, Tea. We are the only two Dark asha in Kion. I can—"

"The *azi* took too much out of you," I interrupted her. "Please, Lady Mykaela. I love you like a sister. I really do. But you brought me here to help you, to send daeva back to their graves. And I was scared at first, even resentful. But now I see how important we are. I'm ready. I'm willing. I survived one daeva. I have more experience dealing with the Dark now than all the other asha combined, except you. Everyone has trained me for this. Let me show you what I've learned."

"You still have a duty to your patrons," Mistress Parmina said. "You cannot abandon your responsibilities, not when you have been booked months in advance—"

"Asha ask to be excused from entertaining patrons for official duties all the time," I pointed out. "I'm sure most of them will understand." I'd come prepared, placing a stack of papers in front of Mistress Parmina. "I asked Ula for an accounting of my record. As I have been working at least six hours every night for almost three months without taking an evening off, I've earned three times what an average asha might make in a year. Despite the substantial debt I owe the Valerian, I have almost repaid it. All I ask is some time off to hunt the *azi*, and as soon as I return, I will work another three months. Please think of this as a small investment in my future, Mother."

I could practically see Mistress Parmina's mind calculating the amount of money she could make, the fame I could bring. The price I command for entertaining guests, already exorbitant, would shoot up. Behind her, I could see Lady Mykaela smiling at my ingenuity, though not without reluctance.

"Very well," the old woman said, "I will give you a month's leave. No more, no less. But if the *azi* is not at Lake Strypnyk as you claim it is, then you are to return immediately, and you shall no longer waste my time with any more of these foolish wild-goose chases."

"That was smooth," Polaire murmured to me after the old woman had left the room, still clutching at the papers. "You struck her where it would hurt the most—at her purse strings."

"This is too dangerous," Lady Mykaela objected. "I should go with you. If something goes wrong, it would be good to have another Dark asha with you."

"Absolutely not," Polaire returned. "You're still too weak to travel. You need another year's worth of rest, and the only sure thing to come out of traveling with us is that it will take longer for you to recuperate. I don't think your presence will help us in any way, not in the condition you're in."

"Us?" I echoed.

"Naturally I'll be coming with you, little idiot. I'm at the peak of health, and I could use a leave of absence from all those parties myself. Althy would come if she could, but Princess Inessa is fond of her, and her role as her protector isn't as easy to take a leave of. Shall we get to packing?"

·· ⟩∕⟨ ··

Polaire had spoken too soon; the asha-ka association had approved our request for an audience, but it was the only thing they were willing to grant.

"Absolutely not," one of the old women thundered—Mistress Hestia of House Imperial. Her heartsglass glimmered burgundy and teal, Mistress Parmina's slight regarding the Falling Leaf *cha-khana* still rankling her. "We deny your request to leave for Odalia. The Deathseekers have agreed to assume this responsibility, and it is no longer our concern."

"There are twenty of them dead in Odalia," Polaire said, who had volunteered to speak on my behalf. Councilor Ludvig was with me, and I had hoped his presence would help sway them to our cause. We stood on the very same stage which I had danced and sang for them on, the same stage where I had refused to burrow into their minds to take a silver hoop off a piece of string above my head. "And there will be countless more if we don't act. This is not a common daeva, Mistresses. This is an *azi*, the most powerful of the darkspawn. Not even the Five Great Heroes have ever defeated it, and its lair remains unknown to this day. It is a reclusive beast that goes out of its way to avoid humans, but its sudden appearance at the *darashi oyun* indicates some new evil at work. It must be neutralized as soon as possible— that will require the talents of a Dark asha, not a Deathseeker."

"Deathseekers are aware of the risks they take whether they face off against an *azi* or a tiger cub, a monster or a human. All the rulers of the Eight Kingdoms have agreed that this must be left up to the men. They are prepared to sacrifice their lives; we are not prepared for you to do the same."

"But why? Isn't that what I'm here for?" My bitterness echoed through the large chamber.

"Yes, but at a time of our choosing. You are still too young and too inexperienced to handle a daeva of this magnitude, and to send you to the *azi* is tantamount to suicide. We have not invested this much in you to send you off according to some foolish whim. Perhaps when Lady Mykaela is well enough—"

That was the last thing I wanted. "But I have faced it down before, and I can do it again! I understand that there are risks, but you must agree that even places like the Willows can be attacked.

If I am safer here than I would be anywhere else, it would not be by any large margin. If there's a chance we can find the daeva, then it's a chance I'm willing to take."

"Foolish girl!" The words rang out in the deserted hall. "Do you now know better than us just because you wear an asha's hua? You are fifteen years old, still a child. We have been here far longer than you have been alive, little girl. We have survived worse years than you could dream of, and we will continue to flourish. Return to the Valerian, and rid your head of such idiocy. And you too, Polaire! I am surprised that you would allow this waif to convince you so easily! What idiot put such thoughts into your heads?"

"This 'idiot' did," Councilor Ludvig said with unnatural calm, "and I wager I speak with more experience than the lot of you put together. The longer we delay this hunt, the more casualties we will incur, and it will not bode well for the rest of the kingdoms. Our enemies are crafty and find solace in subterfuge. They will not be intimidated by this show of strength, which will give us nothing but a foolish waste of the Deathseekers at our disposal. They believe the news will leave us in disarray. We must take advantage of their presumption to strike when they least expect it. The faster we take down the daeva, the faster we seize back the advantage."

"We are aware of your reputation, Councilor Ludvig" was the cold reply. "However, you have no say in Ankyon affairs and even less within the Willows. Isteran politics is not our politics, and you must allow us to handle all Ankyon interests in our own way."

"Sometimes I just want to throttle them," Polaire fumed as

we exited the building. Fox waited for us by the entrance. Judging by the look on his face, he had already gleaned the associations' decision from my mind. "They care for nothing outside of Kion; all they want is to save their asha-ka and their reputations and not necessarily in that order."

I was despondent. I had thought for sure that I could sway them to the urgency of our request.

"I presume they rejected your offer."

Zoya was still garbed in black, still in mourning for her friend, Brijette. She was paler than usual and for once wore none of her acerbity for all to see.

"And what does that have to do with you?" Polaire asked, wary.

Zoya shrugged. "I'm not stupid. I can make a guess at what happened inside. I could have told you that they would refuse your request and spared you the energy and the time. I also know that you all are not the type to give up so easily. Whatever you're planning, I want to be a part of it. It's better than staying here, with little else to do but wait."

"What do you think?" Fox asked Polaire.

"We do need all the help we can get," she admitted reluctantly.

"That's an understatement if I ever heard one." The old man dug at his right ear with a finger. "I've had dealings with those crones before, and quite frankly, I'm not surprised. They're not ones to admit when they're wrong, even when they are."

"What do we do now?" I asked him.

"You have two choices the way I see it. You can abide by their decision, retire to your asha-ka, wait for word of any other battles, and hope they find that daeva without incurring further casualties. Or you can sod off whatever they think and leave anyway."

Polaire, Fox, and I looked at each other. We didn't need to voice our thoughts aloud to know what we had decided.

"You're not being honest with them," Fox murmured as we returned to the Valerian. "You're not doing this just out of the goodness of your heart."

"I'm not doing this because I want to risk my life. I'm doing this for Likh, and I'm doing this for Lady Mykaela. If I—*when* I—defeat the *azi*, they'll make much of me. And I can build my influence, enough to use the elders as leverage. I can force them to accept Likh into the Willows and to have some control over Dark asha affairs in the Willows. Soon I could be in a position where they can no longer refuse me."

Fox only shook his head. "I don't think they'll change their minds even then, Tea."

"I'll make them *change* their minds if I have to."

My brother looked quickly at me, and I softened my tone.

"Not *that* way, of course. But I'll find some other means."

He nodded. He said nothing more, but I wonder if he had sensed that if only for a few seconds, I had truly meant it.

•• ⊱⧸⧹⊰ ••

"Please reconsider," Prince Kance said as Khalad carefully extracted a memory from my heartsglass. "Surely there are other alternatives to choose from?"

"I'm sorry, Your Highness. But I'm the only one who can do this."

"I thought I told you to call me Kance." He smiled, but his heartsglass thrummed with worry.

—his eyes were still the same bright emeralds, and his face still maintained that solemn bearing even as he stood, smiling, to greet us—

Khalad kept a straight face as he gently drew out my memory. "It is a hard reality to accept, Kance, but she is the most logical choice, despite her youth. The possible sacrifice of one life outweighs the lives of your other soldiers—or of a city if the daeva continues its rampage."

"I'm already worried about Kalen. I don't like the idea of putting Lady Tea in any more danger. I have half a mind to report your intentions to my father or to the elders."

I froze. "Will you?"

"As much as I want to, I won't. I promised to tell no one, Lady Tea." He reached over and squeezed my hand. "But it's your turn to promise me something else. I want you to come back safe and unharmed. If it's a choice between saving your life and letting the *azi* get away, I want you to choose the first. Swear on it, Lady Tea."

"I promise, Prince Kance." And if my heartsglass flickered pink for the briefest of instants, it was only Khalad who saw.

*S*HE WAS PALER, MORE WAN *than before—the price of carrying four daeva on her shoulders, with three more to come. But her hands did not shake as she stoppered two more of the vials, and she showed no hesitation as she drank them down. She tossed the bottles onto the sand behind her and stepped out into the waters, toward the bones.*

She summoned the indar *first. The blue bezoar broke in her hands, and the skeleton above us moved. It gained shape quickly enough—a hawklike beast with a gnarled beak and a loud cry that ripped through the air, the sound shrill. It had paws instead of talons and a bear's body made of neither fur nor feathers but of something in between. It shook itself dry and then took to the skies, exploring for several minutes before it remembered its mistress. It landed on the sand before her and bowed its head in acquiescence, as had the other daeva before it.*

The akvan *came next, and it was every bit as grotesque as I remembered, with its protrusion of elephant tusks and its massive trunk. It trumpeted at the sun, no longer gutted and eviscerated. Its tail thumped at the ground behind it, kicking up sand and soil.*

Their black hearts glittered in the air. The girl took them both and pressed them against her own heartsglass.

And screamed. She toppled to the ground, writhing. I ran toward her, but just as suddenly, the spasms ended as they had begun, and she pushed herself up with one hand, breathing hard. Even the daeva showed their concern, turning toward her with high, piping sounds of worry.

She raised her arm when I took a step toward her, concerned. "I'm all right," she insisted. "All I need is a little rest, a chance to... catch my breath."

"What is happening?"

"As...Dancing Wind once gave part of her heartsglass to bring back Blade that Soars...so do I give part of my heartsglass to bring back these daeva. It is like...knives...going through my soul."

"You don't need to do this," I implored her. "There must be some other way."

She laughed. "Did you think I would do this if there was?" She closed her eyes and took a deep breath. "I will rest for a while and tell you more about the azi," she said. "And then I will succeed. Or I will die trying. There is no middle ground."

28

W HAT THE HELL ARE YOU doing here?" was how Kalen greeted us. We found the band of Deathseekers gathered near the lake's edge, setting up camp. The sun glided across the water, sinking past the horizon and turning the sky into a menagerie of pinks and oranges. The creature was close; I could sense the alien presence in my mind grow stronger, though the sensation coming through from the other side of the bond was sluggish.

"We thought we could all use a vacation," Polaire informed him glibly, sliding off her horse. I did the same, patting Chief lightly on the nose and digging into my pockets for a small piece of sugar. Being dead didn't stop Chief from enjoying his share of sweets, and he munched on my offering with gusto.

"Do the elders know that you're here?"

"Would that make any difference now?"

Kalen glared at us and then relaxed. "I suppose not."

"Who's in charge?" Zoya demanded.

"Ostry is. Gerrold died, and Nargal is in no shape to lead us anywhere."

"Take us to him, then. We need to talk."

"Well, hi there," Ostry said as we approached the center of the camp. He had a bandage around one eye; five other Deathseekers displayed similar injuries. He grinned at me. "You've traveled a little farther out than the tearooms of the Willows, Lady Tea. I don't mind the company, although this is not the best of circumstances. On the bright side, I see double of everything, and two of you look just as lovely as the one."

"This doesn't look good," Fox said, surveying the rest of the wounded. "How many are indisposed?"

"A dozen brothers, and they're the lucky ones. We've taken our most seriously injured to the town of Lizzet to recuperate. It's a day's ride away, so they should be safe."

I caught a glimpse of his silver heartsglass, reading its pattern of erratic greens and yellows. "You need to lie down," I told him.

"I'm fine. Alsron changed my bandages only an hour ago."

"Bandages don't do much for concussions. We'll need to get you some ice and a clean cloth."

"There are some fresh strips in my pack." The Deathseeker's fingers moved, and a small block of ice materialized on the ground beside him. "Will this help?"

"And I forbid you to draw runes for the next several days. Let someone else do it."

"That might be harder to do, little lady." He winced when I

pressed the ice against his head at a spot that still looked swollen. "As long as that damned *azi* is out there, I make no guarantees. It's taken out too many of my pals for me to relax."

"We heard," Fox said. "Do you know where it is now?"

Ostry gestured out at the lake. "As far as we could tell, it hibernates during the day and comes out at night. We don't know if it's still there or if it's hunting somewhere else. But the sun's setting, so I'd say you're just in time to find out, which is unfortunate. How did you know we were here at Lake Strypnyk? We'd only figured out its location the night before, and we just dispatched a messenger a few hours ago."

"We have our sources," Polaire said mysteriously.

"Tea here seems confident she can take it on." Zoya nodded at me. "I say she's an idiot, but that's an argument for another time, seeing that we have little choice."

"What the hell are you girls doing here?" Alsron demanded, approaching the campfire with several other Deathseekers.

"Saving your derrière," Polaire said sweetly. "Tea, will it sense you if you try to search for it?"

"I don't think so." The dragon was as used to my mind as I was to it by now, and my nearness caused no alarm, as far as I could tell.

"Do you know where it is?"

"It's inside the lake."

"That was quick," Zoya remarked. "Did you know where it was all this time?"

"I've been looking for it before arriving at the Deathseekers' camp." I strove to keep my heartsglass serene, slowing down my breathing so I would not arouse further suspicions. Sometimes I forgot how perceptive Zoya was.

"Any ideas when it's going to surface?" Zoya asked.

"I don't know. I think I can goad it out if I have to."

"It's more likely to remain in the lake than venture out." The man shrugged. "It's only surfaced once, to our knowledge. You know what happened next." He gestured at the line of wounded. "It attacked us somewhere between here and the village of Indt."

"How did this happen?" Polaire demanded. "You've all faced down daeva before. I'm not saying we've never come away unscathed, but to hear of twenty other Deathseekers dead? This is the worst number of casualties that I've heard of!"

"Seems like it's evolving, studying us. We were not as effective at the *darashi oyun* as you might think. We were barely able to protect ourselves, much less injure it." From his position on the ground, Ostry grimaced. "Fire, hurricanes, quakes, as many arrows as we could put into its scaly hide. Heathal even tried to freeze it. All he got for his troubles was a spike through his heart. We couldn't do much after that but grab the bodies of those who'd fallen and retreat while we still could. It fled, and we tracked it here—I suspect it doesn't want to stray too far from the lake. It would be best if you girls returned to Ankyo. There isn't much you can do here."

Polaire shook her head. "We have to try. Tea, you'll be the one facing it head-on. What do you want us to do?"

I rose to my feet. "I would need a handful of Deathseekers nearby just in case, the ones who aren't injured. I want the others as far away as they possibly can be. I can feel it somewhere underneath those waters, and it feels like it's hibernating. If I'm to seek it out, I want to wrest control before it's fully awake."

"There are six or seven of us with but a few minor scratches to our name," Kalen said. "There's a good chance you'll have about as much success as we had even if you draw in the Dark. And if I were a betting man, I'd stake money that there's a powerful Faceless out there, meddling."

"Choices require risks," Zoya said. "Start evacuating your wounded. They won't want to be here when the fighting starts."

"You're going with them," Polaire informed Ostry, who was trying to stand.

"I can fight," the man protested.

"Spare me the heroics, Ostry. We've been in this long enough for me to see through your *conneries* when you start spouting them! Who's next in command after you?"

"I was the fifth in line, you know. We haven't thought that far ahead."

"Kalen, which of your brothers can remain behind to help us?"

"Terrence, Andres, Kingston, Levi, Farrgut, and I."

"That gives *me* the seniority, then."

"Lady Polaire, I don't think—"

"I'm placing you in charge of the remaining Deathseekers, Kalen, but you're not in charge of me. In the absence of any other senior brothers, I can assume command."

"But you're not on official business from the council, and regulations state…" Kalen trailed off at the look on her face.

"Gibbons has a broken arm but no head injuries. I can put him in charge of the wounded."

"Smart decision. Fox, help the rest of the brothers get to Lizzet."

"No," my brother said. "Where Tea goes, I go."

"There's not much you can do against a daeva, Fox."

"That's not important. I'm not going to go off to safety while Tea remains behind. And if there's one less thing you need to worry about when I'm involved, it's putting an extra life in danger."

Polaire paused. "True enough. I keep forgetting that. Keep Tea out of trouble."

"Tea is already in trouble," Zoya murmured. "So are we for disobeying the council, for that matter."

"Keep Tea out of more trouble, then. Are you sure about this?" she asked me in a softer whisper as the other Deathseekers began making their preparations. "We're treading in unknown territory, and I'd hate to die on a 'maybe.'"

"The runes may not work, but I can still sense it. And I was able to control it to some extent back in Ankyo."

"I hope you know what you're doing," Zoya said from behind us.

"As I recall, you insisted on coming," Polaire pointed out.

"It's never too late to regret things."

"Can you still feel the *azi*?" Fox asked. "How long do we have?"

"Not very long, I think." I could feel it slither along the edges of consciousness. "I think it could wake in another hour's time."

"No sense in delaying, then. Move faster, people!" Polaire

ordered. "Injuries don't give you an excuse to be here once the sun goes down!"

There were more wounded than I had thought. As I watched a few of the Deathseekers borne away on improvised litters, I couldn't help but shudder.

Fox laid a protective hand on my shoulder. "I'm not going to let anything happen to you, Tea."

"I love you, Fox, but Polaire is right—there's not a lot you can do for this fight."

"Enough to drag you out of here if things take a turn for the worse—kicking and screaming if I have to."

Despite their previous assertions, even the other asha showed signs of nervousness. Zoya kept scanning the waters like she expected the *azi* to rise at any instant, and Polaire chewed on her fingernails at intervals, realized what she was doing, and firmly brought her hands down, only to bring them back up to her mouth again after a few minutes.

"Are they going to be all right?" I asked Kalen as we watched the long line of injured Deathseekers begin their journey to Lizzet.

"Let me be blunt, Lady Tea. I'm doing this under protest because Polaire commanded me to and because she's my superior. This does not make us friends."

"What did I ever do to you?" I demanded. "We barely see each other enough for you to hate me. You tell me not to see Prince Kance and expect me to kowtow to what you want without telling me why. Whatever you think about me, you at least owe me an explanation."

He glared back at me, but something in his expression wavered, like he wasn't sure how to phrase it. "I know how you feel about Kance," he finally said.

I felt like a hole in my stomach had opened, and my heart had plummeted right through it. "What?"

"That first night at the party. When you raised those dead rats." He looked down at my heartsglass. "You've been pretty good at hiding your emotions since then but not that first time. Asha aren't the only people who can read heartsglass. It's not mandatory for Deathseekers to learn, but it's a good skill to have."

"Why are you telling me all this?"

"Because I thought you were just another inexperienced asha with a schoolgirl's crush. I've seen enough girls throw themselves at him, and I can see the early signs of infatuation. But then you raised those rats, and I realized you were a lot more than that. I've spent almost all my life protecting Kance from danger, and I knew you would put him there from your presence alone."

"*Conneries,*" I said.

"What?"

"That's what Polaire says when she thinks someone's talking out of their ass. You're right. I do like Prince Kance, but I've tried my best not to let that get in the way of my duties as an asha, and I never intended to let him know, much less do anything about it. You talk about being able to read my heartsglass, but you forget that I can read them as well as you, even better. You lied just now."

He paused. "I don't know what you mean."

"When you said that you thought I was just another inexperienced asha, your heartsglass flickered. You knew I was a Dark asha even before Zoya and her friends told you." And then realization dawned. "You knew who I was as soon as you saw me that first night at the Falling Leaf, didn't you? But when?"

He stared at me, and I watched as his heartsglass shifted color from a dark silver to a deep blue and then back again before settling for a brighter gray tint. "That wasn't the first time we met," he finally said. "When I was fifteen years old and you and Lady Mykaela had come to Kneave to perform the Heartsrune ceremony for my uncle."

I stared at him. "There was a boy in a hooded cloak and a silver heartsglass..."

He frowned. "I wore the cloak, yes. But my heartsglass had not yet turned silver then. I was with Councilor Abadiah when he requested for the king to begin the Heartsrune ceremony."

The boy in the brown cloak accompanying the nervous councilor. The one with the beet-red heartsglass, heavy with anger.

He nodded. "You remember now. Ten years ago, a daeva rampaged through Holsrath, where my family lived. The Dark asha tasked to face it lost her nerve and fled. Other asha managed to put it down, but not before the town suffered many casualties, my mother and Kalen's among them." He paused, then added stiffly, "I don't like my father, but I share his anger at Dark asha. I question how King Telemaine could welcome them with open arms when they caused his wife's death, though I would never turn against him like my father had. But I was angry, and you were the easiest person to lash out at. I owe you an apology for what I said then, but I stand by what I say now. You must stay away from Kance."

"Any minute now, Tea," Polaire said grimly, her head tilted back to watch the sky. She nibbled at a thumb. "I don't want to have to do this in near darkness."

"We can talk later," Kalen said grimly, looking back out at the waters, "if either of us gets through this in one piece."

"For someone who believes I'm powerful enough to have to protect a prince against, you don't seem to believe I can do it."

He glanced back at me and finally allowed himself a small, brief smile. "Good luck, Lady Tea."

"Thanks." I moved toward the edge of the lake, coordinating my breathing with every step that I took. Left foot, right foot. In and out. Left foot, right foot. In and out.

Fox moved beside me, but Polaire put a hand on his arm, forcing him to stay still while I forged on ahead. In and out. Left foot, right foot. My shoes sank into the wet soil, small bundles of vegetation caressing my feet as I moved, waving against the current. I cast my mind around for the presence, embracing it this time instead of shunting it into the furthest corners of my head, and I thought I felt it respond, sensing the change. I waded farther out, ignoring Polaire's alarmed calls for me to stop, and reached out with my thoughts, feeling the spindles of thought gathering around me, giving me all the momentum I need.

I closed my eyes. I had expected the creature to avoid me like it had in the past, but this time the creature's slow advance into my own head was curious, not angry or threatened. It crept out to where I was waiting, almost childish in its naivety. That should have been my first clue that something was wrong—it was far too complacent when it had done its best to avoid me previously.

Instead, I closed my eyes and drew in the Dark, feeling the energy wrap possessively around me, waiting for me to give the order to strike. And when I did, it burrowed into the dark waters, into the monster's underwater lair, wrapping the weaves of my magic around the creature's will.

"*Rise*," I commanded, and I felt the world rise with me—and the most horrible pain I'd ever felt in my life exploded through my body as a new presence reared up from behind the *azi* and attacked my thoughts. It was more painful than the torrent of magic Lady Mykaela had unleashed at my first daeva raising, and I dropped to my knees. My tongue tasted something metallic, blood dripped out of my nose, and the roaring in my ears intensified.

"Tea!" I heard Fox shout from somewhere behind me, heard the splashing of water. I couldn't breathe. Stunned, I fought for control, but a new and sudden presence in my mind was quick to overwhelm me until nothing but blissful darkness remained.

*I*T TOOK HER A FEW *hours to pull herself together, but she appeared well again at its end. "It took more strength than I expected it to," she assured me. "I have taken back control. I am fine. The last daeva should be easy enough."*

I did not share in her confidence. It occurred to me that should controlling all seven daeva be too much for her, the beasts could have turned on us despite their current docility. I broke out into sweat at the thought.

She dismissed my fears. "This last one is different. I have shared in its thoughts, have been in its head longer than I have done with the others. It knows me as well as it knows anyone."

"The azi,*" I said.*

She rose to her feet and removed the cork from the last vial she had. The liquid sloshed inside.

"The azi,*" she agreed and, raising the bottle to her lips, drained it completely.*

The girl closed her eyes.

Underneath us, the ground shuddered.

She screamed.

She was on the ground, writhing again. Her fingers dug into the sand, blood flowing from her lips where she had bitten them. I rushed to her, but she had the presence of mind to raise a hand in warning. "Keep away from me," she rasped.

The pin on my shirt glittered wildly in response.

"I cannot leave you like this," I persisted, tearing off a wad of my shirt and pushing the rolled-up cloth between her lips. Before I could do more, I was lifted by some unseen hand and sent sprawling.

The girl clutched at her head, and her daeva shared her pain. They howled and stamped their feet. For a moment, I feared that she had lost control of them.

"I. Will. Not."

A surge of energy sent me stumbling back. For a moment, the girl was shrouded in a mist of darkness that obscured all in its way. Shadows weaved in and out of the fog, grappling with other unseen things. The daeva roared.

Just as suddenly, the mist was whisked away, sucked in by some vortex at its center, where the girl had knelt. I saw her heartsglass, dead as the night and black as the void, greedily taking in all the vapors, making them disappear into its depths.

An eternity must have passed before she stepped out from the black mist. She was smiling, all traces of pain gone from her face. Behind her, something grotesque and terrifying loomed—a black shape from which three long necks rose.

29

I WAS LOOKING DOWN AT THE body from somewhere up above. It was not moving. It stared back at me with its eyes wide open, mouth slightly agape. There was surprise still stamped across its features, which looked strangely familiar. I saw a human male on his knees by the body's side, movements frantic. I didn't know if the body was alive or if it was dead, only that it didn't matter.

Hate spilled into the air around me, and I reveled in the rage. Wings beat against the wind on either side of me, and I realized they were mine. These were my talons raking through the waters. These were my fangs, snapping at the spray. I had a pair of wings and two pairs of forearms that ended in claws, a long tail whipping out behind me, and three heads. There was something wrong with this, but I couldn't understand why.

I was also screaming, the sound louder than anything I had

ever heard. I was screaming at the humans below me, the bad things who had come to harm me.

I would not let them harm me.

I would kill them.

One of them threw fire, but I barely felt it. I lashed out with my tail, and they scattered. I tried again and caught one in the leg. It fell, and I moved for the final kill. But another surrounded me with invisible winds that cut and stabbed at my skin, and I turned to confront it. The pain was like small pinpricks in my mind, easily brushed aside. I snarled and struck the ground, and they lost their balance, tumbling. I heard a horse shriek in fright, heard more wailing from below.

A sudden need to take flight seized me, and I lifted my massive wings. Still howling, I clawed at the sky with my talons, basking in the dark of the night and the cold wind caressing my scales. I wanted to leave, to soar among the endless clouds and drift away to some place safer, where things did not prick at me with sharp edges.

No, something told me. *We are not yet done.* I felt the message nudging at my thoughts, and with much regret, I submitted to its wisdom. My wings curled back, and I landed a short distance from where I rose, hissing.

The small, frail body on the ground was gone; one of them had dragged it away to a place I could not see. Now the male was back, hacking at my tail with a weapon, a metal clang against the ivory of my bone. One of my heads bent swiftly, and I snatched it up by its middle. My teeth sank into it, and I exulted at the taste of its blood.

But then a new pain started, a sudden blooming against my

skull the instant I had bitten the human. For a few brief moments, there was something else in my head, screaming at me to stop.

No! I dropped the human and thrashed, my other heads bellowing back at me, incensed by my hesitance. The male I had abandoned staggered back to its feet and snatched up its weapon again. But rather than confront me one more time, it turned on itself, stabbing its sharpness into one arm.

The hurt returned, more intense than before. The pain wasn't mine—not exactly; it felt like someone else was in pain and I had access to their thoughts.

Something was wrong.

The human speared itself again, this time in the leg. The pain doubled, a red haze across my vision.

Listen to me! The words came from somewhere outside my mind, but I felt the message pressing into my head, demanding entry. I do not know who the voice belonged to, but every time the human harmed himself, I could feel its agony. *Listen to me!* They were not my words. They were not my thoughts. Something was compelling me to submit, but I did not want to.

Listen to me!

No! The jolt of pain that ran through me cleared my mind enough for me to understand, and I fired back at the unfamiliar presence with a scream of my own.

No! I won't listen!

I felt the presence rear back, the surprise and fury filtering into the beast's mind that we both occupied. With one last effort, I broke through my curtain of hurt and remembered.

I do not have wings and claws and a tail. I do not have three heads that hiss and war with each other. I am not a daeva. I am not a dragon. I am a girl. My name is Tea.

I am not a daeva. I am not a dragon. I am a girl, and I have a name. My name—

One of the other heads, impatient at my resistance, moved to strike on its own, hurtling back toward the male with jaws stretched open.

My name is Tea!

My teeth sank into my fellow creature's neck. It screamed in terror, stunned by this betrayal as blood flowed freely from the wound. I struck again, and the second head turned to defend its brother, distracted from the humans beneath us.

No!

I attacked again but this time with the force of my mind. The head reeled back, uncertain at first, and then attempted another assault. I stormed into its head, and it paused in midstrike.

Obey!

It resisted, whipping its head back and forth like this could somehow stem the tide of my invasion. I did not stop.

Obey!

I felt us stagger back, felt the frantic attempt of the third head, still grievously wounded, to muster another counterattack, but I dodged its flimsy bites, beating it on the side of its neck using my own dragon's head as a battering ram.

Obey!

And then I felt a *second* awareness inside the second head

behind the creature's consciousness, a panicked struggle to wrest control of the creature away from me. Occupied in the same grotesque body, I shared its thoughts. It felt scared and agitated. It was furious and in pain.

It felt human.

Obey.

I took advantage of its confusion and sank into the second creature's mind, cutting away all the strings that other awareness had in place, and I felt him scream as his spell crumbled. I tumbled into the second head's mind, overwhelming its desires and finally finding dominion.

To look out at the world with two heads and two minds while maintaining three was disorienting at first, but it also felt like the most natural thing in the world. I looked down and saw the humans—my *friends*, I thought—looking fearfully back up at me. I saw Kalen raise his hand, a ball of Fire scorching at his palm, saw Polaire stop him, shaking her head. I keened loudly, the emotion of the words I could not say spilling out into that loud sound. I explored and felt Fox and Chief in my head again, wondered how this would feel on their end. My horse was no longer skittish. True to its pedigree, it looked up at me, trusting. Fox was also looking up at me, and his concern and worry shone through our bond.

"Tea?" he questioned.

The three-headed beast gazed down at him and sighed its affirmation.

The other awareness had retreated into the third head, but I could still feel it within the creature, curled in a small ball and trying its best to remain hidden while it licked at its wounds. I punched into its thoughts, felt its fear—its mind felt strongly of soap and marsh water, bitter and root. I formed my own thoughts into a knife, the edges supple and sharp, and plunged it through the strange consciousness. I felt it claw and scream—and then felt it dissipate. Only I remained—and the creature along with me.

Feeling one less burden lifting from its mind, the beast tried to resist again. *Keep still,* I ordered, and it paused. Now in command of all its heads, I guided all three to the ground.

"She did it!" Polaire rejoiced, laughing out loud. "Tea actually did it!"

Kalen was more wary, creeping forward with his sword drawn. Fox was quicker, approaching me/the creature despite wounds that should have been fatal on anyone else. "Are you there, Tea?" He laid a hand atop the middle creature's head.

The *azi*/I turned and nuzzled at his hand.

"How did you know?" Zoya asked him. "How did you know it would feel your injuries?"

"I didn't," my brother said. "I don't feel it myself, and Tea's never felt it on her end either…but I sensed that something else inside the dragon had access to her mind. When the dragon bit me, I felt it screaming in response. It could enter Tea's thoughts, but it wasn't exempted from the pain."

"Provide me with a full account later. Althy might be interested in investigating this further."

"She must kill it quickly," Kalen said. "Before she loses control."

My mind rebelled at such a proposal. Without the malignant

awareness to guide us, we were compliant and docile, almost benign. We did not want to kill the humans; we only wanted to be left alone...

"He's right, Tea," Polaire said to us. "It's the only way to ensure this does not happen again."

"Tea?" Fox's hand felt warm and solid against our skin.

We nudged at him one last time and stood, rising to our full height, wings expanding. Kalen hefted his blade, but we turned away with one last despairing cry, heading into the waters of the lake. We waded deeper, not stopping until the waters closed over our heads until the mud and the dark hid us from view of those waiting by the shore.

The only disturbance along the lake after that was a sudden agitation underneath the surface, huge bubbles rising up to the surface for an extended period of time, only to taper off and fade from view, leaving the waters as clear and as pristine as when we had first arrived.

And I opened my eyes and sputtered. Fox was beside me within moments, placing my head on his lap. The Heartforger's stone around my neck was still glowing.

"Are you OK, Tea? Tea?"

"I am here," I rasped. It was an unsettling feeling, wanting to cough out the bilge water in your lungs when there was none there to begin with. "My leg hurts. You stink."

"So do you." Fox was laughing, and the sound warmed my heart. He scooped me up into his arms despite my protests. "Let's get you out of here."

"Are you OK?" Polaire ran to us as we approached, closing the distance.

"Yes. Thanks partly to this, I think." I touched the stone.

"What happened to the *azi*?"

"Gone." It was still hard to talk, my throat sore. "It won't bother us anymore."

"I thought we'd lost you." It took me a second to realize that as happy as Polaire was, she had also been crying, tears staining her face and ruining her rouge. "You cannot do that to us again, girl! Do you know what it did to me, thinking that you were dead?"

"I'm sorry."

"Sorry isn't good enough! I should have listened to Parmina—almost—after the scare you put us through! I don't know whether to hug you or spank you!" Polaire did the former, throwing her arms around me, and I breathed in her welcoming scent of spice and lavender, trying to rid myself of the putrid memories of my ordeal. Fox gently pulled us apart and set to work bandaging my thigh, the wound I'd suffered there.

Kalen nodded at me, a shade less hostile. His fellow Deathseekers whooped and cheered, staring at me with awe.

I smiled wanly back, forced myself to speak again. "Like Fox said, there was someone else in the dragon's mind. It was—trying to control it."

"A Faceless," Polaire surmised grimly, her arms still locked around me. "We must track him down at whatever cost. He killed the Deathseekers, tried to kill us, and very nearly killed you. He has to pay for everything he's done, and I want to be one of those holding the knife."

"You don't need to," I murmured into her ear, my voice soft enough so the others couldn't hear. My voice felt weaker, and it hurt to get any more words out, but I managed somehow. "I know who it is."

*T*HE GIRL LAUGHED AS THE azi's *three heads vied against each other for the right to be petted, sampling the air with their forked tongues.*

"It is good to see you again," she murmured. She still looked tired, but she appeared to gain strength with every second that passed.

All the world would tremble to see such a sight, I knew—the Dark asha on the shore and the seven daeva she wielded. They were enough to break the land. They were enough to break crowns. How must Hollow Knife have felt when he created such monsters? How must the followers of Blade that Soars have felt to turn and see such horrors at their kingdoms' borders?

The girl turned. The daeva's eyes followed her movements.

"We leave for Daanoris at dawn," she said.

30

THE WILLOWS HAD FINALLY SUCCUMBED to the quiet. Nothing moved, save for the clouds rolling above the asha-ka, across the evening sky. After all the celebrations and all the joy that greeted our arrival, I welcomed the solitude.

Fortunately, Polaire had been insistent, demanding time for me to fully recuperate, and so the jubilation around the Valerian was muted. Mistress Parmina had been ecstatic—no doubt my price would quadruple. Rahim nearly suffocated me in his bear hugs; Likh's and Chesh's were less punishing. Lady Mykaela's happiness was more subdued, her relief more palpable. She said nothing, only hugged me as Polaire had. Her tears came unbid-den, staining her bedsheets, and I, worn and fatigued, cried along with her.

The Valerian household was in disarray. Kana was sick, and Farhi had her hands full trying to get errands done when there were crowds of people packing the streets along the asha-ka. These were not normal visitors to the Willows; these were people not only from Kion, but from nearby kingdoms like Odalia and Daanoris and the city-states of Yadosha, some even as far away as Istera and Drycht—all hoping to catch a glimpse of me. After two days, Mistress Parmina had had enough and enlisted the help of many Deathseekers to clear the roads of people. The revelers were persuaded to take their reveling elsewhere, and for the first time in three days, the streets stood serene and empty, while in other places of Ankyo, the people celebrated.

I made a full recovery after only a night's worth of sleep, though Fox was adamant about letting me rest for a week more, because of the wound on my thigh. Normally I would have lodged a protest, but this time, I agreed with him. Staying at the Valerian would give me a good opportunity to keep an eye on Farhi without attracting any suspicion, and Lady Mykaela was also on hand to ensure nothing went wrong.

Khalad also paid me a visit, using the opportunity to carefully extract my memories of the fight with the *azi*. "The Forger isn't in Kion," he said. "After all the excitement, he thought he'd go and see for himself. New, rarer memories to harvest."

"Are other people's memories all you both think about?" I teased.

"No. We think about heartsglass too." He grinned at the look on my face. "I was joking. I have not extracted memories from my own heartsglass for days, and my mind is clear. Which is a good time to apologize to you."

"But why?"

"You might not remember it, but I was the boy who confronted you at the Odalian palace three years ago—the one who accused Dark asha of killing my mother. Master had just taken me on as an apprentice, but back then I was so full of anger. You were the easiest target for me." He cleared his throat. "I almost didn't remember what I did—until I recognized myself in one of your memories. I am sorry. I know things have not been easy, and it was unkind of me to add to your problems."

"Apology accepted, Sir Khalad," I assured him, smiling, unaware then of the irony of my next words. "If there is one thing I have learned from both our trades, it is that we must always be in the business of forgiveness, lest we become consumed by our anger."

•• ⧹⧸ ••

We had agreed to make our move on the third day after we returned, to give me ample time to rest and to prepare for the confrontation. Tonight, Mistress Parmina and Lady Shadi had left to attend some parties thrown in my honor, and the old woman intended to drag them to as many of them as they were able. This suited my plans; the longer they stayed out of the Valerian, the better.

I waited until it was close to midnight, then headed downstairs, where Polaire, Lady Mykaela, and Althy waited. We ventured into the scullery, where Kana and Farhi were hard at work cleaning dishes. There were four times the number of visitors calling at the Valerian than was the norm, and so both maids were constantly busy. Mistress Parmina had even dipped into her coffers and hired temporary help to handle the additional workload. The first of them would be arriving in two days, which meant we had little time to act.

The girls looked up with surprise when we entered and both dropped a hurried curtsy despite being up to their elbows in soapy water. "Farhi, we need to talk," Lady Mykaela's voice still sounded weak, but with Althy and Polaire at her side, looking grave, it had the desired effect. Farhi visibly gulped, then struggled to dry her hands on the thin apron she wore.

"You, wait in the other room," Polaire commanded Kana. The girl gave her companion what should have been a comforting, reassuring look but came out frightened and half-relieved that she wasn't the focus of their ire. She bobbed her head again and fled the scullery.

"You are in trouble, girl," I heard Lady Mykaela say to Farhi just before I left the kitchen and moved to the room where Kana stood, looking worried. I smiled at her. "Don't look so scared."

"It's just that we're short of hands as it is, milady," Kana said, wringing her hands in dismay. She was still warm to the touch from her brief bout of fever, but she insisted she felt better. "We still have a lot of things to do. The extra help won't come in for another day yet. Did Farhi break something? Did Mistress Parmina learn of the cants you've been giving us?"

"It's a little more serious than that. Lady Mykaela wouldn't be up for something so trivial as a broken plate. She'll still need many more months to recover."

"She shouldn't be up at all," Kana agreed. "And Mistress Parmina has ordered the house be cleaned from top to bottom again tomorrow because she said the Empress of Alyx might pay us a visit. The empress!" She tugged hard at her apron for emphasis. "My nana would be thrilled. I asked the mistress if she could come along and watch—only from the street, mind, not even inside the Valerian. I'm sure she wouldn't mind if there was just one more person outside—"

"The empress's visit is a good reason for causing more mischief," Zoya said, entering the room. She looked stunning. Her *hua* glittered golden, and below her waist, white cranes grazed at silver ponds. Her wrap was deceptively simple: a dark-ochre color with no adornments but spun from the softest silk.

"I didn't think you would come," I told her.

She shrugged. "Lady Mykaela insisted. I have been to four different parties at four different tearooms tonight, and I needed a break."

"You also had another motive for coming here, didn't you?"

"I don't know what you could possibly mean, Tea."

"Kana, there's some tea boiling over the fireplace. Would you be so kind as to pour a bowl for our guest?"

Kana swallowed nervously, then hurried to do just that.

"I've been learning a lot about the Faceless in my history lessons," I continued.

"That is a requirement for all asha, Tea."

"Some of us learn better than others. I've learned that the Faceless can draw runes just as ably. Unlike us, they have certain stones at their disposal that allow them this feat. The seeking stone, for instance. Another stone allows them to speed up the process of raising a daeva so that they do not need to wait years for their resurrection."

"I took the same lessons you did, Tea. I do not need the lecture."

"That's why Mistress Parmina was so insistent that all asha who could potentially enter the asha-ka had to present themselves to the oracle first. The seeress had told her many years ago that a Faceless would try to enter her household, and so she must be vigilant."

"I don't see what that has to do with me."

"Mistress Parmina rejects all applicants who do not pass the oracle's test. You were one of them, weren't you?"

Zoya's heartsglass made a sudden sputter of blue before fading quickly.

"Passing the oracle's test isn't a requirement to be an asha, and so House Imperial took you in. House Imperial has a more lustrous history than House Valerian—it was the first asha-ka, founded by Vernasha of the Roses. But you've always nursed a grudge against the Valerian, haven't you? You were Lady Shadi's childhood friend. Lady Mykaela saw potential in you both and brought the two of you here. Mistress Parmina accepted her but not you. That's why you resented Lady Shadi—it felt like she had abandoned you—and it's why you tried to get me in trouble before I was even considered a novice. You were angry."

Zoya took a deep breath. "I don't deny it. Yes, I've known

Shadi all my life. Yes, it was Lady Mykaela who brought me to the Valerian. Mistress Parmina rejected me because I lied to the oracle. But lying to the seeress doesn't mean I am one of the Faceless. If that were the case, I'd say roughly a quarter of the asha in the Willows are Faceless."

"Should I l-leave?" Kana stuttered, pouring the tea so quickly that parts of the liquid slopped over the bowl and onto the table.

"It's telling, isn't it? You could have hidden the seeking stone at the Falling Leaf, counting on the fact that I was the nearest Dark asha on hand and would succumb to its effects. You were also on hand when the *azi* wreaked havoc on the *darashi oyun*—as I recall, you were angry that Lady Shadi had taken the lead role."

"All other asha were present at the *darashi oyun!*"

"But you were the only asha present who volunteered to fight the *azi* with us, excepting Polaire. You've never wanted to help us before. What better way to keep an eye on your daeva than to be there with us to head off any obstacles—Lady Aenah?"

Zoya took a deep breath. When she spoke again, she sounded almost admiring. "You thought this out thoroughly, haven't you? I'm impressed."

"I had to. Anyone could easily be a suspect if you make a good enough argument for it. And you were the easiest choice."

"That's true. I didn't think about it that way. What about Lady Mykaela or Polaire?"

"Lady Mykaela could have been pretending sickness. When everyone thinks you're asleep in bed, it's easier to move about without being seen. You wouldn't even need an alibi. And like you, Polaire was on the spot for the most part—she could have followed me to the Falling Leaf without anyone else knowing and planted the seeking stone there. Mistress Parmina could have done it for financial gain. Admittedly, I never really thought about Althy as a suspect."

"That makes sense. There's something inherently trustworthy about Altaecia."

"Miladies?" Kana stammered, confused by the sudden turn our conversation had taken.

"Farhi isn't in trouble, Kana. Lady Mykaela and Althy are protecting her right now."

"But I don't understand."

"It's because she's in danger."

"In danger? From the empress?"

"No. From you. We are all taught to block our minds from external infiltration by those who can command the Dark and use *Compulsion*. Even such training may not be successful when facing a strong Faceless, as I had learned. Farhi has no such training, and my sisters are shielding her from you."

Kana looked at me and blinked. "Me? But why? I'm just a—"

"You're just a young girl working at the Willows. That's what you say. A group of people living near the Ankyon marketplace are claiming to be your family. Your father makes a living selling pomegranates at the market, but he doesn't seem to rely on any of the wholesale suppliers in Ankyo for this."

"We're originally from Southeast Kion. My father cuts out

the middlemen and makes the trips himself. A friend of my father's owns a small farm at Amarai and charges him a smaller fee—"

"And what is the name of your father's friend?"

"Ah—Kel."

"There is no farmer named Kel in Amarai," Zoya interrupted.

"That's not possible. I've been to their farm—"

"The lady asha is right," Kalen said, stepping into the room, followed by Fox. "Several of my fellow Deathseekers made some inquiries, and I can vouch for their credibility. There is, however, a merchant named Jeven, who frequents the Cogswheel Inn at Amarai, who supplies the person you call your father with his pomegranates. That merchant has been arrested by the Deathseekers after confessing to being a spy for Acnah, operating secretly in Kion."

Kana stopped, holding herself still. "But that's impossible! I don't know much about father's business, and I might have misheard where he gets his pomegranates. But if that merchant was a Faceless, then my father would never have chosen to conduct any business with him had he known about—"

"You claim to be originally from Belaryu, in southeast Kion," I put in. "Nobody there has heard of you or your family either. None of you thought you would be suspected or that our investigations would be so thorough, did you?"

"You must be mistaken. We have strong roots in Belaryu. My nana's mother's family lived there for generations. She took my grandfather's name when she married; she was a Hescht before that. My grandfather was an outsider; he came from the north—"

"Except you told me months ago that your grandfather's family had lived in Belaryu for generations, not your nana."

"You must have misunderstood me. My nana was a—" And then her thoughts bored into mine, so quickly and so effortlessly that I would have caved if I hadn't been expecting it, if I couldn't feel Polaire from the other room adding to my strength, helping me put up a shield in my mind to prevent her from tunneling her way in.

Kana snarled. All the light went out of her heartsglass; in one instant, it changed from bright red to an impenetrable black. Her face twisted into a mosaic of rage, and she tried again, only to encounter an impervious barrier of our will. Zoya took advantage of her inattention; a quick rope of Wind held her in place, wrapping around her body.

Frustrated, Kana lashed out again with her mind—but this time, it was directed toward Fox. I felt her in his head as easily as I could feel his, and then his presence was gone from mine.

Fox turned, his face wooden. His blade made a metallic, ringing noise as he slid it out from his scabbard.

"Bricky little girl, you are," the girl said. She spoke in a different accent, much like those of the Yadoshan merchants I had met. "Give me one reason why I should not simply use *Compulsion* on you all."

"You are not a match for this many asha," Althy countered. "Surrender immediately."

"I am a match for a dozen of you all at once. In the meantime, I'm thinking I'll kill this one instead." It was easy enough to underestimate Aenah in her guise as a sweet-faced maid working in an asha-ka. The girl standing before us now looked nothing like Kana. Her eyes glittered; her mouth twisted into a cruel smile.

"That's not much of a threat," Polaire said, "as he's already dead."

Aenah laughed. "There is more than one way to die, you fools. Even the dead can feel pain, and I will have him wriggling like live meat on a butcher's hook for all eternity if you do not grant me safe passage outside of Kion. If not, he will suffer. I will make sure of it."

"It was you who shadowed me all throughout Ankyo," I said, struggling to find my link back to Fox. I could see my brother surrounded by a fog of inky blackness, but every time I drew in the rune and directed it toward the mist, I could not break through the Dark barrier. "You were the Drychta woman. You pretended to be the girl who brought me to the Falling Leaf that night. You sent the skeleton after me. When you lost control of the *azi*, I saw into your mind. I know how you were able to compel me."

"Perhaps you can enlighten me."

"The girl from the Falling Leaf told me Lady Shadi would be 'mad as hops' if I were late. That's not a Kion term—it's a Yadoshan one. You told me you were 'all poked up'—another Yadoshan term. A guest from Yadosha used another word you used often—cant. I thought you were joking, that the food we smuggled to you was something you 'can't' have. But in Yadosha, it means 'free food.' Yet you claimed to be from southeastern Kion—why would you use Yadoshan patter? It was only after I encountered your mind within the *azi* and realized why it felt so familiar that I put two and two together."

"Betrayed by the land of my birth, as always. I thought my disguise was perfect."

"How did you learn to be in two places at once?" Althy asked. "In the spirit of scientific curiosity."

"I do not require physical form to find you, little girl. I know more about the Dark than your pathetic little asha friends here. I can do things they can only dream of."

"Including controlling a daeva?" Althy questioned.

"A simple trick. One that I suspect your charge knows all too well." Aenah smiled at me. "It appears that we are at an impasse, my dears. The question remains: How much do you value this Odalian corpse? It would be very easy for me to sever your connection, Tea, and watch him turn to dust before you."

I can teach you more, Tea, her thoughts whispered. **So much more than what they can offer you.**

I don't believe you!

I can teach you spells beyond imagining. We were meant to rule, young one. It is they who deny us our right because they fear our power. I have seen your true heart. We are alike, you and I. I can teach you to heal your brother, to make him truly alive, not this walking corpse.

I hesitated. *You're lying.*

I swear right now, on my blessed mother's grave, that I do not lie.

I will never join you!

Even after they bleed you dry the way they did your mentor? How long will they let you last in the world of the

Willows? Better to die with our will in our blood than their fists around our hearts, child.

"Take one more step," Aenah warned when Althy tensed, "and I will kill him where he—"

With a loud whinny, Chief broke through the wall right beside Aenah. She turned her head, and for a second, I saw an opening through the fog surrounding Fox. It was enough. I drove my will through it, pushed Aenah's presence out of his mind. My brother slumped down.

Kalen was the first to react; his sword came whizzing through the air, but the Faceless reached out and plucked it out of his hands like she was picking flowers along a meadow. Without missing a beat, the Deathseeker sent a ball of Fire toward Aenah's direction, but she repelled it easily, her hand reaching out to absorb the flames.

Polaire and Althy attacked as one; I could see the runes blaze before them, Fire and Wind streaking toward Aenah, combining to form lightning. The Faceless whirled back and stopped both attacks in midair as well. It sizzled a few inches before her outstretched hand, smoking.

"Too slow," she sneered. "Your paltry Runic is nothing compared to what I—"

"Stay out of my head," Fox growled at her feet, rising with his sword in hand. Aenah turned to deflect the blow, the blade skittering across the floor, and I attacked, with Althy, Polaire, and Zoya adding their strength to mine. I used everything I had gleaned from Aenah's mind about *Compulsion* and lashed out.

While she had sought to corrupt my mind little by little in subtle, underhanded ways for years, I needed no such pretense. I poured into her head, using her own tricks against her. She fought off my invasion but never saw Fox coming until his fist slammed into her face, knocking her out.

"The maid," Zoya said with some disgust, staring down at her prone form. "How did we not think it would be the maid?"

"We're too far removed from the time we ourselves worked at our own asha-ka as servants," Althy said. "She was clever. We've assumed often enough that Faceless would choose positions of power and overlooked the people working for us." She bent down and plucked the fake ruby pin from the Faceless's hair. As she did, I stumbled back from the strong sense of magic emanating from her. "Not quite so faux, it seems. It helps to hide her magic from others rather than amplify it. It's like nothing I've ever seen before."

"But why not simply poison the food at the Valerian?" Kalen asked.

"The girl is strong in the Dark, but too many *zivars* and spells are woven around the asha-ka, limiting her abilities," Lady Mykaela said wearily, stepping into the room. "And should someone fall ill or die at the Valerian, she would be easily suspected. She bided her time and waited instead until she could do the most damage—as evidenced when she placed the seeking stone at the Falling Leaf and when she summoned the *azi* to disrupt the *darashi oyun*."

I stooped down to the fallen Faceless. I reached out to her with my mind, assessing, exploring. Twisting. "I wanted to tell you all about her so many times before, but she always compelled me to remain silent," I said, keeping my voice steady. "I believed that they were my own thoughts. I know otherwise now."

"I've never told anyone else about it," Zoya said to me. "That I first came to the Valerian but was rejected."

"Lady Mykaela knew," I admitted, straightening up, "but she never told me. I guessed and confronted her about it. Your dislike didn't just stop with me. You disliked Mistress Parmina, the maids here, everyone in the Valerian except Lady Mykaela. It was like you associated a lot of bad memories with the place itself. And you were always so in control of your emotions, yet every time you looked at Shadi, your heartsglass always betrayed you. I convinced Lady Mykaela that I already knew enough and that I may as well know everything else."

"Was the horse your idea?" Kalen asked me.

"Althy did something similar in the past—but with a cow." Chief simply shook off the blow and wandered out from the stallion-sized hole it had caused in the wall. "Though I imagine Mistress Parmina will charge me for the repairs."

"I think I understand your meteoric rise through the asha ranks," Zoya confessed with a wan smile. She lowered her voice for my ears alone. "And since you know everything, must I implore you not to tell Shadi about my other secret."

I met her even gaze and grinned. "What other secret?"

Zoya laughed.

I CHOSE THE SEA OF SKULLS *for my exile because the bones scattered here serve my purpose," she said. "Because the last person that matters to me lies here. I buried him myself, with my hands and my tears. I raise all these daeva because I intend to have my vengeance for his sake and for the sake of other friends who have fallen. Both asha and the Faceless will pay for taking everything from me—my friends, my love, my identity. The Willows will not protect them. No fortress or stronghold that shields them will be spared, wherever they may be.*

"This is my new family. This is my new identity. I will be the bone witch the kingdom fears, and I will make them pay."

She knelt before the grave one last time. She pressed her lips against the stone and then rose. The daeva flanked her, sensing their mistress' intentions; they were no longer affectionate and playful, now baying and primed for war. Her fingers traveled along the breeze, mapping out a new rune in its wake.

The ground underneath the headstone shuddered, split open. A figure rose from the hole that yawned before us, fingers digging into the dirt. He was tall and garbed in military black; it was obvious from the deep wounds on his chest that he had died fighting.

The girl took something out of her waist wrap. It was the small jeweled case I had seen before on her table, surrounded by the bezoars. Inside lay a silver heartsglass, shining bright as the sun.

"Welcome back, my love."

"Your brother?" I whispered, staring at the boy.

"My brother and I are no longer on speaking terms. He chose to stay behind and defend the Willows."

"But what of the bond you share?"

"An unexpected effect of my black heartsglass is that he can no longer sense me, and the reverse holds true. But for as long as I live, so will he." She smiled. "He might even seek to kill me, though it will cost him his own life. We have come a long way only to fall apart. But if he cannot stand with us, then he must stand against us."

The man in black approached us, cloak fluttering in the wind. He took her hand.

"You can join us if you choose to, Bard. The story is far from over, and we still have many kingdoms to take." She smiled at the boy she had just raised from the grave. "Don't we, my love?"

31

T HEY TOLD ME I WOULD find you here."

My breath caught in my throat. I turned away from the imposing domed roof of the oracle's temple to regard the man standing in the moonlight, regarding me with his solemn face and smiling eyes. He was dressed in dark clothes, an unusual choice for him. I put my hand over my heartsglass, instinctively seeking to shield him from reading the staccato beats his unexpected presence caused. I was thrilled, but I also knew this was not the place I wanted him to see me at.

"Y-Your Highness," I stammered.

"I told you before that Kance is a good enough name for me." He looked to the building. "I've always been curious of what went on inside that temple. Everyone's been rather mysterious about it. I keep expecting some untold treasures tucked away inside, privy only to asha eyes."

"Lord Kance, what are you doing here?"

"Looking for you, actually. I don't think I've seen you since you left to fight the *azi*. And since our first meeting, you've been raised to asha, put down one of the most powerful daeva I've seen in my lifetime, and been instrumental in capturing one of the three Faceless leaders." He grinned at my surprise. "The Faceless may be a carefully guarded secret, but Kalen trusts me. Not even my father knows of the Faceless's capture, though he shall know soon enough. I promised I wouldn't tell another soul of this."

"I don't understand. Why is Your High—why are you looking for me?"

"To thank you for saving my kingdom. The *azi* could have done more damage if left unchecked, more lives lost. And also to apologize. I thought about visiting you sooner, but Kalen convinced me to let you recuperate first."

I made a note to strangle Kalen as soon as I saw him again.

"I had asked both Lady Altaecia and Lady Zoya to keep me abreast of what's been happening with you. They were more than happy to tell me of your remarkable progress, so I decided there was no reason for me not to come and thank you myself." He enveloped my hand in his, warm in the otherwise evening chill. "From the bottom of my heart, you have my thanks, Lady Tea. If there is anything within my power to offer you, on behalf of my father and of Odalia, do not hesitate to let me know."

"A dinner." The words tumbled out before I thought them through.

"A dinner?" The prince looked perplexed.

It was too late to take back my words. "Just…dinner. To ask *you* to dinner for once. Or even a walk would suffice. But not if you're not permitted to—I didn't mean that. I meant not if you have to bring a squadron of bodyguards for protection…" I was babbling. Were princes allowed to walk out with new asha? Did saving his kingdom entitle me to ask him to dinner? Etiquette books were mum on the subject.

"Dinner sounds nice." He was smiling. "It would be my honor. We could do that now if you like."

"I…I can't. Not tonight." My gaze drifted back to the temple. He saw, understood. "I'll wait for you to return."

"I can't possibly keep His Highness waiting…"

"His Highness insists. And I thought I told you to call me Kance." He nudged me forward. "Go on. Take as long as you need to. I'll be here."

"Thank you, Your Hi—Kance."

The thought of the prince waiting outside spurred my pace, despite the stiffness in my right leg. I would suffer a scar there, I was told—a permanent reminder of my encounter with the *azi*. I walked past the familiar corridors, following the snakelike tunnel until it once more opened into the majestic, empty chamber, where the oracle awaited me.

This time, I needed no prompting. Polaire had gifted me with a beautiful turquoise pin set with flutter strips of silver birds at its end. I took a deep breath and threw it into the fire.

"You have taken a living familiar," she said. "And you have taken one that knows neither life nor death."

"Yes." I did not know how far into my future the oracle could see, but I realized I had never doubted her. Not since the first day I entered her realm, even when she asked me time and time again to consign my beautiful ornaments to the flames. Even now, the *azi* stirred in my mind, safe and hidden within Lake Strypnyk.

Even now, I could feel Aenah's thoughts raging while she remained locked away within the dungeons of the Ankyon palace, warded from all magic.

"You have told no one."

"No."

"Why?"

"Because Aenah was right—she holds the key to unlocking the rest of my abilities. There is a way for me to learn how to control daeva without having to sacrifice my life in the process. The asha elders would never have allowed me to do so. Aenah is locked up in the palace dungeons in Ankyo, but if I wish to, I can now command her thoughts the same way she once tried to control mine. Through this, I can learn all I need to know. In time, once I have greater command of these skills, I will tell the others." It was like a dam bursting. Words poured from my lips, desperate to unburden my soul to the nameless, shrouded figure before me.

"Is that why you did not kill the *azi?*"

I swallowed. This was harder to defend than compelling Aenah.

"I do not want to kill it. It only wants to be left alone. Under my control, it won't harm anyone."

"You are dangerous," said the oracle. "Left unchecked, you

can spell the downfall of the Willows, of Kion. The asha should be alerted to the extent of your abilities. And yet—and yet—"

She trailed off. The fires burned lower until they were nothing more than tiny lights dancing above black coals.

"Return to your asha-ka," the oracle finally said, and the fires rose up once more, burning anew. "And may the gods have mercy on the land."

*T*HEY ARE READY.

She was only seventeen. She rose, and the world rose with her. Creatures of nightmares lifted their haunches and howled at the dying stars above us. The girl turned and set her sights on the horizon. Her black heartsglass swung with her movements, and a queer light shone forth from its depths. Her familiar, the boy in black, stood beside her. He laid a hand on her shoulder, and she rested her head against his knuckles. Her fingers found his.

"Let's go, Kalen," she said.

I followed them as they moved across the beach, onto the road that stretched into the kingdom of Daanoris. A cold wind blew from the north, and with it the promise of night—a growing darkness tempered only by the moon above, burning with all the light to see.

The World of *The Bone Witch*:
The 8 Kingdoms

ISTERA

- The coldest among the eight kingdoms
- Has gone to war with Tresea over the Heartsbane Islands in the past and still shares some animosity
- Separated from Tresea by the River of Peace

CAPITAL: Farsun

CURRENT RULER: King Rendorvik of House Petralta

TRESEA

- Composed of mostly dense woods and wide plains
- Population is concentrated mainly in cities, with small scatterings of villages throughout

CAPITAL: Highgaard

CURRENT RULER: Czar Kamulus of House Ambersturg

DAANORIS

- Mild to moderate weather, most populated kingdom

CAPITAL: Santiang

CURRENT RULER: Emperor Shifang

YADOSHA CITY-STATES

- The whole continent was originally the kingdom of Yadosha, but infighting among the royal descendants soon splintered it into several warring states and shrunk their dominion into only its upper continent
- While each city-state maintains a high degree of independence, all share one main government to foster ties and maintain diplomatic missions
- Each city-state has a Second Minister to govern them; every seven years, a First Minister is elected among the Second Ministers to represent Yadosha as a whole

CAPITAL: None

CURRENT RULER: First Minister Stefan

KION

- Once a part of Yadosha; many kingdoms conquered and fought over this land before Kion was able to achieve its independence through Vernasha of the Roses, a legendary asha
- A melting pot of culture and main headquarters of the asha
- Smallest land among the kingdoms

CAPITAL: Ankyo

CURRENT RULER: Empress Alyx of House Imperial

ODALIA

- Composed of plains and forests
- Originally a part of the kingdom of Yadosha but was the first in the continent to rebel and break off into its own kingdom

CAPITAL: Kneave

CURRENT RULER: King Telemaine of House Odalia

ARHEN-KOSHO

- Large group of islands on the Swiftsea, near Odalia and Kion

CAPITAL: Hottenheim

CURRENT RULER: Queen Lynoria of House Imperial

DRYCHT

- Desert kingdom
- Also notable for its austere and extreme perspective generally held in contempt by most of the other kingdoms, but tolerated for the runeberry cloth they provide
- Only the western continent of Drycht is heavily populated; the majority of the kingdom is made of sand

CAPITAL: Adra-al

CURRENT RULER: King Aadil of the Tavronoo clan

Acknowledgments

There will never be enough names on this page, but I will try.

My gratitude to Rebecca, my first and constant cheerleader/agent extrordinaire, who will always and forever rock.

To Annette, Kathryn, and everyone at Sourcebooks for this wonderful, amazing ride.

To Les, who often worries about the strange worlds inside my head despite having married me. "You're weird." "I know, honey."

To my baby, Ezio, the reason this story was completed three months later than expected. Still worth it.

And also to Tom Hiddleston, just because I've always wanted to thank Tom Hiddleston for something. Keep doing what you do, Tom.

TEA'S STORY CONTINUES IN

The

HEART
FORGER

I

*H*E DOES NOT LOOK SO *formidable*, I lied to myself, staring at the warped, decaying body before me. *I can defeat his will. I will break him. It is a wonder what Mykkie had ever seen in him.*

It was not the first time I had deceived myself in this manner. Neither was this the first time I had raised King Vanor from the grave. But if I repeated that mantra enough times, I thought I could finally believe my words.

The dead king refused to look at me, his eyes distant. The royal crypts were built to strike both fear and awe in those who visited, but I had grown accustomed to the stone faces looking down at me with quiet scrutiny from their high precipices. But King Vanor's continued silence unnerved me every time—more than I cared to admit.

"A wise philosopher once said," Fox drawled from the

shadows, "that doing the same thing over and over again while expecting a different result is the mark of a fool."

"Why do I bring you along?"

"Well, a wise philosopher once said—"

"Shut up." My brother had no need to tell me my quest was hopeless. Numerous Dark asha, all more experienced than me, had made the attempt. But I had to do *something*.

"You're in a worse mood than usual. Did Kalen chew you out at practice again?"

"If you don't like it here, why not find some women in the city to flirt with instead?"

"Not in Oda—" He caught himself. "None of your business. Can we get this over with?"

I turned back to the corpse. "Where are you keeping Mykaela's heartsglass?"

No answer. The colossi statues guarding the catacombs were likelier to respond than this infernal sod of a king.

"Answer me! What have you done to her heartsglass? Where did you keep it? Why do you hate her so much?" My headache worsened. Somewhere in the back of my head, I was aware of a shadow thrashing about, sensing my anger. I saw a vision of water, green and murky, before it faded out of view.

I took a deep breath and let it out carefully. The ache lightened and the shadow retreated as I recovered my calm.

"This is a waste of time." Fox folded his arms across his chest. My brother looked to be in peak physical health, though he was no more alive than the royal noble standing before us.

Their similarities ended there; there was barely enough skin and sinew clinging to Vanor to pass for human. That was my doing. The first few times I resurrected him, I had been respectful, taking great pains to restore his body to how it appeared when he was alive.

Now I allowed him only enough muscle and flesh to move his jaw.

"He's not going to talk, Tea. You know that, I know that, and he definitely knows that."

"I will *make* him talk." Many years ago, my sister-asha had fallen in love with this wretched excuse of a ruler. In exchange for her unwavering devotion, he had taken her heartsglass and hidden it so well that no one had been able to find it.

And now, more than a decade later, Mykaela was dying. She could no longer return to Kion. Her health had deteriorated to the point where she had to remain near her heartsglass, still hidden somewhere within Odalia, here in the city of Kneave. It was hard enough to be a bone witch; that she'd survived for this long was a miracle in itself.

I grabbed what was left of the king's shoulders, pulling him toward me. He reeked of death and obstinacy. "Answer me!" My voice echoed off the columns. "Didn't you love her even a little? Or are you so petty that you'd allow her to suffer for the rest of her years? She's *dying*. What grudge do you harbor to hate her this much?"

"Tea."

I froze. So did Fox.

I had told no one else about my weekly excursions to the

royal crypts. Not my friend Polaire, who would have boxed my ears if she'd known, nor Mistress Parmina, who would doom me to a life cleaning outhouses. Only Fox was privy to my secret, which he had agreed to keep despite his own misgivings. And Mykaela was the last person I wanted to find out.

She had aged more rapidly during the last few years since she had taken me under her wing. There was more gray in her golden hair, more lines on her face. Her back stooped slightly, like she struggled under a heavy burden. She had taken to using a cane everywhere she went, unsure of her own feet.

"Mykaela," I stammered, "you're not supposed to be here."

"I could say the same for you," she answered, but her eyes were fixed on King Vanor, her pain obvious. He watched her gravely, without shame or guilt, and my anger rose again. How many raisings had my sister-asha endured, forced to watch while this king refused to speak?

I raised my finger to sketch out the rune that would send Vanor back to the world of the dead, but Mykaela lifted a hand. "Vanor," she said quietly, "it's been a while."

The decaying figure said nothing. His eyes studied her, savage and hungry and ill suited for such an impassive face.

"I apologize for my wayward apprentice. She has been willful and intractable since her admission to my asha-ka and has shown little improvement since. Please return to your rest. Tea, let him go."

Mykaela's words were a steel knife through my heart. Stuttering apologies, I completed the spell and watched as King

Vanor's body crumbled back into dust in his open coffin. Even as his features dissolved, King Vanor never once looked away from Mykaela's face.

"Close the lid and move the stone back in place," she said. I could detect the anger behind her calm. "I would tell King Telemaine to seal his coffin, but even that might not stop you. Whatever possessed you to let her do this, Fox?"

Fox shrugged, grinning like an abashed schoolboy. "I'm her familiar. It comes with the territory."

"Being her familiar is no excuse for being an imbecile! And you! What possessed you to summon dead royalty in the middle of the night?"

"I wanted to help." The excuse sounded weaker when made to Mykaela than to Fox. "I thought that I could control daeva now! You said no Dark asha's ever done that before! That's why…why I…"

Mykaela sighed. "And so by that logic, you think you are different from Dark asha of the past? What you have in ability, Tea, you lack in wisdom. You cannot compel the dead if they are not willing. Wasn't that the first lesson I taught you after you raised Fox from his grave? Arrogance is not a virtue, sister."

I looked down, blinking back tears. Was I arrogant to want to save her? Unlike Fox, Dark asha and all those with a silver heartsglass cannot be raised from the dead, and that permanence frightened me. "I'm sorry. I want to help. But I feel so powerless."

I heard her move closer, felt her hand on my head, stroking my hair.

"It's not such a bad thing, to feel powerless sometimes. It teaches us that some situations are inevitable and that we should spend what little time we have in the company of the people that matter most. Do you understand me, Tea?"

"Yes." I wept.

"Tea, I'm not dead yet." A finger nudged at my chin. "I would appreciate it if you stopped acting like I was. I do not give up so easily, but we must adopt other means."

"I'm sorry."

"It is only an apology if you mean it. This is the last time you will be summoning anyone in the royal crypts, no matter how noble you think your actions are. Promise me."

"I promise," I mumbled.

"The same is true for you too, Fox."

"I promise, milady."

"Good. Now help me up the stairs. My legs aren't what they used to be."

Fox reached down and scooped Mykaela into his arms. "It's the fastest way," he explained. "You've expended enough energy yelling at us."

The older asha chuckled. "Yes, that's always been rather tiresome now that I think about it. Perhaps you should direct your energies toward more productive tasks so I can tire less."

"How did you know we were here?" I asked.

"I've taken to wandering at night. I looked in on Tea, but her room was empty. I detected a shifting of runes nearby and merely followed it to its source."

"I didn't mean to make you worry." The staircase led back to the Odalian palace gardens. For the past two months, Fox and I had been King Telemaine's guests, traveling the kingdom and tending to the sickly. Most of the people here fear and dislike bone witches, though with lesser fervor than before. It is not easy to hold a grudge against someone who has nursed you back to health.

At the king's invitation, Mykaela had taken up residence in the castle indefinitely. But every day finds her weaker, and I feared the palace would serve as her hospice.

"There are many other concerns, Tea. Likh has a new case pending, hasn't he?"

The asha association had rejected Likh's appeal to join, but Polaire had dredged up an obscure law that permitted Deathseekers to train in the Willows until they turned fifteen, which was Likh's current age.

Mykaela glanced over Fox's shoulder, back at the catacombs, then turned away.

She still loves him, I thought, and fury burned through me like a fever. "I'm really sorry, Mykkie."

She smiled. "As I said, only if you mean it, Tea. Get some rest. We've got a busy day ahead."

•• ⧓ ••

I listened until my brother's footsteps faded before sneaking out of my room a second time. I opened the doors of my mind to welcome the hidden shadows; they wrapped around my core, creating a barrier that had for many months prevented Fox from discovering the other sentience I hoarded away, like a sweet vintage I had no intentions of sharing. I couldn't. Not yet.

Chief waited for me at the stables. A lone woman on a horse caused no outcry, and we rode undisturbed out of the city, into a copse of trees that hid us further from view. I climbed off my stallion, told him to await my return, and moved deeper into the forest, into a small clearing that served as a rendezvous point.

I reached out once more to the moving darkness. The scar on my right thigh was hot to the touch. It burned in the cold air, but I felt no pain.

Despite its size, the beast was made of stealth and shadows. Where there was once nothing, it now stood beside me, as if summoned from the air. Three pairs of hooded eyes gazed down at me, forked tongues dancing. Its wings extended, and twilight rolled over me, soothing and pleasant.

Master? It was a voice but not in the manner we think of voices. Our bond gave us an understanding that went beyond language.

I reached out. Its scaly hide was a combination of coarse bark and rough sandpaper.

Play? It sat, unmoving, as I climbed up its back.

Yes.

In the blink of an eye, we were soaring across the sky, rolling meadows and fields of green passing below us. *Turn*, I thought, testing the limits of my control, as I have over the last several months. The *azi* complied, wings curving toward the horizon.

I laughed, the sound joyous and free against the wind, and one head dipped briefly to nuzzle at my cheek, purring.

This is not selfishness, I told myself, *but a responsibility*. Mykaela was partly right; I was arrogant and overconfident, but I was not like other Dark asha. No other Dark asha had been able to tame the *azi*. And riding with it on quiet nights meant it was not rampaging through cities.

But I also knew I had to keep my companion a secret. Raising a dead king was a far lesser sin than taking a daeva as a familiar. *I shall conquer this*, I thought and, in doing so, sealed my fate.

About the Author

Rin Chupeco wrote obscure manuals for complicated computer programs, talked people out of their money at event shows, and did many other terrible things. She now writes about ghosts and fairy tales but is still sometimes mistaken for a revenant. Find her at rinchupeco.com.